JOELLE'S SECRET

3 60p.

GILBERT MORRIS

B&H
PUBLISHING GROUP

2008

Nashville, Tennessee

ISBN: 978-1-60751-495-4

Published by B&H Publishing Group
Nashville, Tennessee

to Johnnie

Chapter One

A SOFT CUSHION OF snow had fallen over the plains of western Tennessee, and as Joelle Mitchell guided her black gelding over the unbroken carpet of glittering flakes, she studied the landscape that surrounded her. The snow had softened the outlines of the hills that lay to Joelle's left and of the tall pines that stood on her right. The ground itself glittered like millions of tiny diamonds as the afternoon sun caught the brilliance of the landscape. The snow also brought a silence to the flat country, cushioning the sound of the horse's progress.

Glancing over her shoulder, Joelle surveyed the trail broken by her horse, the single sign of human occupancy on the smoothness of the pristine carpet. Obviously no one had been out on the road before her, and since the road to River Bend was seldom traveled in the dead of winter, this came as no surprise.

Leaning forward, Joelle patted the horse's neck, saying in a conversational tone, "Well, Blackie, how do you like the snow?" She laughed as the gelding lifted his head and snorted. "You do, I see. Well, I do too. I read a book once about Europe where the snow comes in drifts ten feet high all the way up to the eaves of the house. That would be like being buried alive, wouldn't it now?" Again the gelding blubbered between his lips, and Jo leaned forward and stroked the silky neck. "You wouldn't like it that deep and neither would I. This is just right."

Joelle Lynn Mitchell was "almost seventeen." She always stated her age that way as if that formula would make her. She sat easily in the saddle, her back straight and her eyes constantly searching the road ahead and the trees on each side.

She was not a beauty in the classic sense of the word; her features had strength rather than prettiness, which dismayed her. She had studied other girls and found her own face too plain, yet her features were attractive. She was a full-figured girl with long auburn hair that reached all the way to her waist when she let it down. Her eyes were deep set and wide spaced under long, dark eyelashes. The color was an unusual gray-green that sometimes took the background of whatever clothes she wore. Her face was square-shaped, and her mouth wide. Her chin had a stubborn cast, and she held it up in such a way that seemed to challenge people at times. Her ears were small and set close to her head, and her strong hands were roughened by hard work—cutting wood, plowing, and breaking horses.

Suddenly Blackie humped his back and gave a sideways lurch, almost taking Joelle off-guard. She caught herself, pulled the reins tight, and then laughed. "You'll have to do better than that, Blackie." She leaned forward once again and pulled a burr out of the jet-black mane. "But I like a horse that's got a little meanness in him." She continued to stroke the horse's neck and was tall enough to reach almost to his jaw without leaning forward.

"You know, Blackie, for a long time I was afraid I wouldn't have any figure at all. Remember how skinny I was?" Blackie whickered, assuring her that he certainly did remember, and she laughed. A memory slipped into her mind of a conversation she had had with her mother when she was fourteen. She had been staring at herself in the mirror with displeasure, and her mother had caught her. "What are you frowning about, Jo?"

"I don't have anymore figure than a rake handle," she had said. Her mother had put her arms around her and held her tight and had whispered, "You're just late developing. I was the same way. I cried myself to sleep many a night because the other girls got their figures sooner than I did."

The memory stayed with Joelle along with a tinge of sadness, for her mother's sickness had brought her down so that she had little of her early beauty left. She kicked Blackie into a run, mostly to get rid of the sadness, and delighted in the smooth pace of the gelding. As his hooves threw up snow in a small cloud, she leaned over the pommel.

A memory of her thirteenth birthday flashed into Joelle's mind. Her father had grinned at her at the breakfast table and said, "Well, it's your birthday. You expecting a big gift, I suppose?" He had often teased her like that, she remembered, and then he had laughed and pulled her to her feet. "Come along, Punkin. Your present's out here." She had followed her father, and she remembered, even as Blackie sped along the cushioned road, how he had led her to the barn and said, "There's your birthday present, Jo." Joelle had stared at the black foal, blacker than the blackest thing in nature, with disbelief—and joy. Her throat had filled and grown thick, and she had turned and embraced her father, holding him tight. "Thank you, Pa! It's the best present anybody ever had!"

The thought of her father, dead now for three years, was sharp and keen as any knife as it worked along her mind. Her father had taught her how to ride, hunt, and run the farm. Sadness crossed her features, and she shook her head, forcing herself to think of something else—anything else but the loss of the man who had been her father.

Ten minutes later she entered River Bend, the only town she had ever really known. She had once been to Memphis when she was very small, but all she remembered was that it was a busy place with more people than she knew existed.

River Bend was easy to fathom. It was a small town with no more than two hundred inhabitants. The main businesses, all single-story wooden affairs, occupied the main street—a blacksmith shop, livery stable, and hardware store on one side, and on the other side a bank, a series of shops, and two saloons. As was usual in November, there was little to do for those who farmed or raised cattle, so the hitching racks in front of the saloons were full.

As Joelle guided Blackie down the middle of the street, she passed a few people who gave her a wave and called out. She smiled and returned their greetings. A short, stubby young man in overalls ran up to her. "Hey, Jo, hold up!"

Joelle smiled, for Jerome Ross was one of her favorites. They were the same age and had attended school together. He patted Blackie's neck, and his round face beamed as he looked up at her. "You goin' to the dance Saturday night over at Blevins's, Jo?"

"I don't think so, Jerome."

"Aw, you never go anywhere, Jo. You ought to get out more." Jerome winked lewdly—or so he thought, although the wink was more ludicrous than lewd. "You ought to get yourself a steady feller—like me."

Joelle leaned down and pulled Jerome's hat down over his face, laughing at him. "Sadie wouldn't like that. She's got you branded like a heifer."

"She ain't neither!" Jerome replied indignantly. "But even if I'm took, the country's full of young fellers."

"Full of gophers and possums too."

"Well," Jerome grinned, pushing his hat back up, "if I get tarred of Sadie, I'll come over and set on your front porch."

"My stepfather would furnish the reception." Even as she spoke, a change took place in both their expressions. She knew they were both thinking of how Burl Harper had beaten young Will Conners nearly to a pulp when he had come trying to court her.

"You ought to go to the dance. It'll be fun. You need to get out more."

Joelle shook her head and said, "You have a good time. Tell Sadie if she's not good to you, I'll take you away from her."

She kicked Blackie lightly, and he picked up his pace. She dismounted in front of a faded, weather-beaten sign that said "Dr. Phares Raeburn." She tied Blackie's lines loosely to the hitching post, leaped onto the board sidewalk, and entered the office. There was no one in the outer room so she opened the back door and called out, "Dr. Raeburn, are you here?"

"Come on in." Joelle entered to see Raeburn sitting in a worn, cane-bottom rocking chair. A stove beside him held a battered, blackened coffeepot, and he said, "Take some of that coffee, girl. It's cold as a well-digger's toes out there today."

"I believe I will." Joelle found a cup among the four on the shelf and noted that none of them had been washed. She rinsed it as best she could, wiped it with her handkerchief, then poured the black liquid in. "It looks like tar," she said.

"If you don't like my coffee, don't drink it," Raeburn snapped.

She smiled and tasted the coffee. It not only looked like tar; it more or less tasted like it too.

"Set yourself down there, girl, and gimme some juicy gossip. Since Julie Ann got sick, I ain't been able to keep up with it."

"How is she?" Julie Ann Massey was the woman who served as nurse for River Bend. She had been down with pleurisy lately, and Doc Raeburn missed her. As Joelle sat there, Raeburn, an observant man, studied her face. He had delivered her and had enjoyed watching her grow up from an awkward, long-legged yearling into a shapely, tall young girl on the very brink of mature womanhood. As she sipped her coffee, he leaned back and asked, "How's your mother, Jo?"

"Not too good. I wish you'd come out and see her."

"I'll probably be out that way tomorrow."

"Have you got any medicine I could give her?"

Heaving himself out of the chair, Raeburn walked over to a shelf that contained a variety of bottles of different shapes and colors and carefully removed a small bottle with a brown liquid. "I want you to give her a teaspoon of this five times a day. Early in the morning. Late at night especially."

"What is it?"

"It's medicine. What'd you think?" He spoke with all the force he could, but he saw Joelle watching him and knew that she saw through his words. She got that from her dad—he was that way.

"How much do I owe you, Doc?"

"Nothing. Bake me a pie sometime."

"What kind?"

"Any kind."

"I'll do it. Much obliged for the medicine." She gave him a brief smile, then left the room. Raeburn stared at the door, and a few minutes later his wife, Bertha, came in.

"Was that Joelle I saw leaving here?"

"Yes, it was."

"How's her mother?"

"She's not going to make it, Bertha."

Bertha Raeburn put a sack on the table and poured herself a cup of coffee. She held it for a moment without tasting it and said, "That sorry husband of hers hasn't helped her. If Charles Mitchell had lived, he'd have taken better care of her."

"You're right there."

They both were silent. Then Bertha gave her husband a direct look. "Joelle's afraid of Burl."

Instantly Raeburn looked up. "She tell you that?" he demanded.

"No, she didn't tell me, not with words. But you watch her when he's around. Watch her eyes. She never takes them off of him. She's scared to death of him."

Raeburn began to rock and after a few seconds muttered bitterly, "She's probably got good reason."

$\backsim$

AS SOON AS JOELLE entered Thompson's General Store, she took a deep breath. The smells were always good—the sharp, acrid pickles in the barrel by the counter, the onions hanging from a wire along the roof, and the leather harnesses. She walked up to a big, hammer-headed yellow tomcat on the counter who stared at her with round, golden eyes. She stroked his blunt, scarred head.

"You've been fighting again, Jackson." She continued to stroke the big cat and then smiled. "You're too romantic. You need to leave those lady cats alone and stay out of fights."

"He won't do that." Daniel Thompson, the son of Jesse Thompson, the store owner, had appeared from the back room, carrying a box. He put it on the counter. "Good to see you, Jo."

"How are you, Daniel?"

"Fine as silk. Can I get you something?"

"I need sugar and coffee and some kind of canned fruit."

Daniel quickly assembled the small order, then reached into the glass-covered candy case and scooped hard candy into a small sack. "There. Eat this. It'll make you sweet like me."

The two stood there talking. It was a pleasant moment in Joelle's life. She and Daniel Thompson, along with Jerome, had been good friends all through school. She was not surprised when he said, "How about going to the dance with me Saturday night over at Blevins's? I hear they're going to have some good music there."

"I don't guess so."

"Why not? I'd be proud to take you."

"Harper would never let me go."

8

Daniel noticed that she never called her stepfather any-thing but his last name. His full name was Burl Harper, and Daniel knew she called him Harper to his face too. He reached out and pinched her arm. "Why, you're getting to be an old maid. You're almost seventeen. Other girls your age, like Betty Summers, are already married and have a baby."

"You saw what Harper did to Will Conners when he tried to court me."

"Well, I ain't scared of him," Daniel said loudly. He was a tall young man but thin. Burl Harper, sliced down the middle, would make two splinters like Daniel.

"You should be." She hesitated, then said, "I am."

Daniel stared at her, not knowing what to say, and Jo knew instantly she had said too much. She smiled. "You have a good time at the dance."

She paid for the items, went outside, and walked down the street. She put her purchases in the saddlebags, mounted in one easy motion, and left town.

As she rode home, Joelle was burdened for her mother and afraid for herself. "I'm worried about Ma, Blackie. She never gets any better, and I'm afraid she's going to die." She had long ago started talking to her horse—perhaps because she had so few people to share her thoughts with.

Blackie nodded and glanced back toward her with his dark, liquid eyes. He had learned to recognize the tone of her voice better than most people could. "I don't know what I'd do—if she dies."

She didn't speak to the gelding again, and finally, as she approached the farm, she remembered how much she had loved this place when her father was alive. The snow reminded her of his last winter. He had built a monstrous snowman, and she and her mother had helped. Finally they had made snow cream out of snow, vanilla, and sugar, and she had eaten until she had been half-sick. That was the last good memory she had stored of her father, and she, as always, tried to push it out of her mind. For a long time she had courted memories and tried to store them up, but she had discovered they made her sad, and now sometimes they would come uninvited. More than once tears had come to her eyes as she remembered her father . . .

She rode into the stable, stepped down, and unloaded the saddlebags. Then she unsaddled Blackie. She was talking to him as she scooped grain from a sack, put it in the box, and watched him chew noisily. She slapped him on the rump and turned to go but stopped when Burl Harper appeared. He stood blocking her way, and fear ran along Jo's nerves, as it always did when she found herself alone with her stepfather.

"Where you been?"

"I went to town to get medicine for Ma and some coffee and sugar. We're about out."

Burl Harper was thirty-eight. He had a bold, florid face, hazel eyes, and straw-colored hair. He was a big man, thick and wide. He was a good farmer when he chose to be, but he would rather do other things. He had not been a good husband, and many times Jo had wondered and almost asked her mother why she had married him. Once her mother said, "These are hard times, Jo. We've got to have a man to help us or we'll lose this place." It was not an answer that satisfied Jo Mitchell, but she knew she could never rebuke her mother, for life had been hard after Charles Mitchell had died.

"You sneaked out is what you done," Harper said.

"I didn't sneak anywhere." She faced him and controlled her fear.

"You're meeting a man, ain't you?"

"No."

"You better not. I won't have it. You mind what I say now."

"I didn't sneak, and I wasn't meeting anybody." She moved to get by him, but he blocked the way.

"It won't do you any good to get medicine for Clara. She's not going to make it. You can see that." He suddenly reached out and took her by the arm, and immediately Jo jerked her arm away. Harper laughed. "I like a girl with spirit. Don't you worry, Joelle. I'll take care of you."

"I can take care of myself, Harper!"

"Why do you always call me that?"

"It's your name, isn't it?"

"Well, you stay away from men. You saw what I done to that one that came courting. I'll do it again if another one comes." He reached out for her, but she quickly stepped away.

"Leave me alone," she said coldly. But she saw the gleam in his eyes and knew that he would not.

Moving across the yard, she entered the house, put the groceries in the kitchen, and went at once to her mother's bedroom. No matter how many times she saw her mother, it was always a slight shock. Her mother had been an attractive woman, well-shaped with a full face, and now her face was shrunken, which made her eyes look abnormally large. "I got some medicine from Dr. Raeburn. You got to take a teaspoon five times a day."

There was little response in Clara's face. She didn't protest but swallowed the medicine and said, "Where's Harper?"

"He was out at the barn—" She broke off abruptly when she heard a horse crying out and walked over to the window.

Burl Harper was mounted on the big stallion Napoleon. She watched as he whipped the horse with a quirt, and she saw that he was laughing when the stallion reared up. He lashed the horse and left the yard at a dead run. Burl Harper didn't know how to treat a horse, and Jo knew that he was the same with every living thing.

She moved into the kitchen and made some broth. As she waited for it to heat, she looked around the kitchen—the only home she had ever known. Mom is going to die, and I'll have to leave this place. A bleak future seemed to loom before her, and she steeled herself against it. Forcing herself to concentrate on the care of her mother, she took the bowl in and watched her mother eat a few spoonfuls.

Clara said weakly, "I can't eat anymore, honey."

"You need to keep your strength up."

Clara suddenly reached out and caught Jo's hand. "Jo," she said, "I'm going to die. When I'm gone"—she hesitated and her lips forced the words reluctantly—"you'll have to leave this place."

Both of them knew she was talking about Burl Harper. Clara had already seen the attention he was paying to her daughter, and once she had challenged him. When she had warned him, he had laughed and pushed her away. "You'll have to leave here," Clara repeated to Joelle.

"I don't have anywhere to go, Ma."

"You need to go to Fort Smith to my sister Rita. She's Rita Faye Johnson. They'll take you in."

"All right, Ma." Joelle didn't want to talk about it but knew she wouldn't do it. The thought of asking a stranger to take her in was abhorrent, but she didn't want to argue.

She sat beside her mother and read to her from the Bible. She read well enough, but her mind was not on the words. Her mother had always loved the Bible, and this one was worn and marked on every page, it seemed. As she read on, her mother was listening to the words, but Jo herself was thinking of the day that would come soon enough when she would have to leave River Bend.

❧

MID-DECEMBER CAME, AND THE snow had all disappeared. Joelle spent the days taking care of her mother and staying away from Burl. One day, as she bathed her mother's face, she said, "I'll fix you something to eat."

"Can't eat."

Suddenly Joelle saw something in her mother's eyes, and she whispered, "What is it, Ma?"

"I had a dream last night."

"What did you dream?"

"A dream that God would—send somebody to look out for you. I saw somebody. He looked like my brother Caleb—you never saw him. He was tall and lean with hair as black as a crow's wing. You've seen his picture."

"Yes, he was a fine-looking man."

"He always took care of me when we were kids. In the dream he said, 'Don't worry about Jo, Sister. Someone will take care of her like I took care of you.'"

Joelle felt tears come to her eyes. She didn't believe in dreams, but now she said, "That's a good dream, Ma."

"I believe—it's from the Lord."

Joelle held her mother's hand as the woman drifted off to sleep. Ten minutes later her eyes opened, and she said, "Something I want you to do."

"What is it, Ma?"

"Go into the attic. Look in the old chest that was my mama's. Open the bottom drawer and take it out. Behind it there's a metal box. Bring it to me."

Joelle was surprised, but she was also curious. "I'll be right back, Ma." She left the bedroom and went up the stairs—glad that Harper was gone. She found the old walnut chest, pulled the bottom drawer out, and there it was—a flat metal box no more than two inches thick and probably eight inches square. She put the drawer back and then, holding the box, ran down the stairs. "Is this it, Ma?" she said as she pulled her chair close.

"Open it."

Joelle gasped. "Ma, what's this?" She pulled out a pair of diamond earrings and whispered, "Are these real?"

"Yes, they're real."

Joelle picked up a large ruby ring, a gold necklace and matching bracelets with diamonds in them, and also considerable cash.

"What is this, Ma?"

"My mother gave these to me on my wedding day when I married Charles. Her mother had given them to her."

"What do I do with these, Ma?"

Clara Harper was quiet, and her eyes fluttered as she struggled to stay awake. "Don't let Harper know you have this.

I made a mistake marrying him, but I've been saving money. Don't forget my dreams." She reached down. Her grip was stronger as she held Jo's hand. "God will send a man to help you. He'll be tall and have dark hair and dark eyes."

Joelle sat there, holding her mother's hand and examining the contents of the box. Her mother had fallen into a fitful sleep, and her breathing was shallow. Joelle fastened the box, loosened her mother's hand, and replaced the box behind the drawer in the chest. As she did, she wondered at her mother's keeping this a secret all these years. Somehow it seemed to be a purposeful thing, and she was glad to know the box was there.

She returned to sit with her mother. Two hours later her mother arched her back, uttered a single soft cry, and said, "Charles." Then life left her.

Joelle held her mother's still hand. She was still there when Burl came in. He opened the door and started to speak, but when he saw Joelle's face, he said, "Is she gone?"

"Yes, she's gone."

"Well, where do you want the grave?"

"Under the big hickory tree beside the river."

CLARA'S FUNERAL WAS WELL attended. She and her first husband had made many friends, and now the neighbors came by. The funeral was held in the church, followed by a brief service by the grave. After the pastor read the Scripture, the neighbors greeted Joelle. Edward Campbell, the pastor, came to her. "We'll help all we can, Joelle. She was a wonderful woman. A fine Christian."

"Thank you, Pastor."

Campbell turned away and waited until his wife had spoken to Joelle. The two watched as Burl Harper turned and went to the house. "That's a sad story building there," Campbell said.

"Yes, Harper married Clara for her farm, and he's got it now."

"I'm worried about Joelle. She's afraid of Harper. Doc Raeburn told me that we've got to do something about it."

"Can you do anything, Ed?"

"We'll try, but she's not of age. Harper's her legal guardian." Campbell brushed his hand across his face as if to push a thought aside, and the two were silent for a long time. When they turned to leave, Campbell glanced back toward the house. He saw Joelle Mitchell standing on the porch in the cold, looking toward her mother's grave.

Chapter Two

FOR THE FIRST WEEK after her mother's funeral, Joelle spent a great deal of her time outside the house. She went for long rides on Blackie, hunted rabbits, cared for the stock, and found solace in the cold December air. Christmas was only a few days away, but it meant nothing to her now.

As she came back from the barn, bearing the bucket of milk from Bessie the cow, she remembered the times as a small child when her father had made a great deal out of the Christmas season. She remembered his taking her out into the woods, and not just any tree would do. It had to be a very special one. "You can't just chop a tree down for Christmas," he had said once, a grin decorating his face. "You've got to have one just the right height and just the right shape, and it has to smell like a Christmas tree. Cedar is the only thing for that."

The snow had disappeared, but the air was cold, and as these memories flooded through Joelle, she looked up to see a large jackrabbit dart away, leaping from right to left. The antics of the rabbit amused her. "I'm not after you or your lucky foot either." She remembered her father had been somewhat superstitious and told her once, "The only rabbit's foot that's any good for luck is the right rear foot. The rest of them are nothing. But you take a right rear—why, you got something there, Punkin."

She passed the corral, and at once Blackie trotted up, hanging his head over the fence. She reached into the pocket of her apron and pulled out an apple. She cut it into quarters with the large pocket knife she always carried and fed him one of them. "Don't eat so fast you'll ruin your digestion," she said. She rubbed the silky nose of the gelding and fed him the other quarters. Blackie had become almost as necessary to her as air or food or water. She had always loved the horse, but now that she was alone, she spent more time than ever grooming him and riding him through the second-growth timber that flanked the farm.

"That's all you get. If you're a good boy, I'll bring you another one later."

She picked up the milk pail and walked to the house. In the kitchen, she transferred the milk to a gallon jar and looked to see how much butter they had. There was very little. "I'll have to churn, I guess." She got the crock out, added the thick fresh milk, pulled up a chair, and began churning. The regular motion seemed to calm her nerves, but from time to time her eyes would go to the hall that led to her mother's room, and the sight always brought a feeling of sadness, grief, and loss.

Suddenly, a small movement caught her eye, and she swiveled her head quickly and saw a mouse had come from somewhere and was eating on a fragment that had fallen to the floor. "What are you doing here? Mice are supposed to be outside the house," she said and smiled, for the mouse propped to a sitting position, held the morsel of food in its tiny handlike paws, revolving it rapidly and taking tiny bites. The sight of the tiny creature pleased Joelle, for she loved all living things. Harper had gone on a rampage once trapping mice, and she remembered how grieved she had been at the mangled bodies he made her retrieve from the traps. She leaned forward and studied the underside of the mouse.

"Why, you're a nursing mother," she said and then smiled. "How many little ones have you got? The house will be full of your crew, but I don't care. I wish your family would all grow up to be nice, fat, plump mice, and I'll leave some cheese out for you tonight. Nursing mothers have to watch their diet pretty carefully."

Finally the churning was done, and she put the butter into a mold, one she had seen her mother fill thousands of times. She turned it over and studied the geometric perfection in the beautifully wrought yellow mound. It gave her satisfaction to make small things like this. She stepped outside to the spring house. The air was cold, and she put the butter inside. When she came back in, she saw that Harper had returned. He was wearing a heavy coat, and his cheeks were flushed from the exercise.

"I've been hunting," he said. "I didn't get nothing though."

Joelle nodded but didn't answer. She started toward the bedroom door, but as he passed by, he reached out and caught her arm. "Ain't you ever going to talk again?"

"Don't have anything to say, Harper."

"I don't like it when you call me Harper," he said. "I never have." His eyes narrowed, and then he grinned, his thick lips twisting upward at the corners. "One of these days you'll call me something a lot sweeter than Harper." She didn't answer.

He was so strong that she knew she could not break away. "People die, Joelle. You just have to get used to it."

Suddenly Harper reached out and caught her in a bear hug. His strength was frightening, and all she could do was turn her head to one side so that his lips missed her mouth. "Let me go, Harper!" He was very strong, and she drew back her foot and kicked him in the shin. She was wearing sharp-toed boots, and the pain caused him to turn her loose.

"Ow!" he cried. "You little vixen!"

He advanced toward her, and Joelle backed away. Her eyes lit on the kitchen knife that lay on the table. She picked it up and said, "You stay away from me or I'll cut you!"

Harper was big, but he was quick. His hand shot out, and he grabbed her wrist. He wrenched the knife away from her and said, "I'm going to have you one way or another, Joelle. I promised your ma I'd marry you. She said that would be good."

"That's a lie! She never said that!"

"Sure she did. I'm telling you."

"I'll never marry you!"

He stared at her, and his eyes glowed like miniature furnaces with the lust that was always barely below the surface. "You're going to be in my bed, Joelle, married or not. Better we marry, and that's what we'll do."

Joelle saw the determination in his gruff, blunt features. She twirled and ran out of the kitchen. He called out to her. "Make up your mind to it. I'm going to have you, Joelle!"

$\backsim$

THE REVEREND EDWARD CAMPBELL sat at his desk, working on a sermon for Sunday. He wrote slowly with the Bible and a concordance on the desk before him. A small kitten on the desk was as white as the snow that had fallen lately, and she kept snatching at the pen as Campbell wrote.

"You're a pest, Charlotte. Go away." He shoved the kitten, but she came back at him and threw herself on his hand. Campbell smiled, leaned back, and watched the kitten as she struggled to hold his fist. He loved animals, and for a time he watched her until a knock came at his door. He crossed the room that served as his study and as a Sunday school room during the Sunday morning church meeting.

When he opened the door, he saw Joelle Mitchell. "Why, Joelle, come in." He saw the strain on the young woman's face and said, "Sit down over here. I made some coffee. Would you like some?"

"No, thank you, Pastor." Joelle took her seat and clasped her hands together. They were not steady hands, Campbell saw, and as he took his seat, he thought he knew what the young woman was going to say. Her face was pale, and there was a twitch in her lip that revealed her unsteadiness. "I've got to talk to you, Pastor."

"Of course, Joelle. What's the trouble?"

"It's—it's my stepfather." She tried to speak, but she turned her eyes away from his staring as she twisted her fingers. "He—he says he's going to make me marry him. He can't do that, can he?"

"I don't think so, Joelle. I'll have a talk with him."

"He won't listen to you."

For a moment Campbell sat there and then nodded. "You're right, but I think he'll listen to Judge Robertson. I'll go talk to him about this. Tell me everything now, and then the judge and I will have a talk with Burl."

&

"I DON'T THINK THIS is going to do much good, Preacher."

Judge Harlan Robertson was in his middle fifties. He was a short man and somewhat overweight. His hair was an iron-gray, and he had a pair of sharp gray eyes. He had been at his home when the minister had come by and explained the situation. Now as the two bumped on the wagon seat along the rough road that led to Joelle's home, the judge shook his head. "He's the legal guardian of the girl. No getting around that."

"There's some getting around his forcing her to marry him, I hope."

"He can't force her to do anything. This is a free country."

"I wish you'd seen her, Judge. She's scared to death. She told me that Harper said he would have her in his bed with or without marriage."

"That can get a man hanged in this country."

"How are you going to prove it? It'll be her word against his."

"I guess you're right." The judge stirred in his seat as they approached the house. "We'll have to make it pretty strong, Brother Campbell. Burl's a tough nut."

"Make it strong as you can, Judge. I'm worried about that girl."

Campbell pulled the buggy in front of the house and tied the horse to the hitching rail. The two men started toward the door. Campbell knocked, and almost at once Burl Harper came out. He stared at the two men silently, but there was a smoldering anger in his eyes. "What do you two want?"

"We're going to talk to you, Harper," Judge Robertson said, his voice soft but with a hint of steel underneath. "We can do it here, or I can have the sheriff bring you in. It's your choice."

"I ain't done nothing. You can't arrest me."

"I guess it'll have to be the sheriff then. Come on, Preacher."

"Wait a minute," Harper said. He knew the judge was a hard man, and having stood before him more than once on charges of drunkenness, he said, "Come on in, but I don't know what you want with me."

The men went inside, and Harper turned and stood in the middle of the floor. "What is it?" he grunted in his surly voice.

"We're here about Joelle," Campbell said. "She came to me with some complaints about the way you've spoken to her and the way you acted."

"I haven't touched that girl. She never could tell the truth."

"That's not so," Campbell said. "She's a good girl."

"What'd she say about me?"

Harlan Robertson said, "You told her she was going to have to marry you."

"She needs to get married. A man and a young woman can't live here alone. You know that."

"She's not going to marry you," Campbell said firmly. "You can rest on that."

"You ain't her kin, Preacher. None of your business."

"Some of my business though. If you force that girl, I'll see you hanged for it." Robertson's voice was almost pleasant, but there was a steely glint in his eyes. "I've hanged men for rape before."

"I ain't touched that girl."

"But you've threatened to. She told us that much."

The judge did most of the talking. He never took his eyes off Burl Harper's face, and finally he said, "I've told you what's going to happen. If you want to dangle on the end of a rope, you just try me on this. You touch that girl, I'll see you hanged, Harper."

The two men left, and Burl watched them with a baleful light in his eyes. He left the house and went to the stable where Joelle was grooming Blackie. "So you had to go spill everything to that preacher."

Joelle turned to face him at once. "Yes, I did, and he said he was going to bring the judge and tell what they'd do to you if you don't leave me alone."

Suddenly he laughed. "There'd have to be a witness to that. You and I are here all alone. You thought you'd outsmart me, didn't you?" Anger flared in his eyes. "Well, you didn't. You make up your mind at this, girl. I'm going to have you. If you don't marry me, I'll have you anyway." She turned her back on him and stiffened, for she would not put it past him if he attacked her right then. He didn't speak again, however, and she leaned over and put her head against Blackie's glossy hide. Her legs felt weak.

"What am I going to do, Blackie? What am I going to do?"

e͠

HARPER HAD GONE TO town, and Joelle could not get away from his words and knew that he had enough evil in him to do exactly what he said. She paced the house, tried to pray, and finally went into the main room. Over the front door was a shotgun she had often used for hunting rabbits. She pulled it down and took two shells from the drawer of the table beside the wall. She placed the shells inside and clicked the barrel into place. Then she went into her room and placed the shotgun beside the door. She studied the door for a time. *I've got to lock that door,* she thought.

She went to the barn and soon found a hasp but no lock. Going back into the house, she fastened the hasp on the inside of her door, then she took a railroad spike that had been a souvenir of her father's and tried it. It made a snug fit. She removed it and felt somewhat better. He can't get at me through that door, and if he does, I'll shoot him. She didn't know whether she could shoot a man or not, but she knew she would have to do something.

She spent most of what was left of the day outside and took a short ride on Blackie. Afterward she went into the house and fixed a supper of eggs, fried ham, and biscuits left over from breakfast. She went to her room. It was not late, but she felt safer after she had fastened the hasp. She took her mother's Bible and began to read. A frightening thought came to her: *I feel like I'm on a desert island with nothing here to help me or to love me—and a savage is out there waiting to get at me.*

She picked up the book Miss Harrelson, her teacher at the school, had given her and began to read. It was Shakespeare's play *As You Like It*, and she had liked it so much she'd read it repeatedly. The plot amused her, a story of Rosalind, a young woman who had to flee her wicked uncle. She had dressed herself as a young man, and in this disguise, had met a young man, who thought she was a boy. Then Rosalind offered to help the young man learn how to win a woman's love—so she (a girl pretending to be a boy) became a girl pretending to be a boy pretending to be a girl! It was foolish and utterly unreasonable, but as Joelle read, for a time she was able to get her mind off her problems.

Finally she put the book aside and began to get ready for bed. She put on her warm flannel nightgown and got into bed. She tried to turn her mind from what might happen and thought of her mother's dream, but Joelle couldn't believe that anyone would come to help her. Her mother had been an imaginative woman, as she was herself, but she had never heard of dreams having much meaning. Hers never seemed to. She left the lamp burning for a time and read a chapter of the Bible, but she didn't grow sleepy.

Finally she heard a horse approach, and she stiffened. She lay there frightened and heard the front door close. She waited and heard the heavy tread of Burl Harper coming down the hall. "Let him go by this room," she prayed in a thin whisper.

But that didn't happen. She heard the steps pause outside her door, and then she heard Burl Harper say, "You awake in there?"

Joelle threw the cover back. She got the shotgun and backed away from the door. "Go away, Harper. Leave me alone."

She heard him try the door, and he cursed. "You think you'll lock me out? You think a door will stop me?" She heard a crash, and the door sprang back, the hasp ripped out. Burl stepped inside. His face was flushed with drink, and his speech was slurred. "You can't lock me out. Ain't no door will stop me." He took one step toward her and then stopped. "Put that gun down, girl."

"Get out of here, Harper. I'll shoot you. I swear I will."

Harper wanted to advance, but the shotgun was steady and pointed right at his chest. He knew the damage a 12-gauge shotgun could do. He had seen it.

"Get out of here!"

Harper laughed harshly. "You can't have that shotgun all the time. That's OK though. I like spirit in a woman. Be like breaking a horse." He laughed crudely and said something profane, then turned and moved unsteadily out the door. Joelle shut the door at once. The hasp was broken, and she knew she would stay up all night, or at least until he went to sleep. She sat down in a chair and saw that her hands were shaking.

"You can't let him do this to you, Joelle Mitchell," she whispered. "You know you've got to be strong, so stop whimpering and stop shaking." She watched the door and was listening as she heard Harper thumping around in his room. Something tipped over and made a crash, and she heard him curse. Finally all grew quiet, and Joelle Mitchell sat alone in a house that she had learned to fear and dread.

Chapter Three

THE OIL LAMP CAST an amber corona of light over the bedroom, and silence possessed the house, which was ominous and frightening. Joelle was standing at the window, looking out into the darkness while still holding the shotgun, which was still loaded. A sudden shadow outside caused her to react, and straining her eyes she saw a large owl float by noiselessly. It disappeared, and Joelle turned away from the window and looked at the door. With the hasp broken there was nothing to keep Harper from coming in.

I can't stay awake forever. The thought came to Joelle quickly, and she gripped the barrel of the shotgun tighter. Finally she walked over to the door, lifted the shotgun, holding it in the crook of her arm, and put her finger on the trigger. Opening the door slowly so that it didn't creak, she stepped out into the hall. She wore heavy woolen socks and moved like a wraith down the hall until she stood before the bedroom where Harper slept. She put her ear close to the door and heard heavy snoring.

Relief rushed through her. He always passed out after drinking, and turning quickly, she moved back down the hall.

As soon as she entered her bedroom and shut the door, she moved to the table and leaned the shotgun against it.

Sitting down in the rocker, she picked up the Bible. It fell open almost by itself, and she saw that her mother had put a marker and drawn a line beside the third psalm, or part of it. Something was written faintly in the margin, and she leaned forward and held the Bible up to the light. It was dated two days before her mother had died, and beneath the date was written in a spidery handwriting, "For Joelle."

Tears rose to Joelle's eyes, and she allowed them to run down her cheeks. Life had not been pleasant for her since her father had died, but her mother had always been there. Now she was gone, and the sense of isolation and loneliness seemed to envelop her like a sable cloak of sinister darkness.

She whispered as she read out loud, "Psalm 3. A Psalm of David when he fled from Absalom his son." Joelle knew that story well, and the pastor had preached on it only a few weeks ago. She remembered his stressing how David had loved every-thing he had, including his son who had turned on him and was trying to kill him. She began to read, whispering the words in a faint voice: "Lord, how are they increased that trouble me! Many are they that rise up against me. Many there be which say of my soul, there is no help for him in God."

The next verses, 3 and 4, were underlined, and she read them slowly: "But thou, O Lord, art a shield for me; my glory, and the lifter up of mine head. I cried unto the Lord with my voice, and he heard me out of his holy hill."

For a moment she sat there, and then she remembered that Brother Campbell had read verse 5 and said, "Here is a man who had lost everything. He was running in fear for his life from his beloved son Absalom. His whole life had collapsed about his head, and now he who had been king of Israel and had it all had nothing. And what did he do? As we just read, he cried unto the Lord. And then what? You read verses 5 and 6, 'I laid me down and slept; I awaked; for the Lord sustained me. I will not be afraid."

Suddenly, from a source that had to be God, Joelle Mitchell felt a sense of peace and security. "I will not be afraid," she read again, and as she read it, she suddenly knew that God was in the room. She read through that verse again and again, and as she read it, something began to form in her mind: *David had fled, but the Lord sustained him. I have to leave here—and I have to believe that God will take care of me.*

The thought came almost as clearly as if it were printed in heavy black type against a luminescent white background.

"I have to leave here!"

She spoke the words aloud, and for the first time since her mother's death a sense of rightness of direction and of decision came to her. She read the entire psalm again, then closed the Bible and put it down. "Ma, you told me to go stay with Aunt Rita in Fort Smith," she whispered, "and that's what I'm going to do."

With the decision formed in her mind, Joelle rose and for a moment was thankful that Harper was in a drunken state. She dressed quickly in a divided riding skirt she had made for herself and her high-heeled boots. She put on a woolen shirt and then a fingertip-length coat that she had bought earlier in the winter.

She knew she was going to take Blackie, so she moved into the living room. She lit the lamp on the table, and going to the desk that contained all the papers, she searched through them until she found the bill of sale. When her father had bought Blackie as a foal, he had named her as the owner, and she had been so proud!

There was a great deal of money in the box with the papers, and she stared at it for a moment. Then without hesitation she closed the box and put it back in the desk. Picking up the lamp, she went down the hall to the stairs. She knew that the fourth step that led to the attic always squeaked so she skipped it. Going into the attic, she retrieved the hidden box, put the bottom drawer back, and went downstairs. She knew she could not take a suitcase so she retrieved a canvas bag she used from time to time to carry supplies on long hunting trips. It had a drawstring, and she packed one dress, underclothes, and a few other things.

A thought came to her. She returned to the living room, opened the desk again, and stared at the chrome-plated .38 with a beautifully designed ivory handle that had been her father's. She picked it up along with a box of cartridges. Going back to her room, she put the gun in the sack, then her mother's Bible.

She carried the lamp into the kitchen and set it on the table. She selected what food she could carry, mostly canned goods, but also a large portion of smoked bacon. She added a frying pan, saucepan, tin plate, sharp knife, fork, and spoon. She put in the coffee she had bought that day and closed the sack. She gave one quick look around the room, then without hesitation doused the light and moved toward the door.

As she stepped outside, the cold bit at her face. At the corral she called softly, "Blackie." Instantly the horse came to her. She opened the gate, and he followed her into the barn. She lit the lantern, saddled Blackie, packed what she could in the saddlebag, and hesitated for a moment. She filled a feed sack halfway with the grain Blackie would need. Balancing it over his back, she tied it down with the thongs attached to the saddle, doused the light, and then stepped into the saddle.

"Come on, Blackie, we're going." The gelding immediately obeyed. Joelle Mitchell didn't look back as she left the yard, though she knew full well she was saying good-bye to many things she had treasured.

She guided the horse by the faint light of the crescent moon overhead. Looking up, she could see that the stars were cold and brittle like frozen diamonds in the sky, but she paid no heed. She spoke to Blackie and touched him with her heels, and the big black horse broke into a fast walk. She touched him again, and Blackie broke into a gallop.

Chapter Four

OVERHEAD, BRILLIANT STARS WERE beginning to fade, and as Joelle looked over her shoulder, she saw a faint line of light on the eastern horizon. She had ridden at a fast pace since leaving the farm, and now she was beginning to feel the tension that had built up since making her decision. Five minutes later she ran across a small creek that had thin ice across the top. She moved off the road for thirty yards, stepped down, and then took out Blackie's nose bag and fed him from the grain. She tied him on a long line and began to gather sticks. She made a small pyramid, and striking a match, she waited until a small flame was blazing, added more fuel, and took out her cooking utensils. She filled the coffeepot with water from the creek, added coffee, and put it on to boil.

The air was cold, and she shivered from time to time, drawing her coat closer and pulling her hat down over her head. She didn't want to think about the future, nor was the past something to dwell on, so she concentrated on frying bacon, and when it was crisp, she let it cool on the tin plate. The coffee was boiling so she poured herself a cupful, then sat down to eat.

She chewed slowly, and the coffee seemed to warm her all the way to her bones. When she finished, she quickly cleaned her utensils and pulled the map out of the saddlebag. The light was stronger now, but she had to wait until the sun came through the trees and fell on the map.

Blackie nudged her, and she removed the feed bag and smiled. "I hope you enjoyed your breakfast." He whickered and nodded his head as if he understood. She went back to studying the map.

"We've got to cross the Mississippi up in Memphis, Blackie, but I don't know how to get to Fort Smith." She searched on the map, but it wasn't marked. She stared at the map, nodded, and spoke again to the gelding. "There's got to be a railroad that goes from Little Rock to Fort Smith. I've always heard they were the biggest towns in Arkansas. I wonder if they take horses?"

She pulled out her mother's Bible. She read the Twenty-third Psalm aloud and nodded. "Blackie, that's a good psalm." She got to her feet, packed her gear, and then mounted. "We've got to cross the Mississippi River on a ferry at Memphis, and then we've got to get to Little Rock. I hope we can catch a train from there, boy." She touched him with her heels, and he moved quickly back toward the road and broke into a gallop.

MEMPHIS WAS A HUGE place to Joelle. She had been there once before, but that had been years ago, and she had been only nine. Her father and mother had brought her, and she remembered they had gone to a circus. She remembered every detail—the clowns, the acrobats, and the elephants. Those memories had lived all of these years.

But now the city seemed to have grown. She moved into town cautiously, half-afraid someone would call out to her, for she knew that Harper would not give up. He would find a way to try to get her back.

Finally she asked an old man hobbling on crutches where the ferry was. He had looked at her with sharp black eyes. "Right down there, girlie. You gonna cross the river?"

"I guess so." She hurried away quickly, not wanting to get into a conversation. The old man's vague direction proved to be accurate. She came upon the Mississippi River and was awed at the width of it. It nearly took her breath away. Steamboats were coming and going, the smoke from their stacks rising in tall columns into the sky. As she approached, she heard the cries of men. To her left was a vessel with *Lady Belle* painted on the side. It was an ornate steamboat that carried passengers. She ignored that and moved down the line until finally she found a man wearing what looked like a captain's hat.

"Excuse me, sir. How can I get across the river?"

"If you got fifty cents, you get on that boat right there. Give it to that fellow wearing the tall hat."

Following his instructions, Joelle paid her fifty cents and led Blackie onto the deck. It was a side-wheeler, and they had to wait for two hours, but finally the engines began to roar, and the wheel began to turn. She stood beside Blackie, holding him. His eyes were wide as the boat trembled beneath his hooves. Finally the ferry landed, and she got off. The man who opened the gate looked at her, and she asked, "Do you know how far it is to Fort Smith?"

"Fort Smith? Why, that's a long way. You're in the eastern part of Arkansas. Fort Smith is way out there to the west. Roads are pretty bad. Besides, a woman don't need to be traveling through there. Some folks can be dangerous."

"Well, how would you get there?"

"Was I you, I'd go to Little Rock. It's near about a hundred miles or so. The road ain't too bad, and there's a railroad that goes from Little Rock right into Fort Smith." He cocked his head to one side and said, "Ain't you got a pa or a husband maybe?"

"No, I don't."

"Then you be careful, missy. Lots of bad folks around, especially around Fort Smith."

"Thank you." Joelle swung into the saddle and rode Blackie off the ramp, and soon found the road that led to Little Rock. She rode until dark, stopping at noon to rest and to eat from her sparse supplies—more bacon, biscuits, and peaches from a can. As it grew dark, she pulled up beside a house that was off the road about a hundred yards. It looked run-down, but when she called out, a woman came out on the porch.

"I'm looking for a place to stay the night. I can pay."

"You can stay the night. Put your horse in the barn."

"Thank you." Joelle led Blackie into the barn, fed him, and went into the house.

"You et yet?" the woman asked. She was a tall, raw-boned woman with worn features and weary eyes.

"Not yet."

"I just made some venison stew. It ain't bad. I got some fresh bread."

"That sounds good."

"I'm Elmus Jeeter."

"I'm Jo Ann Jones." Joelle made up a name quickly and then at Mrs. Jeeter's bidding sat down at the table. "This is good stew," she said as she ate hungrily and accepted another bowl.

"Where you bound for, missy?"

"Oh, I'm going to Little Rock."

"You got family there?"

"No, not there. I'll be going farther on. What are the roads like?"

"Well, they been snowed-under, but that's mostly melted. Bad time to be on the roads."

Joelle ate the stew and then a big wedge of apple pie and washed it down with coffee. She made her excuses and went to the bedroom that Mrs. Jeeter showed her. She had not brought a nightgown so she took off her outer clothes and shivered under the blanket but went to sleep almost at once.

℮

JOELLE WOKE UP THE next day feeling rested but still nervous. When she went downstairs, Mrs. Jeeter said, "I got ham and some eggs. Day before Christmas. Not much of a Christmas meal."

"It smells so good." Joelle ate the breakfast, paid the woman, and asked, "What's the next town?"

"Forrest City. Ain't much of a town though."

"Thank you, Mrs. Jeeter."

Joelle saddled Blackie, mounted, and left. She rode all that day, passing through Forrest City, and late that night she found a vacant barn. She wanted to see as few people as possible so if Harper put out word on her, nobody would remember her. She made a fire inside the old barn. The house itself had burned down, leaving only a chimney standing, pointing like a skinny finger at the sky. She was getting low on supplies, but she ate what she had and wrapped herself in her blanket. She lay awake for a long time and thought, *Tomorrow's Christmas.*

As usual, when she thought of Christmas, she thought of her father who took such a delight in the holiday when she was growing up. She remembered stringing red berries with a needle and thread for decoration. The thought of her father made her sad, and then the loss of her mother came home to her, and she resolutely turned over and forced herself to sleep.

She rose at dawn and passed through several very small towns consisting mostly of a few stores and scattered houses. The road was firm, and she rode all day. She slept in another abandoned barn. Blackie's food was gone, and Joelle knew she would have to stop and buy supplies.

The next day she passed through a few more small towns but got into Little Rock late at night. She didn't know what to do, but finally she found a livery stable and had a young boy take Blackie, saying, "Grain him and rub him down, will you?"

"Sure will, ma'am. You staying long?"

"No, I'll be pulling out in the morning. Do you know if there's a train that leaves here for Fort Smith?"

"Yes, ma'am. Leaves every morning at 8:33."

"Thank you."

"Need a place to stay? There's a boardinghouse right across the street."

"Guess I'll look into that." She moved across the wide street and soon rented a room for the night from a very fat woman who said, "We got grub if you got a dollar."

"That would be nice."

She ate greasy pork chops and boiled potatoes for supper and went to bed. She dreamed that night of her mother and then of her father, so her night was restless.

The next morning she got up and didn't want anymore cooking at the boardinghouse. It was only six o'clock, and the train would not leave until 8:33 so she found a café and had breakfast there. Afterward she walked down the street and passed by an office where two men were talking. One of them said, "Boy, that'd be easy money, wouldn't it?"

The other man, a tall, thin individual wearing a plaid mackinaw, said, "Yeah, five hundred dollars. Think what we'd do with that, George!"

"Read that to me again."

Evidently the smaller man could not read, for the other said, "Joelle Lynn Mitchell, age sixteen. Auburn hair, blue eyes. Probably riding a black gelding. Wanted for grand larceny. Reward five hundred dollars. Contact Burl Harper, in care of sheriff's office River Bend, Tennessee."

Joelle froze, then hurried away. The two men were still talking about the reward. "We better keep our eyes peeled for her. I'd purely love to have that money!"

Joelle returned at once to the stable, and the boy was gone. She sat down on a box, and her mind whirled. *I'll get caught*, she thought. *Sure as the world, somebody will see me. I'll have to do something. He'll have a poster at every town along the way.*

She sat there for a long time, confused and frightened. Then she began to pack and took out her mother's Bible. As she did, the copy of Shakespeare's play *As You Like It* was there. She held the book tightly and tried to think, but her mind was nearly paralyzed. She looked down at the book, and suddenly the story leaped into her mind. Rosalind disguised herself as a man! *I could do that. If I were a man, nobody would notice me!*

Joelle had a quick mind and a fertile imagination. She began to think at once how it could be done, and her idea fell into place. She went to the general store. The clerk, a fat man with several cuts on his face, where he had recently shaved rather unskillfully, was grumpy. "What can I do for you?"

"I need to get some clothes for a young fellow. Just working clothes."

"There they are, right over there."

Quickly she found a pair of overalls too large for her, a pair of wool pants, also too big, and two shirts. Everything she picked was oversized. She also bought a fingertip-length mackinaw that looked warm. She found a wide-brimmed rather shapeless hat. She tried it on and cast a glance at the clerk who was reading a newspaper and paying no attention to her. The hat was for a small man evidently, but its broad, floppy brim would come down over her face. She bought two pairs of underwear, making sure that the tops were too small. Gathering the things together, she went back to the counter, and the man added up the cost. "That'll be twelve dollars and sixteen cents."

She paid the man and asked, "Do you have a sack I could put all this in?"

"I reckon so."

"Oh, do you have a pair of scissors?"

"Right over there in the hardware section."

Joelle picked out a pair of inexpensive scissors. He added, "That'll be another fifteen cents."

Joelle paid the man, took the sack, and left. She went at once back to pick up Blackie. The young boy was there, and he said, "You want me to saddle your horse?"

"Oh, I can do that. Here, how much do I owe you?"

He named a price, and she gave him a coin, then she said, "I've got to wait for a little while."

"Well, I got to leave. I'll be gone for about two hours. Make yourself at home."

Joelle watched the boy go and went into the back section. The stable was deserted, and she laid out the clothes and then took the scissors. She sheared her hair, cutting it roughly. Her heart was grieved, for her hair, she had always thought, was her best feature. Then she stepped out of her dress and riding skirt and put on the trousers she had bought. She put on the tight knit underwear, which flattened her upper body somewhat, one of the shirts, and finally the coat. She pulled the hat down over her eyes. She felt suddenly like a fool. "This will never work," she muttered, "but I've got to try it." She packed her things quickly, including the dress and the riding skirt, saddled Blackie, and moved out.

She rode directly down the middle of the street until she found the railroad tracks, and there to her left was the station. She approached and noticed a man standing at the corral, looking at a group of horses inside. She had been worried about how to get Blackie to Fort Smith. She pulled over and said, "Howdy."

"Hello, bub." The man, tall, lean, and tan, was probably in his late fifties. "That's a nice-looking horse you got there."

"Thanks, he's a good one."

"I'm taking this bunch to Fort Smith."

"That's where I want to go. I didn't know how to take my horse though."

The man suddenly laughed. "They'll skin you alive. It's scandalous the prices they charge for me to move these horses to Fort Smith."

"Well, I don't have a lot of money."

"Tell you what, bub. What's your name by the way?"

Joelle had a sudden thought. *If I call myself "Jo," people will think it's "Joe," and I'll be hearing a name some have always called me.*

"Joe Jones," she said.

"I'm Al Tompkins. Tell you what, Joe, why don't you put him in with my horses there? I've got to load 'em myself. They'll never count 'em. That way you won't have to pay."

"Well, that wouldn't be honest."

"It's my business how many horses go in there. I paid for the car. I'll put in as many as I want."

"Well, that'd be nice, Mr. Tompkins."

"They'll be moving the stock car back in a minute. What you going up to Fort Smith for?"

"I got some relatives there, Mr. Tompkins."

"A funny time to be traveling. A man ought to be home with his family at Christmas."

"I think that's right too."

The two talked, and Joelle was thankful she had a deeper voice than most women and felt relief that she had passed herself off as a young man so easily. In her baggy clothes and the floppy hat, he couldn't see much of her to be sure.

Thirty minutes later a train shuttled the car in, and Tompkins said, "Come on. Get that gelding in there. You can unsaddle him when he's loaded."

Joelle slipped off and put Blackie with the rest of the horses. He was nervous, but there was no time to worry about that. The two loaded the small herd into the car, and Tompkins slammed the door shut. "There's the feed section down there. It's walled off. If you want to, you can just stay there instead of paying their outrageous prices to ride this no-account railroad."

"Is that what you're going to do?"

"Not me. I'm going to ride in the passenger section, but a young fellow like you can rough it. Sleep on some of them feed sacks."

"I believe I'll do that."

And that's what Joelle did. As soon as Tompkins left, she unsaddled Blackie and put all the gear and her belongings into the feed room. Then she waited, anxious to get away from Little Rock. The whistle blew, and the train started with a jerk. The horses moved nervously. She went to Blackie. He put his head down, and she stroked his jaw.

"It's OK, boy," she whispered. "We're going to Fort Smith free of charge."

The train began to move and picked up speed slowly. Soon it was rolling over the rails with a clickety-clack sound. Joelle, who had never ridden on a train in her life, stared out at the landscape as it flowed by.

Suddenly she was afraid. She realized she hadn't the slightest idea what she was going to do. Her plan was to find her mother's sister, Rita, but she didn't know the woman. The future looked bleak indeed at the moment. She sat on some of the sacks of feed, and finally she grew sleepy. She made a bed, of sorts, on top of the sacks and curled up on top of them. The rhythm of the train wheels going over the rails with the regular clickety-clack lulled her to sleep, and her last thought was of the dream her mother had told her about. She had a moment to reflect as she went to sleep. She prayed, *Lord, I wish You'd send that man Ma saw in her dream.* Then she dropped off.

Chapter Five

"HEY! GET UP THERE, boy!"

Joelle came awake instantly and swung out at the hand that held her by the shoulder. "What!" She found herself looking up into the face of Mr. Tompkins.

"Well, you sure wake up mad, Joe." Tompkins peered down at her with a crooked grin. "You must have been having a bad dream."

"Sorry," Joelle said. "It scared me a little bit."

"Well, it would scare me, too, to get woke up out of a sound sleep, but we're almost to Fort Smith. Thought you'd want to wake up. You can go in the passenger car and wash up if you want."

"No, I'll just wait."

"You sleep pretty hard, don't you?"

"Not usually, but I was pretty tired."

Joelle dusted the straw from her clothing. She was still wearing the heavy, bulky mackinaw and the pants. She reached down for her hat, and Tompkins stared at her. "You need to find a new barber. That's as sorry a haircut as I've ever seen."

"Well, it was free." She shrugged and gave him a smile. "I want to thank you for your help. I am a little short on money."

"I don't mind gouging this railroad. They got plenty of my money. Say, you got folks here?"

"An aunt."

"Well, you take care of yourself. That's a mighty fine hoss you got there. Don't guess you'd want to sell him."

"No, I guess I'll hang on to him."

"Well, a good hoss is hard to find."

The train slowed, and as soon as it came to a screeching halt, Tompkins jerked open the doors. While he unloaded the other horses, Joelle saddled Blackie and led him outside. "Thanks a lot," she said again.

"Good luck to you, boy."

"And to you too."

Joelle led Blackie down the ramp, and he tossed his head up. "I bet you're thirsty, boy." She led him to a watering trough and let him drink noisily. "Guess we have to see if we can find out where my aunt is."

She moved down the street, taking in the sights. It was a rough town, rougher than River Bend. Every man, it seemed, wore at least one gun. Some carried rifles and a few carried shotguns. Indians were everywhere. She knew that west of Fort Smith was Indian Territory where the government penned up all the Indians. She stared at the Indians curiously for she had never seen one before. *They look like a pretty sorry bunch*, she thought. *Maybe they look better when you get to their land.*

She walked down the main street, which was busy indeed. The air was cold, but the sun shone brightly, bringing warmth to the cold earth. She stopped and stared at a man who sat in front of a general store in a cane-bottomed chair. It was tilted back, and he was concentrating on peeling the finest shavings he could from a piece of cedar with a razor-keen knife.

"Excuse me. Can you tell me where the post office is?"

The man looked up and shrugged, staring at her. "Right down that street over on the other side." He looked down the street and added, "Look at that. Got a wood boardwalk. Didn't have none of that ten years ago. What we did have was thirty saloons. Was about the wildest place you'd be wantin' to see."

Joelle stared at the rough-looking people. "Still looks pretty wild to me. Look how many men are carrying guns."

"They use 'em too. You watch yourself, young feller."

Joelle felt rested after sleeping most of the way from Little Rock, but she was anxious to find her aunt. Going into the post office, she waited until a couple mailed a package, paid, and then stepped aside.

"Yes sir. What can I do for you?"

"I'm looking for a woman named Rita Johnson."

The mail clerk scratched his jaw. "Well, there was a Miz Johnson around here, but her husband died. She don't live here no more."

"Do you have an address for her?"

"Not that I know of. Of course, things are in a mess around here. I'll look and see, not now though. Come back after while."

"Thank you."

She had little to do so she walked down the street until she found a livery stable. "Got to find a place for both of us, Blackie," she whispered slapping him on the neck. He made a blubbering sound with his lips, and she said, "I'll bring you some apples. You be a good boy now."

She walked into the stable and found a middle-aged man arguing with a customer. The customer didn't like the price, and the owner, a tall, bulky man with sharp eyes and a cavalry-type mustache, said, "If you don't like it, get out of here and don't bring your horse back anymore."

"Fine with me. It ain't much of a stable anyhow."

The man left, leading his horse, and the owner turned. "You want to stable that horse?"

"Yes, I do. He needs to be grained."

"A fine-looking animal. I'm Ben Phillips."

"I'm Joe Jones."

"Well, a good-looking animal. I'll have to take care of him myself. I lost my stable hand here. How long you aiming to stay?"

"Not sure, but I'll pay whatever you charge."

"Well, that's good news. People think I'm running a charitable institution here."

"I came looking for my aunt, Mrs. Rita Johnson."

"Oh yeah, I knew the Johnsons. The husband was a shoemaker. Died a couple of years ago. She married another fella. I've forgotten his name. Got a farm up in Canada. Don't know exactly where."

The news was discouraging. Joelle left the stable and walked for an hour. She stopped beside a gallows where a couple of young boys were staring up.

"You see that gallows?" one told the other. "I seen five men hanged at one time on that gallows right there."

"Aw, you didn't neither."

"Yeah, I did. They was Mexican, so it didn't matter much."

"Judge Parker, he's a hard case, ain't he?"

"They call him the hanging judge. I'd hate for him to get his hands on me."

Joelle stared at the gallows and shook her head. She had heard stories about Fort Smith. Judge Isaac Parker was in charge of the Indian nations. He had a group of marshals who patrolled the Indian country. It was a dangerous and lonely job, she had heard.

She quickly turned away and found a restaurant where she could buy breakfast. A sign over the counter said, "If you don't like our grub, don't eat here." The surly aspects of the sign made her smile. The waitress—a young woman with a full figure and a pair of snapping black eyes—said, "What do you have, sir?"

"I'll have whatever you got."

"Well, we got steak and eggs. Does that sound good?"

"Yes, and plenty of coffee and some biscuits if you've got them."

"Oh, we've got all that." The young woman moved closer and put her hip against Joelle's shoulder. "You here for long?" she asked.

Joelle looked up, startled. The girl was smiling at her. "Well, I might be here for a while."

"Well, we'll see each other again. This is the best place to eat." She hesitated and then said, "I get off at six."

Why, she's flirting with me, Joelle thought with astonishment. Nearly speechless, she kept her old hat on but pushed it back and said, "Well, I'll keep that in mind."

"My name is Millie. What's yours?"

"Joe Jones."

"I'll get your food, Joe. There's a dance tomorrow night at the town square."

"Well, I'll have to look into that."

Millie winked at her. "We'll both look into it."

Joelle was stunned. *Well, I guess my disguise is better than I thought if I got women making up to me!* She had looked in a mirror at herself and wondered how she could fool people. Of course, the bulky clothes concealed all the femininity of her figure, and the shaggy haircut helped, but she had no sign of whiskers, of course, and had smoother cheeks than most young fellows had.

Millie brought the breakfast, which was huge, and nudged Joelle again with her hip. "Don't forget about that dance."

"I won't."

Joelle ate slowly and put Millie out of her mind. A farm in Canada. *I'll never find Aunt Rita*, she thought. *Now what am I going to do?*

She finished the meal, put a dollar down, and added a quarter to it for a tip. She moved out the door when Millie said, "'Bye, Joe. I'll be looking for you."

"Me too," she said wryly.

The sunshine was bright now, but the air was still snappy. Somehow winter might lurk over the peaks, and she had heard about the Arkansas weather in the Ozark Mountains.

She walked around the town aimlessly and finally returned to the stable. Phillips was there, looking flustered. "I grained that hoss of yours."

"Thanks, Mr. Phillips."

"I lost my stable hand, dad blast it. What's your name, boy?"

"Joe Jones."

"You moving on, Joe?"

"No," Joelle said, making up her mind instantly. "I'm going to stick around for a while."

"Well," Phillips said quickly, "I could use a man. Young fellow quit. Got gold fever. Headed out for California. If the Indians don't get him, something else will. Besides, them wagon trains to California don't start until early April."

Joelle thought quickly. *If I went out there to California, Harper would never find me, and a working man wouldn't attract much attention here.*

"How much does the job pay?"

"Two dollars a day, and there's a room fixed up in the back. It's pretty filthy, but you can clean it up. Even got a little stove in there you can cook some meals on."

"I'd like to try it."

"Well, you're pretty young, Jones. Usually an older fellow does the job. You know horses?"

"Yes, I know horses."

"The job don't pay much, but you can stay with your hoss free. I'll give you a try. You stay on for a week, and we'll see how we suit each other."

"That suits me fine, Mr. Phillips."

Joelle went to the corral, and Blackie came to her at once. "I'll get you that apple right away. It looks like we got a home, Blackie." She petted his jaw, and he reached out and plucked her hat off her head by the brim.

"You stop that, you hear me?" She grabbed the hat back, and Blackie drew his lips back. He seemed to be grinning at her. "You're a comedian, you are. Leave my hat alone!"

❧

THE WEEK WENT QUICKLY, but after Joelle had been there five days, Ben Phillips said, "You're doing a good job. You just take over."

"How do you know I won't rob you?"

"I don't, but I wish you wouldn't."

"I won't do that, Mr. Phillips."

"I tested you out, you know. The fellow who came in with that big bay? He gave you twice as much as I usually charge, and you jotted it down. He's a friend of mine. If you was going to steal, that would have been the place for it."

"I'm not one for stealing," Joelle said.

"A good way to be. You take care of the livery stable. I'll take care of the card playing, and I'll raise your wages to two and a half a day."

"Thanks, Mr. Phillips."

Joelle watched him go. She felt a moment's relief. She knew she would have to be careful, but this seemed to be a place to wait. *But wait for what?* she thought. Then she realized she didn't know what she was waiting for—unless it was the man in her mother's dream. But she put little stock in that. She went to feed the horses.

Chapter Six

MANNY NOVIS LEANED BACK against the stone wall at the head of his bunk and studied his cell mate. He had shared this cell with Owen Majors for two years, and in all that time had never gotten to know the man. He spoke cheerfully now, a smile on his sharp features. "Well, Owen, you're gettin' out of this dump today. You ought to be jumping up and down."

Owen Majors was staring out the small window. The cold wind that entered didn't seem to bother him, and he didn't answer for a moment. His eyes were fixed on the bleak world surrounding the Arkansas Territorial Prison. He had looked out this window every day for two years, and it looked as ugly now as it had the first time he'd viewed it. He turned abruptly, leaned against the wall, and shook his head.

"I guess I'll save my jumping for when I get something to jump about."

Novis studied the man, as he had often. He was a tall man, six feet two, and everything about him seemed made for hard use. There was a puckered scar over his left hip, Novis knew, and another on his back high up. The face was not handsome, but coarse, jet-black hair and deep-blue eyes centered in a

V-shaped face gave him some sort of intensity. He had a wide mouth and a scar at the left corner, and he didn't smile often.

"Two years out of a man's life seems like a waste," Majors murmured, his voice low, and he coughed at the end of the sentence, a deep cough that seemed to rack his chest.

"You need to go to the doc about that cough you got, Owen. But I guess you can do that when you get out of here. That sawbones here don't care whether we live or die." Novis hesitated, then got to his feet and faced Majors. He had to look up at the tall man and said, "Two years? Why, that ain't nothing. Some guys have been here for twenty years, and they'll be here until they dump them in the lime pit."

"Guess that's right." Resignation, defeat, and despair were melded together and thinly disguised as Majors spoke. He tried to smile and shook his head. "Don't need to be complaining. Be good to be out of here."

"Well, you just shot the wrong feller. The next time you shoot somebody, make sure he ain't the son of the lieutenant governor of this sorry state."

"I'll do my best to watch out for that."

Suddenly, footsteps sounded in the corridor, and a blunt-faced guard stood outside. He said roughly, "OK, Majors, time to go."

Owen Majors gathered the few belongings he had accumulated during the two years and shoved them into a sack. "Take care of yourself, Manny. You'll be out in another year."

"I shore will. You go see a sawbones 'bout that cough."

"Maybe."

The heavy-set guard opened the door and gestured with his head. "The warden's waiting for you. He wants to talk to you."

"All right."

Majors walked down the double row of cell blocks. He knew most of the inmates, and several of them called out as he passed.

"Watch out for them women out there, Majors."

A thicker voice said, "Don't try to drink all the liquor in the world."

Owen smiled slightly and nodded his head, giving a final farewell to the prisoners. The guard, whose name was Morley, said, "A big day for you, Majors."

"Yes, it is, Mr. Morley."

"You're lucky to be getting out in two years. Anybody else who'd plug a big shot like you done would be here for ten."

"I guess the judge was feeling charitable."

"Nah," Morley grunted, "it was all politics. The judge was a Democrat. He wasn't about to give no hard sentence to anybody who shot a Republican." He laughed at his own wit, and when they reached the end of the corridor, they passed through a locked gate that was opened by a hatchet-faced guard. "So long, Owen. Be good now."

"Sure will, Mr. French."

As Owen walked down the hall, his mind seemed to be frozen. The two years he had spent in this place had been the worst thing that had ever happened to him. He had always been a man of the outdoors, loving the wide spaces, the tall mountains, the rivers and streams, the forest. All those had been taken from him the moment he had pulled the trigger that sent him to prison. He knew that although he might be leaving Arkansas Territorial Prison physically, part of it would always be in his mind—in the dark part that kept bad memories and recalled them during the black night and sometimes when the sun was shining brightly. Some of his other memories weren't pleasant either, but these last two years were the worst.

Morley walked with Majors down another hall and through an unlocked door. As Owen stepped inside, Warden Howard Remington was waiting for him. Remington was sixty years old but didn't look it. His hair was thick and glossy, and he had sharp brown eyes. He was not a big man, but even the roughest of criminals instantly recognized his imposing demeanor.

"Hello, Owen. Big day for you."

"Yes, Warden, it is." Owen had always found Warden Remington to be a hard man but fair. He played no favorites, was quick to reward obedience, and was just as quick to come down hard on disobedience.

"What are your plans?"

"I guess I'll go to Fort Smith, Warden. A friend of mine is there I'd like to hook up with."

"Yes, I thought that's what you told me, but there's a storm building up out there. It's likely to get worse. Cold as a well-digger's toes."

"I'll make it, Warden, and I want to thank you for all you've done for me."

"Well, I like to show a little favoritism to the men who try, and you've been a model prisoner. You haven't talked much."

"Not much to say." Owen grinned and coughed deeply.

"You don't sound good. If you'd like, you can stay in the prison infirmary. We'll have the doc look you over. Stay until you get better."

"Much obliged, Warden. That's thoughtful of you, but I'll make it."

"Well, I've got some good news for you. Here. You came here in the summer wearing lightweight clothes. They'll not do you much good in this weather, so I had some of the guards prowl around, and here's some of the things that were left. They probably won't fit, but they'll be warm."

Owen moved closer to the table where the warden was standing. "Why, that'll help a lot, Warden. I appreciate it."

"Well, here's some warm, long-handled underwear you'll be needing. Some thick woolen socks and a pair of wool britches that'll be too big for you, I guess, but they'll keep the cold out. A couple of wool shirts, and here's this buffalo overcoat. I think it must have come from one of the soldiers. Bulky, but it'll keep the cold out. And here, here's a pair of heavy gloves and a cap."

Owen felt a surge of gratitude toward Remington. "You didn't have to do this, Warden."

"I know it, but I don't want to see you back in this place, and I don't want you to freeze out on the road."

"I'll not do that."

Warden Remington put his brown eyes on the big man with an intensity that was almost physical. Owen made a tall, sharp shape in the prison uniform. It was too small—snug around his shoulders and chest. He was a strong man and had done his work without complaint. Now Remington said, "Well, one other thing. I'm sending the wagon to Fort Smith to pick up some prisoners. You can get a ride out there. I've thrown a couple blankets in so you can roll up in the back. It'll be cold, but not as cold as that driver will be outside."

"It seems like I'm having to say thank you a lot, Warden."

"Come on. I'll take you down to the kitchen. We'll fill you up with something hot to keep you going. And here's something else."

Owen took an envelope the warden handed him. "The state gives every man at least ten dollars. I've added ten more to it."

Owen felt warmth suddenly, something he had not felt for two years. It was as though his heart, mind, and thoughts had been put in a freezer and all life drained out of them. But now Remington's actions brought a sense of gratitude that caught him off-guard. "I won't forget you, sir."

"Stay out of this place, Majors. It's no good for you."

$e\sim$

OWEN HAD EATEN VERY well. The warden had instructed the cook to feed him a steak and everything that goes with it. The cook, a skinny man, an albino with a sour look, had obeyed. "Wisht I was gettin' out. What you going to do?"

"Don't know, Leslie."

"Well, sometimes I reckon I'd just as soon stay inside. I tried it outside twice, and it wasn't no good for me."

Owen finished his meal and hot coffee. The warmth made him sleepy, but he came awake at once when Remington entered. "The wagon's ready to go, Owen. Like I say, it'll be cold."

"I'll make out with the blankets and these warm clothes."

"Well, come along then."

Owen followed the warden outside to the yard. The prison wagon was waiting. It was a simple flatbed wagon that had been converted with stout walls and barred windows. The driver had to sit outside, and already his face was blue from the cold.

"You've helped me a lot, Warden. I can't figure it out. You're not this thoughtful to all inmates when they leave, are you?"

Remington paused, looked down at the ground for a moment, and then returned his eyes to Owen's face. "You remind me of my son. He was killed three years ago, fighting the Indians with the Seventh Cavalry. Stay out of here, Majors."

"I'll promise you that, Warden."

Owen got into the wagon, and the guard slammed the door shut. "I have to lock her or it'll flop around," he said.

"That's all right."

"Wish I could get in there with you. It's cold out here."

Owen watched as the warden stood back, and when the guard climbed back up into the box, he kept his eyes fixed on the man. *Not many like him in the world*, he thought. He raised his hand and gave a salute and a wave to the warden, wishing he could say more. The warden nodded briefly, then turned and walked back into the prison.

OWEN WAS WEARING ALL the warm clothes the warden had given him and was wrapped up in two blankets. It was a bone-aching cold, and he was aware that snow had begun falling again. He woke several times, and once the wagon stopped, and they stayed overnight at one of the stage stations. The meal was bad—greasy pork, lumpy potatoes, and half-baked bread, but Owen ate it, not knowing when he would get his next meal.

The next day Owen spent the journey trying to blot out the last two years of his life. The snow fell hard for the first two hours and then stopped. They were in the foothills of the Ozarks now, and the hills were rounded. As the sun came out, they glistened as if covered with tiny diamonds. It was a beautiful sight, and Owen Majors feasted his eyes on it. After the gray world he had been in, it was like magic. He felt himself beginning to separate himself from the two years that had been taken from him.

But the cough continued, and he felt worse and worse. At midday the guard gave him a drink of whiskey that seemed to warm him, but it didn't help the cough. He finally went to sleep and didn't awaken until he heard the wagon creak to a jolting stop. The driver suddenly appeared. His name was Lon Allison—a big man with a red face and hands like hams. "We're here, Majors. Get up."

Majors got to his feet, stamped them to bring feeling back, and then moved outside. "Come on. I'm going to eat. I'll buy you something."

"You don't have to do that, Mr. Allison."

"No trouble."

They went into a café, and the place was rough, but the food was good. Majors and the guard talked, and once when Owen broke into a coughing fit, Allison turned to him, his eyes narrowing. "You sound bad, Majors. You better go see Dr. Crandell."

Owen smiled briefly. "Does he work for nothing?"

"Not likely, but maybe you could work it out with him. Maybe he's a good guy."

Majors turned to the woman who was serving. She was a short, round-bodied woman with a pair of steady brown eyes. "You know where I might get a room here?"

"There's a rooming house right down the street. It's on the left. Got a sign says rooms for rent."

"Thanks."

The driver and the guard turned to go, and Allison said, "Stay away from that prison, Majors."

"That's exactly what the Warden said. Thanks for the ride."

As soon as the two left, Owen put on his heavy coat and went outside into the biting cold. Before he reached the rooming house, he was coughing again, and he could tell he was worse. When he knocked on the door, a tall, gaunt woman answered. "What do you want?" she said.

"I need a room."

He began to cough and the woman said, "You're sick."

"I guess so. I got a bad cough here. Not catching though."

"Be two dollars a day in advance."

Owen reached into his pocket and paid the money. She led him upstairs and said, "I don't allow men to bring women into their rooms."

"Fine with me."

"I serve breakfast at seven o'clock. It'll cost you fifty cents."

"Thanks." Owen waited until she shut the door then came out of his coat. He stripped off his outer clothes and turned the covers down. He put the blankets the warden had given him on top and got under them. The room was cold, and he felt a chill coming on. His teeth began to chatter, and he lay there trying to generate warmth. He realized it wasn't only warmth for the body he needed but also warmth and hope for his soul. He knew he needed something good that he had missed out on somewhere. He went to sleep thinking about it.

℮〜

"I'VE GOT TO HAVE my money. You've been here three days."

"I paid every day."

"You got to pay in advance. I've got a man here who wants to rent this room by the week."

Owen had dressed and eaten breakfast, and now Mrs. Williams was staring at him. "You'll have to move on," she said.

"All right." Owen didn't argue. He went upstairs to his room, gathered his belongings, and left.

As he passed Mrs. Williams, she said, "I don't mean to be hard, but this ain't a charity institution. You need to be in a hospital."

"In that you'd be right," Owen said. He felt that his chest was compressed, and he could barely breathe. When he tried to breathe deeply, it brought on a fit of coughing.

As soon as he stepped out, he saw that the weather was worse. Snow was coming down in long swirling strips, and he had no idea, for the moment, which way to go. He had no destination, and his mind seemed to be paralyzed. *I've got to do something.* He had a few dollars left and thought he would go to a doctor. He started down the street and noted only a few brave souls out in the swirling snow. The flakes bit at his face. He had not shaved for three days, and the stubble made him look rough. He made his way down the street, looking for someone to ask.

He finally passed a man bundled up to the eyes and asked, "Is there a doctor somewhere around here?"

"Yeah, you go down to the next corner and turn left. You'll find the doctor down there. Better get out of this weather. It's a real blizzard."

Owen started to walk, and he realized he was light-headed. The man's voice sounded as if it had come from far off. He felt as if he were in some sort of box where the sounds were muffled, and he could hear the beating of his own heart. He began to cough and had to stop and lean against a building, for the coughs seemed to be tearing him in two. He reached the alley and found he couldn't remember whether the man had said to turn right or left. It was dark, and he turned to his right, hoping that was the way to go.

He had not gone far when he realized he couldn't continue. He leaned against the building and began to cough. The cough tore through his chest, and he coughed until there seemed to be bright lights flashing in front of his eyes. He fell forward into the snow and tried to struggle to his feet. He got to his knees, and then the bright lights disappeared, and he felt darkness closing in on him. The darkness grew even darker, and that was all he knew.

e~

JOELLE WAS FINISHING HER work and was cooking her supper when she heard a voice calling her name. Joelle moved to the door of the small room and opened it. She saw Pete Nelson, a big cowboy with broad features and a pair of twinkling blue eyes, come in, his hat and shoulders covered with snow. "How about a cup of that coffee, Joe?"

"Sure, Pete," Joelle smiled. "I'm just fixing me some stew, and I've got plenty of coffee. Come on in."

The big cowboy swept his hat off, revealing a mass of red hair set off by the freckles across his face. "That smells good. What is it?"

"It's my catch-all stew. I put everything I had in it, and it's different every time. Sit down, Pete."

Nelson threw himself into one of the two chairs, and Joelle ladled him a big bowl of the stew. "I got some crackers here. You want some hot sauce and ketchup to go in it?"

"No, that might spoil the taste." Pete began eating eagerly. "This is good stuff, Joe."

"You're an easy man to please."

She poured him a cup of coffee and said, "I hear that Big Ed Masters has beaten your time with Sally."

"Why, that ain't so! Who told you a lie like that?"

"Everybody's talking about it. You'd better get on the ball or you'll lose that girl."

"I ain't losing nothing! You just wait. I've been laying to give Big Ed a whipping. You think I can whip him or what?"

"He's a pretty tough fellow."

"I may have to use a two-by-four on him."

Joelle laughed. She liked the big cowboy and was pleased that she had been able to pass herself off as a young man. As a matter of fact, she had tried ever since she had taken the job to enhance her image. For one thing she had learned to walk with big strides and swagger like some of the men did. She also roughened her speech, throwing in a mild profanity every once in a while. She always wore the big floppy hat and the clothes that were too big and hid her figure well enough.

"Get yourself some more stew if you want it. If you'll watch the stable for me, I'll give you some apple pie when I get back."

"Sure, Joe."

Joelle put on her heavy coat and left the stable. The job had proved to be fairly easy. Mostly, it meant feeding horses and currying them when the customers were willing to pay for it. Phillips was hardly ever there. He came by to settle up once a week and had nodded saying, "You're the best stable man I ever had, Jones. Don't you run off and leave me now."

"Don't plan to, Mr. Phillips," she had said.

The snow had stopped, but it was still bitter cold, and the night had closed in on Fort Smith. She knew the saloons would be filled, for they served as a social club for the men of the town. She turned down the alley, hoping to get to the store before it closed. Her thoughts were on her errand, and it was very dark. Suddenly, her foot caught in something, and she fell sprawling.

"What in the—!"

She pulled herself up and leaning forward saw a man covered with the snow. Fear came to her, and she thought, He's dead! But when she leaned closer, she heard his raspy breathing. She brushed the snow from his face and said, "Wake up, mister. Wake up!" But the man didn't stir.

Quickly she rose and ran back to the stable. She burst into her room and said, "Pete, there's a man out in the snow. He's freezing."

The big cowboy rose to his feet. "Where is he?" He grabbed his hat, jammed it on his head, and followed Joelle as she ran down the street. When they reached the fallen figure, Pete leaned over and said, "He's a big one. You know him?"

"No, I don't think so. We've got to get him inside. Can we carry him?"

"Well, what do you think? Of course I can." Pete pulled the still figure into a sitting position, gave a lurch, and came up with him over his shoulder. "Well, he's a tall guy, ain't he now?"

"Come on, Pete. We need to get him in out of this weather." She led the way, and when they reached the stable, she said, "Put him on the bed there."

Nelson put the man down and said, "He would have froze out there if you hadn't found him, Joe."

"He probably would."

"You want me to go by and get Doc Crandell?"

"I think you'd better."

Nelson left the room at a run, and Joelle went closer and stared down at the man's face. He was indeed tall, nearly lapping over the small bed she used. He was covered with snow, but she decided to wait for the doctor before she did anything.

It was a short wait actually, for the doctor's office was only a block away. She heard the door close, and then Dr. Faye Crandell came in, followed by Pete Nelson.

"What's this you got, Jones?"

"I found him out in the alley. Pete carried him in."

Crandell was a spare man in his sixties. He had gray hair that came out from under the hat and a pair of direct blue eyes. He put his head down and listened to the man's breathing. He straightened up and shook his head. "I think he's got pneumonia. Is he your kin?"

"No, I never saw him before."

"Well, he'll either live or die."

This didn't sound good to Joelle. "Well, tell me what to do. Is there a hospital or something?"

"Wouldn't do him any good. Nothing much you can do for pneumonia. We need to get him undressed and put some blankets over him. Pete, you'll need to help me. He's a big one."

The three started undressing the man, and Crandell said, "Pull his britches off, Jones."

Joelle flushed and then quickly grabbed the cuffs of the man's trousers and tugged at them. It took a struggle because they were too small. She was relieved to see that he was wearing long underwear.

When the man was undressed, Dr. Crandell said, "Cover him up now. If he gets some fever, that's to be expected." He straightened up and shook his head. "I'll come back tomorrow to see if he's still alive."

Pete watched the doctor leave and said, "It's a good thing you found him. He'd have died sure out there in that freezing weather. You want me to stay with you, Joe?"

"No, it'll be all right. Did you get some pie?"

"I ate a big hunk of it. It was good too."

Pete left, and Joelle looked down at the man, wondering about him. He was big-boned and long-armed. There wasn't any fat on him. His jaws were sharp, and his nose had a small break at the bridge. He had not shaved recently, and there was a rough look about him. His cheeks were sunken as if he hadn't eaten regularly. He looked vulnerable for all his apparent toughness.

Joelle studied him, wondering what would come of this, and something began to creep into her mind. The man somehow looked familiar. "That can't be," she muttered. "I've never seen him before." He had jet-black hair and a V-shaped face. She struggled to remember, and suddenly it came to her.

"Why, he looks like my Uncle Caleb, the one my ma talked about so much!" She had never seen Caleb, for he had died young, but she had seen pictures of him, and her mother had said, "He had the blackest hair you ever saw and kind of a funny-shaped face, broad at the top and down to a sharp chin." This man looked like that, and for one moment Joelle remembered her mother's dream. *A man will come to help you just like my brother helped me.*

Joelle tucked the covers around the man more securely. She filled a bowl of stew and sat down to eat it slowly, staring at the man and wondering what these events all meant.

Chapter Seven

SOMETIMES COLD SEIZED HIM, with an iron icy grip, making him tremble from head to foot and his teeth chatter. It was not a cold like any he had ever experienced, for it seemed to go clear to the bone, and the pain that came with it made him want to cry out—which he thought he did from time to time.

But at times the crushing, bone-squeezing cold would leave, and he would heat up like a furnace. His face would feel as if it were burning up and crinkling as if thrown into a fire, and the rest of his body was gripped with the heat as well.

Occasionally he would come out of the darkness as if he were a man trying to escape from a prison far underground filled with pain. Sometimes light hurt his eyes. The sound of a voice floated to him from a far distance, and someone's hands would touch him—but then he would go back down into the hole again.

Now the heat and the cold were gone. He heard a sound he couldn't identify. He knew he was lying flat on his back, and as he tried to sort out what was happening, he realized that he heard a sizzling sound and over that was a voice of someone singing. He didn't know the voice or the tune, nor did he know what the sizzling sound was, and he felt himself slipping away again.

Determined to stay in the land of the living, he forced himself to open his eyes. At first he couldn't see and was aware that a lamp mounted on the wall was casting an amber light over the room. He was staring up at a ceiling made of loosely jointed boards, and the roughness of the blanket over him caused him to move to avoid it.

Throwing the cover back, he lifted his head and saw that he was in a small room and that someone was standing beside a stove cooking something. That explained the sizzling sound. He tried desperately to think where he was, but he could remember only his cell in the prison. He studied the cook who was dressed in a pair of baggy pants and an oversized shirt. He couldn't see the face, and he called out in a voice that seemed to creak with lips that were dry as parchment.

"Where—where is this place?" His voice was rusty, and he tried to sit up.

"Well, you decided not to die."

Owen licked his lips and peered at a young man who turned from the stove, put a fork down, and came over to him.

"What's wrong with me?"

"You've been sick. Real sick. Didn't know whether you were going to make it or not."

"Can I have some water?"

"Oh, sure. You must be dry as a bone." The young fellow moved across the small room to a bucket, picked up a large white cup, and dipped it in. He came back and said, "Here, hold your head up." Owen felt the hand pulling his head upward, and then the cup touched his lips. He swallowed noisily and with his hand forced it up higher.

"You're going to strangle. You can have all you want, but maybe not all at one time. What's your name?"

Owen licked his lips again and said, "Majors—Owen Majors."

"Well, welcome back to the land of the living. I'm Joe Jones."

Owen focused his eyes on the face that was very close to his. It was a youthful face with a stubborn chin and a rough-cut head of auburn hair. Emerging from the unconsciousness, he saw that the hands were brown and the skin was as smooth as a youth's.

"I guess I've been sick."

"I'll say. Do you remember anything?"

His memory was returning. "I remember walking in the snow and falling down, trying to get up and couldn't make it."

"I found you out there. It's a good thing I did. The temperature dropped to ten below that night."

Owen said, "Could I have some more of that water?"

"Yes." Owen waited until the young man called Joe Jones returned with more water. He drank it all and then said, "How'd you get me in here?"

"A friend of mine helped carry you. The doctor came, and he said you'd either live or you'd die, but I'm glad you made it."

The smells of straw, horse manure, and leather were strong. He looked around and said, "I don't guess I know where I am."

"This is Ben Phillips's livery stable. I live here and take care of it for him. Are you hungry?"

Suddenly Majors realized that he was indeed famished. "Yes," he said, his voice almost breaking, "I am."

"I don't think you'd better try to eat anything too hard. You ain't had much to eat in four days, but I'll get you something."

Owen lay his head back on a rough pillow and watched as Jones quickly moved back to the stove. He emptied the skillet into a plate, and Owen saw that he had been frying bacon. He took some eggs out of a bucket, cracked one of them, and dumped it in the bacon grease. He stirred it with a fork and then dumped it into a small bowl. He put salt and a little pepper on it and then came over and said, "Here, you start on this, and I got some biscuits I just made. You think you could eat one?"

"I could eat anything."

"Don't eat too fast," Joelle said.

"All right." He ate slowly, forcing himself to chew each bite, and by the time he had finished, Joelle brought biscuits smeared with butter. "Here. Can you eat another egg?"

"At least. Maybe two more."

"We'll start out with little bits at a time. I'll make you one more, and then maybe in an hour we'll see."

Majors ate slowly, and Joelle filled a glass. "Got some fresh milk here to wash it down with."

"Thanks." Owen took the glass and drank thirstily. "I've never been so hungry in all my life."

"Well, I guess not. Doc Crandell thought you were going to die."

"I been here four days? I don't remember any of that."

"You had fever. It was pretty bad. Dr. Crandell came and looked after you some."

Joelle watched as he ate the last of his egg and began slowly eating on a biscuit. "You want me to put some jelly on that?"

"Yes."

"I got blackberry."

"That sounds good."

She spread a layer of blackberry jelly on each biscuit. "You chew that up good now. Your stomach is probably pretty tender."

Majors ate slowly, and when he had finished, he drank the rest of the milk. "That was good," he said. "I'm beholden to you."

"Sure."

Owen was thinking more clearly now, and he studied Jones carefully. "Why are you doing all this for me, Joe?"

"Well, somebody had to do it."

"Not always." He tried to get up, but Joelle pushed him back. "You're not going anywhere. Where are you from, Owen?"

For a moment Owen hesitated, but this young fellow deserved well of him. "Well, originally from Kentucky, but I moved away from there and went west a long time ago. Lately I've been a guest in the pen."

Owen saw Joelle's eyes widen. "The penitentiary, you mean?"

"Yes. Was there for the last two years."

"What'd you do?"

"Got into a ruckus, shot a fellow."

"You killed him?"

"No, I didn't kill him. They thought he was going to die. As a matter of fact, it was with his gun. He pulled it on me, and I tried to take it away from him, and he got shot in the scuffle."

Owen saw that Jones was staring at him with a strange expression. "It wouldn't have mattered so much, but he was the son of the lieutenant governor of Arkansas. Wrong fellow for me to shoot."

"I guess that was pretty bad being in jail."

"Worse thing I can think of. I think I'd die before I'd go back there."

Owen found himself getting sleepy. "Could I have a cup of that coffee, do you think? I'm getting sleepy again, and I want something to keep me awake."

Joelle filled a cup with coffee. "You want milk and sugar?"

"Just sugar."

Joelle added a spoonful of sugar, stirred it, and came back. "I doubt this will keep you awake," she said. She watched as he drank it and then took the cup. "You lie down there. I'm going to go get Doc Crandell and have him look you over. You haven't coughed for a time. I thought for a while you were going to cough your lungs out."

"So did I." Those were the last words Owen could speak. He knew there was something he ought to say, and as he slipped off, he suddenly remembered. He lifted his hand and whispered, "Well, thanks!" He drifted off then, and this time the hole was not as black nor as frightening as it had been.

ℰ∽

"STAND STILL, GENERAL. YOU'RE too feisty! Look out! Don't nip me like that!"

Joelle was talking to a long-legged sorrel she had been grooming. She had become an expert groomer, and this horse belonged to the sheriff so she was extra careful with it. He was finicky about his horse and gave her specific instructions about his hooves and how he had to be groomed just so. She ran the curry comb over General's back, then moved over to get some of the special feed the sheriff had provided.

"That sheriff sure spoils you. Wish somebody would take such good of care of me." Joelle carefully dipped the scoop, put grain in the feed box, and watched as General thrust his nose into it and began crunching. "You don't have very good table manners, but you're a handsome devil. I guess you know it too."

Joelle had formed the habit of talking to the horses she cared for. As she moved to the next horse, she was thinking about Owen Majors. It had been three days since he had come out of his fever, and he had been slow to recover. Dr. Crandell had said, "He got pretty well dehydrated. Hard to get fluids to a fellow that's unconscious, but he's going to be all right."

Joelle had fixed a bed for herself in the loft. The cold had broken so that although it still got into the lower twenties at night, she was all right. It had been interesting taking care of the big man, and she was still amazed at how much he looked like the description of her Uncle Caleb. She was a girl of vivid imagination and had heard stories all of her life about miracles happening.

Her grandmother had told her once about an "appearing" of her husband, Joelle's grandfather: "He was off working in the coal mine, and I was shelling peas, and suddenly I turned around, and he was standing right there. Like to have scared me to death. 'What are you doing here, Albert?' I asked him. He just smiled at me and didn't say a word. I didn't know what to do, and I closed my eyes, and when I looked up, he was gone. I knew something was wrong with all that, and when they come to tell me he had been killed in a cave-in, I tried to tell them I seen him. They thought I was losing my mind, but I know what I seen."

Joelle had heard her grandmother tell this many times, and she had been thinking about what her mother had said about her dream—that someone would come and take care of her exactly as her brother had taken care of her.

For a time she felt she was in a forest without a road and didn't know which way to turn. She knew it was dangerous for her to stay in a big town like Fort Smith, for Harper would not give up. She was convinced of that. But she couldn't think of another place to go. She didn't know where in Canada her aunt was, and she didn't want to go there anyway.

Finally she finished grooming the horse and washed her hands. She thought, with a touch of pride, how successfully she had concealed her sex from everyone. Most people called her Joe. As for the last name Jones, it was handy enough, and she was satisfied with it.

She walked to the back of the stables, opened the door, and stepped inside. She found Owen Majors sitting on the cot. He was wearing his long underwear and gave her a smile. "Where's my pants?" he said.

"I washed them and your shirts too. You need to get out of that underwear."

"I want to get out of this bed."

"If you think you're strong enough, you can."

"Anything to get out of that bed. I'm sick of it." Joelle watched for a moment as he began unbuttoning the top of the long-handled underwear and turned quickly. "You get all changed, and I'll think of something to eat."

She moved outside and waited for what she felt was plenty of time, and she then went back in. He was fully dressed, sitting on one of the chairs and pulling on his boots. "I didn't know how good a pair of pants would feel."

"You sure you're strong enough for this?"

"Sure." He suddenly stood up, and she was aware how very tall he was. The clothes were clean and smelled sweet, and he ran his hand over one arm of it. "It's nice to have clean clothes." He moved across the room and stood in front of her. Suddenly he reached out and put both hands on her shoulders and smiled at her. "How much do I owe you for all this care you've given me?"

The touch of his hands frightened Joelle. She didn't have the strong muscles of the young man she pretended to be, and she was afraid for him to get too close. "Nothing," she said, pulling away from his hands. "What do you want to eat?"

"You're a good cook, Joe. Anything would be fine with me."

"How about some pork chops?"

"Sounds good."

"You set." When he sat down, she gave a sigh of relief. She filled his coffee cup and shoved the sugar bowl at him. "How about some fried potatoes to go with it?"

"I could eat a horse."

She laughed. "No, we don't eat horses here. We just groom 'em." She had bought the pork chops from the butcher, knowing he would be hungry, and quickly she peeled four potatoes and sliced them into big chunks. She fried the pork chops, put them aside, then fried the potatoes and placed them on two plates. She had given him two chops and she had one.

"You make me feel like a hog, Joe."

"You need to get your strength up. You were pretty sick, Owen."

"Sure was. First time I was ever really sick in my whole life."

Suddenly, she heard her name being called. "That's Mr. Phillips. I'll be right back. Don't be eating my pork chop."

"Can't make no guarantees."

Joelle stepped outside and found Ben Phillips there. "Hello, Mr. Phillips."

"You get all the horses curried?"

"All done."

"Well, let's settle up."

"Well, I was just fixing to eat. It's all cooked. Could we do that later?"

"Sure. I'll stop by later." He turned to go and said, "What about that fellow you fished out of the alley?"

"Oh, he's better. He's up and dressed now."

"Well, I don't handle charity cases."

"It doesn't cost anything. I buy his food," she said quickly.

"What's his name?"

"Owen Majors, he says."

"Where's he from? Do you know anything about him?"

For an instant Joelle hesitated and almost said, "He's been in prison." But she decided that would not have been fair to Owen. "He's from Kentucky."

"What's he doing here?"

"I don't know, Mr. Phillips. I think he's looking for work."

"Well, you can't keep him forever."

"I think he'll be leaving pretty soon."

"He's just a bum, Joe. Don't let people take advantage of you." Phillips turned and left without another word.

Quickly she went back inside. Majors was still eating, and she sat down and began eating her dinner. "Maybe I can give you a hand with some of this work around here."

"Oh, there's not that much work to it, Owen. Just mostly feeding the horses and once in a while brushing them out."

"Well, I can clean up."

"Maybe in a day or two. You're still not back to full strength."

"Well, I don't like to take your bed. Where have you been sleeping?"

"Oh, I made me a bed up in the loft. Since the cold broke it's not bad."

"Well, that's all of that. You can show me when you finish eating."

She ate and then remembered that Phillips had asked what he did. She had not asked too many questions of the tall man, but now she said, "What do you do for a living, Owen?"

"Whatever I can. I soldiered in the dragoons for a couple of years, trapped beaver in the mountains, drove a freight wagon." He smiled and added, "I was even a deputy sheriff for a time."

"You were a lawman?"

"Just a deputy."

"Will you go back to that, do you think?"

"I don't think there's many towns that would hire a jailbird to be their deputy."

"Wasn't your fault, you said."

"That's what I said at the trial, but it didn't do any good. Nobody believed me."

"Do you have any folks?"

"No, not really. My folks died of cholera on the trail to Oregon, both of them. I was handed around until I got old enough to take care of myself."

"What do you think you'll do now?"

"Find a job somewhere. What about you?" he asked suddenly. "You don't tell much about yourself. You got folks around here?"

"No, I'm like you. I lost my ma and pa."

He suddenly leaned forward and studied her face, saying finally, "How old are you, Joe?"

"I'm seventeen."

"You don't look it. You've not even shaved yet, I don't think. You got smooth features for a fella."

"Yeah, my pa said he was that way too," she said quickly, then tried to change the subject. "You could ask Mr. Phillips if there's any jobs around here."

"Maybe I'll do that. I think I'll take a walk around town."

"Put your heavy coat on. It's still chilly out."

"I hate that buffalo coat. I think I'll just put on both shirts."

He slipped the second woolen shirt on, then picked up his hat, and said, "I've got to get another hat. This one makes me look like an idiot."

He left the room, and as he stepped out into the bright sunshine, he thought, *That Joe Jones is a funny young fella. Doesn't look very tough for a place like this or for a job like this.* He began to walk down the streets of Fort Smith and wondered about Joelle's question. *What am I going to do now?* he asked himself, then realized he had no idea whatsoever. He had always been a man of independence, and nothing had kept him down long although he had had some hard times. The pale sunshine felt good, and the air was sharp and crisp. He was thankful to be out of that cell and thankful that he hadn't died.

e⁀

THE WINTER MOVED SLOWLY away from the earth, and spring began to show signs of returning. It was early March.

Owen Majors stepped inside the stable and found Joelle currying her horse. "You sure take good care of that hoss, Joe."

"I guess I do."

"Well, I like to see a horse well treated. That's a fine one too. Got good news." Joelle watched as he pulled up a chair and sat down. "Got a job."

"Really? That's good. What will you be doing?"

"Not much. Just room clerk down at the hotel. Night shift. Not much going on. Doesn't pay much, but I get a room for it."

"Well, you'll be moving out then."

"I guess so." He studied her and noted that she always wore the same clothes, the baggy pants and the shapeless shirt that seemed to swallow her. *I wonder why he doesn't buy something that fits him better. Maybe he's broke. This job can't pay much.* "I got just about enough to buy us a meal down at the café."

"You better save your money."

"Oh, I'm a man of means, Joe. I'll soon be making money at that hotel. Come on. You cooked enough for me." He saw Joelle's eyes suddenly crinkle and he rose. The two sauntered down the street to the Café Delight. They got a table, and the waitress came over. She was a small, well-shaped woman with attractive brown eyes. "What can I get you gents?"

"What do you have, Joe?"

"What have you got?" Joelle asked and looked up at the waitress.

"We got some good steaks, hon."

It made Joelle feel odd that the waitress called her "hon," and she flushed a little.

"I'll have a steak."

"Same for me and any kind of vegetable you can rake up, sweetheart."

"You bet."

The waitress left, and Owen leaned forward. "I think she's stuck on you, Joe. You made a conquest there."

Joelle said, "She's just foolin'. She probably calls everybody hon."

"She didn't call me that." Owen smiled, and she saw that the color had come back into his face, and her cooking had filled in some of the sunken spots that had formed in his neck and cheeks. He had rebounded miraculously from his brush with near death.

"I'll tell you what," he said. "We'll ask if she's got a sister. If they do, we'll take them out for a dance or something."

"We don't have any money for that kind of thing."

"You're right about that, but eat all you want. I'll start out broke at my new job, but something will turn up. It always does."

℮〜

A WEEK AFTER OWEN left for his job, Joelle discovered she was lonesome. Taking care of the big man had filled a part of her life, and now, although he had come by twice, it wasn't the same. She had cleaned the stables and curried and fed the horses. Now she stepped outside. The courthouse was right down the street so out of boredom she walked toward it. It was a crowded street for the weather had turned warm, and Fort Smith was a busy place. There was going to be a hanging the next day, and people always came to see the spectacle. Joelle had thought about going, but it disgusted her.

She got to the post office and turned to look at the posters. It was filled with wanted posters. Some had hand-drawn portraits of the wanted men, and some were simply printed in large block letters. Most of them were for felons and offered a reward.

She was about to turn when something caught her eye. She moved a poster that half-covered the one beneath and took a deep breath. There it was. Harper had raised the reward to a thousand dollars. Fear gripped her, and she looked around. Nobody was watching so she jerked the poster down, crammed it into her pocket, turned, and fled down the street. *He's after me! He'll get me sooner or later.*

℮〜

JOELLE HAD GONE TO her room and sat there nervously, not knowing what to do. "I need to get out of this place. There'll be another poster. I know there will," she said aloud. She started when she heard somebody calling her, but she recognized Owen's voice. She stepped outside. "Hello, Owen."

"Hey, Joe. I got some news here." He pushed into his pocket and pulled out a letter. "I got a letter from an old friend of mine. His name is Harry Jump."

"That's a funny name."

"It is. Never knew anybody named Jump before. The letter went to the prison, and the warden knew I was coming here, so he had it sent."

"You've known him a long time?"

"Yes, quite a while." He opened it and said, "It says he's going to California to look for gold. He says he'll wait for me in Independence, and that maybe we could hook on to a wagon train." Owen read part of the letter aloud: "'You could probably get a job as a guide since you know the trail, Owen. We could maybe put together enough cash to buy a wagon. We could strike it rich out there. Ask for me at the post office when you get to Independence.'"

Owen laughed and shook his head. "Harry was always an optimistic sort of fellow. Just the kind of get-rich-quick scheme he'd jump at."

"I've been reading about the gold discoveries in California. How do you get there?"

"Well, if you're on the East Coast, you can get on a ship and go down to Panama, cross on land, then get on another ship. Or go around the Cape. Takes a long time to get there. Costs a bundle. Or you can go to Independence and tie up with a wagon train. You've got to have a wagon to do that though."

"You think you'll go?" Joelle suddenly had an idea and hope began to kindle within her.

"I think I will. Not that I am expecting to find gold, but I'd like to see old Harry again. And there ought to be jobs there around San Francisco somewhere. I have to save a little money first."

"I'd like to see California myself."

"Pretty hard making that trip in a wagon."

"You've done it?"

"Sure have, but I wasn't in a wagon."

Joelle only half-listened as Owen spoke of the trip on the Oregon Trail. "But why do they call it the Oregon Trail if it goes to California?"

"It goes both places. The trains leave Independence and get about two-thirds of the way there. Those that want to go to Oregon take the north route. Those that go to California break off and go through the Donner Pass."

Preoccupied, Joelle asked several more questions. Owen left, and she began to walk back and forth within the stable. She began to put a plan together. *If I got to California, Harper would never find me there!* The thought of such a thing frightened her, but then she stopped. I'll bet Owen would look out for me. He's done it before. The thought possessed her, and that night before she went to bed she found herself praying, *God, if this is all right with You, I sure would like to get away from here. Make a way for us to get to California, me and Owen.*

Chapter Eight

JOELLE WAS FRYING LIVERS on the small stove, and the aroma was rich as it filled the small room. Majors sat at the table reading the paper. Joelle had invited him to eat with her, saying, "We can share the cost of the food. It's too expensive to eat at those cafés." He had agreed at once, and the meals had become times she looked forward to. When the livers were done, she put them on a plate along with beans. She had baked fresh bread, too, and she filled their glasses with milk and said, "Let's eat."

"All right. Sounds good."

The two began to eat, and finally, when they had finished the meal, Joelle got up and said, "I made peach pie today."

"You're a fine cook, Joe. Where'd you learn to cook so good?"

"Oh, I just picked it up, I guess." She cut two pieces of the pie, a large one for him and a small one for herself.

He took a bite. "That is prime." He finished the pie, and the two sat there drinking coffee. Owen seemed restless. "I got something to tell you, Joe. I'm going to be leaving."

The news caught Joelle off-guard. "Leaving? Where you going?"

"Well, look here." He reached in his pocket and pulled out a roll of bills. "Three hundred dollars there."

"Where'd you get all that money? Not from being a hotel clerk!"

"No, I got lucky in a poker game. It's about time, I guess. I'm going to buy a horse. Maybe Phillips will sell me that bay I like so much."

"He probably would. I'd get you a good price for it. When will you be going?" She suddenly felt lost, as if she were going down steps and one of the steps was missing. It had been only a short time since Owen Majors had come into her life. She hadn't realized until this moment how much she depended on him.

"Next week, I guess. You talk to Phillips about that horse for me."

"What's it like on a wagon train, Owen?"

"Dangerous, uncomfortable, and lots of hard work."

"What's dangerous about it?"

"The Indians for one thing. Plenty of them between here and California, and the worst kind—Kiowa and Sioux. But mostly it's just uncomfortable. Long stretches with no water. Lose cattle that way. Of course, me and Harry won't have a wagon. We'll just tag along and maybe bring some game in to the train. They always have to have hunters."

"Where will you sleep?"

"On the ground. I did it when I was in the dragoons. Not my favorite place, but that's the only way I'm going to get there."

"Well, I hate to see you go."

He got up and moved his plate and cup to the table where she washed them in a dishpan, and when he came back, he reached down and grabbed her hair. He had never done that before. He pulled her head back and looked down in her face. "I guess I owe you a lot, Joe. You saved my bacon. I'd be decorating a grave somewhere if it wasn't for you."

Joelle was nearly paralyzed by his touch. "Let go of my hair. You're pulling it."

"You're a finicky young fellow, but I meant it. I'll write you when I get to California and tell you what it's like. How about that?"

"All right. That'll be good."

e

ALL DAY LONG JOELLE thought about what was happening. She knew she wanted to go to California, and finally she said, *Well, Lord, I don't know what to do, but I'm going to go. And I'm asking You to help me and Owen get there. Don't let us get scalped.*

She made a plan. From under her bed she retrieved the metal box with the jewelry and cash her mother had given her. She stuck the cash in her pocket, and taking the box she left the stable. She went at once to a jewelry store. A small man with thick glasses and silver hair said, "Yes. What can I do for you, sir?"

"I've got to sell some jewelry. It belonged to my mother. I need the money."

"Let me see. My name is Abe Goldman."

"I'm Joe Jones."

Goldman looked at the jewelry very carefully. He had an eyepiece that he seemed to screw into his right eye and stared at it. "Have you had these appraised?"

"No, I never have. They came from my grandmother."

"I'll make you a price, but you ought to get another offer or maybe two."

"Is there anybody else here?"

"There's a man down the street by the blacksmith." Goldman sniffed. "You might ask him."

"You don't sound like you got much confidence in him."

"He calls himself a jeweler," Goldman shrugged. "Let me figure." He took out a piece of paper and stopping to look, he wrote calculations. "I can let you have five hundred. You might get more in a big city."

"You think the other man would offer more?"

"Half as much, but you go see, young fellow."

"All right." Joelle left the store. She found the other jeweler who offered her three hundred. He was a fat, greasy-looking man, and Joelle didn't like him. She returned to Goldman's store and said, "You were right, but there's one thing. I want to keep this ruby ring."

"In that case it'll be four hundred."

"Can you give me the money now?"

"Of course." He handed her the ring, moved to the back of the store, and came out holding some bank notes. "You shouldn't carry this much money around, young fellow."

"I'll put it in a safe place."

She took the money, thanked Goldman, and left. She had a sense of loss for she would have liked to have kept the jewelry, but at least she had the ruby ring. She had never seen her mother wear it, and it gave her some satisfaction to know that it had belonged to her grandmother.

⁓

JOELLE STOPPED BY THE hotel, but Owen was off duty. She went back to the stable and paced impatiently until finally he came in for supper that night. She had bought some ribs and cooked them, and while he was eating, she said, "When are you leaving, Owen?"

"Day after tomorrow, I think."

Joelle took a deep breath. "Let me go with you."

She saw the surprise wash across Owen's face. "You mean to Independence?"

"No, all the way to California. Look, I've got some money. It's four hundred dollars. Maybe we could get a wagon and join the train there."

"Well, sure, Joe. It'll be rough though."

"I don't care. I just want to go."

"Well, that makes life a little bit easier. Tell you what. Let me shop around here and see if I can find a wagon and some stock. If not, we can pick them up in Independence." He talked with excitement, his eyes flashing, and finally when she got up, he rose, put his arm around her, and gave her a hug. "I didn't know you were an heir," he grinned.

Joelle was paralyzed. He was hugging her, and she was terrified. She could disguise her femininity with clothes but not when someone was holding her close. She pulled away and said, "I wish you wouldn't hug me like that."

Owen laughed. "You're finicky, Joe. You got four hundred, and I've got three so we'll see what's to be had."

"When can we leave?"

"Well, most of the trains leave the first of April, just about now. If we find stock and a wagon, we can get to Independence maybe in less than four or five days. Then we hook on to one of the trains."

"Will they take us?"

"Oh, they always want to have as many wagons as possible. Keeps the Indians scared off."

"I'd like to get out of this place. I don't like it."

"Well, you may not like California either. What'll you do then? Can't go any farther. The ocean's there."

"I know, but I can't stay here."

"You know, that's about the way I feel, Joe. I'm going to start looking out. Phillips knows stock pretty well. He may know of some good buys in oxen."

"You don't want horses?"

"No, nor mules neither. Oxen are the best on the trail, but the wagon is what we really need."

❧

JOELLE COULDN'T SLEEP THAT night, and the next day she was waiting when Owen came for breakfast. She fixed ham and eggs, and then he said, "I talked to Phillips. He knows a fellow that's got some stock to sell. Good oxen. Get them cheap, too, and the best news is that Phillips put me on to a good buy in a wagon. I picked it up for a hundred. A real bargain."

"Good! When can we leave?"

"We'll be ready in the morning."

"I hate to leave Mr. Phillips, but he can get somebody." She smiled and exclaimed, "It's going to be fun, Owen!"

"Hope you think so when we're halfway there," he grinned. "Know what? I think I've got me a pretty good partner, Joe Jones!"

THE STARS WERE BRIGHT overhead, and Owen had hobbled all the oxen they had bought. He had bought eight head, which would be enough, he said.

"You mean to pull one wagon you need eight oxen?"

"Four is usually enough, but you have to give them a rest. When an ox gets tired, he just lies down and won't go anywhere, so we'll have two teams."

They had left Fort Smith and traveled steadily all day until they camped for the night. Owen had bought the bay that he liked for fifty dollars, and she had ridden Blackie. Joelle had been surprised at how the oxen were guided. One of them walked alongside the lead beast. Owen had told her, "Lots of folks ride the lead oxen, but I just as soon walk." They had traveled hard for three days, and now he said, "We ought to be in Independence tomorrow."

The days of travel had not tired her, but Owen, like all men, had rough manners on the trail. They had built a fire and cooked a simple meal, and Joelle said, "I can't sleep. I'm too excited."

"Good thing to be excited."

She rolled over and stared at him. "You never say anything about your past. What about your family?"

"Well, my pa and ma died of cholera on the way to Oregon, like I told you, when I was only five. I had two older brothers and two younger sisters. I took off on my own when I was sixteen."

"Did you ever see them again?"

"Never did."

He said no more, and finally she asked, "So you made out all right?"

"Sure, I made it fine. We're going to be all right. We're going to go to California. We may not find any gold, but we'll see the ocean."

They were quiet for a long time, and she was shocked at how his story had touched her. Finally he said, "You OK?"

"Yep."

"Good-looking young fellow like you is gonna have a good time. Girls like young fellows like you. Why, that waitress in Fort Smith was in love with you."

"She was just silly, and she went for everything in pants."

"She liked you though. She couldn't keep her hands off of you. Always called you 'honey' or 'sweetheart' or something. And you never gave her a tumble."

"Didn't like her."

"Well, there'll be some more."

"What about you? Have you ever been married or anything?"

He suddenly laughed. "Never been married. I guess anything suits my love life. That just about says it."

"You sound like you don't like women."

"Well, I had one give me a pretty hard bump. I guess I'm careful. Hard for me to trust any woman now." He suddenly laughed. "You and me, Joe, we'll be crusty old bachelors. OK?"

"OK, Owen. That's what we'll be."

Chapter Nine

LONG SHADOWS GROWING EVER longer were thrown by the buildings that lined the front street of Independence, Missouri, as Owen and Joelle entered the town. Joelle was tired, for the days had been long on their journey and the nights short. Owen had wanted to make good time, and although the oxen lumbered along at a snail's pace, they had traveled from sunup to nearly dusk, stopping only in time to cook a meal.

During the time when Joelle sat across the fire from Majors, she had become more interested in him. He was like no man she had ever met, and constantly she was thinking about how her deceit would disgust him if he knew she was a young woman and not the lad he thought. She hated to deceive anyone but especially this man she had grown fond of. The fondness troubled her at times, but she realized that was because she had nursed him back to health. He had been so dependent on her that she could not help but think of him as weak. But he certainly wasn't weak now.

"Well, it looks like Independence has grown up a bit."

Joelle glanced at Owen. "You been here before?"

"Oh, sure. Been awhile though. When I came through, there wasn't half a dozen houses and a couple of stores. She's humming now. This is the jumping-off place for all the wagon trains headed for California or Oregon. I liked it better as it was."

Joelle took in the main thoroughfare of the town, which, in essence, differed little from most small towns in the South. There was a brick courthouse with a dignified steeple, surrounded on three sides by a white picket fence. All around the square buggies and horses were tied to hitching rails. She saw that, for the most part, the town was composed of two-story frame buildings with steep roofs. There were a general store, hardware store, bank, hotel, livery stable, laundry, blacksmith shop, post office, and a sheriff's office. There were also three saloons and a small weather-beaten church wedged in between a dentist's office and a doctor's office.

"Whoa!" Owen called, and the oxen stopped obediently.

"What do we do now, Owen?"

"I guess we find Harry Jump. Let's take these critters to the edge of town where we can stake them out. We can't take them with us."

Fifteen minutes later they found a spot, and it was obvious that outside the town itself the wagon trains were forming up. Joelle spotted at least three as she watched Owen take the oxbows off the stock and tie them to a tree. She gathered food for them, put it in a box so they could feed, and then shook her head.

"They could break those ropes if they wanted to."

"They won't though. Oxen are pretty nice critters. Lots nicer than some humans," Owen grinned. "At least I know what to do with you if you act rambunctious. I'll tie you to a tree like I did old Delilah here." He slapped the brown and white oxen on the shoulder, reaching up to do so.

"You're not tying me to a tree."

"Why, I might if you don't behave yourself." His eyes danced with fun. He suddenly reached out and grabbed her. "I'm bigger than you are, so you better mind me."

Joelle was powerless. He held her by the upper arms, and she knew he could pick her up if he wanted to. Quickly she said, "Turn me loose, Owen. Stop your foolishness."

"All right. Well, come on. Let's go see if we can find Harry Jump." He turned and led her back into the town, and as they walked down the wood boardwalk, they passed a café. "That grub smells pretty good. Let's try to have a shot at finding Harry. If we don't find him tonight, we'll come back here and get a cooked meal. Be nice to set down at a table instead of squatting alongside a fire, won't it?"

"Yes, I'd like that."

Owen stopped several men and asked them if they had ever heard of a fellow named Harry Jump. None of them had, and finally Owen turned to Joelle. "I guess we'll start with the sheriff."

"The sheriff? Why would he know where Harry is?" Joelle didn't want to go to the sheriff's office, for she feared there might be a reward with her description on it. She had had a nightmare about this more than once, but she saw that Owen was determined.

He said, "Well, sheriffs know almost everybody. They're elected officials so they have to be pretty good politicians. Come on. I saw the sheriff's office down here."

They made their way down the boardwalk, and the streets were less crowded now. It was growing dark although the April sun was setting later. When they reached the sheriff's office, Joelle's eyes darted quickly to the board as Owen turned to go in. She had only time for a glance, but she had to know. She scanned the board.

"Come on. You're not going to capture any of those criminals, Joe."

Quickly Joelle turned and followed Owen. Inside she saw a tall man seated at a desk, leaning back and reading a book. He put it down and came to his feet. "Can I help you folks? I'm Sheriff Moseby."

"Maybe, Sheriff. My name's Majors. This here is Joe Jones. We're looking for a man."

"A wanted man?" Moseby had direct gray eyes and a very steady gaze. He was examining the two as if he would to describe them later on, probably a habit with the man.

"No, not that I know of, but we thought maybe you had heard of him. His name is Harry Jump."

"Harry Jump? You're a friend of his, I take it."

"Sure am, Sheriff."

"Well, you've come to the right place." Moseby gave his head a sideways jerk. "He's one of my guests here."

Joelle saw that Owen was not too surprised. "What's he done?" he said without much trace of emotion.

"Oh, the charge is disturbing the peace. He got into a ruckus at the Shady Lady Saloon."

"Well, he does drink too much, and he gets a little bit ambitious. He thinks he can whip anybody, but as far as I know, he never has."

"Oh, he was sober, Majors. He started preaching."

"Preaching? Why, Harry's no preacher!"

"Well, he thinks he is. In any case, he got to preaching, and Bing Taylor took an exception." The sheriff grinned broadly. "Said he had come to gamble and get drunk, not listen to a preacher. He told Jump he'd break his head if he didn't leave."

"I take it he didn't."

"No. He just kept on so Bing lit into him. From what I hear, Jump tried to talk his way out of it, but Bing's a rough cob. The two of them flew at it. Finally a chair got thrown that broke a mirror behind the bar and wasted some good whiskey. My deputy arrested both of them. Bing paid his fine, but Jump says he won't do it. He said he wasn't disturbing the peace. All he was doing was preaching."

Owen removed his hat and wiped his forehead. It had been a hot day, and his shirt was damp with perspiration, and his hair was limp. "I don't know about this preaching business, but he wasn't a preacher when I knew him. Far from it. As a matter of fact, he was about as big a sinner as I was."

"They had a revival meeting come through here a couple of weeks ago. A lot of people got religion. I reckon he was one of them. He told me he got baptized, and he's been preaching at meetings." Sheriff Moseby grinned. "I've been a Christian since I was twenty-two years old, and he flies at me like I was Judas Iscariot! He'll preach at anybody that will stand still."

"Well, is there a fine?"

"Yeah, the trouble is Judge Harlen owns half the interest in the Shady Lady Saloon. He said I had to get the damages before I turned your friend loose."

"How much?"

"Eighty-five dollars. He's got the money, like I say, but he's stubborn. He won't pay it."

"Well, I'll take care of it, Sheriff." Owen reached into his pocket, pulled out a leather sack, and fished out some bills. "Here you go."

"OK. Let me get a receipt."

"Oh, I don't reckon I need that. Just get him out here."

"Sure, I'll bring him right out."

Moseby left by a door in the back of the office that evidently led to the jail. Joelle said, "You never told me he was a preacher."

"He's not—at least he wasn't when we were running together. Jump's about as superstitious as a man can be, but he didn't have any religion that I could tell. No more than I did."

The two waited, and finally the door opened. The man who came through was not impressive, Joelle decided. He was no more than five-eight, probably weighed a hundred thirty-five or forty pounds, very spare. He had a shock of blond hair and a pair of bright blue eyes. His clothes looked wrinkled, he had bruises on his face, and a cut was healing over his eyebrows.

He grinned at once. "Well, what took you so long, Owen? I've been waiting for you to come and get me out of this."

The sheriff shook his head. "He paid your fine, Harry. Here's your belongings." He went to a shelf and pulled out a gun belt and several smaller items. "Do your preaching someplace else besides the Shady Lady. You hear me?"

"Can't promise that," Harry grinned broadly. "If the Lord moves me to do it, that's what I'll do. I didn't finish preaching to you, Sheriff. I got some more Scripture for you."

"You get him out of here, Majors. If he pulls a stunt like this again, I'll throw him in the insane asylum."

"Come on," Owen said shortly, shoved his hat on, and left, followed by Joelle and Jump. As soon as they were outside, Owen turned and said, "What in the world is going on with you? What's this about you being a preacher?"

"Why, I done been washed by the blood of the Lamb, Owen. Sure wish it had happened a long time ago." There was regret in his voice, and he shook his head sadly, but then he brightened up. "There was this here revival meeting, and I went to make fun of the preacher. But something happened to me."

"Like what?"

"Well, I was just getting ready to mock the preacher when suddenly something started happening on my insides. I got scared, Owen. I saw myself dying and going to hell, and suddenly I found out I was about ready to squall like a baby, but then I fell flat on my back. Don't know what happened to me. While I was lying there, I fell under the power, and I called on God, and He saved me. Ain't it wonderful?"

Owen smiled and shook his head. "Well, I guess it is if you say so. Just don't try your preaching on me."

"Oh, I've got to do that."

"Well, are you still aiming to go to California, or are you going to stay here and convert Independence?"

"Why, I'm going. The Lord told me so." He turned and stared at Joelle. "Who's this?"

"This is Joe Jones."

"Have you been washed in the blood of the Lamb, Joe?"

Joelle liked the man who appeared to be somewhere in his early thirties. "I've been a Christian since I was fourteen years old."

"Well, that's great!" He put his arm around Jo and gave her a hug. "You and me, buddy, can get Owen into the Kingdom. He needs the good Lord bad."

"I reckon I'm a lost cause, Harry," Owen smiled.

"No, you ain't. You may go kicking and screaming, but you're one of the elect. Why, Owen, God picked you out to be saved before you was born."

Owen saw that Jump was poised to deliver a full-fledged sermon and said quickly, "You find somebody else to preach to, Harry, or I'll soak your head."

"Why, I can't give up on you, Owen. But we got to get to California right enough. I got some money, and we need to get outfitted."

"I had some good luck, Harry. We got eight good oxen and a fine Conestoga wagon. Not new, but it will do to make the trip."

"Well, you see how God's already working. Let's go take a look."

"No, we'll take a look later. I'm starved."

"Me too. The grub was a little skimpy in that jailhouse."

"There's a café down here."

"Oh, I know that. I've eaten there several times."

"Why didn't you pay your way out? You had the money, didn't you, Harry?" Joelle asked.

"Need that money for converting the heathens at the California gold camps."

Jump talked constantly until they reached the restaurant. When they entered, Joelle saw that the place was almost full, but there was a table by the back wall. When the waitress, a tall, raw-boned young woman in her early twenties, came to them, she said, "What can I get you folks?"

"Are you a converted woman? The Lord's handmaiden?" Jump demanded, staring up at her, his eyes almost on fire.

"Am I what?"

"Are you saved? Converted? Born again?"

"No, I ain't. Do you want something to eat?"

"I want to talk to you about your soul."

The waitress gave him a hard look. "We serve food here. If you want something, order. If you don't, get out."

"Why, let me do the ordering," Owen said quickly. "What's your specialty?"

"We got steak and potatoes and peas and fresh bread."

"Bring us all a bunch of that," Owen said.

As soon as the waitress left, Joelle said, "You scared her off, Harry." She was amused by the man. "You can't hit people right between the eyes with the gospel like that."

"Why, John the Baptist did. He called them a bunch of snakes and said they had to repent. If it's good enough for John the Baptist, it's good enough for me."

"Are you a Baptist?" Owen asked, studying his friend carefully.

"I reckon I am. The preacher, he was a Baptist, and he baptized me so that makes me a Baptist."

Owen listened as Harry gave a steady stream of talk, describing his conversion and how he had set out to witness to everybody he met. "You're going to become a public nuisance if you do that."

"Jesus was a public nuisance."

"Well, you're not Jesus," Owen said, "so why don't you sit back and listen awhile. Before you start preaching, you need to know what you're preaching about."

Joelle listened as the two argued. She could see that Owen had a real affection for the smaller man. There was a warm light in his eyes, and he smiled most of the time.

Finally the food came, and the waitress kept her eye on Jump. He opened his mouth, and she said, "I don't need none of your preaching. You're the guy that broke up the saloon, ain't you?"

"That wasn't me. That was Bing."

"You was arrested for it. Don't you break nothing in here. This is my place. If you break any of our furniture, my husband will take your head off. That's him over there. He'd make two of you, and he does everything I tell him."

"That must be a nice arrangement," Owen grinned. "Did you two agree on that before you got married?"

The waitress gave Owen a hard look. "That ain't none of your business. We serve food, and we don't need any help running our lives."

"The food looks good," Joelle said quickly. She tasted the steak and said, "It's tender."

"We serve good grub here." She glared at Harry. "If you don't like our grub, don't eat here."

Harry watched her with surprise. "I don't know what she's upset about. I'm just trying to get her on the right road."

"I think you need a little tact," Joelle said. "Don't jump on people right off."

Harry shrugged and argued, but at the same time he ate like a starved wolf. After they had finished and were working on slices of apple pie, Harry said, "You're probably wondering why I didn't pay my fine."

"I was wondering about that."

"Well, like I told you, I'm going to the gold camp. You're going, too, ain't you?"

"I don't know, Harry. All I'm thinking of is getting to California."

"Well, God's told me to go to the gold camp, and He's my partner so I guess we'll both go. You can dig for gold, and I can dig for souls."

"Sounds like a good arrangement. What about the money?"

Jump leaned forward and waved his hands as he talked. "Well, here's what we're going to do. You've got the wagon and the oxen. All these folks headed for Oregon are farmers. They got their wagons loaded down with tools and stuff. What we need to do is buy some kind of lightweight goods that we can sell at a big profit when we get to California. Stuff like clothes or maybe hats and boots. Maybe some fancy canned stuff but nothing too heavy."

Owen listened as Jump outlined his plan to load the wagon down, and finally Jump said, "We won't need any money out there on the trip so we'll buy everything we can here. Stuff is pretty high but not as high as it is in California."

"Sounds all right to me. What do you think, Joe?"

Joelle was startled. She didn't feel she had anything to contribute. "Well, I guess Harry's got a good idea. Sure won't need any money on the way."

"We'll need some. We'll be stopping at army posts. You always run out of stuff," Owen said idly. He was leaning back, lifted the coffee cup, and drank steadily. Finally he asked, "What about a train? Have you got one staked out, Harry?"

"Well, there's three trains, or was. One of them is leaving in the morning. We won't be ready for that. One of the others is going to Oregon, which we ain't. That leaves only one, but it's headed for California."

"Made up of people wanting to get rich quick, I'd guess," Owen observed.

"Not really. Most of them are farmers, but they don't like the sound of all that wet weather in Oregon Territory. They like the sound of that good climate in California and aim to get into farming there. Got a few men who want to get to the mines and some gamblers and saloon hall girls."

"Doesn't sound like a typical wagon train," Owen said.

"Well, mebby not, but it's headed for where we want to go. Wagon master is a big fellow named Ralph Ogden. Only eighteen wagons, but there may be more by the time they leave. They've been trying to find a guide before they pull out."

"I wish it was a larger train," Owen said quietly.

"Why do you want it to be larger?"

"The bigger the train, the less likely the hostiles will attack."

"They're not going to get us, them hostiles. God's already got it all planned. He's in charge of everything. Why, Owen, I didn't know this, but He's got a Book, and everything we do is writ down in that Book."

"So we don't have anything to say about it?"

"Oh, we have to get in the wagon, but as long as we're following the Lord God Jehovah, we're going to be all right. We'll get to the gold camps, and we'll preach the gospel."

The three finished their meals and left, and when they returned to their stock and the wagon, Harry said, "I can't see too good, but they look like good stock. The wagon looks fine. I'm going to sleep. You got some blankets or something?"

"Yeah, but you better get your own."

Jump took the blankets Owen fished out of the wagon, crawled underneath, and soon was snoring.

"Is he always like this, Owen?"

"Well, he never was before. Like I said, he had about as many sins as I did. Maybe it's just a phase. He's good about getting excited about something, but then he gets tired of it."

"Well, I think this phase might last," Joelle smiled. "I'm going to bed. I'm tired too."

"We'll go talk to the wagon master tomorrow." He reached over and ruffled Joelle's hair. "You sleep good, Joe."

"Don't paw me!" Joelle said sharply and pulled her head back.

"You are finicky! Good night, boy."

❧

"OWEN, THIS HERE IS Ralph Ogden and his wife. Ralph, this is my old partner Owen Majors and our other partner, Joe Jones."

Ralph Ogden put out his hand, which Owen took and found his own swallowed by the man's enormous paw. Ogden was a huge man, sideways and in depth and in height. He obviously was a strong individual. He had a pair of mild brown eyes and light brown hair and smiled readily. "Glad to know you, Majors, and you, too, Jones. Harry's been waiting on you. You plan to join the train, I hope."

"Looks like it."

"Well, we'd be glad to have you."

"You're not married, Mr. Majors?" Cleo Ogden was a tall, attractive woman with a pair of steady gray eyes.

"No, ma'am. Haven't had that good fortune."

"Well, you're a young man. There's time yet." She glanced over and said, "That's my sister over there with that little girl. Her name is Lily Frazier. That's her daughter, Rachel."

"Looks like they're having school," Joelle remarked. The two were seated on boxes and had a tablet. The woman didn't look up although the girl did. They both had the same auburn hair, Joelle noticed, and Lily was very attractive.

"Well, when we pulling out, Ralph?" Jump asked.

"I expect we're all ready. I'm sorry they picked me for a wagon master. Don't feel up to it."

"You always put yourself down, Ralph," Cleo Ogden said. "You're as good a man as anybody else on the train."

"Why, sure you are," Jump said. "A big fellow like you. If anybody acts up, you just squash them like a bug. Either that or I'll preach at them."

Ogden smiled and said, "Well, I hope one or the other will work." He turned to Owen and shook his head. "We've been waiting for a guide, and finally we got one just yesterday. A fellow called Mace Benton."

Joelle happened to be looking at Owen's face, and at the mention of the guide's name, she saw something pass across his face. *He knows him*, she thought.

"I know Benton," Owen said.

"You do?" Ogden said.

"Yeah, we trapped together in the mountains."

"Is that a fact? I guess you've never made this trip before."

"Sure, I made it about five years ago. All the way to the coast."

Ogden was excited. "Now that's good news! We need experienced folks. Somebody that's been over the trail will help."

"I was on horseback. Getting wagons there will be different."

"Still, I hope you come along. We sure need some experienced help, and three more guns would be a real blessing."

"Most trains head for Oregon. A little surprised that you folks aren't going after that free land."

Ogden shook his head. "From what I hear, it's a killing trip to get there. I heard you have to build rafts and float down a pretty bad river. And from what I can pick up, the climate's pretty wet. We decided to go where the sun shines."

"Might be a wise choice. Well, we can be ready to leave when the train pulls out."

"Really good to have you with us, Majors."

Owen nodded, and Joelle and Jump said their good-byes, and they started out of the camp. They passed by half a dozen wagons, and suddenly Joelle heard a woman's voice call out, "Owen—Owen Majors!"

Joelle turned quickly and saw a woman come from one of the wagons. One look at her revealed her calling. She was an attractive blonde with large green eyes. Something about her dress proclaimed she wasn't a homesteader. She was wearing jewelry, and despite it being the early part of the day, her face was made up with powder and lip rouge.

Joelle watched as the woman came forward. She judged her age to be late twenties, and when she stood before Owen, Joelle looked her over critically. She was well formed, and her clothes were tighter than was absolutely necessary. *Why, she's a saloon girl!* Joelle thought. She shifted her gaze and saw that Owen was staring down at the woman. He took off his hat, and the sun caught a glint in his coarse black hair. "Hello, Cherry," he said.

"What are you doing here, Owen?" She had to look up at him for she was not a tall woman. She was smiling as if the two of them had a secret.

"Headed for California."

"Well, so am I. Will you be with the train?"

"Looks that way. Surprised to see you here, Cherry. When did you leave Dallas?"

"Oh, about a year ago."

Suddenly Owen turned and said, "These are my partners. This is Harry Jump. This is Joe Jones. Like for you to meet Cherry Valance."

"Glad to know you," Joelle said.

"I'm glad to know you, too, ma'am. Are you saved?"

Cherry Valance stared at Jump. It was a question that had not come up recently. "I'm a dance hall girl, Harry."

"Well, you don't have to be. God can make you all over again, sister."

Cherry Valance laughed and shook her head. "You carry him along to keep you from the dangers of dance hall girls, gambling, and whiskey, Owen?"

"That's it. I pay him a small fee for keeping me pure."

"Well, I doubt if it'll work." She would have said more, but Owen suddenly nodded and said, "I'll be seeing you, Cherry."

"Good to see you again, Owen."

As they left, Joelle was filled with curiosity. She knew there was some kind of history, and she asked impulsively, "You've known that woman a long time?"

"It's all ancient history."

"She's very pretty."

"Oh yeah. Cherry's always been pretty."

"Where did you know her?"

Owen suddenly turned and grinned. "Why are you so interested?"

"I'm just nosy, I guess."

Harry Jump had been thinking. "That woman needs to be saved. As a matter of fact, there's two kinds of folks on this train. Most of them are farmers, but two or three wagons was filled up with gamblers and—"

"I know." Owen slapped Jump on the shoulder as he interrupted. "That will give you something to work on. Maybe you'll leave me alone."

Joelle said no more, but all that day she wondered about Cherry Valance. She cooked a simple supper, and after eating, Jump wandered off. As soon as he was gone, the two of them cleaned the plates and then sat down before the fire cross-legged. "I guess you were surprised to see your old . . . friend."

"You mean Cherry? Sure was."

Joelle waited for him to continue, and when he didn't, she said, "I guess you've met a lot of people traveling around."

Majors reached down and picked up a small stick. He held it in the fire until it caught flame and then watched it as if it had some meaning. His voice was soft as he said, "I guess about all I've got is memories, Joe. I remember once outside of Shreveport, Louisiana. I was walking down the street, and there was a young girl no more than seven or eight years old. She had light blonde hair and a blue dress that matched her eyes. She was playing with a fuzzy black and white kitten. As I passed by, I stopped to look at her, and she held the kitten up to her cheek, and she said, 'Her name is Pickles. Ain't she pretty?'"

Owen blew the flame out, tossed the twig into the fire, and then turned to look at her. "I guess that's all my life is, Joe. Just some pictures that I keep, memories of people and things. Not much behind me and nothing much that I can see in front of me." He sat for a minute, then rose, and said, "I'm going to bed."

Joelle watched him go. For a long time she stared down into the flame, her eyes going to the still form of Majors as he lay under the wagon. Something about his last speech had saddened her. *He's a sad man really. I wish he weren't.* She got up then, found her own blanket, and went to sleep.

Chapter Ten

"WE BETTER STOCK UP as well as we can with the necessities, Joe. Won't be a general store along the way."

"We stop at some army posts, don't we?"

"Oh sure. Fort Laramie and some others, but they don't have much, and what they have is high as a cat's back. I'll tell you what, you make out a list of groceries, and I'll look it over. While you're doing that, I'll make sure we've got plenty of ammunition."

"All right." Joelle took a piece of paper out of her pocket, sat down on top of a pickle barrel, and wrote industriously. It helped to be able to look around the store, and finally Owen came back.

"You about finished?"

"I think so." She handed him the list and said, "This is all I could think of."

Owen stared at the list, and his lips turned upward at the corners in a smile. "We're not going to China, you know. Last time I went, all I had was my rifle. I shot game along the way."

"I'm not going to eat tough jackrabbit all the way to California. We need all this stuff."

Looking down at the list, Owen saw a string of items. He read them out loud. "Flour, bacon, coffee. That's all good. There's baking soda, cornmeal, hardtack, dried beans, dried beef, dried fruit. What do we need all this dried fruit for?"

"To make pies with."

"Well, I reckon that's OK. Molasses, vinegar, pepper, eggs." He stopped and said, "How we gonna haul eggs without getting them broken?"

"We'll get fruit jars and pack them in cornmeal."

"How do you know about that?"

"Never mind. What about the rest of the items?"

"Salt, sugar, rice, and tea. Well, that ought to keep us from starving to death."

"What about what you bought?"

"Well, I bought you a rifle. Harry and me both got rifles of our own. Can you shoot?"

"Of course I can shoot."

"Well, come over here." He picked up a rifle. "This one ought to do you. It's a Spencer. I'll give you some shooting lessons."

"I don't need any."

He grinned at her and then pointed out the other items. "Let see. I got gunpowder, lead, a bullet mold, a powder pouch, a bullet pouch. Got enough ammunition here to kill half the Sioux nation."

The two wandered around the store, and Owen suddenly gave Joelle a searching look. "You're going to burn up in that outfit. You need to get rid of those heavy clothes and get you something lightweight."

"I'm cold-natured. I like a coat." Joelle had deliberately worn her large clothes, mostly to hide her figure.

"Well, we'd better both get some underwear and socks. What size you wear?"

"I'll pick out my own stuff. You buy yours."

"You're one finicky young buck. Well, be sure you don't buy too much. We don't want to load the wagon down with personal stuff."

"I think Harry about filled it up with stock to sell when we get to California, but I'll tell you one thing," Joelle said, "I'm going to sleep in the wagon. I'm making a bed on top of all that gear."

"I may just crawl in it with you if it rains."

Owen saw that this idea didn't appeal to Joe. "Harry will probably crawl in there too. We'll be snug as three bugs in a rug."

Joelle didn't answer, but she knew that would never work. She shooed Owen off and bought a few things she would need—personal supplies Owen would never think of. A woman needed things a man didn't.

They were interrupted when Jump came in, his eyes bright. "We spent all the money you turned loose of on stock. We're going to get rich when we sell that stuff."

"I've heard you sing that song before. You never did get rich."

"Well, don't need to be rich," Jump said. He turned and walked over to a glass cabinet and said to the clerk, "Give me a big sack full of that there hard candy." He waited and then asked, "Have you got any sunflower seeds?"

"No, we don't have that. What would you want with sunflower seeds anyway?"

"You don't know they're the secret to health? I carry my own stock. The sunflower seeds got everything a man needs to keep him healthy."

"I get tired of seeing you chew on those things and then spitting out the hulls," Owen said. "They're just seeds. What do you think you are, some kind of a bird?"

"I'm telling you they're good for your health. That and garlic." He turned to the clerk. "Give me some garlic."

The clerk sighed, came out with the item, and said, "How much you want?"

"You better give me all you got. We got a long trip to go."

"You'll keep the Indians away when they smell your breath," Owen grinned.

"I'm getting enough for all three of us."

"I'm not eating any of that mess," Owen said. "Come on, Joe. If you're going to be the cook, you probably need some utensils."

The two wandered toward the back of the store where she picked out a Dutch oven, a three-leg skillet called a spider, a sharp butcher knife, and several other items.

Jump wandered around the store, holding the garlic and the sack of candy, one sack in each hand, and he looked over and saw the young woman, Ogden's wife's sister. *What is her name? Well, that little girl she's got there will like candy.* He moved over, and the woman had her back turned. He said, "I'd like to give your girl some candy."

He waited, but the woman didn't turn although the girl leaned over and stared at him. She was a pretty girl, and she looked up into the face of her mother.

The woman turned to face him, and Jump said, "I said I want to give your girl some candy. What's the matter—you deaf?"

The woman turned suddenly, and he saw that she had light brown hair with a touch of gold in it and green eyes. Her daughter had the same coloring. "Yes, I'm deaf. What do you want?"

Jump was embarrassed. *Why didn't somebody tell me she was deaf?* he thought. "Well, I just thought your girl might like some candy."

"You stay away from my daughter." She turned away and left, pulling the young girl after her.

"She's right sensitive." Jump turned to see Cleo Ogden standing there. "I didn't mean no harm."

"I'm sure you didn't."

"How long she been deaf?"

"Since she was six. She had a high fever, and it went into her ears. Hasn't heard a sound since."

"Where's her husband?"

Cleo Ogden stared at Jump and said evenly, "She don't have one. She went to work as a housemaid for a man, and he got her in trouble. She loves Rachel better than anything else. She's afraid to let her be around men."

Jump had taken his hat off, and now he ran his hand through his hair. "Well, I just wanted to buy her some candy. I do that for most kids I run into. A man did it for me once when I was no older than that girl there. I ain't never forgot it."

"Well, you won't get anything out of Lily. She's afraid of men. She doesn't like any of them, and she keeps them away from Rachel."

Jump didn't answer and waited until Owen and Joe were through, then he helped them carry their purchases to the wagon. He was quiet for a while, so quiet that Joelle said, "What are you so quiet about? Are you mad?"

"No. It's that woman—Mrs. Ogden's sister. Did you know she was deaf?"

"No, I didn't know that."

"And she ain't got a husband either. A man got her in trouble. She had that baby."

Joelle saw that Jump was troubled. "Some women have a hard time, don't they?"

"Some of them do. You reckon she'll ever marry?"

"I don't know. Do you think so?"

The three walked along, and finally Owen said, "You always want good things to happen, Joe. Mostly they don't. I'm glad you feel that way. I hope you always do."

Joelle looked up at him. "Think you'll ever get married, Owen?"

"Nope."

"Why not?"

"I don't know, boy. Why you asking?"

"I'm just wondering."

"I've kind of given up on something like that." He was quiet for a moment as they finished loading, and finally he leaned against the wagon. She saw that he was pondering something.

"What's wrong?"

"Just thinking about married folks. You know, Joe, a man without a woman, he's not much. I don't know the Bible, but I know the first thing, almost, that God said to Adam was, 'Son, you need help.'"

She laughed. "He didn't say it like that. He said you need a helpmate."

"Well, God was right. By himself," Owen said, his voice soft as the summer breeze, "a man doesn't have much purpose. Just like that wind blowing out there with no idea where it's going. But when a man finds his woman, he sees himself, and he knows what he is. I guess that's what I'm looking for."

This was the most profound insight that Joelle had heard from Owen Majors. She saw that there was a loneliness in him that he kept well hidden. She studied him carefully until finally he turned and met her eyes. "What about you, Joe Jones? Are you looking for the woman you need?"

Joelle was confused and said, "No, I'm not."

"Well, you got plenty of time. On this trip maybe I'll educate you."

"What do you mean educate me?" Joelle asked. "About what?"

"Why, about women, of course. I'll give you the benefit of all my vast knowledge about women."

His words stirred something in Joelle. "Is that Cherry Valance what you want in a woman?"

Owen turned to face her. "You ask too many questions. Come on. Let's go to the meeting. It will be the last time we meet before we leave in the morning."

"All right."

Owen called to Jump, and the three of them headed for the center of the train.

When they got there, the meeting had already started. There was already an argument going on about the leader, and they stood beside a man whose family they had met. His name was Caleb Taylor. He was a bulky man with thinning brown hair and muddy blue eyes. Not a very forceful man. His wife's name was Pearl. She had reddish hair and big eyes and was still an attractive woman even in her late thirties.

Joelle was standing close enough to hear Pearl say, "Caleb, I didn't want to leave Missouri."

"We had to leave. There's no future for us there."

"Of course we got to go, Ma." Danny Taylor, age sixteen, had yellow hair and blue eyes. He was a lanky young fellow very uncertain about himself. He fancied himself almost grown but, in fact, he was not.

An older woman with steel gray hair and a pair of alert dark eyes was standing nearby. She said, "How are you this morning, Joe?"

"I'm all right, Miss Ketura." Ketura was Caleb Taylor's mother. Joe had met her briefly and was impressed with the spirit of the woman who seemed ancient to her.

"It'll be a long trip, Miss Ketura."

"You think I'll wear out, boy, 'cause I'm too old to make it?"

"Oh no, ma'am, I didn't mean that at all! You're right sprightly."

"Well, I am a little bit long in the tooth, but Danny will take care of me, won't you, Danny?"

"Sure I will, Grandma. I won't let the Indians get you."

Pearl turned to her husband. "Caleb, I'm not sure Ralph Ogden's the right man for a wagon master. Maybe Lyman Riker would have been better."

"No, he wouldn't," Ketura said. Her lips drew into a fine, white line. "He's a tyrant to his family. He'd be the same to the whole train."

Maggie Taylor appeared and stood next to her brother Danny. She was fifteen now and was already showing signs of young womanhood. "When are we leaving?" she asked her father.

"As soon as everything gets straightened out, I guess," Caleb said. "You anxious, Daughter?"

"Yes."

At that moment Ralph Ogden stood up and said, "All right, folks, gather 'round." He had a high tenor voice, strange in so large a man, and said, "We'll be leaving in the morning. We've got to get everything straight today."

"One thing we need to get straight, and that's how much gear and food people have." The speaker was Lyman Riker. He was fifty-three with black hair and dark eyes—an imposing man and the richest in the train. His wife, Edith, was much younger than he, and she stood beside him along with two of his sons, Clyde and Sid. They were not Edith's children but children of Riker's first wife.

"What do you mean, Lyman?" Ralph asked.

"We've got to put a limit on who can go. People have to have some cash and have to have plenty of food. Some people don't have it." He turned and nodded. "The Picketts over there don't have it. I say they can't go."

The Pickett family was standing out of the circle. Delbert Pickett was a small man with thin blond hair and faded blue eyes. His wife, Ada, had mousy brown hair. She was tall and thin. Their daughter Jennie, age sixteen, was different from either parent. She was blossoming like a flower in the desert, a pretty girl. The three smallest Picketts were barefoot and dressed almost in rags.

Joelle listened as Riker humiliated them, saying that the Picketts were all for charity.

"I wish I could shut that man up, that Riker!" she muttered under her breath.

Owen looked down at Joelle and grinned. "I think you're right." He spoke up and said, "The Picketts will be all right. I'll see to them."

"What do you mean, you'll see to them?" Riker asked.

"I made this trip once. The country had plenty of game. I reckon it still does."

"That's not good enough," Riker said.

A big man approached. He wore buckskins and a fur cap. He had blunt features and a pair of sharp, dark eyes. "I've seen the day you couldn't bring in enough grub to feed yourself, Majors."

"Hello, Mace."

Riker glared at Ogden and said angrily, "It won't do! I won't have them on the train."

"Well, now. I guess if Owen says he'll take care of their food, he will. It's good enough for me."

"I want a vote," Riker said angrily. "How many are in favor of leaving the Picketts?"

Only a few hands were raised, and Riker, who hated to be crossed, then glared at the family. "Don't be coming to me when you get hungry!"

The meeting went on for some time, and when it broke up, Cherry Valance approached. A tall man, handsome and well dressed, was with her. He had chestnut hair and hazel eyes. "Owen, this is Ash Landon. He's a good man. Just don't play cards with him. This is Owen Majors, Ash."

Landon smiled and put out his hand. "Glad to know you, Majors. Glad you stood up for the Picketts there."

"They won't be any trouble."

Cherry said, "I remember you talking about Mace Benton. You had some trouble with him when you were in the mountains, didn't you?"

"A little bit."

"He better watch his manners, or Owen will stop his clock," she said to Ash.

"Is that right?"

"Are you going to Oregon to farm?" Owen asked Ash. "You don't look much like a farmer."

"Nope, going to California. Just letting the breeze blow me."

Owen had spotted Ash Landon's trade. He was obviously a gambler, and even though a wagon train promised rough circumstances, he was still carefully dressed.

Cherry Valance laughed and took Owen's arm possessively. "You going to find that pot of gold at the end of the rainbow?"

"I never did believe that story. I expect I'll break my back digging dirt and come up with nothing but gravel."

Ash Landon laughed. "Well, I'll find my pot of gold at the faro table." He stopped and said, "You think Benton can get us there?"

Owen shrugged. "He knows the way."

          e⁓

JOELLE WOKE UP, STARTLED by the sound of a gunshot. Frightened, she sat straight up and hurriedly pulled her clothes on. She tumbled out of the wagon and found Owen folding his blankets. "What was that shot?" she said.

"It means it's time to get up and get ready to roll. They'll start every day off like that."

"Will I have time to cook breakfast?"

"You bet. We need a good one too. It'll be a hard day until we get this train prepared and ready to roll."

Harry Jump crawled from his bed, scratching and yawning hugely. "I'll fix you a fire, Joe."

Twenty minutes later the three were eating the fried ham and eggs Joelle had put together. "I'll make some biscuits if we ever stop early enough," she said.

"That'll go down good," Owen said. He stretched, and they began to clean to their plates. Joelle packed everything while Owen and Jump hitched the oxen. "Guess maybe we'll just take it easy today. You want to ride in the wagon, Joe?"

"All right." Joelle climbed up in the wagon, and thirty minutes later the wagons went into motion. All morning long she sat there until finally at noon the train paused.

"How far did we come?" she asked.

Harry Jump had been walking beside the oxen. Now he grinned at her. "About seven or eight miles. Not a bad morning's walk. I'll bet that wagon seat has about pounded your bottom to pieces, hasn't it?"

He reached over and slapped Joelle's bottom and laughed when she jumped. "Ow! You stop that!"

Jump laughed again. "Why don't you get that black horse of yours saddled? It'll rest you a might."

"All right. I won't have time to cook anything much, but we can eat some sandwiches."

Owen returned from riding with the men who were taking care of a large herd of beef cattle and milk cows. He stepped out of the saddle, saying, "Well, we better have a good meal here."

"There's a creek over there. See that line of trees?" Jump said. "I'll go get us some fresh water."

"I'll fix the sandwiches," Joelle said. "Have it ready by the time you get back."

Jump moved quickly across the open field and came to the trees. He stopped abruptly, for there fetching water was Lily Frazier. She turned to face him and stood there, obviously on her guard. Jump dropped one of the buckets, reached up, and jerked his hat off.

"Howdy, Miss Lily." The woman didn't answer, and Jump chewed his lower lip and said nervously, "I didn't mean nothing by what happened in that store. I always give candy to the kids when I can."

Lily spoke up then, and her voice was somewhat louder than he expected. He realized she had no idea how loud she was speaking or how softly. "I'm careful about Rachel," she said. Rachel had come up beside Lily. She reached up and took her mother's hand.

Jump smiled at her. "That's a fine-looking girl you got there."

"Thank you."

"I still got some of that candy left. You reckon she can have a bit?"

"I—suppose so."

Jump reached into his pocket and pulled out a crumpled sack. "Almost melted," he said. "It's been a hot day. Here, Rachel. You take one; I'll take one." He opened the sack and held it out. The girl watched him warily and then came forward.

"Thank you," she said, taking a piece.

"You're right welcome, and it'll make you sweet like me." He grinned and then turned to see Lily staring at him. "You like candy, ma'am?"

"No, thank you."

"Well, I'm sorry I offended you. You got a good, fine girl there." She didn't answer, and he took the buckets and filled them. "Can I carry one of those back?"

"No, thank you."

Jump got back to the wagon, and Joelle saw that he looked troubled. "What's wrong?"

"That Lily Frazier was there with her girl. She's still mad at me."

"I feel sorry for her. It must be awful to live in a world like that. Can't hear the birds singing or the voice of a friend."

Jump looked at the woman and the child now crossing the open spaces and heading toward the Ogden wagon. "Yes, she's had a rough time, I guess. May never get over it."

Joelle knew Jump was concerned, and she liked him better for it. He had a good heart, and she said quickly, "She'll find a man."

"With that handicap it might be hard."

"If a man loved her, he wouldn't care."

Jump looked at Joelle, and his face was more sober than she had ever seen it. Finally he said, "I had a sister who was handicapped. One leg was withered and she had to use a crutch. She was so pretty, but she never married." He turned and walked away, picked up a sandwich, and bit into it.

Joelle glanced at Owen who was watching. They didn't speak of this for the rest of the day, but she sensed that a feeling passed between them.

Chapter Eleven

JOELLE PLODDED BESIDE THE oxen, her hand resting, from time to time, on the rough coat of Big Daisy, her favorite. The week on the trail had given her complexion a light golden tan and brought out scattered freckles across the bridge of her nose. From time to time she glanced across the wagons spread out on each side of her. She had always had the idea that wagon trains would go single file, but at Owen's suggestion the wagons made a long line, side to side.

"No sense anybody eating dust if they don't have to. It may come to that," he had said to Ralph Ogden. "There'll be some places where we'll have to go in a line. In this kind of country it might be better to spread out."

As Joelle strolled along, weariness caught up with her. It was her time of the month, and she was in considerable discomfort but couldn't show it, of course.

It had taken an entire week to get the train in order, for none of them except the guide, Mace Benton, and Owen had ever been over this territory before.

A sound of laughter caught her ears, and to her right she saw youngsters running through the fields, plucking wildflowers, shouting, and playing. The sight pleased her. She had grown quite close to some of these children. She glanced up and saw that Owen, who had been hunting most of the day, had returned with game tied across the back of his saddle. He was talking to Cherry Valance. Even at this distance Joelle could see that the woman's face was bright, and she was laughing at something Owen had said.

Looks like he'd have better sense than to fool around with a saloon woman. The thought came without volition, and she tried to shake it off. *It's none of my business what Owen Majors does. If he wants to make a fool of himself over a woman like that, let him do it.* The thought displeased her, however, and she forged along and was glad, an hour later, when Ogden signaled a stop. The big man had been almost helpless at first, but he had learned quickly, and now the wagons were drawn in a circle. She took her place, and as soon as the circle was completed, Harry Jump appeared to take the yokes off.

"I tossed some dry wood in the back of the wagon, Joe," he said. "I'll build us a fire. I'll cook supper, too, if you want."

"No, I'll do it, Harry." She straightened up and arched her aching back. After Harry built a small fire, she began pulling together the elements for a meal. The late-afternoon air was filled with the cries of children playing, oxen lowing from time to time, and the voices of the travelers. She had not yet started the supper when Owen pulled up. He had an antelope slung across the back of his horse, and as he swung to the ground, he grinned.

"Fresh meat," he said. "Antelope is about the worst meat there is, but it was all I was able to get."

"Well, it's better than shoe leather but not much," Jump grinned. "Here, let me dress that thing, Owen."

"I sure will. I hate to dress antelope. They're a pain." He unsaddled his horse.

In a short time, Jump, who was good at dressing wild game, came to Joelle. "How about these steaks? They're kind of lean, but they're fresh. I like mine rare."

Joelle smiled at him, took the steaks, and threw them into the spider that she had placed over the flame. They began to smoke at once, and she shifted them with a fork. She had drawn up a box to use for a seat in front of the fire.

"There's a creek over there," Harry said. "See that line of willows? We need some fresh water."

"I'll get it, Harry. You watch the steaks."

Quickly she grabbed a bucket and headed for the creek. She found the creek was small, no more than eight or nine feet across, but the water seemed to be clear. She removed her hat and knelt down to wash her face. *I'd like to plunge into this and wash all over,* she thought. *But I don't guess that would do unless I came back after dark.* The lack of bathing was troublesome for she always cherished a warm, hot bath. Now that they had been on the trail for a week, she felt dirty, gritty, and grimy. She reached down to scoop up a bucket of water, but then suddenly she was aware of a man who had appeared with two buckets.

"Hey there. That water any good?"

"It looks good, and it tastes all right," Joelle said.

"I'm Davis Hall. I reckon you're with Majors."

"That's right. It's a good thing we got him along. I believe he's a better guide than the one we've got."

Davis was a tall man with tawny hair and blue eyes. He was roughly handsome and stood there for a moment, then leaned over and took a drink. "Long way to go. What you say your name was?"

"Joe Jones."

"Well, Joe, you ever been to California?"

"Never have."

"Me either. My wife and I are having a fight about it. I want to go to the gold fields, and she wants to keep on farming. She wins most of the arguments so I'll probably grub around in the dirt."

The two of them talked for a few moments, and then one of the dance hall girls appeared with a bucket. "Hello, Bonnie."

"Hello, Davis." The woman was more than average height and full-figured. There was a bold look about her, and she smiled professionally, it seemed to Joelle.

"I brought some clothes down. Everything I've got is filthy."

"Well, Bonnie, let me give you a hand with that."

"Men aren't supposed to wash clothes."

"Why, for a pretty woman I'll do just about anything."

Joelle was surprised. She knew Davis Hall had mentioned his wife, and here he was flirting with a saloon woman. She turned to go when another woman arrived. Joelle had seen her before and knew that her name was Aiden.

The woman took in the man kneeling down beside Bonnie Martin and said in a chilling tone, "Well, you don't change, do you, Davis?"

Instantly Hall got up, his face flushed. "Aiden, I was just—"

"I know what you were 'just'!" The woman walked over to the creek, filled her bucket with water, and turned around without another word.

Hall hurried after her, and as soon as they were out of hearing, Bonnie turned and winked at Joelle. "It looks like I broke up a happy home. When you get a wife, Joe, be sure you don't get caught cheating. I guess I'm lucky. Some women would have shot me." She looked at Joelle carefully. "How old are you, Joe?"

"Seventeen."

"I bet you've got a sweetheart somewhere back East."

Joelle didn't know how to answer. "Not really," she said. "Well, I'd better get back."

"You're not afraid of women, are you?" Bonnie Martin called and then laughed as Joelle fled from the creek.

℮

WHEN AIDEN HALL RETURNED from the creek, she found her son Benny waiting for her. "I could have gone and gotten that water, Mom."

"You do more than your share, Benny. Oh, you got the fire all laid."

"Let me light it, Ma."

The twelve-year-old took the matches from Aiden, and she watched him as he knelt carefully. He was a handsome boy with his mother's blond hair and gray eyes. He was thin but healthy. He looked up and smiled. "What do we have for supper, Mom?"

"I guess it'll have to be bacon and beans."

137

"I've been soaking the beans all day in that pot like you said."

"It'll take awhile for them to boil, but we'll have a good supper. You take good care of your old mother, Benny."

"You ain't old," Benny said.

"Well, I appreciate that kind remark."

"This is fun, ain't it, Ma? It's a lot better than being stuck back in Missouri."

"Fun so far, but we've got a long way to go. It's going to be thirsty at times."

"You reckon we'll get attacked by Indians?"

"I hope not."

The two busied themselves; Benny set the beans on a tripod over the fire and put a skillet alongside it for the bacon. Aiden sat back and watched him. She had seen other boys his age who were wild, but Benny had a mild and good spirit about him. She turned suddenly to see Davis coming back. He had a hangdog look, which saddened her. She had had high expectations of marriage, and they were mostly gone. There had been a brief period when she had been wildly in love with Davis, but he was a weak man. She had learned that from the start, and now there was grief in her heart as she looked at him.

Davis could not meet her eyes. He stood over her and said, "It was nothing, Aiden."

"It never is with you."

Aiden found herself saying things she didn't really mean. "Why don't you go back to the creek? I'm sure your lady friend is still there."

"I was just passing the time of day."

"I know what you were just doing, Davis, and the only rea-son I came on this trip was because you begged me. You prom-ised me you would change." She kept her voice low so that Benny would not hear.

"I will."

"No, you won't, Davis." Davis reached out and touched her as she drew away. "Stay away from me. Go to your cheap women."

Davis watched as she got up and walked away. His shoul-ders slumped, and he had a worried, defeated look on his face. He knew she was right. He couldn't keep his hands off women, and he couldn't understand why. Aiden was a good wife, fine-looking and strong—stronger than he was, he knew that. Finally he walked over and squatted down beside Benny, saying, "Those beans look good, Son."

"How long will they have to cook do you think?" Benny looked up, and there was trust in his eyes. Davis felt a pang because he knew, for whatever reasons, the boy loved him and even admired him—Aiden had not been able to keep the whole truth from their son. He ruffled Benny's hair. "We'll just sit here and watch them until they soften up."

"WELL NOW, OWEN, THAT'S mighty handy."

"Antelope is about the worst kind of meat there is, Delbert, but at least it's fresh."

Owen stepped out of the saddle and handed the quarter of antelope to Pickett. The small man had faded blue eyes and the air of failure. Owen had seen it many times, not always in small men. Sometimes in big powerful men who had missed their way somewhere. The aura of failure to him seemed to have almost a smell to it, and now he felt a touch of grief for the Pickett family. He turned to Ada who was a few years younger than her husband but had that same air.

She said, "Thank you, Owen. This will cook down pretty good."

"How are those babies doing, Ada?"

"They're doing fine. I ain't got enough milk for two. Never planned on that." She gestured over to a box where the two six-month-olds, Johnny and Esther, were kicking their feet and waving their arms.

Owen went over and bent down. "Look at you," he said. "You've got a whole lifetime in front of you."

"Do you like babies, Mr. Majors?"

Owen turned to see Jennie Pickett. She was a well-formed girl with a wealth of yellow hair and bright blue eyes. She had already begun to blossom out. "Well, I was one myself, Jennie, so I guess I have to like the breed, don't I?"

"They sure are hard to take care of."

"Maybe you can get Burke Townsend to help you. I notice he's usually handy."

Jennie stared at him, and her face turned rosy. "He wouldn't like babies."

"He likes you though, Jennie."

Jennie Pickett was a shy girl. "No, he doesn't like me. Anyway, I don't like him."

"Why not?" Owen said peering down at the girl with interest in his expression. "Pretty good-looking young fella."

"He's not nice like—"

"Like Danny Taylor?"

"Don't you tease me, Mr. Majors."

"You can call me Owen. I like it when young women call me by my first name. It makes me feel young again. An old codger like me, we need all the help we can get."

"You ain't old!"

"Well, I feel that way sometimes."

Owen reached out with both hands and offered each twin a finger to pull. One of them took it and hung on, and the other stared up at him, then began to cry. "Well, one of them likes me and one of them don't," he said. He laughed, pulled his finger back, and said, "You folks enjoy the meal. It won't be long until we'll be in buffalo country. Then we'll get something really good to eat."

"I expected to see a big herd of buffalo," Delbert Pickett said. "Read stories about them."

"They don't stay on the trails much. We'll see some big herds as we go." Owen swung to his saddle. "You folks eat hearty."

He went over then to the wagon where Cherry Valance was cooking something over a fire. "Brought some fresh meat," he said.

"What is it?" Cherry said.

"Antelope." Owen got down and pulled out some steaks. "Got enough for all your girls."

All of the dance hall girls gathered around, and one of them named Dora pulled at Owen's sleeve. "What's a good-looking man like you doing without a wife?"

"Nobody will have me, Dora," Owen said lazily, shaking his head with mock sadness. "I'm just a forlorn old bachelor and doomed to be."

"Not likely," Dora said. Her eyes were bright, and she had a lively look. "You and me will have to talk about that. We might make a real team."

"You might as well forget that," Cherry said. "Owen's not husband material. I ought to know." She winked at Owen. "I gave you your chance, didn't I?"

"You sure did, but I wouldn't saddle a lovely lady like you with a bum like me."

Owen enjoyed talking with the women. He knew they were bad. Some of them had a vicious streak, but he always felt a grief for a person's being trapped in a life that could not end happily. He stayed until Cherry had fried the steaks, and the others left to eat. As soon as they were gone, she said, "You want a steak, Owen?"

"No, I ate back at the wagon. Antelope's not much."

Cherry didn't seem to hear his words. She was watching him with a curious expression, and finally she said, "Owen, do you ever think about the time we were together?"

"I guess so. I was telling someone the other day about all a man has is memories. Yes, I remember those days, Cherry."

"So do I." She hesitated, then added, "We could have that again, Owen."

Owen stared at her, not knowing how to answer. He had fancied himself in love with Cherry Valance at one time, and he had even offered to marry her. But she had refused him. He wondered why she had lied to the girls about it and then decided that was the way of a woman.

"A friend of mine used to read philosophy," he said quietly. He turned from her and studied the horizon as if it had some mystical meaning. The stars were beginning to come out, and the darkness was falling fast. "He said one time there was one of those philosophers. His name was Heraclitus, I think. This friend of mine said he came up with the smartest thing he ever heard. He said, 'You can't step in the same river twice.' I reckon that's about the extent of my wisdom."

"I don't believe that. I believe you can go back to a better time and a better way."

"Well, you may be right." Owen smiled at her and touched her cheek. "We have a long time to talk about it. Nights get pretty long on the trail." He suddenly pulled her forward. His voice grew husky, and he said, "Sure I remember those times. I remember everything about it." He pulled her close, and she came to him willingly. Her body pressed against him, and she put her arms around his neck. He remembered, in the days when they had been together, there had been a wild sweetness in her caresses, but the sweetness was missing now.

He released her and laughed shortly. "I've got to get back. I'll see you tomorrow. We'll get some buffalo soon. It'll be better than this antelope." He led his horse away as she watched.

"Some old history there, Cherry?" She turned to see Ash Landon who had stepped out from behind the wagon.

"You keeping track of me, Ash?"

"Couldn't help seeing. Raking up old ashes, maybe hoping for a fire?"

Cherry Valance stared into the darkness where Owen Majors had disappeared. "He's a good man. About the only one I ever saw, I guess."

"Makes me feel small."

She turned and laughed. "We're what we are, Ash. You and me—and Owen."

"You getting tired of the life?"

"Been tired of it for years."

Ash Landon stared at her and then shook his head. "I guess most of us are. Nothing to do but keep on, is there?"

"No, I guess not."

❧

LYMAN RIKER FINISHED HIS supper and glanced around at his family. "Well, we didn't make much time today, did we?"

"No, we didn't." Edith Riker's brief answer disturbed Lyman.

"Why don't you talk more?"

"I wait until I have something to say."

The three sons of Riker—Clyde, Sid and Artie—were finishing their meal. Clyde and Sid were the sons of Emily, Riker's first wife. They were alike in many respects; each had black hair and a tall, muscular build. Artie, the son of Riker's second wife, Jennie, had her blond hair and mild blue eyes, and Lyman was displeased with the boy.

Lyman threw his plate down and said, "I'm tired of this food already. Didn't you two see any game at all?" He had sent Clyde and Sid out for fresh meat, but they hadn't found any.

"We didn't see nothing," Sid shrugged. "It was scared off by the wagons."

"Majors brought in something," Lyman challenged them.

"Well, he was a mountain man." Artie spoke up.

Both Clyde and Sid were insulted. "He was just lucky, that was all," Clyde snorted.

"Artie, go butcher a yearling. We're going to have fresh meat."

"Yes sir." Artie left at once. Lyman Riker watched him go and then shook his head. "He's weak like his mother."

Edith didn't argue. She picked up the plates and began cleaning them. Clyde and Sid disappeared, and Riker watched her for a time. His eyes glowed with a sudden burst of lust, which came to him often. He went over to her and said, "Put them dishes down. Come on in the wagon."

She put the dishes down, and he grabbed her and kissed her roughly. She didn't respond but stood there waiting. Lyman Riker had a short, fiery temper.

"You got no feelings. You're like a block of wood."

"You married me to keep your house, Lyman."

"A woman should show something to her husband. A little love."

Edith stared at him, unmoved. "You never mentioned love when you asked me to marry you."

Lyman Riker had chosen this woman; she had looks and some property. He had married her for both, and though he had gotten the property, he was constantly angry with her for her lack of response. He whirled around and said, "You're not a fit wife for anybody!"

Edith watched him go. She stared after him. She had long since given up grieving over the poor choice she had made in a husband. She finished cleaning the dishes and went to where Artie had killed the yearling and was now dressing it. "That'll be good tomorrow. I'll tender one of those steaks for you, Son."

Artie looked up. "I wish," he said quietly, "I could be what Pa wants, but I'll never be as tough as Clyde or Sid."

Edith put her hand on the boy's shoulder. "You're a better man than either of them."

Artie looked at her with shock in his eyes. "Why, no, I ain't. They can both whip me anytime they take a notion."

"That's not all there is to being a man, Artie. There's a goodness in you that Clyde and Sid don't have and your father either. I think you got it from your mother." She kissed him on the cheek. "There, your old ma has told you the truth." She turned and left.

Artie Riker stared after her in disbelief. "I don't know why she said that. It ain't so." He thought about it for a long moment and then shrugged and went back to butchering the yearling.

Chapter Twelve

THE DAYS ON THE trail were routine. At four o'clock each morning, the wagon master fired a single shot, signaling the beginning of the day. Shortly afterward, slow columns of smoke rose from the campfires, and half a dozen men rode out to move the stock toward the camp. From six to seven, breakfast was eaten, wagons reloaded, and the teams yoked. The wagons moved out promptly at seven, leaving each camping ground, so recently full of activity, to sink back into the profound solitude that reigned over the broad plain. Hunters went out each day, and some of the men fell behind to herd the stock.

At noon the teams were not unyoked but simply turned loose from the wagons while a quick meal was eaten. By late afternoon the men and beasts were tired so a campground was chosen. All of the drivers grew expert at drawing the train into a circle so tight it formed a barricade. Everyone joined in to cook the evening meal, to pitch tents for some, and to prepare for the night. For the first week everyone had gone to bed as soon as the meal was over, but as the travelers grew accustomed to the routine, each evening the sound of talk and low laughter scattered in the air as the women gathered in small groups and the men carried on card games beside their fires.

For the first two weeks rivers had marked their progress. They crossed the Kaw River and a week later the Big Blue. They reached Sandy Creek and hit the Little Blue early in the afternoon. The Blue was a changeable river that could be forded sometimes and fortunately was low at this time in April.

"What's up ahead, Owen?" Joelle turned to look at Owen who had joined her out in the advance of the train. The two horses ambled along, stopping to crop the grass from time to time.

"We'll be reaching the Platte River pretty soon."

"The country looks a little different here."

"A little bit I guess, but still plenty of grass and water. No trouble." Indeed, what timber there was mostly had been burned by the Indians in small-game hunts and survived mostly in the river on sandy islands.

"How far are we from California?"

"Why, boy, we've barely just gotten started. It'll take us four months to get there. You in a hurry or something?"

"I'm curious. I've never been anywhere."

"You never mention your folks or your home." Owen turned to study her, and Joelle flushed slightly. Indeed she had kept her background a secret out of necessity.

"It was in Tennessee, but I don't have folks any longer. They both died."

"That's tough. I lost mine when I was pretty young too."

To Joelle's relief Owen said no more, and she quickly changed the subject. "Will there be a town pretty soon?"

"Fort Kearny. We'll probably get there tomorrow. It's not much. Don't get excited. These army forts are always a disappointment to folks who have never seen one."

"What's it like?"

"Well, mostly a bunch of logs stuck in the ground and a few buildings inside." He suddenly laughed. "Outside there are drunk Indians, and inside there are drunk soldiers."

"Surely not all of them!"

"No, not all, but it's a pretty lonesome life for soldiers. I'm glad I never had to do that sort of thing."

Owen fell into silence, and Joelle was accustomed to this. She wondered what went on in his mind when he stopped talking; he seemed to be lost in another world. In a way she was glad because she didn't have to guard her own words about her past and what she was doing in this part of the world.

An hour later it seemed the wildlife was more common. Owen pointed out a grizzly that was some distance off the main trail. Joelle asked, "Are bears dangerous?"

"Sure. You get between a mama and her cub, she'll wipe you out."

A few minutes later she said, "What are those mounds?"

"Prairie dog villages. Sometimes they cover as much as five hundred acres."

"Are they good to eat?"

"Better than hawk."

Joelle gave him a startled look. "You've eaten hawk?"

"Once. It was hawk or nothing."

"What'd it taste like?"

"About like shoe leather soaked in rancid oil, but we'll hit the buffalo in a few weeks. That's when the good eating will start. The first one I shoot I'll give you the liver. It's better if you just eat it raw."

"I'm not eating any raw liver," Joelle protested.

"Well, I'll eat it then. I'll give you the second best part, the tongue."

"That might be all right, but I'll want to cook it first."

The horses ambled on, and high overhead a group of seven buzzards circled in the leisurely fashion of their kind. The air was clear, and the sun was hot, but Joelle liked it. She reached forward and patted Blackie on the shoulder, and as she did, Owen said, "I been meaning to warn you. You better be careful about them pretty ladies hanging out with those gamblers."

"What are you talking about?"

"Well, you're downright pretty, boy. Got smooth cheeks and good color. Not very big, but them girls ain't particular. I think you'd better stay away from them."

"I don't notice you staying away from Cherry Valance," Joelle snapped.

"Well, it's too late for me. I'm done ruined, but you're not. You're young and innocent, and I aim to keep you that way."

"You like that kind of woman?"

Owen grinned. "I liked her once pretty well. Man's a weak creature and full of sins and flaws. She was downright gorgeous, and when she fluttered her eyelids at me, I went after her like an ox to the slaughter. I'm just a downright sinner, Joe."

"I don't see why you have to be."

"Why, Joe, it didn't happen all at once," Owen remarked. His eyes never stopped but moved from point to point. He was cautious about things like that, Joelle had noticed, but he continued in the same teasing way. "A man don't lose his honor all at once."

"What do you mean?"

"I didn't wake up one morning all fresh and innocent and green like you and say, 'I guess I'll become a bad man. Throw away all my Sunday school teaching. I'm going to do all the bad things I know I'm not supposed to.' Nobody just wakes up and decides that."

"How does he get there then?"

"Well, it's like I lost my honor a little bit at a time, you know like a little mouse crept in and got just a little morsel of cheese. Then the next night he comes again, and this time he brings a friend with him, and they get two morsels. Sooner or later, he loses it all just a little tiny bit at a time. So that's the way I became a bad man. I lost all my goodness just a bit at a time."

"That's foolish!" Joelle said scornfully.

"I guess it is. Don't ask me about things like that. Talk to Harry. He's the one that's on the glory trail."

"I like Harry," she said defensively.

"Why, so do I," Owen said. He gave her a surprised look. "He's a good man. Always has been. Of course, this religion kick of his gets a little tiresome at times, but you have to put up with your friends when they've got annoying habits like that. I put up with yours, don't I?"

"I don't have any annoying habits."

"Oh yes, you do. I just don't want to mention them to you. See, you're so sensitive and all. If I mention them, you'd get mad at me."

"What bad habits do I have?"

"Well, you wash too much, Joe. Every time we stop at a creek, you're out washing your face. Of course, I do, too, once in a while, but bathing is a serious business."

"You're a fool, Owen!"

"Next time we come to a creek I'll tell you what. We'll get some soap and we'll go out and soak all over. We'll get cleaner than a granny's washing. Would you like that?"

Joelle could not answer for a moment. "I'll take care of myself, Owen."

"Well, you need somebody to scrub your back. Bound to be plum filthy." He reached out suddenly and put his hand on her back and rubbed it back and forth. "I can just feel the dirt and grime rolling around your skin."

"You—you get your grubby hands off me!" Joelle struck at his arm and kicked Blackie in the side. He snorted, crow-hopped, and moved away from Owen.

Owen began to laugh. "You're a finicky young fellow. You really need to be back in New York City doing something that clean-favored young fellows do. Maybe you could find you a rich old woman and make up to her. You could marry her, and she'd give you all her money. You'd be nice enough to her, but could have all the lady friends you wanted until the old lady died."

"You have a foul mind, Owen Majors!" Joelle kicked Blackie in the side, and he shot ahead.

Owen laughed loudly and shouted after her, "I'll tell you some more about yourself after supper tonight." He grinned and shook his head. "He sure is a shy young fellow. Must have been raised in a monastery or something."

ALL AFTERNOON AS THE train moved slowly, everyone was looking hungrily ahead. Joelle was feasting her eyes on a panorama of sky and land, the borders of which met along a seam that was nearly invisible. By late afternoon she saw something that broke the monotony of the prairie. As the wagons grew closer, she heard someone shout, "There it is. That's Fort Kearny!" Everyone speeded up as much as oxen can be speeded. Distances were deceitful, and it was late when they reached the fort. It was shining white in the sun, high up on a bluff. Joelle spotted white objects, and as they grew closer, she discovered they were teepees. Ralph Ogden called a halt. The wagons drew into a circle although there was no need for it at this time since no hostiles were going to attack a wagon train within the shadow of an army fort.

As soon as the oxen were unyoked, Owen said, "Let's take a look inside, Joe."

"Have you been here before?"

"I stopped once a few years back." She followed, as did Harry, and they walked toward the walls of the fort. As they entered, Joelle was disappointed. There was a drab monotony about the collection of log huts that occupied the interior of the long rampart. "Well, at least I'll be able to sit down in a real chair. I hope we stay here a week."

"No, we'll be pulling out probably tomorrow, day after at the most. We better get our supplies today before they get picked over." Owen grabbed Joelle's coat. "Get rid of this here heavy coat. You need something lightweight. Come on. I'll help you go pick it out."

"I'll pick out my own clothes, Owen."

"Well, you better get some underwear. Get something lightweight. It's going to get pretty hot. Maybe I'll help you pick that out too."

"I'll pick out my own clothes."

As they started toward the general store, Cherry Valance approached them. She smiled at Owen and said, "There's a saloon down here. Are you feeling frolicky?"

"Frisky as a frog ready to jump." He turned to Joelle and said, "You go get that underwear, Joe, and get me some too." He handed her some money and said, "Get something unusual to eat."

"Like what?"

"I don't know. Chocolate covered ants or frog legs or something different from antelope. Come on, Cherry. Let's go investigate the morals of Fort Kearny."

Harry Jump said, "Cherry, the good Lord is watching you. I done preached at you about the way you're living."

"Preach on, Harry. Maybe it'll do some good, but I'll have all the fun I want. Then when I'm on my death bed, I'll get converted."

"That's foolish talk," Jump frowned. "It don't work." But Cherry was already gone. Harry shook his head. "That poor woman is headed for a fall, and all the rest of them too. It's bound to be worse when we get to the gold camp."

"You really have any hope for women like that, Harry?"

"Why, of course I do. They ain't no worse than I was. They ain't no angels, but then I wasn't either. Come on. Let's go spend some foolish money and get something real unnecessary and good to eat."

Joelle moved with Harry toward the general store, but her eyes followed the tall form of Owen as he and the woman left. She noticed that Cherry's arm was around him, and as she watched, his arm went around her. "There's some more of his honor being carried off by rats," she said.

"Rats? What are you talking about?"

"Oh, never mind." Joelle smiled. "Come on. Let's go find something good to eat."

℮

OWEN HAD NOT INTENDED to drink much, but somehow with Cherry he found himself becoming drunk. It had been a long time, and he more than once protested, "Cherry, tomorrow I'll have a head that feels like a stick of dynamite went off."

"Don't worry about tomorrow. You're having a good time, aren't you?"

"I guess so, but all I think about is the headache. Liquor don't agree with me. You're leading me astray." But then Owen said, giving her a sober look, "You always did."

They stayed at the saloon for another hour, and Owen got into a poker game. There was a rough-looking man who was winning most of the pots. His name was James Sanders. When Owen started to win, Sanders began hinting that Owen was dealing from under the deck.

"No, I'm not doing that. That wouldn't be honorable. I'm an honorable man, James."

"You ain't all that honorable. I'll bet you was rotten even when you was a kid."

Owen leaned back and winked at Cherry who was perched on the arm of his chair. "I was so honorable. When I was a kid, I went to Sunday school every Sunday, and I helped old ladies across the street, and I never said no bad words. I bet you wasn't that honorable, was you, James?"

"Shut up and play cards!"

The card game went on, and even half-drunk, Owen was a good poker player. He won a great deal of money and finally he said, "Well, I'm pulling out."

"You ain't leaving the winner!" Sanders growled.

"That's the best way to leave a game." Owen scraped the money across the table and knocked some of it to the floor. Cherry picked it up, and he stuffed it into his pocket. "I'll come back tomorrow and win the rest of your money."

Sanders stood up so abruptly his chair fell backward. He came around the table very fast for a big man and caught Cherry by the arm. "You take the money, and I'll take your woman."

"Take your hands off that woman, Sanders."

"Why don't you make me?"

Owen swung a blow, but his reflexes were slow. Sanders laughed and suddenly struck Owen a hard blow right in the mouth. It drove him backward, and he scrambled to his feet in time to meet the rush. *I wish I wasn't drunk. He looks like a rough old cob.*

℘

IT WAS LATE, AND the stars were sprinkled across the sky. From far off came the lonesome cry of a wolf, always a sad

sound and rather frightening to Joelle. She had been waiting
for Owen to come back, but Harry had gone to bed, saying,
"He'll come in when he gets ready if he don't get beat-up."

A slight sound came to her, and Joelle stood up. It was
a bright night with the moon round, shining, and silver and
throwing gleams all over the flat plain. As she expected, she
saw a tall form and knew it was Owen. Then she saw Cherry
beside him, and he was leaning heavily on her. When they got
close enough, Joelle saw that Owen had blood on the front of
his shirt.

"What happened?" Joelle demanded.

"Well, I suppose you think I've been drinking," Owen said
pugnaciously. "Well, I ain't. I ain't had a drop."

"I expect you need to go to bed, Owen," Cherry said.
"You're going to feel pretty bad in the morning."

"No, it's too early to go to bed."

Cherry laughed. She was half-drunk herself. "You better
put him to bed, Joe. He's had a hard night. I'll see you tomorrow, Owen."

Owen swayed on his feet, and Joelle pulled him toward the
fire where she could see his face. "Sit down," she said shortly.

"I ain't had a drop."

"You're drunk as a skunk. Who beat you up?"

"Nobody. I ain't been in no fight."

Joelle had packed a medical kit, and she got fresh water
and washed the blood from Owen's face. He had a bad cut
over his left eyebrow, but she didn't think stitches were called
for. She patched it up, ignoring his grunts. He grew quiet while
she did her work, and finally he said, "Joe?"

"Yes, what is it?"

"I have so been drinking. I got in a fight and I lost it too. I'm just no good, Joe"

"Come on. You need to lie down. Here, let me give you some laudanum. It'll make you sleep."

Owen was agreeable enough. He took the medicine, made a face, and stumbled over to where his blankets were. He lay down on one, and Joelle pulled a cover over him. She saw he was already going off to sleep. "I'm just no good, Joe. No good at all."

She reached down, nearly touched his hair, and then pulled her hand back quickly. "Good night," she said sharply, turned, and left. "He should have had better sense. That woman will get him killed one of these days!"

*

"WELL, YOU SURE MADE a plum fool out of yourself with that scarlet woman. Look at your face. You look like you've been hit with a bunch of wet squirrels or something."

"I don't want to hear all this, Harry." Owen's head was killing him. He had awakened feeling sick with a terrible headache. Not wanting to face Joe and Harry, he had left before breakfast, but later in the day Harry found him in front of the train. Harry left, but his place was taken by Joelle who had been watching them.

"Well, you made a fool of yourself, didn't you?"

"Don't you start on me, Joe! Yes, I made a fool of myself. I've done it before, and I'll probably do it again." He glared at her saying, "You're just a kid. One of these days you'll make a fool out of yourself over a woman. Every man does."

"No, I won't ever do that. I've got better sense." She turned and left him angry clear through.

⟡

OWEN STAYED SILENT FOR the next two days. He got up early, ate a quick breakfast, and then went back to help the men herd the cattle. It was a job he didn't like, but he didn't want to face Joe or listen to Harry's preaching. By noon he was tired of it, and he circled the train and went out looking for game. He was headed back with an antelope. They were easy enough to pop. All he had to do was tie a white rag onto a sapling and hide himself, and the silly creatures would get curious. They'd move closer and closer, sniffing at the flag, and he had shot one.

As he headed back, he was berating himself. "Owen, you're old enough to know better. Why do you have to make a fool of yourself every chance you get?"

He paused suddenly and drew up his horse's head. "What's that? Looks like a man," he muttered. He spurred the horse forward, and sure enough there was a man lying on his face. "Don't look like the Indians got him." He dismounted and dropped the reins. Captain, his horse, was trained to stay where the reins were dropped, so Owen bent down and turned the man over. "Not dead," he said, "but he sure looks bad." He went back to the horse and got his canteen.

Raising the man up, he said, "Here, partner, take a drink of this." The man's eyes opened slightly. They were both puffy with blows, and his lips were swollen where they had been cut against his teeth. One of his ears was torn nearly off his head, and he cried out when Owen moved his body. "Somebody beat you and left you for the wolves. What's your name?"

"Logan."

"Well, we'd better get you back to the train. What happened to you?" The man didn't answer, and Owen pulled him to his feet. "Come on. You can't walk. Here, I'll help you on the horse." Fortunately Captain was a placid animal, and he stood stock still as Owen hoisted the battered man into the saddle. He picked up a carpet bag that had been thrown aside, and swung on behind him, saying, "OK, Captain, take us home."

e⌒

"WHO'S THAT WITH OWEN?" Harry said.

"I don't know. It looks like he's been through the mill though." The two hurried, and others were gathering to meet the pair. Ralph Ogden spoke first. "Who you got there, Owen?"

"Found him on the trail."

"He looks dead," Edith Riker said. "What's he doing out here in the middle of nowhere?"

"He's not able to talk much. Some of you fellows take him."

Caleb Taylor and Ralph Ogden helped the man down. "What's your name, fella?" Ogden demanded.

He got no answer.

"He said his name was Logan. I don't know if it's the first or last," Owen said.

"What's he doing out here?" Ash Landon demanded. He was dressed as if he were in the finest restaurant in St. Louis and shook his head. "It looks like he's not going to make it."

"Well, we'll have to do something with him," Ogden said. "He'll have to ride in a wagon."

No one volunteered, and then Edith Riker said, "We've got plenty of room in one of our wagons. Bring him on."

"You can't take him in," her husband said. Lyman Riker didn't believe in showing much charity. Edith paid him no attention. "You don't have to worry about him. I'll take care of him."

Riker threw up his hands and said, "I give up on you, woman. If you'd show your husband a little more attention, you wouldn't have it to give to a beat-up stranger who's probably some kind of a crook."

"Bring him to my wagon, Ralph. He'll need to be cleaned up."

℮〜

HE FELT SOMETHING COOL on his face. Something had changed and it confused him. When he opened his eyes, the coolness touched his face again, and he started to sit up and uttered a cry of pain.

"Lie still. You've been hurt."

Logan opened his eyes and saw that he was under canvas. It was a wagon. It was bumping along, and the woman was sitting beside him. "I patched you up as best I could, but I think you've got some cracked ribs."

"Who—who are you?"

"I'm Edith Riker. What were you doing out in a shape like this? . . . Doesn't matter."

Logan lay quietly and said, "You should have left me to die."

161

Edith shook her head. "You've given up. Don't be a coward, man. You're young enough to make something out of yourself."

"I'm no good to anyone."

Edith Riker studied him. It was difficult to discern his features since his eyes were puffed shut, and his lips were swollen, but he seemed to be a higher type than most men. At least she felt this. "A man's meant to find out what he's put here for."

"Not me. I wish you had left me there to die."

Edith stared at him for a moment, then jumped off the back of the moving wagon. Artie Riker asked, "How is he, Ma?"

"He'll be all right physically, but he sure is in bad shape in other ways. Says he wished we had left him to die."

Artie was shocked. "Why would a man wish that? He ain't hurt that bad."

"Something's wrong with him on the inside. I guess we'll have to wait until he gets better before we find out what it is."

The train moved on slowly under the inverted bowls of sky, and as Edith followed the wagon, she thought about the man Logan. She didn't know his full name, but for some reason she was interested. Ordinarily she paid men no attention. Her marriage had soured her on the breed. She never had very high expectations of marriage, and the few she had had been shattered by her union with Lyman. Now she shook her head. "You can't be much of a man if all you want to do is die."

Chapter Thirteen

LOGAN TEMPLE CAME OUT of unconsciousness with a spastic motion. The movement sent a white-hot, searing pain through his head, and immediately he realized his entire body was in pain. His tongue was so thick and dry that he couldn't even lick his lips.

Sounds began to come to him—the creaking of wagon wheels and the far-off moaning of a coyote. Closer than these was the sound of a woman singing an old hymn he remembered from his childhood:

> I will arise and go to Jesus,
> He will embrace me in His arms;
> In the arms of my dear Savior,
> O there are ten thousand charms.

The memory of the hymn was a good one, but it immediately faded, and bleak memories began to rise like ghosts. They seemed to come out of a dark, malevolent box, and one of them was recent. He winced as he thought of a thick-set man named Yates cursing him, striking him with hamlike fists, and beating him into unconsciousness.

For a long time Temple lay still and wondered whose wagon he was in. He was waking up in a strange place, and he dreaded facing the world. As he lay there, a wagon wheel dropped into a ditch or a hole, shaking his whole body and making him clench his teeth against the pain. *I wonder when was the last time I woke up happy and ready to face the day with joy?* The question had no answer, and he felt that happiness and joy were as far back in time as the antediluvian period or the Flood.

He wanted desperately to return to the black hole of unconsciousness, but that time had passed. Finally he heard a voice cry out something, and the wagon ground to a stop. It was time, he knew, to rejoin the world. He struggled to his elbows and managed to get into a sitting position. Looking down, he saw that he was naked to the waist and that his chest, stomach, and arms were dark with bruises, some violently yellow and others fading into a garish violet. He ran his hands over his chest and winced.

Moving cautiously, he eased onto his knees and moved toward the back of the wagon. Pushing the canvas aside, he stuck his head out and at once was blinded by brilliant sunlight. It was nearly as powerful as a physical blow, and Temple shut his eyes and waited. He finally opened them a mere slit. He was staring at a wagon train.

Slowly he lowered his legs over the edge and with one impulsive motion shoved himself out. His feet hit the ground, but there was no strength in his limbs. His legs folded and threw him facedown, causing him to utter a painful grunt. He lay there, nearly helpless, catching his breath. He heard footsteps, and then hands were turning him over. He was still staring into the brilliant heavens, but he saw a woman. "You shouldn't be doing this," she said.

Temple couldn't answer for his tongue was thick. He felt her strong hands help him into a sitting position. He caught a glimpse of bright hair rising from her temples, making a mass on her head and caught into a fall behind. She had gray-green eyes such as he had never seen before, and he knew she was full-figured as she held him to keep him from falling. She said, "Here, lean back against this wheel," and he obeyed.

She left for a moment, and he tried to collect his thoughts, but all was confusion. She was back in a moment, kneeling beside him and holding a cup to his lips. The water was tepid, but he drank it eagerly. Some of it ran down the sides of his mouth onto his chest, and the woman said, "Drink slowly. You can have all you want but a little bit at a time."

Temple drank all the water, licked his lips, and felt better. "Thank you," he whispered, his voice hoarse and rough.

The woman stared at him. "I'm Edith Riker. What's your name?"

Temple started to speak and had to clear his throat. It was still difficult to talk. "Temple," he whispered roughly. "Logan Temple. Could I have more water?"

She went to a keg on the side of the wagon, filled the cup, and returned. "Can you hold it yourself?"

"I think so." His hands were unsteady, but he drank the water more slowly than he would have liked. When he handed the cup back, he thanked her again.

Edith Riker stared at him. "How did you get out here in this place in such bad shape?"

"Where was I?"

"We found you on the trail." She touched the bruises on his chest. "Who did this to you?"

Temple looked down and then lifted his eyes. "It doesn't matter," he murmured.

His answer didn't please Edith. She was not satisfied with a man who would take such a beating as if it were nothing. "Where were you headed?"

"No place important. Doesn't matter." He added, "It'll be just like the last one."

Edith noticed something in the man's face, especially in his eyes. He had light hair, not blond exactly but close to it. His eyes were blue, and as she studied him, she saw loneliness and a pain most people would not show. She felt compassion for this bruised, beaten member of humanity. This was a strange thing for her, almost an alien thing, for her marriage had hardened her against most men. But this one seemed different, and she couldn't determine why. It troubled her that she felt like this. It made her feel a softness she thought she'd lost.

"I'll get your shirt," she said abruptly. "I had to wash it."

Temple watched as she moved away. He was aware of people at the next wagon staring at him, and he didn't meet their eyes. When she came back, he leaned forward and reached for the shirt, but the pain made him grunt.

"You must have hurt your ribs. Here, let me help you."

Edith put one arm in the shirt, draped it over his shoulders, and then put the other arm in. She pulled it together in the front, and as she buttoned it up, she studied his face. She had noticed that he was no more than average height and rather thin. She was used to rough men—farmers, hunters, and trappers—but this man had none of their roughness. He had almost aristocratic features with a short English nose and a clean-cut jaw. What little she had heard from his speech gave him away, for it was not the speech of a rough farmer.

"I'll get you something to eat." Rising quickly, she moved back to the fire.

His mind was clearer now, and he studied her while she couldn't notice his attention. She had clean physical lines, and as badly as he felt, he also noticed the smoothness of her body within her dress. She was shapely in a way any man would notice. She returned carrying a bowl and spoon and knelt beside him again. "Can you feed yourself?"

"Yes, I think so. Thank you."

He had fine manners, and her curiosity grew as she watched him eat. He was half-starved, that was obvious. Most men would have gobbled the stew down, but he ate slowly and without spilling any of the food.

She took the bowl when he handed it back, and when he said, "Thank you. That was good," she, once again, was struck by his language and by his attitude. *He doesn't belong out here,* she thought.

Hearing a noise, she turned and saw that her husband had rounded the wagon. He came up at once and stared down at Temple's battered face. "Well, has he told you who he is?"

"His name is Logan Temple."

"What are you doing out here on the prairie, Temple?" Riker demanded.

"I got left behind."

"Who left you? Who beat you up like this?"

"I guess it doesn't matter. I appreciate your taking care of me."

"It wasn't me. It was her." Riker turned his eyes, glowing with accusation, toward Edith. "You've fed him and put him back together, but he can't stay here."

Temple noticed Riker's harshness and got to his feet, swaying. "I'll be moving on," he said.

"You're not going anywhere," Edith said. "You wouldn't get a hundred yards."

"I don't propose to take him to raise, Edith."

"He'll be no trouble, but he's got to have some care until he's able to take care of himself." She stared at her husband with challenge in her green eyes. "You wouldn't begrudge a wounded man the little food he'll eat, would you?"

Lyman Riker never liked to be challenged by anyone— man or woman. He had married Edith not for love but for her property. He had learned quickly that she was as strong as he was, and now an angry reply leaped to his lips. He saw that she was waiting for it, and instead he shook his head and said, "Well, he can't stay forever." Stiffly, he turned and walked off.

Logan Temple stared at the man and then looked back at Edith. She saw something in his expression that told her that he understood what was between herself and Lyman Riker. She was not accustomed to this kind of sensitivity. Somehow in a brief encounter, Temple comprehended all about her marriage, and that disturbed her.

But she said only, "You're not ready to go anywhere yet."

"I don't want to make trouble, Mrs. Riker."

"My trouble was made long ago." The answer came from Edith's lips before she had framed it with her mind, and she knew she was not telling him anything he had not seen for himself. "Here, you sit down and eat more of this stew." She guided him back to a sitting position. "Eat all of this, and when the train starts, I'll help you get back in the wagon."

She saw him smile for the first time as he took the bowl. "I guess you hate bossy women," Edith added. "Most men do."

Logan looked at the stew, and when he looked back up, there was a strange expression in his eyes, but he said gently, "No, I don't mind at all."

⁓

TWO DAYS AFTER TEMPLE had been found, the heat of the journey was broken by a prairie storm. It broke at dusk with streaked lightning and long booming drums of thunder. It turned the sky black, and the wind whistled ominously. Joelle had seen storms before, but not like this one. With nothing as a barrier on the prairie, the thunder smote the earth like cannon fire, deafening and clattering, dying away only by slow degrees. The sky was marred by streaks of brilliant lightning branching down and seeming to grab the ground, a vivid, dangerous sort of thing that frightened Joelle. The rain came suddenly in a solid sheet, dense and massive enough to flood the earth, it seemed.

But by morning the sun came out again, and Joelle and the others took a deep sigh of relief. Joelle took the Ogdens biscuits she had made before the rains came. She had made too many, and now she said, "Mrs. Ogden, you folks like biscuits?"

Cleo Ogden smiled. "Of course we do, Joe. You didn't make these yourself?"

"Sure did. I learned how when I was real young."

"Most men think cooking is a woman's job."

Joelle immediately grew defensive. "Well, I expect that's about right." She changed the subject abruptly. "What do you think about this fellow Temple we picked up?"

Cleo brushed her hair back from her face. She had beautiful auburn hair, thick and lustrous, and very sharp blue eyes. At only twenty-eight, she still had traces of girlhood beauty. "He's a strange fellow. Edith says he's quality. She ought to know."

Joelle caught something in the woman's words. "What do you mean by that, Mrs. Ogden?"

"For land sakes, Joe, why don't you just call me Cleo? It makes me feel like an old woman to be called Mrs. Ogden. What do I mean by that? Well, it don't look too good."

"What doesn't look good?"

"The way Edith took that fellow in."

"She was just trying to help him."

"Maybe so, but that's not the way Lyman saw it. That husband of hers is jealous. What I heard is he tried to get her to run him off, but she wouldn't do it."

"They're a strange couple, aren't they, Cleo?"

"As strange as you know, boy." Cleo shook her head and seemed to be thinking. "Lyman Riker wouldn't help anybody. It's all Edith that's doing that. That's a bad marriage there, the Rikers."

"They don't seem much alike."

"Alike! Why, they're as different as night and day! I've seen women like Edith before. She was bound to have been one of those sprightly girls all the men wanted to dance with. She's still fine-looking, but she's lost most of that. I guess living with Lyman Riker would cause any woman to lose her bloom."

"Why did she marry him?"

"She didn't show good judgment. Women are weak. You be careful. Look at the Halls."

"What's wrong with them?"

"Boy, don't you have eyes in your head? He's a womanizer, and Aiden knows it. And that boy knows it too. He's ashamed of his daddy, and he ought to be."

Joelle had not thought about these things. The wagon train was small enough that she knew everybody on it. She had thought the Halls had a good marriage. Davis was tall and fine-looking and could sing well. Aiden, his wife, was a beauty, and Benny was a fine-looking boy. "I always thought they had a good family."

"Open your eyes, Joe. You just be careful when you get you a woman that she's the right one."

Joelle felt tremendously uncomfortable with talk like this, and she merely said, "I guess I'll be thinking about that."

"Men are always thinking about that. You ain't very old yet, but don't tell me you haven't thought about the girls because I know better."

Joelle suddenly laughed. "I guess I got more things to think about than that." She left, feeling that she would have to steer clear of conversations like this.

eↄ

THE LAND WAS A sea of mud after the rainstorm, so the train made only six miles that day. Several times wagons bogged down, and extra oxen had to be hitched to pull them out.

Finally, by the time they pulled into a circle near a large creek, now swollen and muddy, everyone was gloomy and short-tempered.

Delbert and Ada Pickett were weary of the trail. Both of them were small and undernourished. It was a mystery to everyone how Jennie, their sixteen-year-old, could blossom into such a well-formed, pretty girl. She looked nothing at all like her parents, and more than once one had asked if she had been adopted. Her youthful figure was the target of men's eyes already.

"Ma, you want me to go down to the river and get some water?"

"I guess you'd better, honey. It'll be muddy, but we've got to have water."

"Ma, I'm worried."

Ada Pickett looked at her daughter. "Worried about what?" She herself was worried all the time. Being married to Delbert had worn her down. He had been a failure at everything he had ever tried, and she had given up any expectations.

"I'm worried about getting a husband."

"Why, girl, you ain't got no worries there, pretty as you are!"

Jennie wanted to say, *But a man will take one look at you and Pa, and he won't want me.* She was accustomed to being low on the pecking order. She had not been an attractive adolescent, and the girlish beauty had come only in the last year. But the early years had scarred her, and now she said, "Nobody will want me, Ma."

"Stop that foolish thinking. You got plenty of time. Now go get the water. I'll start supper cooking."

Jennie didn't respond. She walked down to the river, filled the buckets, and looking up, saw that the sky was clear of clouds. "No more rain," she said. "That's good." She turned to see a coyote trotting along the riverbank. He had a frog in his mouth, and the sight amused her. "Well, froggy, you had a bad day. Too bad." She turned and walked back toward the train. It was growing darker now, and an unexpected voice nearly made her drop the buckets.

"Hello, Jennie." Mace Benton, the guide, appeared from a group of scrub trees. He was a big man with a dark complexion and thick blunt features. His lips were thick, and when he came nearer now, they twisted in a grin. "Let me carry them buckets for you, girl."

"Oh, I can do it, Mr. Benton."

Benton reached out and touched her hair. "You got the prettiest hair I ever saw."

Jennie didn't know how to handle men, especially men like this. If he had been smaller and younger, she might have known what to say, but she was afraid of the man. "I got to get back with this water." She turned and walked quickly away. She could not get away from the man who let her get almost to the wagons and then caught her arms.

"What's the matter? I'm not good enough for you?"

"Please let go of me."

"Sure I will. You just give me one kiss, and I'll let you go." Jennie could not resist. He pulled her close and kissed her. She dropped the buckets and tried desperately to get away.

"Let me go!" she cried.

"You need a man. That's what you need, Jennie."

"Let her go, Mr. Benton."

Benton whirled suddenly to see Artie Riker, the youngest son of Lyman Riker. "Get away from here, boy!"

"Sure I will, but you let Jennie go." Artie was eighteen. He would be a big strong man one day, but now he was merely tall. He had none of his brothers' bulk.

Jennie, frightened, suddenly turned and ran toward the camp. She had reached the edge when Benton caught up with her. He grabbed her again and said, "Don't be running away from me, girl!" He felt his arm suddenly jerked free, and he turned to see Artie Riker facing him.

"Don't bother her," Artie said.

Suddenly, without warning, Mace struck. His blow caught Artie in the chest and drove the young man backward until he sprawled in the mud. "You're going to get hurt if you don't get away, boy."

Artie got to his feet. His face was pale, and he obviously had little confidence in a fistfight with this big, bruising man, but he said, "I don't want to fight, but you've got to leave her alone."

Benton looked around and saw a crowd gathering. A fight always gathered a crowd, and he saw Riker and his two burly sons, Clyde and Sid. This gave him pause. "The boy interfered with me."

Riker stared with disgust at his son Artie. "Are you going to take that, boy? When are you going to become a man?"

Clyde and Sid, both huge, muscular men, were grinning. "Come on, show him what a man you are, Artie."

Mace Benton saw at a glance that he would have no trouble with these three. He turned to face Artie and said, "You get along, boy. Come back when you get growed up." He slapped

Artie with the flat of his hand. It staggered the boy, but Artie came back and struck the big man in the mouth. He was a strong young man for his size, and the blow broke Mace's lip. He uttered a curse and threw himself forward. Artie Riker had no chance at all. He was beaten to the ground and rose several times staggering.

Lyman Riker heard a voice. "Are you going to let him do that to your boy, Riker?"

Riker turned to see Owen Majors watching him. "He's got to learn to fight."

"Not with a man like that."

"You keep your nose out of it, Majors," Sid said. "None of your business."

Majors gave him a long, level look and then turned to see that Mace Benton had knocked the boy down. Artie was trying to get up. Mace drew back his foot to kick the boy, but Majors leaned forward and drove a blow into the big man's kidney. The punch to such a vulnerable spot brought a cry of agony. Mace turned and saw Owen standing there. "This ain't none of your business, Majors."

"I guess I'd better leave my mark on you, Mace—as I did once before."

The words fell like acid on a raw wound for, indeed, Owen Majors and Mace Benton had had a terrible fight on the Little Missouri River when they were trapping. Both men had been marked, but Mace had been left unconscious and battered in body and face. His anger had been building for years, and now he took a step forward and drove a blow at Owen's face. Owen managed to dodge and instantly returned the blow. It caught Mace Benton in the mouth, drove him backward, and Majors followed with a left-handed shot that turned Mace around. He watched as Mace staggered and slipped to the muddy ground.

"What's the matter, Mace? You getting old?" Majors said. "You never were much of a man."

Mace got to his feet. He looked around and saw everyone was watching and waiting for him to take it up, but he had felt the power of Owen Majors's blows, and they were no less than they had been back at the Little Missouri River. He tried to gear himself up for a battle, but he remembered how it had taken him weeks to recover from Majors's earlier beating. He stared around and said, "I ain't fighting you, Majors."

"Then get out of camp."

The words were flat and deadly. Mace Benton started to argue, but he saw the light of battle in Owen's eyes and turned quickly away. Everyone watched him go. He mounted his horse and headed back east away from the train.

"Good riddance, I say," Ralph Ogden said. "He wasn't no guide of any kind anyhow."

There was a murmur of assent, for no one had been pleased with Mace, but Edith Riker had come and watched this with cold eyes. She turned to her husband and said, "You're a coward, letting your own son be beat like that."

"You keep out of this, Edith!"

"Yeah, it ain't none of your put-in," Sid said. Neither he nor Clyde had ever liked their stepmother, and now both glared at her.

But she faced them fearlessly. "You're both no-good bums, letting your brother get whipped like that. If I were a man, I'd whip you myself."

"Well, you ain't no man so you ain't whipping nobody."

"I might take on that job." Riker suddenly stared at Majors who had come to stand before him. He saw that Majors was challenging him, and he glanced to see if his sons were ready. Although Majors was a ferocious fighter, Riker had no doubt that three of them could handle him.

"We'll just take you on."

"No, you won't," Caleb Taylor, a huge, bulky man, said at once. He came to stand beside Majors, and Ralph Ogden, the biggest and strongest man on the train, came with him. "We'll just make it three and three," Caleb said. He smiled suddenly. "That way, Lyman, you and Majors can have at it. Have your own brawl."

Lyman Riker was imposing, but he had seen the power in Owen Majors, and knew he would have no chance with the young man.

"This ain't none of your put-in, Ogden."

"It was your place to help your boy," Ralph Ogden said. "I ain't got no respect for a man that lets his kin be whipped by a bully. Now either fight or git."

For a moment the matter seemed to be up in the air, but then Riker stared at Artie, who was struggling to his feet. Edith had watched Majors carefully. The scene had blown up like an explosion almost, and now she thought, *Everyone knows what Lyman is, and his sons, too, and I'm glad.* She knelt down in the mud. "Come on, Artie. You need some looking after."

"I'm all right, Ma."

"No, you come with me." Everyone watched as Edith led the boy away. When she got to the wagon, she found that Logan Temple had followed her.

"That's a bad cut. That eyebrow needs some stitches."

"I don't think I can do that," Edith said.

Logan stared at the woman and seemed to come to a decision. "I'll do it." He reached into the wagon for the black bag she had noticed. When he opened it, Edith watched him take out medical supplies, and she saw medical instruments. Instantly she knew the truth. "You're a doctor, Logan."

"Used to be. Here, sit down, Artie. We'll get you fixed up."

Edith watched as Logan treated the boy's wounds. He sewed up the eyebrow with skill. Finally Logan said, "You're going to be a little bit sore, but you'll be all right. Here, take a spoonful of this before you go to sleep tonight." He handed Artie a small bottle and then changed his mind. "No, Edith, I guess you'd better give it to him."

"All right, Logan."

Artie was staring at Logan Temple and said, "Thanks, Doc." He turned to his mother and said, "I did the best I could, Ma."

"You did fine, Son. I'm ashamed of your father and your brothers. You're the best of them though."

"Aw, Ma, that ain't so."

"You better go lie down awhile."

As soon as Artie left, she turned and said, "If you're a doctor, what are you doing out in this forsaken place?"

"It's a long story, Edith, and one I don't like to talk about."

She started to question him but saw that it was a painful matter. She suddenly put out her hand, and he took it before he thought. "Thanks for helping Artie. He's a good boy."

"Yes, he is, and I'm glad Benton's gone. He wasn't a good fellow."

"No. We'll have to have a guide now. I think I know who that'll be."

❧

OWEN'S TIME HAD BEEN claimed by Cherry, and she asked about the fight. Joelle was standing close and saw Cherry approach.

"Did he hurt you, Owen?" Cherry asked.

"No, he didn't."

"What you need," Cherry said, "is a woman to take care of you."

Owen laughed. "No woman would put up with me, I guess."

"I think you could find one if you looked hard enough."

The two walked off, and Joelle felt a strange pang. He ought to stay away from her. He's a smart man. *Doesn't he see what kind of a woman she is?*

The thought troubled her, and later on that evening as she was talking to Aiden Hall, she remembered what Cleo had said about Aiden's marriage. Joelle was curious, and finally she brought up the matter of the fight and worked it around to talking about the Rikers and their marriage.

Aiden turned and faced Joelle. "Joe, I don't want to hurt your feelings, but you're a man, and all men are weak. But I hope you've got better sense than to go to a bad woman. It makes me sick to watch Owen chasing after Cherry. She's a saloon woman." Aiden shook her head and said, "You find a good woman and be true to her if it kills you, Joe."

❧

THE NEXT DAY, ARTIE was gathering wood as the train moved along. He made a habit of picking up dead sticks and placing them in the back of the wagon. He moved rather stiffly for the fight had taken a lot out of him. The laudanum had made him sleep, however, and he had gone over and over the fight in his mind and wished he could have done better. He heard his name and turned to see Jennie Pickett. She came up to him, and he saw that her face was flushed. He had always thought she was a pretty girl although he had never really spoken to her.

"What is it?" he asked.

"I . . . I just want to tell you"—she bit her lip—"thank you for taking up for me."

"Well, I didn't do much good, Jennie. I got stomped."

"You're not grown yet. When you're full grown, you'll be able to take care of yourself, but you tried. That's what counts." Her voice grew soft and her eyes warm. "It's the first time anybody ever really took up for me."

She suddenly reached out and touched his cheek. "I'm sorry you got hurt," she said, "but I thank you." She turned and ran away.

Artie Riker stood watching her. He felt something turn over in his breast and suddenly grinned. The movement of his facial muscles brought some pain, but he said, "Well, I guess that was worth taking a licking for."

Chapter Fourteen

"I SEE AS HOW that Townsend girl is plum gone on you, Joe."

Joelle turned in the saddle to give Owen a disgusted look. The two of them were riding far ahead of the train, having left Harry Jump to lead the oxen. "Don't be silly," Joelle snapped. "She's man-crazy."

Her answer came sharply for she was well aware of Leah Townsend's attentions. The girl was indeed wild about men. That was easy for Joelle to see. Leah Townsend had bright red hair, fair skin, and freckles. She was attractive, and she was obviously out to get any man who gave her a look.

"I don't reckon so," Owen murmured. "She's setting her cap for you. I expect she'll catch you too. Girls with red hair have a way of getting what they want."

Joelle sniffed but didn't answer. She looked around the country instead, for there was a different quality to the terrain. They had come to the Caw River and were watering their horses. Overhead the fleecy clouds were delicate and fine as they drifted along lazily.

"How much farther to California?"

"A long way," Owen shrugged. He turned to face her and studied her carefully. "You sorry you came?"

"No, I'm glad."

The horses drank thirstily, and Joelle took the opportunity to study Owen. This had become habitual with her. He was a man of loose, rough, and durable parts. A thought occurred to her: *Why, he's like a machine that's made to do hard things. There's nothing fine or smooth about him.* She studied the long mouth that was expressive only when he smiled and the rather short straight English nose. His hair was coarse and black as night itself. He was looking off in the distance. His intense deep blue eyes fastened on something far off. Joelle learned that he had the best vision of any man in the train, able to see things the rest of them couldn't even glimpse. She noted the wide mouth and the scar at the left corner, wondering how he got it.

Ideas sometimes came over long periods of time in small increments. Joelle's mind usually worked like this. She had been thinking of Owen Majors a great deal ever since she had stumbled over his inert body, and caring for him as she would for a child had sharpened her interest. As she sat loosely in her saddle, however, a realization struck her forcefully. She straightened, and her lips drew tighter.

Why, I'm too interested in Owen!

The single thought shook her, and she pulled her floppy hat down farther over her forehead as if to hide her expression. The troubling thought came firm and solid. For years she had been unable to think of any man in this sense. She had a streak of romance, but her efforts to help her mother and to fight off the unhappy advances of Burl Harper had driven most romance out of her system. Now, however, she knew that this feeling had been building deep inside for some time, and involuntarily she shook her head. *I can't be thinking thoughts like that.*

"It's too deep to cross here," Owen murmured. "Come on. We'll find a better spot." He turned his horse to the left, and Joelle followed him. Her thoughts still lingered on the astonishing revelation, and with it came a sudden bitterness. *He couldn't be thinking of me. He doesn't even know I'm a woman, and he's had other women in his life.*

She pulled her horse closer to him and said, "You've known Cherry Valance a long time, haven't you?"

"Why, you're downright interested in my love life."

Joelle turned red and glanced at Owen. He was smiling at her. "I guess most young fellows are interested in women. I was, I know. When I was about your age, I followed them around like a hound dog follows a coon. I was scared of them and didn't know how to act."

"Well, how did you learn how to act?"

Owen suddenly leaned forward and slapped his horse's neck, and there was amusement in his intense blue eyes. "The same way any fellow learns, I guess. Trial and error."

Owen's eyes were searching the river, but Joelle was not finished yet. The thought that she was attracted to this man troubled her, and at the same time her curiosity caused her to ask, "Are you in love with her?"

Owen pulled up his horse and turned to study her. His face was deeply tanned without a wrinkle, and he seemed taller and heavier than when she had first met him. He had a rider's looseness about him, and his features were solid, and his flat, angular shape was that of a man who made his living in hard ways. Her question seemed to trouble him, Joelle saw, and he searched for an answer. She had learned, at times, he would become absolutely still, and she had learned to recognize the expressions on his face when he was thinking deeply.

"I thought I was once," he admitted finally.

"Are you still?" she persisted. And then suddenly she blurted out, "She's only a dance hall girl, you know. She's not the kind of woman who's fit for a wife, Owen."

Owen suddenly grew serious. He pushed his hat back, and a lock of black hair escaped from the brim, falling over his forehead. "She's no angel," he said finally, "but neither am I."

"You're better than she is."

"Don't be making snap judgments, boy. You aren't old enough for that." Her words seemed to trouble him, and finally he straightened in the saddle, pulled his shoulders back, and shook his head as a thought seized him. "A man wants a woman to be better than he is," he said finally. "I know that probably isn't right, and maybe it's unfair to women, but a man has to get out and rassle with the world, and he does things he shouldn't have to do just to stay alive. When he comes home at night, he doesn't want a woman that's wallowed around the dirt like he has. He wants her to be gentle and full of goodness. He wants one that won't lie to him."

"Have women lied to you?"

"You're plum full of questions. Yes, a woman lied to me once. She fooled me pretty bad. I was young, and I found out she had been deceiving me. Ever since that time, I've been a little bit careful about how much faith I put in a woman. Maybe I'll always be like that."

Owen's words troubled Joelle. *Well, I'm deceitful, and I'm fooling him just like that woman did. Maybe not in the same way, but he's got a hard streak in him that I hadn't noticed before. He seems happy enough, but that woman, whoever she was, put her mark on him, and now he'll never be able to accept a woman as good. He'll always remember her.*

"This ought to do." Owen broke into her thoughts and indicated a spot on the river where the banks gently sloped. "We'll check the water here. Come on. Let's tie these horses off."

"What for?"

"Why, it's time to have a bath." He glanced back and saw that the wagons were a far distance. "They won't be here for thirty minutes." He tied his horse, but Joelle sat on hers. He turned to look at her, and as he pulled off his shirt, he said, "Well, come on. You're bound to be as dirty as I am." He sat down, pulled off his boots, and then stood up and started to unbuckle his belt.

"I don't want a bath," Joelle said. Hurriedly, she turned Blackie's head around and touched him with her heels. He went galloping off, and she heard Owen calling after her.

"Why, you dirty boy! Don't you ever take baths?"

Owen watched the horse and rider disappear. He stripped off all of his clothes and plunged into the river, ducked his head under, and came up sputtering. The water was warm, and he would have preferred one of the colder mountain streams, but a man used what he had at hand. He watched the rider as she grew smaller and then laughed. "That's one funny kid. He'll have to toughen up before he makes it out here."

∽

THE TRAIN HAD SETTLED down for the night. The smell of cooking meat was in the air, and fires dotted the darkness with bright yellow tongues. The wagons had traveled farther than usual, and everyone was tired but not too tired to eat. A fiddle started up, and then the sound of singing reached Ash Landon. He was sitting on a blanket across from Lonnie Tate, who was the bouncer in his gambling casino when he had one. Also there was Tom Jordan, a lean gunman, with the grace of a panther and the same yellow golden eyes. Two miners had joined them, and they were losing money steadily. Finally one of them, a tall lanky man named Henderson, said, "I must have left my mind somewhere back on the trail, trying to beat a gambler at his own game."

"Try again. I'll take your IOU, Henderson." Landon smiled, but the miner got up, and the short, chunky man with the unlikely name of Bill Og threw his cards down. "That goes for me too. You done cleaned me out."

"Come back anytime, boys. We never close."

Lonnie Tate laughed as the two left. He was a broad man in every way. His face had the blunt features of a bare-knuckled fighter, which he had been at one time. "They got to be pretty stupid to play cards with you."

Ash suddenly smiled. His fine dress and appearance were lacking in the other members of the train. He was only of medium height, but he gave the impression of being larger. His chestnut hair was carefully trimmed and had a definite curl. His deep-set, well-shaped eyes were hazel. He looked down at the cards in his hands and shrugged. "It's a good thing men are fools or else I wouldn't have any way to make a living."

He got to his feet and saw Cherry standing by herself, gazing into the darkness. He moved over to stand beside her and was silent as he studied her. He could feel a turbulence in her spirit as a man might feel strange currents across the waters of the sea. Her face was a mirror that she usually used as a mask, but now he saw that something had loosened in her, and for the moment, at least, she was vulnerable. *She's as alone as any woman I've ever seen.* Her expression stirred his curiosity, and he tried to identify her feelings. It was something like the gravity that comes when someone has seen too much—like the shadow of hidden sadness.

Cherry turned to him, and her eyes reflected a thought he couldn't read. She watched him silently, and Ash knew that a woman's silence could mean many things. He wasn't sure what it meant in Cherry Valance, but then he had never understood her. She was meant for better things and, perhaps, had them once, but she had taken a wrong turn somewhere. And now he knew that she was as alone as he himself. Her head turned slightly, and he followed her gaze to see Owen Majors. Landon knew that the two of them had been more to each other than either of them admitted.

"Cherry, I can't believe a fellow like Majors looks better to you than I do." His tone was jocose, but he saw no answering smile on her face. She moved her shoulders in a gesture of impatience.

"I'm getting too old for this kind of life we lead, Ash."

Her words surprised Landon. "What else is there?" he said. "Get married and have a houseful of squalling babies? You wouldn't last a year at that."

"What difference does it make?" She turned, and her voice was hard as flint. "You'd never marry me or any woman, Ash."

"I might. You never know."

"I know you."

Ash said suddenly, with an abruptness that surprised him, "You're going to try to get Majors. I doubt if it will work. He's not your kind of man, Cherry."

"It might work. You never know until you try."

The thought of the woman's past floated into Ash's mind. He was not in love with her in the least, but in some strange perverse way he admired her, for she was as hard as he himself in some ways. He shook his head and put his hand on her shoulder. "Good marriages have happy endings. Why, those things are just romances in books or on the stage. I figured you would have learned better by now, Cherry."

Cherry Valance didn't answer him. Finally she shrugged, and her voice sounded flat and filled with a grief he had never heard in it. "You don't like this life either, Ash."

"It's the only life I know. The only life you know too."

He was surprised when she turned abruptly and moved toward the wagon. He knew he had touched a nerve in her that he had not known existed. His eyes went back to Majors, and he studied the big man carefully. It was his business to know men, for his was a dangerous trade, and one mistake in a man's character or inclination could prove fatal. He knew Owen Majors was hard, tough, and sometimes dangerous. As far as Majors's affairs with women, Ash knew nothing except that he and Cherry Valance had once fancied themselves in love, or so he supposed. He struggled for a moment and finally gave it up. "A man never knows about a thing like that," he murmured and then turned back toward the fire.

~

AFTER WEEKS ON THE trail, the wagons had traveled 460 miles west of the Missouri River, passing the confluence of the Platte's north and south forks. High water had caught them once, and wagon wheels had to be removed, and the wagon box turned into a flat-bottom boat that could float. Some of the wagons were not watertight and nearly sank, but fortunately none were lost. Others had to be double-teamed, using eight yoke of oxen for each wagon. The wagons plunged into the river, taking a diagonal course, and it took three-quarters of an hour to reach the opposite shore.

The country had changed as they moved westward. It began tilting uphill. For twenty-two miles, the train crossed a high, waterless tableland. The wagons passed Hash Hollow, and the going was so difficult through sandy ground that the wagon wheels sank deep, and the oxen were exhausted by the end of a hard day.

At noon Joelle turned to Owen and said, "What's that?"

Majors turned in the direction of her gesture. "That's Chimney Rock. Pretty big hunk of rock, isn't it? About five hundred feet high."

"Did anybody ever climb it?"

"Oh, lots of people. They get up to the top and carve their names in it. You want to go?"

"I don't think so. Sounds like a lot of work for nothing."

"I always thought so myself." He suddenly grinned at her. "You missed your chance at having a bath. Now I'm all nice and clean, and you're dirty. Didn't your mama teach you to take baths, Joe?"

"That was a week ago. You're as dirty as I am."

He suddenly laughed. There was a freeness to his laughter when it came, which was not often. "Next time I'm going to strip you off and scrub you down myself. I can't stand having a dirty partner like you."

Furiously Joelle turned away, her face flaming. She heard him laughing as she turned Blackie away and went over to where Edith Riker was fixing a quick meal for the men. Joelle liked Edith a great deal and also the youngest son, Artie, but Edith's husband Lyman reminded her somewhat of her step-father Burl. Lyman had a cruel streak, and he had passed it along to his two sons, Clyde and Sid. She dismounted and approached Edith who was slicing bread.

"Have a sandwich, Joe."

"That would be good." She studied Edith carefully. Despite the hardness of the journey, there was a glow of health in Edith Riker's face. Edith had impressed Joelle as being a woman of considerable unhappiness. Taking the sandwich, she waved it toward the high country.

"Owen says that's five hundred feet high. He says people climb to the top and carve their name in it."

"I'd like to do that."

Lyman Riker, who was chewing steadily on a sandwich, gave his wife a look of disgust. "That'd be a waste of time. Who's gonna see it?"

"Somebody will. A hundred years from now," Edith said, "people will climb that rock. We'll all be dead and gone, but they'll see a name, Edith Riker, and they'll say, 'I wonder who she was? I wonder what she was like?'" She gave a self-conscious laugh and shrugged her shoulders. "That is foolishness, I guess." Suddenly she said, "I'm going to climb that rock. I want a coal chisel, Lyman."

Lyman stared at his wife. "Just the kind of a fool thing you would do. Ain't you got enough work to do?"

Edith met his gaze steadily. "I'm going to climb it. Why don't you come with me?"

"Not me. I've got better things to do."

Edith stared at her husband as he rose and stalked away.

Artie was eating a sandwich. His face looked young and vulnerable. "I'll go with you, Ma. I'd like to have my name up there too."

Clyde Riker laughed. He had his father's black eyes and black hair. He was a good-looking man but rough and aggressive. "You ain't got enough to do, Artie." He stalked off, and she said, "I'm going anyway. You want to come, Joe?"

"I guess not. You tell me about it when you get back."

"Probably won't be much to tell."

After the meal was finished, Edith found a hammer and a coal chisel in the box of tools. She saddled one of the stock, swung into the saddle, dress and all, and then moved out. Fifteen minutes later she was at the foot of Chimney Rock. There were mounds of broken rock at the base, and she tied her horse off and began the climb to the top. By the time she did reach it, she was out of breath.

She found a prominent place and began to read the names of others. She was so intent on reading some of them, which had dates attached, that she forgot her problems. Finding a clear spot, she began chiseling her name. The rock was soft, not hard as she had feared, and she had gotten her first name engraved when suddenly a sound caught her attention. She turned to find Logan Temple who had come up beside her. He smiled and greeted her. "Hello, Edith. Doing a little name carving?"

Edith was embarrassed. "I suppose it's ridiculous. My husband says no one will ever see it, but it's something that I wanted to do."

"I thought I'd do the same thing. I got a hammer and chisel from Harry, so if you don't mind, I'll put my name right here."

Edith shrugged and continued, and as the two worked silently, the only sounds came from the cries of a bird circling overhead and the striking of the hammers onto the chisels.

Time moved on slowly, and occasionally Edith would steal a glance at Temple. She had not known many men like him, but something distinguished him off from others.

Finally Logan finished, and she turned to see that he had simply abbreviated his first name. "L. Temple," she said. "You going to put a date on there?"

"I don't guess so. My hands are soft. Look, I've worn blisters on them." She looked at his hands and knew that no other man on the wagon train had hands this well formed, not toughened by hard work. She put the chisel down and looked at their names. She read them aloud, "L. Temple and Edith Riker." She suddenly laughed.

He looked at her and said, "It's sort of like a marriage, isn't it?"

Edith was struck by his reply. The thought would never occur to her nor to any of the men in her family. "How do you mean, Logan?"

"Why, we're joined together as long as this rock stands. Wouldn't a wedding ceremony say something like that?"

"Have you ever been married?"

"Never have."

"Why not?"

The question seemed to trouble Temple. He looked into the distance, and a long silence ensued. "I don't know. Just too busy to get married, I suppose. Hard to get to be a doctor, you know."

"It's a good thing to be a doctor."

"It wasn't for me."

Somehow Temple's words shocked her. "Why not?" she said. "You get to help people."

From far off came the howl of a dog, then it was cut off abruptly as if someone had struck or killed the animal. He turned to face her, and she saw that the marks of his beating had faded and noted how handsome he was. His face was lean and narrow, and his hair was fair—someone had cut it recently so that it was rather stylish. His eyes were warm brown, expressive, deep-set, and well shaped. There was a quick intelligence in the man, lines of wit around his mouth, and a hint of a temper around his brows. It was the face of a proud man who could have unusual charm and revealed an ability she had already seen in a man of this type.

"I killed a woman."

Logan's words shocked her. "How'd that happen?" she asked.

He threw his hands apart, and his lips drew into a thin bitter line. "I was drunk, and I operated on her, and I killed her just as surely as if I put—" He broke off and could not finish the sentence for a time. "Just as if I put a bullet in her brain."

Edith Riker was suddenly startled when she saw tears form in Logan Temple's eyes. She was not used to men crying. It wasn't done by the men she knew, but somehow she understood that Logan Temple was not like the men she had known. A tremendous compassion came to her, and she moved beside him and took his hand. "Thank you for telling me, Logan."

Temple shook his head, and an abysmal sorrow came to him then. "You—you must despise me. Men don't cry."

"I like you better for it," she said. They were standing close, and he looked deep in her eyes. Suddenly he was drawn to her. At that moment Edith recognized what was passing between her and this man. They were close, and suddenly she reached out and put her hand on his upper arm. She saw her touch moved him, and he put his arms around her. Edith didn't resist. He kissed her and then stepped back, shock in his eyes.

"I—I didn't mean to do that. The last thing I want to do is take advantage of you, Edith."

Edith Riker knew that she was as moved as Logan, and she said, "I guess we're entitled to one mistake." She picked up the chisel and hammer and turned to say, "Try not to be so bitter. You have so much to give." She turned then and walked away, and he watched her go. As she left, she was thinking, *I'll remember that longer than I should.* She was a woman who needed love as most women need air, but life had cut her off from it. *I wonder what would have happened if I had married a man like that?* The thought troubled her as she moved down the steep slope toward the camp.

Chapter Fifteen

MOST OF THE TRAVELERS had become accustomed to the hardships of the trail. Now the evening campfires burned brightly, and the camp was filled with the sound of cheerful laughter and often music.

Gerald Townsend and his wife, Hattie, were both fine musicians. They were in their early fifties, and each had the youthful look that some older people still maintained. Both of them were rotund with rosy cheeks and ready smiles. Gerald played a fiddle with great enthusiasm, and Hattie accompanied him, either on the mandolin or sometimes on a mountain dulcimer that made the most plaintive music some of the travelers had ever heard.

"I'm sick of this grub, Ma," Leah Townsend said. She was seventeen years old with a wealth of flaming red hair and sparkling blue eyes. Her brother Burke grinned at her across the fire. He was chewing on a tough antelope steak and said, "I hear we'll be hitting the buffalo anytime now. They say that's the best eating there is."

Leah tossed her head and shoved the remnant of the steak back on her plate. She then picked it up and tossed it to a lean, mustard-colored dog that bolted it at once and looked eagerly for more. "That's all you get, Butch," Leah said. She got up and stretched, and the thin fabric of her dress revealed the youthful contours of a rapidly maturing figure. She was no longer an adolescent but not quite yet a woman. She spent a great deal of her time thinking about making herself attractive and had a reputation of a flirt among the men on the train.

"Why don't you play something, Pa?" she said plaintively.

"I'll just do that, Daughter."

Gerald Townsend unwrapped his fiddle, ran his fingers up and down the neck, and drew the bow across it. "She sounds mighty sweet tonight. Let's do 'Arkansas Traveler,' Hattie."

"That's a right sprightly tune." Hattie pulled the mandolin out, and immediately the camp was filled with the sound of lively music. Soon a group had gathered in the area around the Townsends, and some of the dance hall girls began dancing with the men who approached them.

Leah's eyes went from man to man, and finally she settled on the young Joe Jones. *He's shy, but he's right good-looking. Kind of undersized, but I don't mind that.* She threaded her way through the dancers, and when she reached Joelle, she smiled. "How come you never ask me to dance, Joe?"

Joelle was caught off-guard. She saw the boldness of Leah Townsend's eyes and said quickly, "I don't know how to dance."

"Of course you do. Come on, I'll teach you what you don't know."

Owen, who was standing alongside Joelle, grinned. "Go on, boy, don't be so bashful. She won't bite you, or if she does, it won't hurt much, will it, Leah?"

Leah flashed him a brilliant smile and considered him for a moment, but then her attention returned to Joelle. She tugged her by the arm. "Come on, it's easy."

Joelle wanted to refuse, but several people had their eyes fixed on her, and she knew she had to do something. She actually was a good dancer, but as Leah pulled her into the center where the fire cast its beams over the dancers, she made sure that she kept the girl at arm's length. When the dance was over, she said, "Well, that was nice," and turned to go away. But at that instant Gerald and his wife began playing a slower tune.

"That's the kind of dance I like," Leah grinned. "Come on now." She put her arms around Joelle, and Joelle was startled. She had been able to fool everyone by wearing large clothing, but this young woman had sharp eyes, and she might be able to tell instantly if she held herself against Joelle. Joelle began to talk and held the girl away. "I like this country, don't you, Leah?"

"It's all right, I guess. It'll be better when we get to California. I thought you said you couldn't dance."

"Well, I don't much."

"You're different from most men. They always try to hug me."

"Well, I guess I got better manners than that."

Leah laughed. "You're green, aren't you? You don't know much about women."

Joelle smiled. "Not a whole lot," she said, "but I've got time to learn."

"How old are you?"

"Seventeen."

"Why, so am I. We ought to become real good friends being the same age and all."

Joelle continued to spar with the young woman who made it difficult, and finally when the dance was over, she said, "I've got to go help the night herders, Leah. I'll see you later."

Leah watched as Joelle disappeared. She shrugged. "He's green as grass. He ought to know more than that at his age."

Harry Jump had been watching the dancing. He saw that Lily Frazier and Rachel were standing back, the girl in the circle of the woman's arms. Lily often put her arm around Rachel as if protecting her, and this touched him. He had been paying more attention to the woman and her daughter as the days passed. He felt saddened by Lily's handicap, and he had often wondered what it would be like not being able to hear anything. Even now he was thinking, *She's watching the dancing, but she can't hear a thing. That must be pretty bad. Just one more thing that she misses out on.*

He saw that Rachel was bright-eyed as she watched the dancers, and he got an idea. He approached the two. He saw Lily's eyes come to him at once, and he spoke not loudly but using his lips more than usual. He knew she was an expert at reading lips, and now he made it a point always to face her so she could understand what he was saying.

"I sure would like to dance with a pretty girl."

Lily's eyes opened with surprise. "I can't dance," she said.

"Oh, I didn't mean you, Lily. I mean this girl here. I'll bet she's a great dancer." He smiled down at Rachel who looked up and fastened her eyes on him. "Why, I don't know how to dance."

"I'll tell you what," Jump said. "I'll teach you if it's all right with your mama."

"Can I, Mama?"

Lily hesitated, then she saw the eagerness on her daughter's face and nodded. "It's all right."

"You come right this way." Jump took the girl by the hand and led her to a place that wasn't crowded, and he began to move, smiling and talking constantly to the child.

"I never did dance before." Rachel giggled. "It's easy, isn't it?"

"Well, it is if you got good talent, and I can tell you're going to be a fine dancer. Why, when you grow up and get to be good-looking and big like your mama, the young fellows are going to be coming all over the place."

"They will not neither!"

"Oh, yes, I can tell. I'm going to have to give you lessons in dancing and other stuff that young ladies need to know."

"You have any little girls or boys?"

"I sure don't, honey. I really don't."

"Why not?"

"Well, I haven't been lucky, I guess. Your mama is lucky to have a fine, pretty girl like you." Jump continued to speak and was rewarded by the animation on Rachel's face. He glanced up once and saw Lily watching them closely. He winked at her and nodded, and she smiled and nodded back. *She's worried about this girl,* Jump thought. *Afraid she won't make it, that she's not a good enough mama, but she is.*

Lily was startled when Aiden Hall suddenly stood beside her. She turned to face her, and Aiden said, "Harry Jump's a nice fellow, isn't he, Lily?"

"Yes, he is. He seems to be very good with children."

"That's a little odd, isn't it? I don't think he's ever been married. He doesn't have any children."

"I guess he just likes children. Rachel will be talking about dancing with him for the next week."

"He's a good man." Aiden hesitated then added, "I'm sorry for your trouble, Lily. I know you miss a great deal."

"I've gotten used to it." The words came quickly, but Aiden saw that the woman was troubled.

"A good man wouldn't mind a handicap like that. You've got everything else that a man wants."

"I'll never marry."

Aiden almost said, "You should. Your daughter needs a father." But she didn't. She waited until Jump returned with Rachel, and she said warmly, "I didn't know you were such a good dancer, Rachel."

"Mr. Jump is teaching me. He's going to teach me some more kinds of dances too."

"Well, that's fine. Harry, I didn't know you were a dancing instructor."

Jump shoved his hat back on his head. His light blue eyes were bright now, and he said, "Well, the Lord gave us feet to dance on so I'm going to do it."

"Some Christians think dancing is a sin." Aiden smiled at him.

"Well, that's plum foolish. King David was the best man there was, and he danced before the Lord with all his might."

"I remember that story," Lily said suddenly and smiled. "His wife told him he was foolish."

"Yes, she did." Jump laughed, his bright teeth flashing against his tanned skin. "But he fixed her. He shut her up, and she never had no more children. A woman's got to be careful about things like that."

The Townsends started another tune, and Jump said, "How about you, Miss Lily? I believe I could teach you to dance too."

"No, I couldn't really."

"Shucks, it's easy."

"It is easy, Mama. Go on," Rachel urged.

Jump held out his hand, and Lily hesitated. She saw Aiden watching her and Rachel as well. Lily allowed Jump to lead her to the dance and discovered that he was indeed a good dancer. She couldn't hear the music, but she could feel the rhythm. Jump whirled her around and said, "Why, you're a fine dancer, Miss Lily."

"It's the first time I ever danced."

"Well, ain't that fine! You and me will have to do lots of dancing. They have this hoedown every night, and me and you and Rachel will have a heap of fun."

"I never saw Mama dance before," Rachel said. She was staring at her mother and Jump and looked up at Aiden. "I didn't know she could."

Aiden put her hand on the girl's shoulder. "Your mama can do just about anything she wants to, I expect."

℮

"I'LL BE GLAD WHEN we get to the next fort," Joelle said. She eased herself out of the saddle, pressing her foot against the stirrups and arching her back. "How much farther?"

"That's it right over there."

Joelle stared in the direction Owen indicated, but she could see nothing. "You can see farther than any man I ever saw."

"Pretty handy when you're out in this kind of country," Owen said mildly.

"What's it like in this fort?"

"Like all the rest of the forts out here in the West. It's all filled up with drunks and prostitutes and Indians looking for a handout."

Suddenly Owen lifted his head and said, "There's something I didn't expect to see."

"What is it, Owen?"

"Indians. Sioux, I think. Could be worse. Could be Comanche."

The two watched as a group of horsemen approached. There were not more than a dozen, but they were coming at a full gallop.

"They're charging us," Joelle said. "We'd better get back to the train."

"They won't give us any trouble."

"How do you know?"

"Because the fort is right there. They're good Indians as long as the soldiers are around."

Joelle watched nervously as the Indians charged to within a hundred feet. They rode magnificently, and she mentioned this to Owen, who replied, "They say that Comanche can outride the Sioux, but I don't think anybody can."

Joelle watched the Indians and saw that one of them had a rifle and others had bows and arrows. "What do they want?" she said.

"I guess they just want to race their horses. They can do that until we make them stop. They think they got a right to race their horses."

Joelle turned to Owen, who looked sad. "You don't like what's happening to the Indians, do you?"

"No, I don't."

Joelle had heard Owen's comments before and had been surprised to find out that he felt a sympathy for Indians that other men on the frontier didn't have.

"I spent part of a summer with them once. Got to know them pretty well. They're just folks like we are. All they want to do is hunt buffalo and be left alone." He suddenly pulled his hat down low on his forehead. "But they're a doomed race, Joe. Their way of life is gone. Taken from them. That's always sad."

The Indians didn't remain long. They wheeled their horses and disappeared. Joelle didn't speak until they were at the walls of Fort Laramie. She was eager for civilization, and as soon as Owen directed the wagons into a circle, she said, "I'm going inside and see what it's like."

"I already told you," Jump grinned. "The soldiers are inside, most of them drunk, and the Indians are outside, most of them drunk too."

Jump's words seemed prophetic. Indians were scattered in their teepees thrown up outside the fort. Smoke from many Indian campfires wound its way in tall spirals and blended with the rapidly falling dusk. As they passed an Indian camp, Joelle was astonished when she saw an Indian woman take a fat, squirming puppy and strike it on the back of the head, breaking its neck. She did it quickly without a sign of remorse.

"She killed that puppy," Joelle said.

"Sure did. You see a lot of that. You might even have puppy dog stew if you're lucky enough to get invited to a meal."

"I would never eat a puppy!"

"Don't say that. I've seen a time when I would have given everything I had for a good puppy dog stew."

The inside of the fort was barren of trees. Soldiers moved back and forth, some of them the worse for drink.

"The general store is over there, Joe. Why don't you get what we need?"

"You come with me."

"No, I'll be around." Joelle turned to see that Cherry was walking toward them. She wore a green dress that brought out the color of her eyes. She smiled at Owen.

"Come on, Owen. Let's go have some fun."

"I reckon we deserve it. You go on and get the supplies, Joe. Get Jump to help you carry them back to the wagon."

"All right." Joelle's reply was terse. She watched the two and then moved toward the store. *Owen Majors is a fool to let a woman like that into his life.*

Owen turned and shook his head as he watched Joelle moving toward the store. "He sure is a funny kid."

"Why'd you pick him up?"

"Well, I didn't. He picked me up." Owen related how Joe had practically saved his life, and by the time the story was finished, they reached the saloon. Cherry went in on his arm, and soon the two were seated at a table. The clientele was rough—trappers, soldiers, and some of the men from the wagon train, including Ash Landon and his entourage.

GILBERT MORRIS

Cherry began speaking of gold camps and asked Owen if he was excited about getting there.

"Not really. I tried prospecting once. Broke my back at it. I could have made more as a day laborer."

Cherry leaned forward. "Tell me about it."

"Nothing much to tell. Back-breaking work. Lots of disappointments. Sounds like life, doesn't it, Cherry?"

"Life can be better than that. We had it better once, didn't we?"

He turned to meet her gaze, and something passed between them. He felt the attraction of a woman as he always had. He sat still and didn't answer for a moment.

"What is it you want, Owen?" she probed.

He knew she was aware of feelings he kept hidden from others. No words could completely describe what he felt or what he wanted, and even if he found the words, he knew this was not the woman who would understand him. He wanted her as a man wanted a woman, but he could not bring himself to go back to where they had been. This woman had been everything to him once, but now as he looked across the table, he thought, *There's no backtracking. A man can't go back and pick up where he left off years ago.* He couldn't look at her without a feeling of ownership of what had once been the most vital thing in his life. He saw in her eyes that she was his for the taking, that though they had been parted for a while, part of what they had had together was still with her. It was with him, too, but he had developed a tough wisdom throughout life and knew this was not the way for him to go.

207

As for Cherry, she was falling in love again with Owen Majors. She felt a piercing regret, knowing that although they had been together once, she had let something come between them.

The two sat quietly until Joelle entered. "Come over here, Joe. Have a drink," Owen called.

Joelle came over, and Owen saw that the boy's eyes went at once to Cherry Valance, with disapproval. But Joelle said only, "I've got to have some more money, Owen. I didn't have enough."

"I'll go with you."

"Don't leave, Owen," Cherry said.

"I'll come back. We need to get those supplies. We'll be pulling out pretty early tomorrow." He got up, and one of the saloon girls grabbed Joelle's arm. "Come on, honey. Let's have a dance."

She laughed at Joelle's expression and glanced up at Majors. "Well, big man, did you bring your son with you? I got a friend that's even younger than he is. It'd be the four of us."

Owen grinned and shook his head. "I have to take care of my boy. I'm teaching him to be a respectable citizen."

"I doubt it will take," the girl laughed.

Owen shook his head and said, "Come on. We'll get the groceries. I'll see you later, Cherry."

As they walked out the door, Owen was grinning broadly.

"What's so funny?" Joelle said.

"That girl thought I was your pa. I kind of like that. I'll tell you what. You call me 'Pa,' and I'll see that you grow up to be like me. I'll keep these saloon women off of you too."

"You're not my pa."

"Well, I am in a way."

"You're not old enough. Anyway, I think I'm the one that needs to keep the saloon girls off of you. Your taste seems to run in that direction."

Owen was surprised. He had been merely teasing the boy, and he said, "Why, Joe, a man has foolishness in him, and it's bound to come out. I don't think—"

"Owen—Owen Majors!"

Owen and Joelle both turned to see a tall, well-built man dressed in buckskins coming toward them. Owen at once let out a yelp and said, "Why, you no-good scoundrel! What are you doing here, Chad?"

"Just waiting for the moon to change, I guess. You ain't changed a bit, Owen."

Owen suddenly turned. "Joe, this is Chad Hardin. Don't believe a word he says. Chad, this is my partner, Joe Jones."

"One of you two is in mighty bad company, and I expect it's you, Joe. Glad to know you though. I'll put you onto Owen's pernicious ways."

Chad Hardin was in his early thirties, Joelle estimated. He was more than six feet tall, lean, but with broad shoulders and an aura of strength. He had auburn hair with silver at the temples and rough good looks that would draw women. "Glad to know you, Mr. Hardin."

"Well, you've got better manners than some I could mention." Chad grinned. "Chad's good enough for me." He turned and studied Owen. "What in the world are you doing here in the middle of this sorry fort?"

"Taking a train through to the gold camps, Chad. What about you?"

"Well, I went trapping, but the beaver's about gone. Guess I'll find me a new occupation. Maybe I'll become a dentist."

Owen laughed. His eyes sparkled, and Joelle could tell that he had a real affection for the man. "You'd never make it," he said.

"You say you're going to the gold camps in California?"

"That's the rumor. Why don't you come along with us?"

Chad's eyes opened. "Why, you know I might as well. You think I could get hired on as scout?"

"I'm the scout and the guide. I'd be your boss."

"You'd never boss me, you son of a gun." He turned and grinned suddenly at Joelle. His skin was burned to a golden tone. He turned his head to one side and shoved his fur cap back on his head. "I'm going to warn you about this fellow. He could lead you astray. He's a real ladies' man, or thinks he is."

"Never mind about that. Come on. Let's go celebrate. Joe, take this money. Me and Chad's got some catching up to do. You and Jump get the supplies."

"All right."

As Joelle left, Chad said, "He's pretty young to be your partner."

"Yes, I have to look out for him. He's at that bad age. You remember how we were when we were seventeen? Ready for anything and found trouble without looking."

"A golden childhood. Come on. Let's go have a drink and tell me about this here wagon train."

Chapter Sixteen

THE TRAIN HAD ASSUMED some of the characteristics of a small, insular town. Having grown up on the outskirts of a small town, Joelle knew the inhabitants' propensity for gossip and how their attention sharpened and fastened on anything or anyone new. She realized that when Chad Hardin attached himself to the group, he would be the center of attention, and so he was. The young, single women were drawn to his rugged good looks, and mothers with marriageable daughters were weighing him on the scales.

All of this amused Joelle, but she also was interested in Chad. Not because she was drawn to his looks, but because he knew more about Owen than anyone she had met. For this reason late one afternoon when the train was an hour or so from camping for the night, she pulled her horse up next to Chad, who was riding leisurely a hundred yards in front of the train.

"Hello, Joe," Chad smiled. "What's for supper tonight?"

"You're always interested in your stomach, Chad. I guess it'll be stew, and I may make an apple pie. I have some dried apples left."

"Sounds good. Where'd you learn to cook?"

"Oh, there was an old man at our place who had cooked for harvest hands. He taught me a few things when nothing else was happening."

She studied Hardin, noting there was no fat on him. He was big-boned and long-armed, and his teeth looked white against his tanned skin. She noticed he had a slight indentation on his nose and wondered if it had been broken at some time. He was a fighting man, she could tell, and also, Owen had said once, in speaking of his friend, "Chad's a whirlwind in a fight. Rather have him at my side if a bunch of Apache hit than any man I know." She studied him silently and saw that his eyes were never still, going from point to point in the distance ahead.

"Are you expecting Indians?"

"Always a chance of it, but not likely until after we get through the South Pass. You ever fight any Indians, Joe?"

"No, never did."

"Hope you never have to."

Joelle spoke with the man as the horses ambled along, and the air was full of the sounds of creaking wagons, lowing oxen, and shouting men. The sun was getting lower, and overhead a group of black birds was circling as if seeking prey.

Finally she said, "I guess you've known Owen a long time."

"Yep. We go way back. We were partners trapping beavers on the Little Missouri. You get to know a man pretty good if you spend a season with him."

"Did you know him when he was a boy?"

"No, and he never talks about that much either."

"It's a wonder he never got married."

Chad shrugged. "Well, he came close once."

"Was it Cherry Valance?"

"No. Before that. There was a woman named Irene. He was real gone on her, but she let him down."

"What did she do?" Joelle asked quickly.

"Ran off with one of his best friends. It hit Owen hard. He didn't talk about it then, and he still doesn't. But you can still hear the echo walking around inside him if you know him well enough. Doubt if he'll ever trust a woman again."

"That doesn't seem very fair to blame all women because of what one did."

Chad Hardin laughed and slapped his horse on the neck. "I guess you ain't noticed, but life ain't very fair," he said. "If it was, we would all be born to rich daddies. How come you're so interested in Owen?"

"Oh, we're partners, you know, but I don't know much about him."

"He told me how you fished him out of the snow and saved his life. Said you took care of him just like a nurse. Fed him like he was a baby. Says he probably would have died if it hadn't been for you."

Joelle hesitated then shook her head. "He'd probably have made it, I guess."

"He don't figure so."

The two continued to speak for a while, and finally Joelle turned Blackie away, saying, "I guess I'll go back and see if Owen wants anything special for supper."

"Why, boy, you're treating him like a wife ought to treat a husband."

Joelle flushed and knew she had made a mistake. "That's foolish. I like to do things right."

"Well, I'm for that."

Joelle moved back past the wagons and found Owen, one of the three men heading the herd of horses and spare draft animals. She pulled up beside him and said, "We're stopping pretty soon, aren't we?"

"Yep. Thought I'd just give the boys a hand here. Gets lonesome and dusty back here."

"Not many scouts would eat dust. They'd be out in front."

"Just shows what a wonderful man I am."

Joelle suddenly laughed. "Were you always so good, Owen?"

"Good?" His eyes suddenly danced with humor. "I was so good I went to church every Sunday when I was just about your age. Helped old ladies across the street. Mamas from miles around came to point me out, telling their daughters, 'That's the kind of man you need to get.'"

"I'll bet!"

"Why, you don't think I'd tell a lie, do you?"

"I sure do."

"In that," Owen said, "you're probably correct. Don't believe anything you hear me say."

The two rode along, making conversation. Knowing that Owen would soon leave to pull the wagons into a circle, Joelle asked a question that had entered her mind many times. "Do you believe in God, Owen?"

Owen shot her a look of astonishment. "Do I believe in God? Well, of course I do. You don't take me for a fool, I hope."

"Well, you're not a Christian man, are you?"

"No, I'm not."

"Why not?"

Owen found it difficult to answer. He was quiet for a long period of time, and she saw that he was handling the reins of his horse nervously. "Well," he said finally, "I couldn't tell you, Joe. I came up the hard way, and you don't find too many Christians among trappers or in the dragoons either. Soldiers and rough people like that, hard for them to find God.

"One thing has been in my mind for a long time. I had a friend named Larry Tolliver. We worked together on a ranch for a while. Larry was a fine fellow, a good Christian. Kind of a rarity. Most of the hands made fun of him. He took a lot of ragging from them, and finally he got sick. Something wrong with his stomach. He got worse real quick. Suffered a lot, but he never complained."

A long silence followed, and finally he continued. "We all thought he was going to die, and the fellows stopped ragging him then. I remember when he died. I was with him. Most men would be bitter and scared at dying so young in such a painful way, but not Larry. He went out smiling. It's one of those memories I'll always have, I guess. Before he died, he whispered, 'I'll see you when you get to heaven, Owen.'"

Joelle waited for Owen to say more, but he didn't. "That bothers you, doesn't it?"

"Yes, it does. Some folks who call themselves believers don't have much religion except on the outside, but Larry had religion all through. Whatever he had, it was enough to take him through a mighty tough time and keep him sweet." He broke off then and shook his head almost angrily. "A man's a fool to live without God." He spurred his horse and broke into a gallop.

Joelle stared after him. She had been surprised by what she heard, and she saw there was a depth to Owen Majors she hadn't expected.

$$e\!\sim$$

SUPPER HAD BEEN COOKED, and the women had cleaned the dishes, preparing for breakfast the next day. The Townsends had played some music, and quite a few travelers had come to listen and make requests.

The gamblers who ranked themselves around Ash Landon had played cards, as usual. They played for small stakes, and Jack Benbow had lost. He was a lean man with light blue eyes and brown hair. He wore two guns, which was unusual, for most men didn't want to weigh themselves down. Benbow prided himself on his reputation as a fighting man but not with fists. He was too small for that, but he was lightning quick with a gun. A rumor had circulated that he had killed three men in one fight in Dallas, and he himself fueled the rumor.

Cherry had come to sit in. She was a better poker player than most men, and she finally said, "Jack, this is not your night."

"I don't have any luck."

Ash glanced at the gunfighter. "There's a little more than luck to poker. There's skill involved."

"No, it's just luck. Come on, Cherry, let's me and you go take a walk."

"I guess not."

The other members of the game glanced at each other, and Ash hid a smile. Jack had been after Cherry from the time he had seen her, but she paid him no attention. Any other man would have taken that and moved on to another woman, but Benbow was not a man to take a slight from anyone, male or female. He gave her a bitter look and said, "I know what you're doing. You're trying to get your hooks into Majors."

Cherry gave him a cool look. A quick flare of anger touched her eyes then as she considered the man. "Jack, let me give you some free advice. Don't butt into a woman's business." She glanced over across the open space to where Majors was outlined against the fire, talking to members of his group. "Owen is about the only man I'd ever trust with anything anytime."

Ash said with asperity, "That's pretty hard on me, Cherry."

She gave a short laugh and shook her head. "You'll live, Ash."

"I'm a better man than he is," Benbow said.

Cherry gave him a contemptuous look. "Don't try to prove it. Men have tried before. They're not around anymore."

"Tough, is he? He may be a good scout, but I can shade him with a gun."

"Well, don't you try it," Cherry said shortly. "You've led a full life, I guess, Jack."

The card game continued, and finally Cherry was surprised to see Owen come over. He nodded to Ash and said, "We're going to be leaving a little bit early tomorrow, Ash, if you can get your folks ready."

"Sure. What's the hurry?"

"Pretty long drive from here to the next water. May be a little late getting there. The animals will be thirsty."

Benbow was watching Owen Majors. "Sit down. Take a hand, Majors."

"Pretty late, Jack. I guess I'll pass."

Benbow leaned back. There was something in the coiled, skinny body that reminded everyone who saw him of a serpent. He was thin but not unhealthy, strong enough for his weight, but there was something sinister about the man. He smiled and said, "A man that won't gamble ain't much, Majors."

Majors suddenly turned to face Benbow. He recognized the challenge, but his voice was calm as he said, "I guess we got different standards. I don't measure a man by whether he can turn a card or not."

"You scared of losing your money?"

"Nope. I'm just not in a card-playing mood."

Benbow smiled, at least his lips drew up at the corners, but there was no humor in his expression. "Won't make any difference to me. I'll bet on anything."

"Anything?" Owen said, lifting one eyebrow. "That's hard to believe, Jack."

"Try me."

"All right. I got fifty dollars here that says that I can give you a glass of iced lemonade in twenty minutes."

Every eye turned to Majors, and Benbow said, "That's crazy. We've been sweltering out here under this heat. There's not any ice any closer than Fort Laramie and probably none there."

"I thought you wanted to gamble, Jack. Fifty dollars says I can do it."

"I'll cover you." He reached into his pocket, peeled off some bills, and said, "There's my money."

Owen reached into his pocket and pulled out some money. "Well, Cherry, you hold the stakes."

Cherry didn't understand what was happening. Reluctantly she took the cash and studied Benbow. He was smiling slightly, and he said, "You ready to start the count?"

"You got a watch, Ash. What time is it?"

Ash pulled a watch out of his vest pocket and glanced at it. "It's three minutes after eight."

"Go on, big man," Benbow jeered. "You got twenty minutes to give me some iced lemonade."

"You got any lemons, Cherry?"

"We got a few."

"Mix up some lemonade while I get the ice."

"I want to see this," Ash grinned. He didn't know what was in Owen's mind, but he realized that Majors was never foolish in the matter of gambling.

"I'll be right back. Come along," Owen said, "anybody that wants to go to the icehouse with me."

"You got twenty minutes," Jack repeated.

Cherry went to the wagon, pulled a lemon out, squeezed it into a pitcher, and put in sugar and water. She stirred it with a spoon and returned quickly to the men. A half dozen were there, and she saw that Owen had a pickax. He got clear of the camp, and in the moonlight there was still enough light to see by. He raised the pick and started digging.

Benbow jeered, "You going to dig through to China and find out if them Chinese have any ice?"

Owen didn't answer, but suddenly the crowd heard his pick strike something. "You hit bedrock, Owen," Ash said.

Owen struck furiously, and then he bent down and picked up something. "How about this?" He handed something to Cherry.

Astonishment showed in her features, and she gasped, "Why, this is ice!"

"Sure is. Here, I'll get some more, then we'll go wash it off. Still got fifteen minutes."

He struck several more chunks of ice and returned to the wagons.

"I can't believe it!" Cherry gasped. "What's ice doing here?"

"We're in the high country. They call this the Ice Slough. Ice here the year-round, just a foot or so down. Everybody who passes here knows about it." Owen turned then and said, "It looks like you lose, Jack."

Even in the growing darkness, by the flickering light of the fire, all of them saw that Benbow's face was flushed. He said not a word but turned and walked softly away in the darkness.

"Here," Cherry said shoving the money toward Owen.

Owen took it and separated the bills. "I guess I ought to give this back. It wasn't a good bet."

"Never give money back to a man who bets like a fool," Ash said. He was thoughtful for a moment, and then he added, "Jack's a bad man to get even. Watch yourself, Owen."

"I try to."

He turned and walked toward his wagon, pocketing the money, and Cherry said, "He's always doing things like that."

"Remind me never to play poker with him."

Owen dug more ice and took it in a bucket to where Jump, Joelle, and Chad were drinking coffee. "How about some iced lemonade?" he said. He laughed at their expressions and explained where he found the ice. "Let's wash this off. Some iced lemonade would be pretty good. I'll wash the ice if you fix the lemonade, Joe."

Ten minutes later they were sipping lemonade, and Jump said abruptly, "I'll take some of this over to Lily and Rachel. I guess they'll be surprised." He made his way to the Ogden wagon where he found Rachel listening as Lily read to her. The child looked up and said, "Here's Harry."

"Got a treat for you," Jump said, always remembering to face Lily when he spoke. "Iced lemonade."

With a half-startled glance, Lily's eyes widened, and color came to her cheeks. She leaned toward Jump with sudden interest.

"You got any cups?"

"Yes, what's in the pitcher, Harry?"

"Lemonade. Ice cold." He saw the expression on her face and laughed. "It's hard to believe, but we're standing on ice right now. Owen told us about it. Get some glasses. Let's enjoy this."

The three were soon drinking lemonade, and Rachel said, "This is so good."

Jump sat down beside the fire and described how Majors had dug up the ice. "He's all kinds of a fellow, that Owen Majors," he said.

"He knows this land," Lily said. Her voice didn't sound quite normal, but it was pleasant enough for a woman who could not hear herself speak. They talked for a time, and Rachel finally leaned over and said, "I'm sleepy, Ma."

"Well, go to bed."

"Good night, Ma." She kissed Lily on the cheek and left.

"That's a sweet child, Lily. Pretty and smart. Going to make some man a wonderful wife."

Lily asked the question that had been on her mind. "Were you ever married, Harry?"

"Me? No."

"Why not?"

He handled the cup awkwardly, turning it around in his hands, drank the last of the lemonade, and then looked up at her. Sadly, he said, "I'm too worthless for a good woman, and who wants a bad one?"

Lily considered him and said, "There are lots of women who would like to have a good man like you, Harry."

He didn't answer. Something was moving within his chest or in his mind, he couldn't tell which, and finally he said, "What about you, Lily?"

A startled expression disturbed her features. "Me? What do you mean?"

"Would you have a worthless fellow like me?"

"I don't think you're worthless. You've been so good to Rachel and me too."

"That's not hard to do. You're both fine ladies."

A flush touched Lily's cheeks, and she turned away for so long that Jump worried he had hurt her feelings. When she turned back, however, she was smiling and said, "Go along with you, Harry. We start early in the morning. Thanks for the lemonade."

"Good night, Lily." He walked back to the wagon, lay down, and for a long time studied the stars, but he was thinking of the light on Lily's face.

$e\!\sim$

"WELL, THAT'S THE SOUTH PASS."

Joelle stared at the hills and said impulsively, "Doesn't look like much, Owen. I thought there would be huge mountains and a little narrow gap."

"Most people are disappointed, but it's the only way to get through the big mountains. They get higher as you go farther west."

The South Pass was the gateway to the West. It was nothing like the dramatic gorge that most people envisioned. Instead the trail rose slowly over broad, grassy plains and then sloped downward to the west.

They had come five miles ahead of the train, and Owen said, "Let's rest up here until the wagons get here. We'll probably get on through later today."

He led the way to a small creek where they watered the horses and then tied them to shrub bushes. Owen suddenly laughed at her and said, "It'd be a good time for that bath I threatened to give you."

"You stay away from me, Owen!"

The corners of Majors's lips turned upward, and he said, "I'd do it, but I'm too tired. I'm going to stretch out and take a little nap." Without another word he lay down, and soon the sun was in his face so he rolled over on his stomach.

Joelle saw how quickly he was able to go to sleep. A thought came to her. He's so ticklish. Chad poked him in the side one time, and he nearly jumped out of his skin. Without much thought, she crept forward, reached down, and grabbed his sides, digging him with her fingernails. She got more than she bargained for, for Owen gave a screech and rolled over, carrying her down. He grabbed her by the front of her loose shirt said, "You fool, kid! You know I don't like to be tickled. I got a good mind to throw you in the creek."

"Don't do it, Owen!"

His hands suddenly dropped, and he was tickling her, gouging her in the sides. Pure terror filled Joelle. She knew that with one touch he might recognize her sex. She shoved her arms down, hugged herself, and said, "No, don't do it, Owen!"

Owen stopped tickling her and shook his head. "You are a foolish boy. Don't you ever tickle me like that again."

Joelle gave a sigh of relief. "I'm sorry, Owen," she said. "I was just funning you."

"Well, fun me some other way," he said grumpily.

He rolled over and faced the east. "Look, there's Chad. The train doesn't need two scouts. He's as good a man as I am."

"You really think a lot of him, don't you?"

"Sure do."

"The women sure keep their eye on him."

"Always been like that," Majors said. "Women always like Chad."

"Better than you?"

"Of course better than me." He turned and studied Joelle. "Yep, women are always after Chad. It'll be that way with you pretty soon."

"No, it won't."

"Why, of course it will. You know"—he was smiling—"I've been meaning to give you a little help on how to handle women now that you're getting to be the right age."

"I guess I know all I need to know."

224

"No, you don't. You got to be careful around women, boy."

"Why is that?"

"'Cause they're all out to tame a man. They just want to get him and rip his manhood from him. Never fails. So, what you have to do is make sure they know who's the boss. Teach them there's one king in a castle, and you are it."

Joelle knew that Owen could be intensely serious, but he also had a sense of humor. She could always tell when he was getting ready to tease her. "I don't think I need any lectures on women from you."

"Oh, sure you do," Owen said. "But anyhow, before you settle on a woman, I want to test her out."

"Test her out? What are you talking about?"

"Well, you know the Bible says a woman is made out of a rib. Now you wouldn't expect a rib to be uppity, would you? But they get that way sometimes. Anyway, I'll see if you know that part of the Bible that says that a woman is supposed to obey her husband, be submissive to him and all."

"Submissive?"

"Yeah. You know what that means?"

"You mean a woman always lets a man have his way?"

"Well, you hang on to that idea. Now listen. The first thing you got to understand about women, Joe, is that they got a bad start. They got us in all this trouble. The whole mess started when Eve started listening to that snake."

"So men don't have anything to do with what's wrong in the world."

"Well, I'm just telling you what the Bible says, so you got to watch out. Women got ways to get a fellow on the wrong foot."

"Ways like what?"

"Oh, they take lots of baths so they smell good."

Suddenly Joelle laughed. "Is that bad if somebody smells good?"

"Well, it makes men weak. They use perfume to make themselves smell even better. They do it to draw men into their clutches." Majors was lighthearted and enjoying himself. "Well, you watch out, too, when they start leaning on you."

"What do you mean 'leaning'?"

"Well, you know, they're soft and round, and they know that if they lean on a fellow, it'll make him weak."

"You found out about that."

"Oh, I've been leaned on a time or two. The thing is you got to be wise to them, boy. You got to keep them in their place firmly, and that's what it takes. Got to give them discipline just like breaking a horse."

"I see. And have you had to discipline many, Owen?"

"Oh, it wouldn't be proper of me to speak of it—not to a young fellow like you. Just take my word for it. Women are a snare, but I'll be giving you lessons from time to time."

Joelle laughed. "I appreciate it, and I hope that you'll help me when women start crowding in on me."

"Oh, I'll do it. Well, come on. Let's mount up. What's for supper tonight?"

Chapter Seventeen

THE WEATHER HAD BEEN hot and stifling, and the nights were little better than the days. Joelle slept in her oversized, heavy clothes for fear of being caught and her secret found out. On this particular night, she had tossed and turned, and her heavy clothes were damp with perspiration. Half-asleep, sometime in the middle of the night, she sat up and took off her heavy shirt and then slipped out of the oversized pants. She always kept the canvas flap of the wagon down, which allowed for no breeze at all, but, at least, wearing only a pair of cotton drawers and a tight-fitting undershirt was like coming into a cool room. She lay down and went to sleep instantly.

Suddenly she heard Owen calling, "Joe, get out of bed! You can't sleep all day."

Joelle made a wild grab for her shapeless shirt, but before she could get it on, the canvas at the end of the wagon flew up. A hand seized her ankle and started dragging her out of the wagon. She made a wild grab at the ribs of the wagon and managed to catch hold, but Owen was laughing and saying, "You sleepyhead! Come out of there right now."

If he sees me like this, he'll know I'm a woman!

Joelle kicked at him, and Owen yelled, "You crazy kid! Get out of there. We got to get moving."

"I'm coming. You just leave me alone." Joelle was relieved when she heard Owen leave. She pulled on her pants and the shirt. When she pulled aside the canvas and stepped out, she saw that it was late, and she had overslept. She jumped out and saw Harry Jump grinning at her from the fire. "Hey, sleepyhead."

"First time I overslept like that, Harry."

"Well, it won't hurt you. I've been making biscuits. Made two big bunches here. Too many for us." Jump made a rough shape as he squatted before the fire. His hat was pushed back on his head, revealing the tawny hair, and his blue eyes seemed bright, almost, in the midst of the tanned face. "You must have a good conscience, Joe, to sleep like that. We've been making enough racket to wake the dead."

"I guess I'm just worn out from this trip."

"Can't blame you for that." Jump gestured at the biscuits and said, "This is the last of the eggs. If we don't get to the fort pretty soon, we'll be going hungry."

"I'll cook the eggs and the bacon." She began fixing breakfast, and when it was ready, she and Jump ate. Owen was already gone, and looking at the large mound of biscuits, Joelle said, "You know, Harry, I think I'll take some of these over to Edith Riker. She was feeling poorly for the last couple of days."

Harry gave her an odd look and turned his head to one side. "Be careful, kid. Her husband is jealous of her. I thought he was going to shoot Phil Strickland over her, and the two were just talking."

Joelle avoided smiling but was amused. "I'll do the best I can not to make him jealous."

She gathered up the biscuits in a sack and walked across the camp. Most of the women had finished breakfast, and the men had eaten and were leaving. When she reached the Riker wagon, she found Edith trying to cook breakfast, but her face was pale.

"Mrs. Riker, I brought some biscuits over. Harry made too many of them." She handed the sack to Edith who said in a weak voice, "Thank you. That'll help."

"You don't look at all well. What's the matter?"

"Oh, some kind of stomachache. Probably something I ate."

"Well, you go sit down. I'll fix breakfast. You got any eggs?"

"Yes, we have a few left."

"Well, I'll soft boil a couple for you. That's always good for an upset stomach."

"I don't want anything."

"You need to eat. You go sit down."

"I'll be all right."

At that moment Artie Riker came around the end of the wagon. "Hi, Joe." He took Joelle's greeting and then looked at Edith and said, "Ma, you look terrible."

"Just a stomachache."

"You go lie down. I'll take care of the driving today."

"What's the matter here?" Lyman Riker appeared, accompanied by the two other sons.

"It's Ma. She doesn't feel good."

"What's the matter with you, Edith?" Lyman asked. "You ain't no better?"

"I'll be all right."

Lyman glanced at Joelle, and his eyes narrowed. "What do you want, boy?"

"We made too many biscuits. I thought I'd bring some over for you folks."

"We can cook our own grub, I guess," Riker said shortly. His manner was surly, and his face showed displeasure.

"Pa, she's been sick for two days."

"You keep out of this, Artie. Women have aches and pains. There's nothing really wrong with her. Now you get to work." He gave Joelle a hard look and was about to say something but changed his mind. He said grudgingly, "Thanks for the biscuits." It was a dismissal, and Joelle left at once.

When she got back to the wagon, she found Harry and Chad at the oxen yoke. Chad turned to her and said, "Hello, sleepyhead." He grinned crookedly, and Joelle thought, *He doesn't know how good-looking he is and how attractive he is to women.*

"I did oversleep." She turned to Harry. "I took some of your biscuits over to Edith."

"Lyman have anything to say about that?"

"No, but Edith is sick."

Chad rubbed his chin thoughtfully. "Reckon we got a herb woman on the train?"

"No, I don't think so," Joelle said.

"Well, maybe she ate something that disagreed with her. She'll probably be all right. We better get moving."

℮↝

THE TRAIN HAD MADE good time by midafternoon, and the men were looking for buffalo. Both Chad and Owen had talked about seeing a big herd sooner or later. Artie Riker had been left alone, and after a time he went in to see how Edith was. She had tried sitting on the wagon seat, but she had been unable to stand the pounding. Artie insisted that she lie down in the wagon. He filled a cup with tepid water, took it into the wagon, and found her lying on covers.

"Ma, drink this. You need lots of water." He helped her to sit up, and when she drank it thirstily, he saw that her face was drenched with sweat. He put his hand on her forehead. "Ma, you're burning up. Where does it hurt?"

"My stomach, Artie. It's killing me." She suddenly arched and let out a moan of pain and grabbed at her abdomen.

Artie stared at her and then said, "I'm going to get some help." He paid no attention to Edith's protest but leaped out of the wagon. He searched for Logan Temple. At first he was afraid that Temple would have gone with the others hunting buffalo, but he found him talking to Ralph Ogden. "Dr. Temple, I got to talk to you."

"What's the matter, Artie?"

"It's Ma. She's real sick. You got to come and look at her."

At once Ogden said, "Did your pa send you?"

"No, he didn't."

Ogden hesitated. He knew that Lyman Riker's jealousy could reach dangerous proportions, and he shook his head. "Better wait until your pa gets back."

"It won't wait, Mr. Ogden. You got to come now, Doctor."

"I'll just go have a look at her. Can't do any harm. You go on back. I'll be right there."

As soon as the boy left, Cleo Ogden came and stood beside her husband. "I'm worried about Edith. She's always been so healthy."

"Well, I'm worried about Riker. He treats that boy Artie like dirt, and Artie's the best of his boys."

"I'll go see how she is. Hopefully it's just something minor."

❧

EDITH FELT THE WAGON give as someone came in. She called Artie's name, but then a voice said, "Not Artie. It's me, Logan."

"Logan, what are you doing here?"

"Artie says you're feeling bad. I need to ask you a few questions."

"You better not be in here in this wagon with me. You don't know how my husband is."

"He couldn't object to my looking at you."

Edith didn't answer for the pain was taking her.

"Where does it hurt, Edith?"

"Right—here."

Temple put his hand on Edith's stomach and pressed slightly. She gave a small cry. "Is that it?"

"Sometimes. Sometimes it's the other side."

Temple felt her stomach, and then he put his hand on her forehead. "How long have you had this fever?"

"I don't know. A couple days. What do you think it is, Logan?"

Logan started to answer, but then he heard horses riding up and heard Riker's strident voice. "There's your husband. I'll go talk to him."

"Be careful!"

Temple stepped outside as Riker dismounted. Artie was waiting for him. "Pa, Ma's worse. I got the doctor."

Riker looked up as Logan stepped outside of the wagon, and his anger flared. He suddenly struck at Artie, hitting him on the neck with a heavy blow that staggered the boy. "You fool, boy! I'll say when somebody goes to the doctor!" He turned and walked over to Temple. "And, you, you can get out!"

"Mr. Riker, your wife is very ill," Temple said in a calm, reasonable voice. "She needs medical attention right away."

Riker began to curse, and in the packed vicinity of the wagons drawn in a circle, a crowd began to gather. Riker paid no attention. "You couldn't wait until you put your hands on her, could you?" He suddenly struck out, and his fist caught Logan in the mouth. It drove him backward.

Still cursing Riker moved forward and drew back his foot to kick the man, but suddenly he was seized by the back of his shirt and jerked away. Furious, he turned and saw Owen.

"You take your hands off me! No man touches me, Majors!"

"Then act like a man."

Chad, Jump, and Joelle had come along. They all saw Clyde and Sid Riker advancing with fight in their eyes and their fists doubled.

Chad stepped in front of them with Harry by his side. "Hold up there, boys," he said.

Sid stared at the big man. "Get out of my way, Hardin!"

Suddenly Harry Jump drew his gun. "You boys are too big to fight, but you ain't too big if I put a slug in your knees. You'll be crawling around for quite a spell."

Clyde Riker stared at the smaller man. Clyde, like his father, could not stand to be crossed. "You won't always have that gun, Jump."

"I'll always have the gun anytime you need it."

Owen held the gaze of Riker for a moment and then turned to say, "What do you think, Temple?"

"I think it's appendicitis."

"What does that mean?" Artie asked quickly.

"Most people call it blocked bowels."

Pearl Taylor spoke up at once. She had drawn close along with her husband. "My little sister died from that." Most of the people from the wagon train had gathered, it seemed.

"My mother died of it too," said Aiden Hall.

"What—what can you do, Dr. Temple?" Artie asked.

"You keep out of this, Artie."

Artie faced his father. "I won't keep out of it, and if you were any kind of a man, you'd be more interested in your wife's health than you are in keeping men away from her."

"You're no son of mine."

Artie Riker was the mildest and meekest of young men, but he had been pushed too far. He was genuinely fond of Edith, and a lifetime of being pushed and bullied by his father and his two brothers suddenly came to a boiling point.

"I don't like being your son anyhow, so suppose we just call it off." Artie's face was pale, but there was a certainty and a determination that no one had ever seen before—least of all his own family.

Lyman Riker stared at his youngest son in total astonishment. Artie had always been a mild-mannered young man, and Riker suddenly grew flushed and said, "Fine. You go your way, and we'll go ours. Don't come running to me when you need something."

"You can believe that." Artie turned and said, "Do what you have to do, Doctor."

"Wait a minute!" Riker said. "I'll make the decisions here."

Owen's voice grated, and his eyes were angry. "Riker, only a fool would act like you're doing."

"It's my family."

"She's your wife, but you're not acting like it," Joelle spoke up before she even thought. She turned and said, "What can you do for her, Dr. Temple?"

"I can operate. Take her appendix out."

"What will happen if you don't?" Chad asked quickly.

"She'll die."

A silence fell over the group, and Lyman Riker never felt such pressure as he did at that moment. He glanced around the circle and saw not one friendly expression. There were scowls on the faces of some and disdain on others, and he wanted to lash out, but he knew he could not.

Chad called out, "I shouldn't have to be saying this, Riker. Your boy is right. What will it be? Will you let her die? And I warn you, if you do, you won't go anywhere with this train. I'll run you and Sid and Clyde off. You can make it to California on your own." With a smile, he added, "The Indians will love that, a single wagon. You won't get very far."

Riker was furious, but he felt intimidated. He hesitated and then shrugged angrily, putting his eyes on Temple. "Do what you want to."

"Fine," Logan said caustically. "I'll need some help. Some people can't watch a thing like an operation. Need someone with steady nerves and clean hands."

"I don't know anything about it, but I'll help," Joelle said quickly.

"That's fine. We'll need a tent."

"You can use ours," Ralph Ogden said. "What else do you need?"

"It would be nice to have something built up about waist high."

"I'll take care of that with some kegs and some boards," Ogden said quickly. He watched Riker walk away. "I can't believe a man would be that little," he muttered and then spoke to Caleb Taylor, his close friend on the train. "Come on, Caleb, let's get this thing set."

THE TENT WAS FAIRLY cool, but sweat was still running down Joelle's face and her body. The men had done a good job, making a table on which Edith Riker now lay on several folded blankets. Her eyes were on Temple as were Joelle's.

"This looks fine," Temple said. He said to Edith, "I don't want you to worry about this. It's really a very simple operation." Edith looked up and studied his face. "Have you ever done it before, Logan?"

"Oh yes, many times. It's not really complicated. The first one I know about was done by a surgeon in the English army. He had to do it without ether, but it was successful. Since then a Harvard doctor wrote it up for the medical journals so now it's fairly common. You're going to be all right."

"I trust you, Logan."

"Good. Well, let's say a prayer, and then we'll get at it." He bowed his head and spoke a simple prayer. "Lord, be with this woman and be with me and give my hands skill. We thank You for Your healing, for You are the healer, and I know that Jesus will be with us. Amen."

Joelle felt a sudden burst of admiration for this man, and she saw Edith's face grow peaceful.

"We've gone over this. All you have to do is put this cloth over the lower part of Edith's face. When I tell you, put on three drops. We'll watch and see. That should put her under," Logan said. "On long operations you have to do it again several times, but not this time, I think. Are you ready, Edith?"

"Yes, I'm ready."

"All right. Begin, Joe."

Joelle put a cloth over the lower part of Edith's face, covering from her eyes down to her mouth. She carefully counted three drops and watched as the woman almost at once began to breathe more deeply.

"She's asleep. You just hold the cloth in place and tell me if she starts waking up, but I don't think she will. This will be very quick."

Afterward Joelle remembered little of the operation. She was studying Edith's face, and only twice did she glance down. The first time she saw a small opening, and the second time Logan was putting stitches in.

"All done," Logan said. "You did fine, Joe."

"It wasn't much."

Logan was staring down at Edith's face. "It's a good thing that we did this. She wouldn't have made it otherwise."

"She would have died?"

"Almost certainly. Well, let's go tell the folks."

The two stepped outside, and Artie was there instantly. "Is she all right, Doctor?"

"She's fine. She'll need someone to stay with her until she wakes up. Shouldn't be any problem." He smiled at the relief on Artie Riker's face. "Don't worry." He turned then and said, "Mr. Riker, she's going to need some care. Do you want me to do it?"

Riker recognized this as a challenge, and Logan was staring at him in a determined fashion. He glanced around and saw that many of the travelers were watching him. "Do what you have to," he grunted ungraciously, then turned away.

"Thank you. I appreciate that," Logan said tersely.

Owen asked, "How soon can we get under way, do you think?"

"I'd like to take the day off tomorrow. The day after be all right with you?"

"Yes, we're still ahead of schedule."

"Someone needs to stay with Mrs. Riker. Can one of you women do that?"

"I'll do it," Aiden Hall said. She entered the tent.

"Guess we can go back to our wagon," Owen said. He started back with Joelle beside him, and he asked, "What was it like?"

"It was so quick, but she would have died if Logan hadn't been here."

"Kind of lucky, wasn't it, picking up a doctor, out of all the men in the world?"

"I don't think it was luck."

Owen gave her a quick glance and smiled faintly. "You think it was God, don't you?"

"Don't you?"

Owen didn't answer, and finally he nodded. "I'm inclined to agree with you. I think God was in it. That Logan Temple is some man."

"Yes, he is," Joelle answered. Her mind was elsewhere. She was thinking of Logan Temple's attitude as he was treating Edith Riker. There was more to it than a clinical interest, and she recalled now that she had seen the man looking at Edith with interest. She had made little of it, but now she thought, *They would have been perfect for each other. Edith has made a horrible mistake, and now it can never be right.* The thought discouraged Joelle, and she went to bed early that night, troubled by the situation.

Chapter Eighteen

"ARE YOU ALWAYS THIS embarrassed when you examine a woman, Logan?"

Logan was checking Edith's incision one more time. Three days had passed since the surgery, and he had no doubt from his past examinations that all was fine. Still, he found himself examining her again. She had given him an odd look when he said, "I need to take one more look at that incision and see how long before the stitches come out."

Edith had paused for a moment and then nodded. "All right. Perhaps we'd better go in the tent." She turned and moved inside the walled tent that Sid and Clyde erected for her each night, rather sullenly, but both men knew that the entire train was watching them for signs of ill treatment of their stepmother. Inside, she unfastened the buttons of her dress and pulled it down. Beneath it, she was wearing only a thin cotton vest. She pulled up the edge of the vest at her waist and watched Logan. He avoided her eyes but leaned forward and took no more than a cursory look at the wound.

"That's fine," he said hurriedly, and when he lifted his eyes to meet hers, he saw she was smiling.

"Are you always awkward examining your female patients, Logan?"

Logan couldn't answer. He felt his face burn. He had long thought he was able to deal with the intimacy that existed between doctor and patient, but he was attracted to Edith. He recognized that, despite the harshness of her marriage, she possessed pride, honesty, and graciousness. Without trying, she had ignited in him the flame of hungers he had thought were long buried. He gave a half-startled look and noticed her small smile.

Suddenly Temple returned her smile. "I thought I had gotten over all that when I studied medicine."

"And I suppose women have tried their wiles on you from time to time."

Her words amused him. He allowed himself to smile. "A few, I suppose."

"I can tell you what happened."

"What do you think?"

"You ignored them."

"How could you possibly know that?"

"It's written all over you, Logan. You're a noble man, a man of integrity. You wouldn't take advantage of a woman's weakness"

"Don't be too sure of that, Edith."

His words brought a puzzled expression to her face. "Why would you say that?"

"I may have been honest and ethical with other women, but that doesn't mean you're safe."

His answer stirred Edith's interest, and she studied him closely as she knew he had been studying her. She saw aristocratic, intelligent features and lines of wit and laughter around his mouth. There was a hint of temper between his brows, but she guessed it was rarely used. She could tell that he had lost something and had encountered deep valleys. His features displayed marks of grief, sadness, and regret. She was curious about the reasons but didn't ask questions. Pulling her dress up, she turned away and buttoned it, then turned back to him.

"I'm sorry. I shouldn't have asked foolish questions."

"I really didn't answer your question," Logan said. He seemed to hesitate as if he was deciding whether to make a safe or a risky move; he was not a man who took risk lightly. She saw him take a deep breath, and then he made his decision. "I shouldn't be saying this, but I care for you, Edith."

Edith Riker had known the attention of men. Before her marriage, she had been a belle and had learned to recognize the devious and the honorable ways of men. She saw honor in Owen Majors and had admired the man. The new man, Chad Hardin, had it also, not to the same degree of Majors perhaps or even Temple, but it was there.

She said evenly, "I know that. Women know things like that."

Her answer startled Temple. "I had never said a word."

"Words are weak things," Edith said quietly. "But I've seen it in your eyes."

"Do you think I'm a man you could ever care for?"

"Oh, Logan," she whispered. There was sadness in her voice. "We're too late. We've missed out on something that could have been very good. Out of all the men in the world, how does a woman find the one who would satisfy her needs and fill her life? I've often wondered that."

"Or how does a man find a woman like that?"

"It happens sometimes," Edith said, "but most of the time it doesn't." Her words revealed a feeling of fatalism, which she rarely allowed to show. She knew she had to end this. "Go now, Logan, and please don't speak of this again."

"I probably will," Logan said, then turned and walked out of the tent without looking back. Edith Riker stood there silently, but her heart told her that she would never forget this moment, not if she lived to be a very old woman. Even then she would be able to bring it back word for word—the sight, sounds, smells, and his facial expressions. She had few memories like this, but she knew she would treasure this one.

❧

"THIS FORT'S NOT MUCH of a place, is it, Chad?"

Joelle had joined Chad Hardin who was walking along the roads of the army post. "Not much." There had been a rain, and the ground was muddy. They'd reached the Wasatch Mountains, which had made for slow going. More than once they double-teamed the oxen to pull the heavily laden wagons up steep slopes.

"Looks about like all other forts. Maybe a little worse."

"Why are you going to California? You weren't headed that way, Chad."

"Why, I don't know, Joe. I'm just like a rolling stone, I guess. You know the old saying: The rolling stone gathers no moss, but I always said who wants to have a bunch of moss?" He laughed and punched Jo on the shoulder. As light as the blow was, it moved her backward. "Sorry," he said. "You're such a small young fellow I forget. How old are you anyway? Seventeen? Eighteen?"

"Seventeen. Be eighteen soon."

Chad Hardin gave Joelle a sideways glance. "Well, you need to leave the West. You belong in the East somehow. You'd make a good clerk or something like that. You're too soft for this kind of life."

"I can handle myself."

Chad grinned but shook his head. "I trust you can."

Joelle was curious about the big mountain man. "Why did you come?"

"I was heading back to St. Louis when I met up with the train, but I remembered what good times I had with Owen. Hard times but good. Decided I'd go on to California."

"You're going to get rich?"

"Get rich, find me a woman, marry her, settle down, and raise a passel of young ones. How does that sound for a plan?"

Joelle laughed. "It sounds good. I'd like to see you do it."

"Lots of Spanish women out there in California. Some of them are the best-looking things you've ever seen. Skin like satin and big, luscious brown eyes. Soft lips. But their families are kind of protective of them. I got shot at once by a Spanish grandee down on the border. Said I was too familiar with his daughter."

"Were you?"

"You bet!"

"You're incorrigible."

"There, you see? How many people you think on this wagon train knows what 'incorrigible' means? Except maybe for Dr. Temple, who knows all, sees all."

The mention of Logan Temple caused both of them to fall silent for a moment. "He's stuck on Edith Riker, which is bad news." Chad shook his head. "I feel sorry for that woman to live with a no-account fella like Riker. I don't know what she married him for."

"Nobody knows about things like that. He may have been different when he was younger."

"I doubt it. A woman is weak. Remember that, Joe. They're easy to fool."

"Your opinion of women isn't very high, is it?"

"I think it is. Just got to know their weaknesses. How you going to take care of them if you don't know that? Well, back to my plan. I can't decide whether to be a rich rancher or go into business and start a saloon."

"Your wife might have strong feelings about that."

"Well, maybe I'll just find a rich widow and marry up with her. Then I won't have any decisions to make. I'll just take her money and have a good time the rest of my life."

Joelle kept the conversation going, for she enjoyed Chad's foolishness. Suddenly she saw Jack Benbow slouching along with Lonnie Tate and Ash Landon. They were headed for the saloon, of course. "I don't like the way Benbow keeps trying to provoke Owen into a fight, Chad."

"He's the kind of fellow who can judge a man only one way," Chad said soberly. "Can he kill him?"

"What a terrible way to live!"

"It seems to be born in some men. He's a dangerous fellow, Benbow is. I've been keeping an eye on Owen's back. I may have to put Benbow down myself."

"Would you do that?"

"In a second. Benbow's never been any good. He's nothing but a killer, and as far as I can see, that's all he ever wants to be."

The two continued until Hardin left her to go to the saloon, and she went into the general store to get a few supplies.

❧

"I HAD A PRETTY good time at the fort, Pa." When Davis Hall looked down at Benny, he grinned. "So did I. It's a wonder all that candy and soda pop didn't make you sick."

Benny Hall turned his fair blue eyes on his father. He was a thoughtful young man. At age twelve, he seemed to have absorbed some mature qualities. "Why'd you buy me all that candy? You let me have all I wanted."

"Well, I guess maybe I wanted to see how much candy a twelve-year-old would hold."

"Ma said she was afraid you'd make me sick."

"Well, I didn't, did I?"

"No, you proved one thing though."

"What's that, Son?"

"I didn't think there was enough candy in the world for me, but while you kept feeding it to me, I didn't even like it anymore. Had to turn it down." Benny shook his head in wonder. "Sure enough thought I'd never turn candy down."

Davis Hall reached down and tousled the boy's hair, the same tawny color as his own. He had taken the boy back behind the train where the stock was driven. It was his turn to lend a hand, and lately he had started taking Benny with him at every opportunity. The two had grown closer, something he had always dreamed of, and now he said, "Well, that's the way it is with most things a man hankers after. Most of the time he comes to the end of it."

"I don't know what you're talking about, Pa."

"Well, I don't guess I do either. Just that things we long after don't always satisfy us. Maybe we're looking for the wrong things."

"I don't know what that has to do with candy."

"Well, it's candy you want now, but you're twelve. Pretty soon you'll be thirteen and fifteen, and then, Son, you'll find yourself chasing after some other things."

"Like what?"

"Well, the things young fellows think they have to chase after. They think they have to prove how tough they are so they start experimenting with drinking and gambling and finally women, of course."

"Did you do that?"

"Sure did." There was regret in Davis's voice. "I wish I hadn't now."

"You don't drink much. No more than any other fella on the train."

"No, not my weakness."

He waited for the boy to ask what was his weakness and realized that Benny never would ask the question. *Why, he already knows my weakness!* The thought shamed him for he knew that Benny had heard, more than once, Aiden bringing him up short because of his tendency toward other women. He wanted now to say something that would form some kind of justification for his life before his son, but he knew there was nothing. *I've ruined it all. There's no way now I can gain Benny's respect, and Aiden will always hate me.*

"Why do you and Ma fight so much?"

This was not the question Benny had wanted to ask. Davis recognized that at once. It was Benny's way at getting at the problem without embarrassing him, and he was amazed at his young son's sensitivity. "Because I've been a bad husband and a bad father too."

The two had stopped their horses, waiting for the stock to get ahead of them. Benny was framing a question that had been troubling him, but it took him a long moment before he could ask. "Why don't you be better, Pa?"

At that instant Davis Hall came face to face with his wrongdoing. He had seen men who never seemed to face up to their problems, but he was a better man than that, all signs to the contrary. He knew he had to make a drastic choice, and he said quietly, "I'm going to try, Son. I'm promising you that."

A light came into Benny's eyes, and his face grew less tense. "That's good, Pa," he said. "You can do it too."

BENNY WATCHED HIS FATHER leave to go on night guard. They had had a good supper, and, as usual, there had been little talk between his parents. Benny had done most of the talking, and finally, when he helped his mother clean up, she said, "Tomorrow, if we stop early enough, I'm going to bake you a pie. I've got just enough dried peaches."

"Gosh, Ma, I'd love to have a fresh pie."

"So would I. Now, let's have us a cup of coffee, sit down, and we can talk."

"All right, Ma," Benny said quickly. He poured the coffee into two cups, no more than an inch in his, to which he added sugar, and then he stirred it vigorously.

"Well, now. Tell me what you're going to do when you get to California? You going to be a miner?"

"Shucks, Ma, I don't want to be a miner. All they do is dig around in the ground."

"Well, I think that's right. Why don't you be a doctor?"

"I'm not smart enough for that."

Aiden reached over and pulled his hair. "Don't you say that. I didn't give birth to no fools."

"Oh, Ma, you know I couldn't be a doctor."

"I don't see why not. Why don't you talk to Dr. Temple? Ask him how hard it is and how to get started."

Benny said, "That would take a long time."

The two sat there, and she realized he had fallen quiet. "What is it, Son? You worried about something?"

Benny turned and said, "I wish you and Pa wouldn't fight so much, Ma. Why do you do it?"

"Just something between grown-ups."

"Will it ever be any better?"

The question hurt Aiden. "I loved your father once, but he wasn't faithful to me, Son. You know that."

"Don't you love him, Ma?"

"Not anymore."

Aiden saw that her reply had quenched Benny's spirit. She didn't know how to soften the blow and waited for him to speak. Finally he looked up, and she saw pain in his eyes. "If I let you down, Ma, will you not love me anymore?"

Benny's reply broke Aiden's heart. She put her arms around him and held him close. "I'll always love you no matter what." But she knew he was afraid—afraid that he'd lose her as his father had lost her.

⁂

BENNY HAD GONE TO bed early, but Aiden stayed up. When Davis returned, he was surprised. "You still up? I thought you'd be asleep."

"I've got to talk to you, Davis."

"All right." He put his rifle into the wagon and sat beside her. "What is it? Is something wrong with Benny?"

"No—well, yes, there is. He talked to me tonight about you and me."

"I didn't know that he talked to you, but he talked to me about that too. Hard on a young fella, isn't it? His parents are his whole world, pretty much. That's all he's got when he's twelve, and his world's broken-up."

"He asked me if I loved you, and I told him no. He said—" She choked up, and when she turned to him, he saw her eyes were glistening with tears. "He asked me if he failed me, would I not love him anymore. Oh, Davis, it broke my heart."

Davis recognized that the wall between the two was his own making. He took her hand and held it in both of his. "I've made so many promises and broken them to everyone, but something's happened to me. I've lost everything that's worth anything in this life, my son and my wife. I've been the world's biggest fool, Aiden, but I've been reading the Bible, and I've been thinking about God, and one thing is pretty clear. God forgives us for anything. I don't know if a human being is able to do that, but if you could forgive me, without any promises on my part, I'd feel mighty good about it."

Aiden studied his face. He was a handsome man, always had been, and now there was a seriousness about him she hadn't seen in a long time. She knew this was the moment that would either destroy her life or give her back something. She knew it was going to be hard as it had been in the past. She had no idea whether he could keep this unspoken promise.

She said, "When we first met, I was so much in love with you, Davis, and when we were first married, I thought no woman had ever loved a man as I loved you."

Davis stared at her, and his voice was husky. "Is any of that love left, Aiden? Any at all?"

In an instant Aiden Hall knew that despite their rocky road, the fights, and all the wrongs she had endured, there was something there. "Yes, Davis, there is."

They sat there, he holding her hand, and then he squeezed the hand, lifted it to his lips and kissed it. His voice was low and husky as he said, "Aiden, I'll die before I'd ever go to another woman. I'll blow my own brains out. I know I don't deserve this chance." He touched her hair. "You always had the most beautiful hair I ever saw."

She suddenly put her arms around him, and he held her. "We'll find each other again, Aiden," he said. "God put us together for always."

She sat quietly in his embrace and wondered, *Can a miracle like this happen? Can he be the man he used to be? Could our love come back again?* And suddenly she knew this was the second chance that some people never get. She breathed a prayer, *God help me to be a good wife to this man.*

❧

OWEN HAD BEEN SADDLING up his big bay horse, ready to go for a hunt, and Joelle said, "I want to go with you."

"All right. Come on."

Joelle had saddled Blackie, and the two of them rode out. It was a mystery to everyone on the train how Majors was able to bring in game when no one else could. They rode several miles from the train, and he led her into a small arroyo. "Tie the horses here." She tied her horse and saw him take a white cloth out of his saddlebag "Watch this, and you'll see the secret of the mighty hunter." He led her away from the arroyo a hundred yards and tied the strip of the rag to a yucca. It fluttered in the breeze, and he said, "There."

"What is that for?"

"Come on, you'll see." He led her back to the arroyo, and they hid themselves in the small gulch.

"Now then we have to wait awhile."

"Wait for what?"

"Wait for the antelope to come. A man's too slow to catch an antelope so the antelope have to come to him."

Joelle said, "You're funning me, Owen."

"No, I'm not. Here, just be quiet."

Joelle crouched beside him, and from time to time he would whisper something about the train, and they carried on a quiet conversation. Finally he looked up cautiously. "There. See?"

Joelle looked up and saw a small herd of antelope. They were nervous and jumping, but they were all looking at the white bit of cloth.

"What are they looking at that for?"

"Just nosy. Curious like a woman, boy. Get your rifle ready. When I count three, you take a shot, and I'll get one too."

Joelle pulled her Spencer out and cautiously leaned over the rim of the gulch. She heard him count. On three, she pulled the trigger and was thrilled to see an antelope fall. She heard Owen's rifle sound twice, and two more antelope fell.

"See how simple it is. Everybody thinks I'm a great hunter. All it takes is a little bit of knowledge. Come on. Let's get these critters back to camp. I like to hunt them, but I hate to dress them out. We'll give two of them away."

They tied the game on the back of their horses, small creatures and not the best of eating, but better than no meat at all.

When they reached the camp, Owen left one antelope with the Picketts. They were always short of grub, and he talked with Delbert and teased Jennie. "A pretty girl like you shouldn't have to skin antelope. I'd make your dad do it if I were you. You just sit around and be pretty."

"You're funning me, Mr. Majors."

"I always flirt with the pretty girls. You watch out for the men in this train. They're not all honorable like I am. Come on, Joe. Let's do a good deed." He stepped back in the saddle. "Let's give this extra antelope to Cherry and the rest of Ash's crew."

"They won't appreciate it."

"No, but it'll make them think what a nice, generous fellow I am. Next time I play poker with Ash, he'll give me a break."

The two crossed the opening until they pulled up in front of Ash's wagon. There was a poker game going on, and he called out, "Hey, Cherry, I've got a Christmas present for you." Cherry had not been in the game, and she laughed.

"It's not Christmas, you fool."

"Well, your birthday then." He untied the antelope, and holding it by the hind legs, he started toward them. "You'll have to get Ash to dress this. He won't mind."

At that instant Jack Benbow rose and cursed him. "We don't need your dumb antelope! Get out of here!"

"Take it easy, Jack," Ash said.

"I'm tired of his ways." Benbow lost his mind when he drank, and it was gone now. He reached down, pulled his gun in one smooth motion, and fired. It missed Owen by a hairbreadth. Owen was not carrying a pistol. He saw Benbow raise his gun to take a steadier aim, and then heard another gun fire. A black dot appeared over Benbow's left eyebrow, and he stepped back, slowly fell to his knees, and then faced forward. Owen whirled to see Chad Hardin lower his pistol.

"Good riddance, Owen. Maybe you'd better start carrying a gun all the time."

Owen started to answer, and then he heard Ash shout, "Look out for the young fellow!"

Owen whirled to see that the top of Joelle's chest was covered in bright, scarlet blood, and even as he watched, she fell limply to the ground.

Owen knelt beside Joelle. "He's hurt bad!" Chad said.

"You go get Temple, Chad. I'll carry him to the tent."

As he turned and picked up the limp form, Ash ran forward. "I hope the boy's all right. I'd have shot Jack myself. He was crazy, but I didn't have a chance."

Owen didn't answer. He went at a half run, conscious of the lightness of his burden. "Come on, Joe, you'll be all right." But the scarlet blossoming on the shirt spurred his worst fears.

When Owen entered Ralph Ogden's tent, he put the limp form on the cot. He saw Temple rip open the black bag and roll his sleeves up. "You got to do something, Doc."

"How'd it happen?" Logan Temple asked, but his hands were working.

"It was Benbow. He took a shot at me, but it missed and hit Joe here."

Temple said, "Blasted shirt he wears!" He ripped the buttons, tore it off, and then suddenly he paused. He stared at the rounded form of the youngster known as Joe Jones and glanced at Owen. "Did you know this is a woman, Owen?" His voice was harsh and accusing.

Owen stared at the curved form. The garment was a tight white chemise, but there was no questioning the feminine gender.

"No, I didn't know," he said slowly.

Logan stared at him and then shook his head. "The bullet hit high."

"She was on a horse, and he was on the ground."

Logan lifted Joelle and ran his hand over her back. "We're lucky," he said.

"What do you mean?"

"The bullet hit high up and missed the lung. It's right here under the skin. Didn't come out." He reached down, got a scalpel, slit the skin, and popped the bullet out.

"I'll wash these wounds," he said. He laid Joelle down, and when he turned to get the alcohol he used to clean wounds, Joelle opened her eyes. Owen was staring at her.

"I thought he killed you," Joelle said weakly. When Owen didn't answer, she said, "I'm glad you didn't get shot."

Owen still didn't answer, and she looked around and saw that her vest was soaked with blood. Realizing that her secret was out, she had a moment of fear. She tried to speak, but Logan was back. He was cutting away the thin, cotton chemise, and he cleaned the wound with alcohol. It burned like fire, but all she could see was Owen's face. She remembered at that moment how he had once been devastated by a woman who had deceived him.

"I—I wanted to tell you, Owen," she began, but he whirled and left the tent, his face tense.

Logan was cutting away the blood soaked vest. "I'll have to bandage you up a little bit. What's your real name?"

"Joelle Mitchell."

"Well, Joelle, you're a lucky young woman." He bandaged the wound, then said, "You'll need something to wear. I'll fetch some of your clothes. You just lie here." He saw that the young woman was trembling and staring at the tent. "He'll be all right, Joelle. Quite a shock for him. He must not be very observant."

Joelle barely heard him. "He knows that I'm not a man. He hates me for it, Dr. Temple."

"He must be blind. I knew you were a woman the first time I saw you."

"You didn't say anything."

"Well, I thought you had a reason, Joelle. If you want to tell me about it sometime, I'd like to hear it."

Joelle briefly told Temple why she ran away, disguised as a man, and tears came to her eyes. "I wanted to tell Owen, but a woman deceived him once. Now I'm the second one. He'll always hate me."

Logan Temple was a healer of bodies, but he saw this young woman needed healing of the spirit. Joelle Mitchell was hurt worse by Owen's look than by the bullet that had torn through her. She closed her eyes to keep back hot, scalding tears, wondering what would come of all this.

Chapter Nineteen

"WELL, LET'S HAVE A look at that scar."

Logan Temple had made his rounds and at last had reached Joelle. It was not yet dark, and the canvas flap was raised so he could see her face plainly. He didn't miss the flush that touched her cheeks and thought, *Why anybody could ever take her for a man is beyond me!* He saw her hesitate and was surprised. As a doctor he had found that most women had some kind of modesty, and he learned to deal with it. In a business-like fashion he said, "Come now. Unbutton that shirt and let me take a look. I need to change the bandage."

Logan rummaged through his bag until he found fresh bandages, and when he turned back, he saw that Joelle had unbuttoned her shirt and pulled it down over her shoulders but kept her breasts covered. He appreciated this because he always liked to see modesty in young women. He began to remove the bandage, and when the wound was uncovered, he examined it closely.

"Why, that looks good. You're very lucky. If that bullet had been a little bit lower, it would have gone through your lungs. Then you would have had trouble."

Still no answer from the young woman, and Logan continued to speak as he applied a fresh bandage and tied it on as best he could. When he finished, she quickly buttoned her shirt.

Logan hesitated, wanting to know more of the girl's story, but he saw that she was pale and probably in no mood to answer questions. "Don't do anything stressful. Ride in the wagon tomorrow. In a few days you'll be as good as new."

"All right, Doctor."

Logan repacked his bag and said, "Good night, Joelle." He stepped out of the wagon and saw that Harry Jump had a fire going and coffee brewing. "I could use a cup of that coffee, Harry."

"Sure, Doc. Sit down here. I'll have some stew ready pretty soon if you want to eat with us."

"Maybe I'll come back. I need to go see that Pickett child. He may have measles. I sure hope not."

Logan sat down on a box, took the cup of coffee, and sipped it. His eyes opened wide, and he gasped, "That's strong coffee, Harry!"

"You know, Doc," Harry Jump grinned amiably, "the worst cup of coffee I ever had in the world was real good."

For a while the doctor nursed the cup of coffee until it grew cooler, and finally he asked, "Where's Owen?"

"Oh, he's out hunting, I guess."

"I guess I'm as curious as everyone else in this train, Harry. What does Owen say about Joe—or Joelle, as she says her name is?"

"I dunno, Doc. He don't say nothing really. Stays gone most of the time. Helps with the critters in the herd. Goes off hunting. Takes night guard."

"A strange situation. Don't know as I ever heard the like of it. Most people think that Owen knew Joelle's secret all the time."

"Well, I don't think he did."

"I know he didn't. When I told him about her, he looked like a man who had been punched in the stomach."

"He's behaving a little strange, Doc. I don't think he's said ten words to her. I don't really know their history. I wanted to ask her, but I didn't figure it was my place. Figured she'd tell me when she got ready."

"I guess she will. Well, thanks for the coffee."

"You're welcome, Doc. Come back after while. This stew is going to be right good."

Harry watched the doctor as he moved off into the growing darkness, then ran his eyes over the campfires that had sprung up. He checked on the biscuits in the Dutch oven. The wagons had stopped early that day, and he'd had time to use his starter mix. He saw they were a nice golden brown on top. A motion caught his eye. He smiled. "Well, Rachel, you come to have supper with me, I reckon."

"I don't know."

"Well, you set right there. I'm gonna give you something like you've never had before." Taking one of the biscuits from the oven, Jump slit it in half. He opened a small glass jar and soaked the tops of the two halves with golden syrup, then closed the jar. Handing one half of the biscuit to the young girl, he said, "That's sourwood honey, the best honey there is. See how you like it."

Rachel bit into the biscuit and smiled. "That's good. Why do you call this sourwood honey?"

"Because it's made by bees that visited a sourwood tree. Oh, it's the best kind of honey." Jump bit into his half of the biscuit and chewed thoroughly. "Always was partial to honey."

Rachel was silent for a time as Jump spoke about making honey, and finally she said, "Where you from, Mr. Jump?"

"Kentucky is where I got my start."

"Did you have lots of brothers and sisters?"

"Had seven. Four brothers and three sisters."

Rachel asked questions between bites of biscuits that Harry kept pulling out of the Dutch oven. Finally she said, "Are you married?"

"Me? Why, no, of course not."

"Ever been married?"

"Nope."

"Why not?"

"What woman would want to marry a no-account, ugly gent like me?"

Jump was watching the vulnerable, innocent little girl. One day she would grow up to be beautiful. In fact, she already was, but her shyness and reticence didn't seem natural. Jump thought, *It must be because she's been around her mother who can't hear. I guess that's it.*

"I wish Mama would get married."

"Do you now?" Jump said with surprise.

"She gets lonesome. When I grow up and get married, she won't have anybody."

"Sure she will," Jump said quickly. "She'll have you and your husband and Ralph and Cleo."

"That's not the same thing."

Jump found no answer. He didn't know much about children, not having had close contact with any. There was something about the young girl that drew him and pleased him. He pictured what she would be like when she was eighteen. *Going to be a pretty young woman,* he thought. *That's good and bad. Pretty women have a good time, but they can have a hard time, too, the way men use them.*

"You think you'll ever get married?"

Jump laughed shortly. "I don't think on that much. It seems—" He turned and saw Lily approaching. He got up and keeping his face turned toward her, said, "You're just in time, Miss Lily. Going to give you some of my own special biscuits with sourwood honey. It's good, ain't it, Rachel?"

"It's real good."

Lily bit into one of the biscuits. "Why, this is the best honey I ever had!"

"'Course it is. Nothing but the best is good enough for us."

"Can I take a biscuit and some honey to Benny, Mr. Jump?" Rachel asked.

"Sure you can." Jump sliced another biscuit, put it on a saucer, and soaked it with honey. "Go on and get that youngster a bite of something good." He watched as the girl scurried off into the gathering darkness and shook his head. "Well, we better hurry up and eat before Chad and Owen get back and eat it all up from us. Sit down there, Miss Lily. I'm going to give you some of my special varmint stew."

Lily had been watching his lips, and now she smiled. "Varmint stew? It doesn't sound very good. What's in it?"

"Any kind of varmint I shot. I had one once that had possum and snake and a little bit of coon."

"Sounds awful, Harry."

"Well, us old bachelors have to do the best we can. I'm a pretty good cook though. Let's eat up." He found two bowls, filled them carefully with big spoonfuls of the stew, and then sat down. "Try it out."

She took a bite and said, "This is good! You don't want to tell me what's in it?"

"No. I eat a meal once with some Sioux Indians. I ate what they had. It was a stew, and I found out later what was in it. Never ate no more with the Sioux."

"What was in it, Harry?"

"Puppy dogs mostly."

"How awful!"

"I remember it wasn't too bad. We'll be in California pretty soon. What do you reckon you'll do out there?"

"I guess I'll help my sister and take care of Rachel."

She was quiet, and suddenly Harry turned and looked off. A coyote sounded closer than usual.

"What was it, Harry?"

"Just a coyote. They sure make a mournful sound."

"I've never heard one."

"I'm sorry about your hearing, Lily."

She leaned forward and held the bowl in both hands, and there was a longing in her face he had seen before. She confirmed that she missed her hearing when she said, "I'll never get used to it. I miss so much."

Jump wanted to reach out and touch her but felt that would be out of place. He leaned forward, and the flames illuminated the craggy contours of his face. He was a rough-hewn man, this Harry Jump, used hard by the West, but there was no sign of cruelty or meanness in him. Somehow he had escaped this, and now he said slowly and thoughtfully, "I had a sister once named Janie. She got kicked by a horse in the back of her neck." He looked down at the bowl and didn't speak, but then when he looked up, sorrow was written plainly on his face. "She was plum paralyzed. We had to do everything for her. She could talk. She used to talk about what she was missing, like going fishing down at the river and going with me when I hunted coon at night. I tried to help, but there wasn't much I could do. That's when I gave up on God."

"You shouldn't have done that, Harry."

"I know it. Foolish, ain't it? Man's a foolish creature full of sinful emotion, but I loved that girl."

Lily straightened and gave Jump a direct look. She smiled, which made her look younger. "You're telling me I ought to be thankful that I can see and walk. You're right, Harry." She got to her feet abruptly and said, "Don't let Rachel be a bother to you."

"Won't ever happen." Jump rose to his feet. "She's like a ray of sunshine. You know this is a pretty dark world, Lily, but some people glitter."

His words delighted Lily, and she gave him a careful look. "What a nice thing to say!" she exclaimed.

"Well, it's true."

"What did you two talk about tonight?"

"Oh, she mostly asked questions. She sure is full of questions."

"What did she ask you tonight?"

Jump was uncomfortable, and she saw it in his face. "It must have bothered you."

"What makes you think that?"

"I can tell by your expression. What was it? What did she ask you?"

"She asked me why I never got married."

For a moment Lily didn't answer, and then she asked, "What did you tell her? I'll ask her what you said so you may as well tell me."

"Aw, Lily, you know. I said no woman would ever have a rough fellow like me."

She whispered, "I guess we're alike then, Harry." She abruptly left, and Jump watched her go. He refilled his coffee cup, but the coffee grew cold while he sat in the flickering light of the flames, thinking long thoughts about women, young girls, and how the two were different.

JOELLE HAD REMAINED IN the wagon after Logan Temple left. Her wound was still giving her considerable pain, but she ignored it. She had intended to get out to fetch water, for her mouth was dry, but she was interrupted when Rachel and Lily had visited Jump while he was cooking the supper. She held herself stiffly, trying to avoid all painful movement, and she was not able to think very clearly. Ever since the shooting, she had felt disoriented and more cut off and alone than ever before. She also felt shame; her secret had been discovered. She thought that what she had done was wrong. Recalling all her actions, she tried to think of another way she could have escaped from her stepfather, but nothing occurred to her.

After Lily and Rachel left, she moved to the end of the wagon. She gave a small grunt of pain as she positioned herself to get down to the ground. At once Jump was there beside her. "Now, what are you doing, missy? You ought not to be moving around."

"I want to get down, Harry."

"Sure. Here, let me help you." Jump simply reached up and lifted her to the ground. "Come on over here and set down on this here box," he said. "I bet you could use something to drink and maybe something to eat."

"I'm so thirsty."

"You sit right there. I'll fetch you some nice fresh water."

Joelle watched as Jump went around to the side of the wagon. He came back bearing a large cup of water. "Here," he said. "You drink this. We hit a fresh river just about right over the ridge there. It's mighty good."

Joelle eagerly took it and gulped the cool water. "Thank you, Harry."

"Tell you what. I got some nice biscuits and some stew here. You set right there and let me wait on you."

"I can fix it."

"No, you can't. You just let me do this now."

Joelle was pleased enough to let Harry wait on her for she still felt confused. He returned with a bowl of fragrant stew and a spoon. "Here, you take this, and I got some biscuits. You might want to crumble them up in there," Harry said. He turned away and came back with a biscuit.

She tasted the stew and said, "This is good."

"Well, that's about the limit of my cooking, I guess. I can fry bacon and make stew." He sat down beside her on the ground, his legs crossed and a curious light in his eyes. "Reckon I'll have to know your name. Can't go on calling you by that boy's name."

"Well, actually a lot of people did call me Jo. My name's Joelle Lynn Mitchell."

"Joelle? Why, that's a right pretty name."

There was a sound of laughter from one of the wagons, and Joelle looked up. "I guess people are talking about me, aren't they, Harry?"

"Well, you know on a wagon train there ain't a whole lot to talk about. So, something like this comes up—it's just people's nature."

"It's something I had to do."

"Sure. We all have to do things like that. Get away from things, so to speak," Harry said.

Overhead the stars were beginning to appear, making tiny, brilliant dots in the sky. "Going to be a full moon tonight. Right pretty."

Joelle was grateful to Jump. "Aren't you going to ask me anymore questions?"

"Reckon you'll tell me when you get ready. I'm not one to poke around other people's business much. Anyways, you're gonna be all right soon. The doctor tells me that that bullet missed your lung. You're lucky there. Could have been a heck of a lot worse."

"I know it. I'm really thankful." She was quiet for a while, and then she said, "I had to run away from my home, Harry."

She told how her stepfather had driven her to run away, and then related how she had gotten the idea of disguising herself as a boy. She ended by saying, "I hated to do it, but I was afraid I'd get caught."

"Why, don't you worry none about that, Joelle. You're gonna be all right. After you get to California that no-account stepfather of yours ain't going to come two thousand miles to get you. If he does, I'll perforate him."

Joelle smiled. "I hope it doesn't come to that, Jump, but I appreciate it." She felt a sense of warmth at the easy way Harry Jump had accepted her. However, her mind kept returning to Owen, and she wondered why he was gone.

Finally Harry said, "I've got to go take over the herd. You be all right here by yourself?"

"I'll be all right, Harry."

"I'll put this stew and these biscuits right here. You get them anytime you get hungry."

"Thank you, Harry."

Joelle waited as Jump mounted his horse and rode into the darkness. The sounds of the camp were the same as always—laughter, shouts, and off-key singing. She ate another biscuit with honey and was surprised at her keen appetite. Overhead the moon was beginning to light up the skies, and she watched it for a time. She grew sleepy after a while, and she pulled a blanket from the wagon, wrapped it around her, and returned to the fire. She put more sticks on it, and after a while lay down flat on her back and stared up at the skies. Finally she drifted into a fitful sleep. She was awakened by a voice, and frightened, she sat up. The sudden move brought pain to her upper shoulder, and she let out a small cry.

"Well, you're upright, are you?"

Chad sat down beside her. The fire was going down, but the moonlight was bright. He pushed his hat back, and she saw he was smiling. "How you feeling?"

"I'm much better, Chad."

"The doc said you wouldn't have to worry any. He says you're going to be fine. Hurts to get shot though. I been shot twice. Didn't enjoy either time."

"We've got some stew here. I can heat it up."

"Why, I am pretty hungry, but you let me do the heating." Chad moved quickly to put the pot back over the fire, fed the blaze with a few sticks, and picked up a spoon and began to stir. "You cook this?"

"No, Harry did it. It's good though, and there are some biscuits in that oven over there and some honey."

"I always like to have my dessert first," Chad said cheerfully. He extracted a biscuit from the oven, split it open with his fingers, and poured honey over it. "Mighty messy, honey is, but mighty good." He chewed thoughtfully, then began telling her how the day had gone, and she knew he was talking to put her at ease. He ate a bowl of the stew. "That's mighty good. Harry's a good cook."

"Chad, I want to tell you what I'm doing here and why I dressed myself up as a boy."

"Why, you don't have to do that."

"I want to," Joelle said hurriedly. She gave him her name and told the story.

"That skunk ought have been shot!" he said edgily. "Don't worry about him. If he ever comes after you, I'll send him back in a basket."

Somehow the big man's encouragement meant a lot to Joelle, as had Harry's. "I don't know what to do, Chad," she said. "I don't know how to act anymore."

"Well, why don't you let me make some decisions. I'm mighty good at making other people's decisions," he said with a smile. "Tell you what I'm going to do. We're going to get you a dress; you're going to put on some makeup and join the world. Show them you're a real woman."

"I don't even have a dress."

"Well, make one, steal one, buy one. Tell you what. I'll get one from that Cherry girl. You're about the same size."

"I don't think I could do that, Chad."

"Sure you can. Just put your head down and run right at it."

Suddenly, to her horror, she felt sadness and regret. She struggled, but the sound of tears in her voice gave her away. Chad put his long arms around her and said, "Now, Joelle, let me tell you. You're a good-looking woman. I guess every man in the train must have been blind not to see it, but you're going to dress yourself up, and every single man on this train will come courting you, including me and Owen Majors."

Joelle felt comfort and relief. Chad's strong arm held her tight, and although she had never needed a man's consolation before, she needed it now. She simply sat there as Chad continued talking, mostly teasing her. Finally he stood up.

"You mind what I say. We're going to dress you up so you're going to be prettier than a pair of green shoes with red laces. I have to git now. Thanks for the stew."

Joelle realized she was fully awake. She didn't know what time it was, but the moon was high in the sky. She heated the stew and ate another small portion and another biscuit. As she drew the blanket around her, she wondered how she would face Owen. That was what hurt her the most. *I can't even think about what to tell him.* She felt lonely and confused for a long time.

She dozed, but the sound of a horse awakened her. Owen was dismounting. He tied the horse and stopped when he saw her sitting beside the fire. "Well, you're up. How do you feel?"

"The doctor said I was fine. Just be a few days."

"Well, that's good." His words were terse, and he studied her with a troubling expression.

"I—I want to talk to you, Owen."

"All right." He didn't sit down.

"I want to tell you why I dressed up like a boy."

"You don't have to tell me."

His words discouraged her. She knew he was angry with her, but she plunged ahead. "My name is Joelle Mitchell," she said quickly. "I had a bad stepfather. When my mother died, he—he kept after me. He was going to make me marry him, he said, so I had to get away. I ran off, Owen, but I knew he'd find me so I dressed up like a boy, and I've been running ever since."

Owen stared at her, and his expression changed. "Why didn't you tell me? You couldn't trust me with it?"

"I—I was afraid."

"I wish you would have told me, but you don't have to worry."

"That's what Harry and Chad said. That he would never come all the way to California to get me." The strain was telling on her, and she felt weak. "I need to lie down. Will you help me get into the wagon?"

"Sure." He helped her to her feet, and when they got to the wagon, he simply picked her up by the waist and set her inside. "I'm sorry about your trouble," he said.

"Others have worse. Thank you, Owen. I'm tired. I think I'll go to sleep."

"The doc left some laudanum here. You want some of that?"

"No, I don't think so. I believe I can rest without it. Good night, Owen."

"Good night."

He started to say more, but she moved back into the wagon and drew the canvas cover over the end. Joelle still felt more alone than ever.

℘

"WELL, WE FOUND US some buffalo," Chad said. "I don't want to shoot 'em this far from camp. They're pesky to haul."

"Tell you what, Chad. We'll drive some of them over toward the train. How about that?"

"OK."

Chad and Owen had been looking for game and were pleased to find a small herd of buffalo. They were a long way from camp, too far to haul an entire carcass, so the plan to drive them close to the camp made sense to both.

The two had not spoken of Joelle, but now Chad, who had been waiting for Owen to speak of the girl, said, "Joelle's going to be fine. That shot could have done a lot of damage."

"Yeah, I'm glad of that."

Something in Owen's tone drew Chad's glance. "What's the matter with you? You look like you're mad at her."

"Well, I just don't like to be lied to."

"Well, don't you know why she was dressed up like a boy?"

"Yes, she told me."

"I think it was pretty gritty of her. Don't be a fool, Owen. She's tough. She did what she had to do. And besides that, she's good-looking. I think all of us are idiots for not seeing that."

"Logan Temple knew it."

"Well, he's got a closer eye than most of us."

"She shouldn't have deceived me, Chad."

"You're a fool, Owen! She's a fine girl. Anybody can see that." He suddenly grinned rashly. "Why, I'm going to court her myself. I've said all the time I need a wife. She'd make a pretty good one."

Owen gave him a tense look and shook his head. "You come up with some crazy ideas, Chad. Let's get that buffalo back to camp."

THE TWO HUNTERS HAD driven the buffalo back to camp, and Chad killed it. The other men came out and at once began cutting up the animal. Afterward, they cooked steaks, and an unannounced meeting was called.

"What's this all about, Ralph?" Owen asked.

Ogden shifted his weight. "Riker wants to take a shortcut to get to the gold camp."

"We better not. Shortcuts can get us into trouble."

"Well, he's asked for a meeting, and I'll have to let him have it."

The three men approached where a crowd had already gathered. Riker had already been talking. "I've been telling these folks just what I told you, Ralph. We can save four hundred miles by taking this shortcut."

"We don't know anything about that shortcut."

"We know it's shorter," Riker insisted. He was a forceful man, always convinced he was totally right. He had the eyes of a fanatic, and now he turned to Owen and said, "You're the guide here. You ever been over that trail?"

"I haven't, but it's been tried."

"Well, it can be done, can't it?"

"Some folks named Donner tried it, and they couldn't make it. They lost their wagons. Got caught in the winter. Turned to eating each other."

"Well, it ain't wintertime. I heard about that, but this is the right time of the year."

Chad pointed out that they'd have to cross very difficult territory on the shortcut. "Some of the wagons won't make it, I can tell you that right now."

Riker could not stand being crossed. "I may just split the party and take them who wants to get to California in a hurry and go on."

"You do as you please," Ralph said, tired of the argument. "I'm not leading the folks into anything that dangerous."

Owen spoke up then. "The Indians are thicker in that region. With a small group of wagons you'd just be asking to get yourself scalped."

The meeting went on for some time, but in the end Ralph said, "The train's going on. Anybody who wants to split does it on their own responsibility. Meeting's over."

Riker was angry, but he knew he had no choice. He turned and stamped away. Logan Temple had been watching him. He neither liked nor trusted the man. He turned and was stopped by Dora Patton, one of the dance hall girls, who had been sick. Nothing serious, but she came up beside him now and said, "Well, Doctor, you going to make a visit to one of your patients?"

"There's nothing wrong with you, Dora. You're as healthy as I am."

"Well, maybe I just want a good-looking man like you to pay me some attention."

"You won't have any trouble," he smiled. Dora was a small brunette with a pleasing figure and was constantly pursued by the men on the train. Temple knew the dangers of a woman like this. "You're healthy as you can be, Dora."

Cherry came over and said, "Leave him alone, Dora."

"All right, but he just looked lonesome to me."

Cherry laughed. "Are you lonesome, Doctor?"

"No more than anybody else, I guess."

"Tell me, Logan. Do you enjoy good-looking patients like Dora there and Edith?"

"Oh, all patients look alike to me."

She laughed shortly, her eyes dancing. "I doubt that. How's that girl doing? What's her name?"

"Her name is Joelle Mitchell. She's fine. The bullet hit high and missed anything vital. Didn't get infected so she's going to be all right."

"Did she tell you why she dressed up like a boy?"

"I couldn't say about that."

"You doctors! Better stay away from Dora. Women like her—and like me—aren't what you need."

"You're all right, Cherry. You're just on the wrong road."

"Well, if you're going to start preaching, I'm going to let you go."

Logan smiled and said, "All right. I've got to wash some clothes. Mine will stand up alone."

He collected some of his clothes and started for the river. He had gone only a few feet in that direction when he found Artie and Edith Riker headed for the river. "Guess we're all going to wash some things out."

Artie was carrying a huge load. "I guess so. How's that girl doing?"

"She's fine. Her name is Joelle."

"That's a right pretty name."

Once at the river, Edith said, "I'll wash the clothes. Thanks for carrying them, Artie."

"I'll come back and help you tote 'em to the wagon." He left and walked along the river, stopping to throw a rock every now and then. Edith watched him go.

"He's the best of the three," Edith said. "His mother must have been a fine woman."

"His mother?"

"Yes, didn't you know? Sid and Clyde have another mother. Lyman had a second wife. Artie was her son."

"I didn't know that. He's different from the other two."

She watched as he began washing the clothes awkwardly. "You haven't washed many clothes, I can see."

"No, I try to stay away from things like that."

The two worked silently for a time, and finally she asked, "What about that girl Joelle? Is she all right really?"

"Well, she's all right physically, but she's got her problems."

"Don't we all."

Logan looked at the woman. "I guess we do," he said.

She was silent for a time, and then she said, "Do you miss your drinking, Logan?"

"No, I don't—which surprises me. I don't know why I did it. Just lack of sense, I guess."

"What will you do when you get to California?"

"Be a doctor. What about you?"

"Nothing exciting. I wish—" She suddenly broke off, and he saw she was troubled.

"What is it you wish?"

"Oh, nothing. Wishing is about all I've done lately."

He touched her hand. It was cold with the waters of the river, but there was warmth in this woman, and he suddenly knew that he was drawn to her as he could not ever remember being drawn to a woman. She looked at him with surprise but didn't attempt to withdraw her hand. They were silent.

"What do you want, Logan?"

He amazed himself when he said, "I want you, Edith."

"You can't have me."

"I don't know much about love, but I feel something for you that I've never felt for another woman."

"It's too late," she said. "We'd have to hide, live a lie. Could you do that?"

"I don't know. I never had to." She was watching him steadily, and he saw something in her eyes he couldn't understand. Finally he said, "Well, I guess we'd better get the clothes washed."

She, however, still was thinking about what he had said. *He wants me, but it's too late for us.*

e-·ɔ

ARTIE WAS SURPRISED TO find Jennie Pickett at the river. As always, he was shy around her. She seemed to have blossomed even more during the journey. "Hi, Jennie."

"Hello, Artie. What are you doing?"

"Oh, I helped Ma take some clothes down. She didn't want me to help her wash them. What are you doing here?"

"I just wanted to get away. I like to be alone once in a while."

"So do I. We'll be in California pretty soon." He tried to think of conversation that would keep her there. "I guess your folks will farm."

"We never had a place of our own."

Artie was aware of the Picketts' situation. He had seen a hundred families or more like them—travelers failing at one place and moving on to the next failure. Somehow the failure had not marred this young woman. "Maybe your family is due for a break. There's good land in California. I hear anybody can farm it."

"I hope so. Will you hunt for gold?"

"I don't know."

"Don't you want to be rich?"

"No, not really, but Pa does."

She was studying him, and he suddenly met her eyes. There was silence. "Well, what do you want, Artie?"

He answered easily. He knew exactly what he wanted. "I want a home place of my own. Not a big place. Just a small one that I can build up." He had never spoken about it aloud. Previously, his future seemed set; he would work for his father as long as his father lived. But now Artie Riker felt a sudden desperate need to be on his own, responsible for himself.

"Is that all you want?"

"Well, I want a family, of course. A son maybe and a little girl."

Overhead, circling birds were making lazy arches in the sky. The thought came to him, and he nearly spoke it. *I'd like to have a woman like you.* But he didn't have the courage. To his surprise she helped him out.

"I guess you want to get married."

"If I could find a woman who would have me, I guess so." Then he took a deep breath. He was a shy young man. "I—I'd like to have a woman like you, Jennie."

"No, not like me, Artie." She turned to go, but he took her arm.

"Don't talk poorly of yourself," he said almost sharply. She was aware of the strength of his hand and turned to face him. Artie saw tears in her eyes.

"You deserve better than me, Artie," she whispered, then she turned and walked away.

Chapter Twenty

"HARRY, I'M GOING TO take Blackie for a ride out along the river."

Harry Jump looked up from the Bible he was reading and said, "You better be careful. Owen says we could get some Indians around this part of the world. Not likely, but it's always possible."

"I'll take my gun along."

Harry Jump grinned crookedly. "That little .38 you carry won't be a good help against a band of marauding Indians, but I reckon it'll be all right. Just don't go too far."

"I won't. I just want to see the river." Joelle saddled Blackie quickly, swung into the saddle, and left the camp. She glanced backward and saw that the train was settling in for the evening. Having reached the banks of the Humboldt River, it had stopped early for the day, and the women had gone to the river to wash clothes. The poker games provided by Ash Landon had drawn most of the men. Joelle looked for Owen but didn't see him and assumed he had gone out on an afternoon hunt.

The river was actually a shallow stream, twenty feet across or thirty at the most. Still it gave Joelle pleasure as she guided Blackie along the banks. She wanted to get away from the crowd and all of the activities of the train so she could think. She had gone about three hundred yards, and the camp sounds had faded. She was surprised to see Cherry Valance walking toward her. She pulled Blackie up and nodded, "Hello, Cherry."

"Out for a ride, Joelle?"

"Yes. I get tired of all the racket." Cherry Valance was wearing a lightweight cotton dress that clung to her figure. No matter what clothes she put on, they seemed to be tantalizing. She now paused, crossed her arms in front of her, and looked up at Joelle.

"Where's Owen?" she asked.

"I don't know. Out hunting, I suppose."

"Let me ask you something," Cherry said. She was a straightforward, direct woman, and her good looks, while not yet fading, were starting to show the effects of her hard life. She paused, first considering what she wanted to say. "I'm going to come right out with it, Joelle. Have you been sleeping with Owen?"

"No!"

"Well, you didn't have to think about that. Everybody thinks you have, of course. They think he knew you were a woman all the time."

"I can't help what people think."

Cherry laughed. "You get upset when I talk about Owen. Women don't get upset unless they got some kind of real interest. But I better warn you, Owen's not much of a candidate for a husband."

Joelle stared at the woman. "I'm not thinking about that." She felt suddenly as if she had lied, for she knew the thought had crossed her mind. She hadn't admitted it to anyone, not even to herself, but now confronted by Cherry, she felt justification was necessary. "I was in trouble, and I had to get away from home."

"What were you running from?"

"I had a stepfather who couldn't keep his hands off of me so I lit out. When he started putting bulletins out looking for me, I had to do something so I dressed up like a boy. That's all there was to it."

"How'd you meet Owen?"

"He got sick and fell down in the snow. I took care of him until he was strong again."

"You don't think he's ever noticed that you were a woman? That's pretty hard to hide, isn't it?"

"I don't think it ever occurred to him."

Cherry turned and looked across the river. For a moment the only sound was the rippling of the waters along the shallows. The sky overhead was blue and looked hard enough to scratch a match on. Joelle watched her. Finally Cherry turned and tried to smile, but she wasn't successful. "I thought he might marry me at one time."

"Would you have married him if he had asked you?"

"Of course I would. I've seen enough bad men to know a good one when I see one."

"We agree on that. He is a good man."

Cherry took a deep breath and turned to leave. After only a few steps, she stopped and said, "I don't know why you are fighting it. It's obvious that you're in love with Owen." She didn't wait for an answer but walked quickly toward the camp.

Joelle was troubled, for Cherry had brought up feelings she had managed to successfully bury deep in her subconscious. Now she dismounted and tied Blackie to a branch of a small cottonwood tree. She began to walk along the banks of the river, thinking about the encounter. It had struck deep in her heart, and she was arguing with herself. *I'm not in love with him. He's just been good to me. She doesn't know what she's talking about.*

She walked fifty yards from where she had tied Blackie and then sat down on a log whitened with age. The sound of the river was soft and soothing, but her thoughts were not soothing. *What am I going to do when we get to California? Owen doesn't have any idea how I feel about him, and he wouldn't care if he did. He told me about getting hurt by a woman who deceived him. He thinks I'm just like she was.*

She shook her head, picked up a stone, and threw it into the water. A sudden sound brought her to her feet. Walking along the bank was Sid Riker. His eyes were fixed on her, and suddenly Joelle was aware of danger. She had witnessed the Rikers' brutal nature and had heard how Sid treated women. She started to leave.

"Wait a minute there, girl." Sid came to stand before her, a big bruising man with a deep chest swelling out his thin shirt. The muscles of his arms revealed his strength. He had a short neck and his face was rough. The look of brutality frightened Joelle.

"I was just going back."

"I followed you out here," Sid grinned. He saw her fear, which pleased him. "You don't have to be afraid of me," he said.

"I'm not afraid of you."

"Sure you are. You don't know much about men. I can tell that about you, but you know enough about Majors."

Joelle turned to go. "I'm not—" But he caught her arm and turned her around. The strength of his grip was frightening. He was like a huge animal, and suddenly he put his arms around her.

She began to cry, "Let me go!"

"Sure, sooner or later. You need to know what a real man is like."

Joelle started to scream, but he put his hand behind her head and pulled it immobile, leaned forward, and put his mouth on hers. He held her so tightly she couldn't move, and then he pulled her to the ground and began tearing at her clothes. "Go on and scream. Nobody's going to hear you."

Joelle started to scream, and he cuffed her across the cheek, the power of the blow turning her head to one side. He tore at her shirt, and she cried, "Let me go, please."

"Go on and beg. It won't hurt you. I've had my eye on you for a long time."

"Let her go, Sid."

For a big man, Sid Riker moved quickly. He rolled over and saw his brother Artie coming toward him. "Get out of here! This ain't none of your put-in."

"Yes, it is. You let her alone." Artie was wearing a gun, as most of the men did, but he made no sign he was aware of it. "Come on, Joelle."

Riker came to his feet at once. "Artie, get out of here before I break your neck."

"I'll go, but Miss Joelle's going with me."

Sid laughed—a crude, brutal laugh that revealed his nature. He shoved Artie backward, and the young man grew pale. "You're crazy, Sid. They'll hang you if you hurt this woman."

"That's my business. You get on back to camp. Keep your mouth shut, you hear me?"

Joelle started to back up, but Sid grabbed her arm and held her tightly. "You ain't going nowhere."

Artie moved forward. He looked thin and slender next to the bulk of his half brother, but so did most men. With surprising strength he grabbed Sid's arm and jerked him around. "You let her alone or I'll—"

Sid Riker suddenly roared and cursed. He swung, and his maul of a fist struck Artie square in the face. It drove the boy backward to the ground, and Artie lay still for a moment. Joelle saw that he was half-conscious. She watched in horror as Sid kicked the boy. "I ought to kick your brains out!"

Artie got to his feet, and though his face was bloody, he threw himself against Sid. He caught the bigger man on the side of the cheek. Sid wasn't hurt, but all of his life he had bullied Artie, and now his anger exploded. He began to beat the boy, and Artie went down again.

Joelle cried, "Let him alone!"

"You shut up! I'll take care of you after I fix him!"

He advanced toward Artie, and Joelle suddenly reached into her pocket and pulled out the .38. "You stop or I'll shoot you!"

Sid saw her holding the gun steadily. "You won't shoot nobody." He started toward her but pulled up as if he had run into a door. A bullet whistled so closely beside his ear he thought he could hear it. He reached for his own gun, but Joelle pulled the trigger again. He felt a burning along his shoulder.

"You get out of here or I'll kill you!" she said.

Sid laughed. "Well, you got spirit. I like that. There'll be other times." He looked at Artie who was bloodied and in poor shape. "Kid, you need to learn to mind your own business." He turned and walked rapidly away.

At once Joelle went to Artie and saw that he was nearly unconscious. His face was battered, and his eyebrow had been split so it was bleeding profusely. She pulled a handkerchief out of her pocket and pressed it on his face.

"We've got to get you sewed up, Artie." His mouth was bleeding, and she didn't know whether he had lost teeth or not, but she knew he was hurt. Quickly she ran and untied Blackie. She led the horse to Artie who was regaining consciousness. "Come on, Artie. Get on the horse." She helped him put his foot into the stirrup and then shoved him upward, but she kept the lines. "Hang on to the horn. You've got to be sewed up."

She led Blackie back toward the camp, glancing anxiously at the young man. He was holding the horn, and his face was pale under a mask of blood. She was only fifty feet from the camp when Edith Riker came running toward them. Her eyes were on Artie.

"What happened?"

"Sid beat him up."

"Why'd he do that?"

"He was—bothering me, and Artie tried to stop him."

Logan Temple approached at a run. "Artie, you have to have stitches. Here, let me help you down." He pulled Artie from the saddle, and supporting him on one side with Edith on the other, they led the boy away.

"What happened to him, Edith?"

"Sid beat him up. He was trying to take advantage of Joelle. Artie tried to stop him."

"Somebody needs to shoot that man."

"Somebody will someday. It may be me."

OWEN CAME IN FROM the hunt, having shot nothing, and he saw the small crowd. He stepped off his horse and moved forward. He saw Temple bending over somebody with a bloody face, and as he came closer, he saw it was Artie Riker. "What happened?"

"The kid got impudent, and I had to shove him around a little bit," Sid Riker said.

Owen stared at Sid's face and saw his smirk.

"That's not the way it was," Joelle cried out. "He was trying to—tear my clothes off. That's how he got those scratches on his neck."

"Let's see your neck, Sid."

"You go to the devil, Majors. You ain't my boss!"

"He was trying to hurt me," Joelle said. Anger had drawn her face tight, and she turned to face Majors. "He would have killed Artie if I hadn't been there."

"She's lying. She's been trying to get hold of me ever since this trip started. She was the one that got me to go down to the river with her. Said she was going to make it nice for me."

"You're a liar and a bully!" Joelle cried.

Edith suddenly moved forward and walked up to Sid. He watched her warily, not knowing what she intended. With a quick movement, she tore his handkerchief away. "There's the scratches. You always were a liar, Sid."

Lyman Riker had been taking all this in. "Edith, you keep out of this. This is a family matter."

"Family!" Edith spat out. "This monster is no family of mine!"

"Shut up, Edith!" Lyman said. It made him furious to be rebuked by his wife in public.

Edith faced Lyman Riker squarely. "Lyman," she said, and her voice was low and as cutting as a steel blade. "Either you make Sid answer for what he's doing, or I'm done with you forever."

"You're my wife. You're my family."

"What about Artie? He's your family." She put her hand on Artie's shoulder, and her eyes were blazing. "You're a weak man, Lyman Riker." She faced Sid. "You better watch yourself, Sid. If I were a man, I'd beat you half to death. As it is, I'll probably shoot you when you're not looking."

"She made up to me. She's no better than any of the other dance hall girls. Just a prostitute. That's all she is."

Owen moved forward to face Sid Riker. He was a powerful man, but the bulk of Sid Riker seemed monumental. "Sid," Owen said in a steady, soft voice, "I'll give you a choice. Either get on your horse and be out of this train in fifteen minutes or take a beating."

Riker blinked in surprise and then he laughed roughly. "You ain't man enough to make me leave, Majors. You had that woman and everybody knows it. She ain't nothing but a—"

Riker didn't finish his sentence for Owen Majors swung a blow and with every bit of his 185 pounds behind it caught Riker in the mouth and drove him back against the wagon. For a moment Sid was dazed. He reached up and touched his bleeding mouth, then stared at his hand.

"I'll kill you, Majors! I'll kick your brains out!" Sid gave a terrible cry of rage and anger and threw himself forward. He was a fearsome man, strong as a bull, and his thick skull was nearly impervious to pain.

His first blow would have ended the fight, but Majors moved to one side and caught Sid on the back of his neck with his forearm. The blow drove Sid to the ground and would have knocked a lesser man unconscious, but Riker was tough. He came to his feet with a bloody mouth, but his eyes glittered with a feral intensity. He approached more slowly this time, and although Majors had avoided one blow, he took the next one in his chest. It drove him backward, and he felt Sid's power. It was all Owen could do to keep his feet.

The two men circled, with Majors backing up and throwing punches that caught Riker in the face. Sid was an easy man to hit, but the punches seemed to have no effect. And Owen was taking several blows, all of them hard and destructive.

As the two fought through the camp, the crowd parted, but nobody left.

"Kill him, Sid!" Lyman Riker called out. He was grinning, for he had watched his son fight before, and he had never seen him lose. The fight went on until both men were exhausted.

At one point Clyde Riker stepped behind Owen and struck him. Owen was staggered, but then Clyde Riker was driven to the ground. He looked up and saw Chad Hardin standing over him. Chad had used his gun to drive Clyde Riker down, and now he put it back in his holster.

"You stay out of this, Clyde," Chad said, "or I'll stop your clock."

Clyde got to his feet. Blood was running down his face, and he said furiously, "I'll get you for that, Hardin."

"You ain't getting nobody! Now shut up!"

Joelle was horrified at the violence of the fight. She saw no hope for Owen, for Sid had the strength of an animal. She gave a cry when Owen fell backward, driven by a blow. Riker shouted in triumph. "I got you now!" He threw himself forward, intending to pin Owen down and pound him senseless.

But Owen raised his right leg and drove it forward. The heel of his boot caught Riker in the mouth and stopped him dead still. He gave a grunting, squealing sound, and blood flowed all around his mouth. He was gasping for breath, and there was a gap in his teeth. Owen got to his feet, and as Sid made a move to lift his hands, Owen picked up a handful of sand and threw it into the man's face. Sid cried out and was helpless. Owen threw himself at Sid who fell into a small cooking fire. He screamed with the pain of the burns, and Owen would have held him there, but Chad pulled him back.

"I reckon that's sufficient. You showed him where the bear sat in the buckwheat." Chad looked at Sid who was crawling out of the fire, his eyes squeezed shut and his mouth a wreck. "He's had enough. It would have been easier to shoot him, Owen."

"I will the next time."

Owen turned and said, "I won't have this man in the train, Riker."

Lyman stared at him, speechless. He was accustomed to having his own way, and now the situation was out of his control. "He's hurt too bad to leave."

"He's your responsibility. If he gives anymore trouble, I'll shoot him first and then maybe you second."

Lyman swallowed hard and said, "Edith, come and help me."

"Take care of him. He's your son. You take one wagon and put him in it. I'll take care of Artie. You never gave this boy a kind word. Now you've got those two you're so proud of, beat-up. I hope you enjoy them."

She turned to Artie and said, "Come on, Son. You need to lie down."

Chad watched them leave, then placed his hand on Joelle's shoulder. "You all right, are you, girl? He didn't hurt you?"

"No, but he would have if Artie hadn't come."

"He's a good boy. Not like the others. We'll take care of him."

Joelle looked up at the big man. "Thank you, Chad. I was pretty scared."

"Well, don't be anymore. You won't hear anymore out of Sid Riker."

"Well, you need some cleaning up too," Logan Temple told Owen.

"I'm all right," Owen said. His voice seemed hollow. He was beginning to feel the hurts. He looked at his hand and saw the skin was split on his knuckles. He didn't know when he had done that. He allowed himself to be led back to his wagon where Jump waited. "You ought to have killed him, Owen."

Temple worked on Owen for a while, and finally he said, "Well, you're going to be pretty sore for a few days. Not as sore as Sid is. The man's a beast."

Owen leaned back against the side of the wagon and tried to smile, but it hurt. "You all right, Joelle? He didn't hurt you?"

"No. Thanks for what you did."

"Had to be done."

"You don't believe what he said about me, do you?"

"No, I know you better than that." Suddenly he reached out and ran his hand over her hair, the first time he had ever touched her in this way. "My life sure has been complicated since you saved me."

Very much aware of the pressure of his hand on her head, she gave an embarrassed laugh. She said, "I'll fix you some stew."

As she turned away, Harry Jump grinned and said, "Well, you done the necessary, Owen. If he had hurt that girl, I would have killed him myself. She's some punkins, ain't she?"

Owen was watching Joelle as she began to fix a simple meal. "Yep, I think she is, Harry."

Chapter Twenty-One

"MA, CAN I ASK you a question?"

Edith Riker looked up from the shirt she was patching and studied Artie's face. His face still showed signs of the beating he had taken from Sid. "I don't know, Artie." She smiled at him. "It depends on what you want to know. A woman's got to have some secrets, you know."

Artie blinked with surprise. "I guess she does," he said. He had taken his hat off, and the midafternoon sun lighted his fair hair and highlighted his lean face. She had always liked his gentleness and sensitivity and often wished she had known his mother. "Go ahead and ask your question."

Artie cleared his throat, hesitated, and then blurted out, "Why did you ever marry Pa?"

The question troubled Edith Riker, for she herself had sought an answer for that ever since her marriage. She was a forthright, honest woman, and now she ran her hand over her light brown hair and said, "I don't have a good answer for that. Mainly, I guess, I needed a home, and your father needed a wife—er, thought he did. Why are you asking, Artie?"

"I don't know, Ma. It just seems like you don't—" He broke off his words and looked at the ground where he was digging the toe of his boot into the dirt. "Are you ever going to go back to him, do you think?"

No one else had asked this question, but everyone on the train was aware that Edith Riker and her husband were no longer sharing the wagon with which they'd started the journey. Edith had taken another wagon. She made no attempt to cook or clean for Lyman. She had expected that he would blow up, but he merely glared at her. Now she saw that the situation troubled Artie.

"Don't worry about it, Artie. I'll make out. People make mistakes sometimes, but this is one I can remedy." She wanted to get his mind off the problem and asked, "What are you going to do in California?"

The question seemed to enliven his features. He looked up, and his eyes were bright. "I'm going to get some money and buy a farm."

"Where do you plan to get all this money?" Edith smiled.

"Dig for gold, I reckon. What are you going to do, Ma?"

"Oh, I don't know. I can hire out as a cook maybe."

"I'd hate to see you do that," Artie said. "I'll tell you what. Maybe you and I can get some money together. We could buy a place."

Edith laughed. "You don't need me, Artie. You need a strong young woman for a wife. Somebody to give you a family." She knew that Artie longed for a family. He had never been accepted by his father or his brothers, and for this reason he had drawn closer to Edith after she married Lyman. He glanced across the circle of wagons toward the Pickett wagon, and Edith could read his mind. "That Jennie Pickett would make a nice wife."

Artie's eyes widened. "I think she likes me."

"Well, why wouldn't she like a fine, good-looking young man like you? She's got lots of sense, that girl has."

Artie started to answer but saw his father approaching. He straightened up and his smile disappeared. He nodded at his father and left hurriedly. Lyman watched him go but paused in front of Edith. She knew him well and was aware that he had made up his mind about something. At first she had admired his determination, for she had a great deal of this characteristic herself, but Lyman's determination had gone the wrong way. He had become stubborn and impatient with anyone who disagreed with him. Now she said briefly, "Hello, Lyman."

"Edith," Lyman said forcefully, "I want to know when you're coming back. You've got to stop this foolishness."

"I'm not ever coming back."

Riker's face flushed as it always did when his will was thwarted. "I'm your husband!" he said loudly.

"You were. The biggest mistake I ever made," Edith said quietly. She looked him full in the eyes and said, "Find yourself another woman."

"You can't make it without me."

"I don't need anything, Lyman."

"You think you're fooling me? You're carrying on with that doctor. That's what you're doing."

"You're wrong about that. Logan Temple's a fine man. He wouldn't have anything to do with taking another man's wife."

"Everybody knows he's crazy about you, and I think you've fallen for him and his fancy education."

Edith said nothing for a moment. "You're a little man, Lyman Riker. I should have seen it before, but now I do. Leave me alone, and if either one of your boys ever touches Artie again, I'll shoot him myself."

Riker threw his head back, and for one moment Edith thought that he was going to strike her, but with a curse he turned and walked away, his back stiff. "Good riddance," Edith murmured. "I'll be glad when this trip is over, and I won't have to look at him."

⁓

OWEN HAD SEEN THE line of wagons at a distance and had spurred Captain forward. The big horse loved to run, and Owen soon caught up with the end of the train. He passed by, counting them—fourteen wagons. *Not a very big train making this journey.* As he pulled up toward the first wagon, a tall, lanky man turned his horse and came to greet him. He had a lined, weather-beaten face and could have been anywhere from forty to seventy years old. His big hands held the reins loosely, and his light blue eyes were fixed steadily on Owen.

"Howdy," he said. "What are you doing way out here?"

"I'm Owen Majors, leading a train through. We're about ten miles behind you."

"I'm Micah Jukes. You know the trail?"

"No, I don't. Never been over it before. Gone on through to other places."

"Well, there's water up ahead. Some good springs and a little creek, but there's a big dry spell that lasts maybe two or three days." Jukes hesitated then added, "We're going to pull up and water the stock good and fill up all the barrels. Might be a good idea for you to do the same, Majors."

"Wouldn't put you out?"

"Not a bit of it. Be glad for the company." A thought occurred to him, and he said, "Maybe we'll have a little celebration. You got any music makers in your train?"

"Some pretty good ones, but I have to warn you, we've got gamblers too. If I were you, I'd warn your people to stay clear of that if they want to hang on to what they've got."

Jukes grinned slyly. "I'll do that, but I'm pretty handy with cards myself. Maybe I'll play a few hands."

"Watch yourself."

"I'll do that. You go tell your folks to come right on in. We'll be at those springs in about two hours."

Owen turned his horse and rode back toward the train. He found Ralph Ogden in front, as usual, and told Ralph about the train ahead of them. "Seemed like a nice fellow, that wagon master. He says we need to water our stock good and fill up all the barrels."

"That's not a bad idea. Be good to have somebody along who knows the way."

"He wants to have some kind of a celebration tonight."

Ogden took off his hat and scratched his head. "I reckon it'd be all right since we are going in the same direction. I'll tell our folks."

e⁓

HARRY HAD SHAVED CAREFULLY and was now combing his hair. He was looking in the small mirror, and Joelle said, "You sure admire yourself, don't you, Harry?" She was still wearing her oversized men's clothing.

Jump stared at his reflection and said, "I am a good-looking fellow. No question about it."

Joelle laughed. "And humble too."

"Well, humble is when you got to be, but when you're a good man like me you don't have to fool around with that. Come on. Let's go to this party. I hear them starting the music up."

"No, I don't want to go."

"You come on with me. You need to join up."

"I'll just wait here, Harry. I don't have anything to wear at a frolic."

Harry stared at her and then shook his head. "You shut yourself off too much, Joelle. People would be friendly, but you've got to reach out to them."

Joelle knew that Harry was right, but she couldn't seem to help it. Finally she said, "I'll come over a little bit later."

She watched as Harry left, and for a time she watched the fires from the neighboring wagon train, which was in a circle five hundred yards from the Ogden train. She could hear the music on the night air. The stars glittered overhead, and the breeze was warm. She felt lonely, and for a time she thought about home, or what had been home. It seemed a hundred years since she had left, and her good memories were of her mother, but she also knew how close to danger she had been. Finally she looked up and saw Harry approaching. He had something in his hands, and he smiled.

"I got something for you, Joelle."

"What is it?"

"It's a go-to-a-party dress." He held it up. "You put this on and come on over to the party."

Joelle wanted to refuse, but her loneliness had become oppressive. She smiled. "All right, Harry, I'll come."

"You hurry now. They got some mighty good pickers and singers over there."

He left, and Joelle moved away from the fire. She stepped out of her clothes and put on the dress—an emerald green. She looked down and gasped for it was much lower cut than any dress she had ever worn. "I'll bet he got this dress from one of those dance hall girls—probably Cherry Valance!"

It was a rather daring dress, and she had reservations. But finally loneliness got the best of her. She walked slowly toward the music, and as soon as she stepped into the circle, she saw Owen straighten up. At once he left where he was standing alone and approached her.

"Hello, Owen," she said.

"Where'd you get that dress?" he asked abruptly.

"I think it was one of Cherry's. Harry brought it to me. I didn't have anything to wear."

Owen shook his head. "You can't come here wearing a dress like that."

"Why not?"

Owen searched for a reply and couldn't seem to find one. "I guess because I say so."

"You're not my father, Owen."

"I know I'm not, but I'm well—I'm like a brother. I'm responsible for you, and that dress could give men the wrong kind of ideas." Joelle knew exactly what he was talking about; she had felt the same fears while deciding whether or not to wear the dress.

"Like what?" she said.

"You know what."

"No, I don't. Explain it to me, big brother."

"I'm not going to argue about it. You're not wearing that dress."

If Owen had spoken more gently and had shown a different spirit, Joelle knew she would have surrendered at once, but his presumptuous words and his attitude that he had charge of everything to do with her grated on her.

"I'm wearing the dress, and I'm dancing, and I'm going to have a good time!"

Owen didn't move for a moment. His eyes took her in, and he realized she was a girl with a great degree of vitality and imagination. He saw the hint of her will, or her pride, in the corners of her eyes and lips. For the first time, he saw her really as a young woman. The dress, at least, had accomplished that! Her fieriness made her lovely and brought out a rich, headlong quality of her spirit, usually hidden by a cool reserve. On the trail he had learned to know her pride and honesty, but now he also saw her physical beauty. And suddenly it woke in him the flames of hungers he didn't want to acknowledge. She was a strong presence standing before him—like fragrance riding the night air or like a melody coming over a great distance. He was struck by the hint of her womanliness, so fresh, turbulent, and strong.

"I don't want you to wear it," he said lamely, not forcefully as he had intended.

"I'm wearing the dress, Owen, and that ought to be good enough for you."

Chad, across the way, was dancing with Cherry. "Hey, look at Joelle!" he exclaimed. "My land! Look at that dress!"

"That's my dress," Cherry said at once.

Chad grinned. "I bet it is. It looks as good on her as it did on you." The dance ended, and he said, "I'm going to get me a dance with that young woman."

Joelle smiled when she saw him. She had always liked Chad Hardin. He had the rough good looks of a man of the outdoors. "My land, Joelle, if you ain't the belle of the ball. You look splendiferous. Come on. Let's dance!"

"I don't feel like dancing."

"What's the matter?"

"I just had an argument with Owen."

"What about?"

"He said I couldn't wear this dress. He said it's not fitting. He really meant it made me look like a dance hall woman."

"Oh, he's just an old grump. Now, you take me, Joelle. I'm known all over the West for being good medicine for young women. Why, one dance with me, and you'll be cut loose from all of old Owen's sayings. Come on."

Joelle laughed and let him lead her to the dance. She was a good dancer, and he was equally good. She enjoyed the music and his bantering as the lights of flames lighted the rough contours of his face.

❧

HARRY JUMP PULLED AT Rachel. "Come on, honey. It's time for me and you to dance."

"I don't remember how to dance, Mr. Jump."

"You can call me Uncle Harry if you want to. A young lady like you has got to learn how to dance, and I'm the best teacher in the world."

Rachel looked up and smiled. She liked Harry Jump immensely, for he spent a great deal of time with her, telling her tales of sidewinders and adventures she knew weren't true. He guided her around, and when the dance was over, he stepped back and said, "You look plum pretty. Come on now. I'm going to dance with your mama."

"She won't dance, Uncle Harry."

"She will tonight." Facing Lily, Jump said, "That daughter of yours is a real dancer. I'll bet her mama wants to dance too. Come on. Let's try it out."

Lily had watched with pleasure as Jump danced with Rachel, and when he asked her dance, she remembered how she'd danced with him once before. "I'd like that, Harry."

As they danced, she could almost feel the music though she couldn't hear it. Finally the dance ended, and she would have rejoined the spectators, but Harry said, "Now they're playing some of that slow dancing music." He moved closer and put his arm behind her and held her left hand. He swayed with the music.

"What are they playing?" she asked.

"Oh, it's a sad song called 'Lorena.' About a sad woman. I don't like them sad songs. They always make me cry. This one does."

"What are the words, Harry?"

Harry had a poetic streak that he kept carefully concealed. He quoted some of the words to her, and when she listened to the sad tale, he saw, with shock and amazement, tears in her eyes. "Why, it's just a song, Lily."

"I know, but it's sad."

Harry didn't speak for a time, but the two moved together. He was aware of her in a way that was strange for him. The fragrance of her clothes came powerfully to him, and he felt the swing of her body, and the soft fragrance slid through the armor of his self-sufficiency. He admired her as a full woman and felt the sensations a man feels when he looks upon beauty and desires it. Jump had known women before, but Lily was different. She seemed to color the air when he was around her. She put something into it, something like a charge of electricity. She had, he knew, strength and dignity, and her femininity touched his senses. It seemed to turn his past barren and made him a hungry man now. He suddenly expressed what he had meant to say for some time.

"Lily." He waited until her eyes came to his lips and then said, "Have you ever thought of me as a man you might marry?"

Lily missed a step and suddenly stood still. She had known troubles, and they hadn't soured her, and now she spoke the truth simply. "Yes, Harry, I have."

His face lighted up, and he said, "You hang on to that thought! When we get to Sacramento, and I get all settled, we'll talk about this some more."

"All right, Harry, if you say so."

℮

THE LAST DANCE WAS over, and Chad was walking with Joelle toward the wagon. Both of them were laughing, for Chad had a way of making a woman laugh. As they stepped close to the wagon, they saw Owen sitting in front of the fire. "You missed a good dance there, Owen."

"I guess I did."

Chad started to speak but saw that Owen was not in a good mood. "Thanks for the dance, Joelle," he said. "I'll see you in the morning. When we get to Sacramento, we'll have some fine times."

"Thank you, Chad. I'll look forward to it."

She watched him as he disappeared into the darkness. She was about to get ready for bed, but she hesitated. "I'm sorry I was so mean to you, Owen. I didn't mean all those things I said."

Owen got to his feet and said quietly, "I shouldn't have meddled with your affairs."

Joelle saw that she had hurt him and was surprised. "I won't wear a dress like that again."

Owen Majors was caught off-guard. He had seen the adamant side of this young woman, and now he saw the soft and gentle side that he had already learned to love. "It's just—well, I feel responsible for you, Joelle. I don't want anything to happen to you except something good."

Joelle felt a warm glow of happiness. He cares for me. It's good to know somebody cares what happens to me.

Something passed between the two, and Owen stepped forward. He put his hands on Joelle's shoulders and pulled her slightly forward. She knew he was going to kiss her. She knew little about men, but that was apparent. She lifted her head, but he released her abruptly.

"Good night, Joelle." He turned and moved away. Joelle watched him. *Why didn't he kiss me?* she wondered. *He wants something I don't have, I guess, and I'll never have.* All the happiness that had come with the dance was gone, and after she went to bed, she lay for a long time, thinking of the look on his face and wondering why he had not kissed her.

Chapter Twenty-Two

"IS THAT A FORT, Owen?"

Joelle was riding alongside Owen at the head of the train as they approached what appeared to be a settlement. As they drew closer, it became obvious that all the buildings were constructed of roughly hewn logs with mud daubing. There was no attempt at stockade walls, and it didn't have the military appearance of other forts Joelle had seen.

"It's the worst looking settlement I've ever seen."

"That's Fort Ruby. Probably the worst fort in the West."

"What's it for, way out here in the middle of nowhere?"

"Nobody knows why some politicians in Washington decided to stick a fort out here. There are few settlers, and the Paiute raiders are pretty bad. But it looks like a pretty poor doings to me." He glanced backward and said, "I'd better get with Ralph, and we'll go see how the Indian situation is for the rest of the trip."

"All right, Owen." She turned, caught his eye, and for a moment the two of them were silent. Joelle was remembering that moment when he had placed his hands on her shoulders and had pulled her forward. She had thought about it incessantly and wondered what made him draw back from her. *Am I not pretty enough? Am I not the kind of woman he wants?* She saw something in Owen's face that she couldn't identify. He was handsome in a rough, masculine way. He had long firm lips, and the rest of his features were smooth. Aware that she was staring at him, she turned away.

"I'll see if I can find a store. We need a few supplies."

"All right." Owen's voice was more curt and short than he had intended. He saw her downcast expression and regretted his sharp tone. He tried to think of some way to tell her what he was feeling, but because he didn't know himself, that was difficult. He turned his horse and rode quickly to where Ralph Ogden was plodding alongside his oxen.

For a moment the thought crossed Owen's mind that the leader of the train was not unlike one of the oxen. He was massively built—the strongest man in the train, a good man who knew his limitations.

Pulling up, Owen said, "Ralph, let's go talk to the commanding officer and see how the Indian situation is from here on into Sacramento."

"That's a good idea, Owen." He spoke to the oxen and turned to his wife. "I guess we'll camp out here tonight, Cleo. You and Lily can cook up a good supper. If they've got any supplies, we probably need to get them for the rest of the trip."

"All right, Ralph."

The two men rode ahead and were met by a tall, skinny lieutenant whose uniform seemed to have been made for a bigger man. His pale skin was blistered, and his eyelids were red with irritation.

"Good afternoon, gentlemen," he said in a high-pitched, raspy voice. "Just coming in, I see."

"Yes, lieutenant. We thought we'd like to find out about the Indian situation. Who's the commanding officer?"

"I'm Lieutenant Rankin, but I'm afraid Major Stewart won't be able to see you."

"What's the matter? It doesn't look like there's a great deal to do out here."

Rankin smiled thinly. "You're right about that. What's your name?"

"I'm Owen Majors, and this is the wagon master of our train, Ralph Ogden. We're headed for Sacramento."

"Yeah, another train went through headed that way just two days ago. You might catch up with them."

Owen looked around the shabby fort and saw a group of soldiers drilling. They seemed to be half-asleep, and the sergeant in charge of them was leaning against a post, calling out the orders in a bored voice. "Looks pretty calm. Don't guess you've got a lot of action here."

"More than you might think," Rankin said. "The Paiutes lately."

"Have the Indians been acting up?" Owen asked.

"Yes, they have. One of their chiefs, Walking Bear, got them stirred up on the warpath. They've hit several settlers."

"Why don't you go out and get them, lieutenant?" Ogden inquired. "Isn't that what you're here for?"

"Trying to catch an Indian is like trying to catch the wind. We know they're out there, but when we take a troop out and get close to them, they all separate, so you got fifteen to twenty trails to follow instead of one. What are you going to do—send one trooper to get one Indian?" He shook his head. "There's no way to fight like these redskins."

"What about your commanding officer? He a fighting man?"

"He was once before he got sent out here. There's something about this place that draws a man down." Suddenly Rankin straightened his shoulders. "Didn't mean to complain. A soldier serves where he's put, but it's a bad fort. There's no question about it." He looked around the bleak, inhospitable place and shook his head. "No lumber to build anything more grand than log cabins. To make matters worse, they built a distillery not too far away. They make a liquor called Old Commissary. Of course, the men get at it. Can't help it. We can't watch them all the time."

Because Lieutenant Rankin looked as if he had been drinking himself, Owen didn't answer. He quickly surmised that the commanding officer was a drinking man too. "Well, we're going to stock up and head out tomorrow morning. Any advice?"

"Nothing you don't know of probably. Camp early and get your wagons boarded up. Keep watch at night. Some fools say the Indians won't attack at night, but these Paiutes will. They pick you off one at a time. Most of all, never let anybody leave the train alone or in a small group. The Paiutes are waiting to pick off anybody like that. It's happened before."

"Where can we buy some supplies?"

"Such as we've got is over there at that painted building." He waved listlessly toward the only painted structure. Most of the buildings were a leprous gray, weathered, and seemingly left over from the antediluvian age. "You can get some basics there. Nothing fancy."

"Thank you, lieutenant, for your help." The two men turned and walked away. "Doesn't sound like a lot of fun, the last leg of this journey, Owen."

"We'll make it. You go back and tell the womenfolk to stock up on supplies. I think this is the last chance before we hit Sacramento. I'm going to see if I can get my horse shod."

⁓

THE TRAIN PULLED OUT shortly after daylight the next day. The women had cooked the breakfast and fixed enough food for nooning. All were anxious to be on their way. Ralph had called a meeting and explained the situation. They all listened as he said soberly, "We're all right so far, but the officer here says that the Paiutes are on the warpath." He went on to explain how they had to be extra careful on watch at night. "We'll all sleep in our clothes with our guns at hand, and we'll have double the guard out. Most of all, nobody leaves the train except Majors."

"What makes him so special? I can take care of myself as well as he can." Lyman Riker had been soured by the beating Owen had administered to Sid. He cast a malevolent look at Owen now, saying, "He can get scalped as quick as anybody else."

"He's had experience none of us have, except Chad there. These two will go on ahead and do what scouting has to be done. Anything to add to that, Owen?"

Owen was leaning against a wagon, taking no part in the meeting. Now he looked up and met Lyman's gaze and said quietly, "I doubt if they'll mount a full-scale attack. They're usually in small bands if it's a war party. They hang around the edges, and when anybody wanders off, especially you women going down to the creek or somewhere, they can get you, and you'll be dead before you know it."

"I guess I'm a grown-up man," Riker growled. "I can take care of myself." He snorted and stalked away.

Edith watched her husband and said to Artie, standing beside her, "He's like a spoiled child in some ways, Artie. You tell him not to do something, but he'll do it or die."

"He might die if he doesn't pay attention to what Majors says."

"He thinks nothing can get the best of him. He's mad through and through at Owen for whipping Sid like he did."

"Well, you heard what he said, Ma. Don't you be running off. Anytime you want to go anywhere, I'll go with you." He smiled at her and said, "We'll be in Sacramento pretty soon. Me and you'll go in the fanciest restaurant there and eat until we can't get up."

Edith smiled. "That'll be something to look forward to."

FOR THE NEXT TWO days, the travelers all had strained nerves. The warning about the Indians had sobered them.

On the very first day out, Chad had come to the campfire where Joelle was cooking supper. "You're always around when there's food cooking, Chad."

"My mama didn't raise no foolish boys," Chad grinned. "I know who's the best cook on this train."

"You're not going to talk me out of anything."

"Why, I can charm the birds out of the trees, Joelle. You ain't never seen me when I had my charm at full pitch. Why, they say that Davy Crockett could just grin a squirrel out of a tree at a hundred yards."

"And you think you can do the same to women?"

"Some women," Chad said.

He was sitting on a small box, watching her cook, and Joelle was conscious, as always, of his strength. He seemed to have springs of power, and the muscles lay banded across his arms and shoulders like woven wire. He wore a battered hat, and his face was bronzed by the sun. No furrows or wrinkles marked his features. His chin was cleft, and his mouth wide. Joelle liked his bantering talk. She knew little about his background, but she was aware he was interested in her. Other men had showed interest, but Chad's interest wasn't troublesome, which wasn't true of the interest shown by other men in the train. He had a quick intelligence and wit, and a hint of temper showed between his brows.

Relaxed and smiling, he told her tales of his days in the mountains, and finally he said, "I've got an inclination. Those things can be bad for a fellow sometimes, but I don't think this one is."

"An inclination to do what?"

"Why, to come courting you, Joelle."

She glanced at him and shook her head. "Don't be foolish, Chad. You don't even know me."

"Well, that'll be half the fun, getting to know you. See, I've decided that you need a good man, and I'm nominating myself for the position."

"You're a fool, Chad."

"Why, I reckon I am foolish about you. I don't like to come at a woman from the sidelines and sneak up on her, so I'm just telling you plain that I'm a candidate." He got to his feet in one swift, easy motion and looked down at her. He was very tall, somewhat taller than Majors, she saw. Although there was laziness in his manner, his eyes were dancing. "I reckon you're about the most appealing woman I've ever seen."

"You've seen a lot of women, I suppose."

"Oh, one or two, but none like you, Joelle." He reached out suddenly and put his hand on her cheek. "You got the prettiest hide I ever saw. You're prettier than a hound dog under a wagon."

The comparison amused Joelle. "Well, thank you for that. I guess it's a compliment."

"Now what I wish is that right now it were night, and the stars were out, and that old moon was sailing overhead, and you and I were here all alone. I'd tell you how sweet you are and how pretty you are, and I'd kind of put my arm around you a little bit like this."

Joelle stepped back and said, "Don't you try to hug me, Chad Hardin!"

"Well, I'm just telling you what it's going to be like. You got romance in your soul, Joelle. Anybody can see that. Yep, you're just what a man like me needs, a pretty woman with spirit. Smart too. I need you around when I get old."

Joelle stared at him. "What are you talking about?"

"Well, when I get old and lose my teeth and can't see too good and can't get around, I need a young woman to take care of me. Kind of like a squaw, don't you see?"

Joelle burst out laughing. "This is what you call courting?"

"Well, I like to set it all right on the front porch, Joelle. I'm older than you are, so you can take care of me when I get to be an old feller."

Joelle said, "Don't you have anything else to do?"

"What could I do that would be more fun than courting you? But, yep, I guess I'd better get on the way. I'll try to bring down a deer or an antelope or something. If I do, I'll bring you the best part. Then you can cook it for me, and I can eat it."

"Get on about your business, Chad."

He smiled and turned away. His foolishness pleased Joelle. She didn't take it seriously, but after she had finished cooking the stew, she grabbed some clothes and went down to the small stream beside which they had camped. She noticed that armed guards were out watching several women who were already washing clothes. She got down beside them, and Edith said, "This may be the last time we have a chance to wash clothes for a while. Don't know how much water there will be."

Rachel said, "I don't care. What good does all this washing do anyway?"

Lily laughed. She had caught the words and said, "You don't want to be a dirty girl. No one will like you."

"Yes, they will," Rachel insisted. "Harry likes me dirty or not."

"That man is spoiling you. That's what he's doing," Lily said. "I'm going to have a talk with him."

"He likes you, Mama."

Lily turned and saw that the other women were smiling at her, and she said, "Harry wants me to marry him."

"Why, that's wonderful," Joelle said at once. "He's such a good man. You'll be happy with him."

"I don't know if I'll marry him or not."

"Why not?" Edith asked. "He's a good man, and you're a good woman."

"It doesn't seem right to make a man put up with my handicap."

"Every woman's got a handicap," Edith said. "Harry will have some too. When people get married, they take the bad with the good." Suddenly what she said brought to mind her own marital situation. She turned away, began soaping the clothes, and said no more.

Joelle said nothing, but she wondered what would happen to Edith Riker. *Will she go back to her husband? I don't think so. She's too strong a woman for that, but it's so hard for a woman alone in this world.* Joelle continued washing the clothes and carried on a conversation with Rachel, but her mind was on other things.

WHEN OWEN RETURNED FROM the hunt, he had two antelopes tied across the back of his horse. He brought them to Jump and said, "Harry, wish you'd clean these and kind of divide it up. Give Edith a quarter."

"Sure. Something happened."

"What is it?" Owen asked.

"It's Riker. Him and Clyde went out hunting."

"He shouldn't have done that. I saw some signs when I was out."

"Riker wouldn't know a sign if he saw it. Neither would Clyde. They're both plum dumb about Indians. I tried to talk him out of it, but he wouldn't. I think he's showing off, trying to prove he's as good a man as you are."

"Which way did they go?"

"Up north, that way."

"Well, they may get by with it, but it's dangerous."

Owen said no more about it, but from time to time that afternoon he kept looking toward the north. By three o'clock he made up his mind. He rode up to Ralph and said, "I think I'd better go have a look for Riker and Clyde. They should have been back by now."

"The fools shouldn't have gone. I tried to talk them out of it, but you know how Riker is."

"They're probably all right, but I'll go take a look."

He mounted his horse, and Artie came over. "Owen, are you going to look for Pa and Clyde?"

"They're probably all right, but they may have gotten their directions confused. It's easy to do out here in the desert."

"Can I go with you?"

Owen hesitated. "It's a little bit dangerous, Artie."

"I need to go. He's my pa after all."

Owen looked at the young man, thinking how much better a human being he was than his father or brothers. After the beating Artie had taken from Sid and the indifference Lyman Riker had shown him, Owen felt the young man deserved a chance. "Well, come on."

They rode out but were joined by Chad who seemed to know what was going on. "Thought I'd take a little ride with you."

"Yes, you always did like to ride for pleasure, especially after riding all day, Chad."

Chad laughed, and Majors spurred his horse. The three moved at a slow trot across the barren land. They found nothing for a time until finally they crossed the trail. "They left the trail here and headed that way. They're up over toward those bluffs, I reckon."

"No tracks coming back," Chad murmured. "Better keep your heads up, fellas."

The three rode on, and thirty minutes later Chad stood up in his stirrups. "I heard something."

"I heard it too," Owen said. "Shooting. Come on. They're in trouble."

The three galloped across the level floor of the desert, and the sound of fire became more apparent. When they topped a ridge, Owen saw a group of Indians circling the two men who had taken refuge at the top of a bluff. "There's only seven of those Indians. We'd better run them off."

Chad pulled his rifle from the saddle boot, and Artie did the same. "You want to sneak up on them or just charge them?"

"I think they'll run when they see us coming. We'll try to knock one or two down before they see us though."

The three galloped hard toward the band, and when they were a hundred yards away, one of the Indians let out a yelp. Owen pulled up. He leveled his rifle and pulled the trigger, and the Indian fell to the ground. He kicked three times and then lay still.

Artie and Chad were firing, too, and the remaining Indians ran to their horses. They disappeared quickly into the brush, and the three men moved up the bluff.

Riker was sitting with his head down; an arrow protruded from his stomach. He looked at the body of Clyde, who had three arrows in him, and whispered, "They surprised us— put them arrows in Clyde before we could get our guns out. I kept them off, but one of them came close enough to put that arrow in me."

"Let me see how bad you're hurt, Lyman," Owen said.

Lyman's eyes were wide with shock. "They got me right in the stomach. Hurts like nothing I ever felt."

Chad and Artie approached the wounded man. The arrow hadn't penetrated to Riker's back. Owen said, "We'd better get you back and let the doc look at you."

"Pull this thing out of me!"

"Can't do that, Riker. The arrowhead might come off. We'll have to let Temple take care of it."

They put the wounded man on his horse and tied Clyde's body to another. As they left, Artie rode alongside Lyman to hold him steady. "You'll be all right, Pa," he said.

Riker didn't answer. He had lost a great deal of blood, and his face was pale. He looked at Artie as if he didn't know him, and then he dropped his head again.

"We'd better get back as quick as we can," Owen said. "If it was in the arm or leg, we could push it through and cut off the head and pull the arrow out, but you can't do that with it in his stomach."

"He's not going to make it, Owen," Chad said softly, shaking his head. "Nothing much the doc can do for a thing like that especially if it was poisoned."

Their eyes locked, and Owen shook his head. "We'll let Doc have a try."

"THERE'S NOTHING I CAN do, Edith." Temple had been examining Lyman Riker, and Edith was watching.

"Can't you get the arrow out?"

"I'm going to try. We can't leave it in, but I'll have to do quite a bit of cutting to get it out, and he's already lost too much blood."

"But he'll die, won't he, if you don't get it out?"

Logan looked down at his feet and didn't answer; he looked up again and said, "I think he's going to die anyway, Edith." His voice was gentle, and he was watching her face.

"Do all you can, Logan."

"I know he's your husband, but—"

"I wouldn't want you to do any less than your best for him. He hasn't been a good man to me or even to himself, but he deserves a chance if you can give it to him."

"I'll do the best I can. I'll get someone to help me."

"I can do it."

He stared at her and said, "I wish you wouldn't. I'd rather have Owen help."

She knew what he was thinking and said, "All right. I'll tell him to come inside."

She stepped outside where a large crowd was gathered. "He wants you to help him with the operation, Owen."

"I'll do what I can," Owen said. He stepped inside, and the flap of the tent closed. Edith could hear her husband moaning and crying out in pain. She stood beside Artie, and he put his arm around her. "Wish we could have got there earlier, Ma, to help them."

"You did all you could, Son."

EDITH WAS WAITING AS Logan and Owen came out, and without asking, she knew the result. Others crowded around. "He didn't make it, Edith. I'm so sorry."

Edith's mind seemed to be frozen for a moment, and then she said, "I know you did your best, Logan."

Logan Temple, at that moment, wanted more than anything else to put his arms around this woman he had learned to love, to comfort her, but he knew that couldn't be.

"I'll take care of him. Owen, will you have somebody open two graves?" He returned inside the tent, and Edith turned away. She saw Sid watching with shock etched across his face. He seemed beyond speech, and with an effort turned and walked away.

Artie watched him go. "Don't worry, Ma. I'll take care of you."

Edith put her arm around Artie, feeling the young muscles that would one day produce a full-grown, strong man. "I know you will, Artie. I'm counting on it."

Chapter Twenty-Three

HARRY JUMP WAITED AWKWARDLY at the head of two shallow graves dug in the sandy ground. The blanket-wrapped forms of Lyman and his son Clyde were beside the open graves. It was early morning, and the sun had turned the eastern sky crimson. Every member of the train had gathered in a circle around Jump, and he ran his eyes over them as he thought about what he had to say. Edith Riker was wearing ordinary clothes as was everyone else. There was no funereal black on any of the women, for they had not brought such things on the journey across the country.

Jump studied Edith's face and noted that she shed no tears, which didn't surprise anyone. *I guess she might be a little bit sad that she had a breakup with her husband just before he died, but I always had the feeling the two of them didn't match together well anyhow.*

His glance moved to Artie, and he could see traces of grief in the young man's eyes, and he admired him for it. The son had received little attention from the father who had favored the older brothers, but even so, Artie seemed to be grieving for his father.

325

To one side by himself was Sid Riker. His face was still puffy and bruised from the beating he had taken, and his eyes were fixed on the two blankets lying beside the open graves. He was staring at them as if mesmerized and still appeared as insensitive and brutal as always. The loss of his father and his brother had hit him hard though. Harry thought, *I wonder what he'll do now that he doesn't have his father around to tell him what to do. It came to a bad end, I'm afraid.*

A sudden breeze moved across the open space, and a tumbleweed rolled in its odd, rhythmic way across the desert floor. The travelers had passed other graves on the way, and now Jump shook his head slightly and knew he had to say something.

"Folks, you all know that I'm no preacher, and I haven't even been a Christian all that long, but since we don't have a preacher, I'll do the best I can. What I'd like to do is to read some Scripture. We're here to bury these two men who were our companions on the trail." He hesitated for a moment and tried to think of something to say. How to eulogize Riker and Clyde had troubled him.

"The ways of God are mysterious. He says in His Book, 'My ways are not your ways, and your thoughts are not my thoughts.' So we are gathered here today to say good-bye to Lyman and Clyde. I didn't know them long, but my heart always goes out to anyone who leaves this earth and goes on to what's beyond this life. This Book"—he held up the Bible, and his voice grew louder—"This Book is full of promises. It offers salvation, forgiveness of sins, a new life, and when we die the promise of a mansion in heaven. I don't know what that mansion is like. I don't reckon words could say it."

As Jump continued to speak, the men, women, and young people grew silent. There were only the sounds of the cattle lowing and a horse snorting and bucking in the remuda. Everyone was thinking pretty much the same thing. *Is Jump going to preach these two into heaven?*

Harry Jump knew what was in the minds of his audience, and as his eyes touched the two still, blanket-wrapped bodies, he said, "As I say, I haven't known these men long nor well. I know they made their mistakes as all men do. It is a grief when any of our number gets killed by hostiles. So I'm not going to say a great deal about these two men. Instead, I'm going to read from some of God's words."

Harry read from Scripture of the death of Jesus and how that death redeemed all who came to Him. Finally he read from 1 Corinthians 15 in which Paul spoke of the resurrection of the dead. Jump raised his voice when he reached the words, "O death, where is thy sting? O grave, where is thy victory?"

Jump looked at the solemn faces and said, "And that is what I have to say today, not just to these two men but to all of us. Every man, every woman, every young person has one big decision in life. Not 'Who will I marry?' as much as that means to a person. Not 'What will I do for a living?' or 'Where will I live?' But 'Will I come to God through the death of the Lord Jesus Christ to get my sins forgiven?' Jesus said, 'I am the way, the truth, and the life: no man cometh unto the Father, but by me.'" Jump continued to read Scriptures, and his eyes fell on Owen Majors. Majors was watching him with a strange look on his face. His expression was tense, and Jump was astonished. A thought raced through his mind, *Well, for once Owen is listening to the gospel. I hope it takes.*

Finally Jump prayed a short and simple prayer and then nodded to the men who were standing with shovels. They put the two forms in the graves and began shoveling the dirt in. Jump moved forward, took a handful of dirt, and scattered half of it on each grave. "A man comes from dust, and he goes back to the dusty earth," he said. He would have said more but was constrained by the obvious lives of the two men who lay dead. He turned and walked over to Edith. "I'm sorry, Edith. I wish I could have done better."

"You did fine, Harry. Just fine."

"Artie," Jump said, "it's a hard blow for a young fella, but you'll make it. You stick with your ma here. You two will be all right."

"I'll take care of her, Mr. Jump."

"I'll bet you will." Turning then, Jump walked quickly to where Sid Riker stood. "I'm sorry, Sid. I know this is rough on you."

Sid's mouth twisted in a grimace. "Pa wasn't a man of God, but he was fair to me and to Clyde."

"I'm sure he was. You'll be kind of alone now, won't you?"

"I reckon so."

"You'll make it. Just learn to look toward Jesus."

Sid looked troubled. "I'm too far gone for that."

"No man is too far gone for the mercy of God."

Sid turned and walked rapidly away. Harry watched him go and shook his head almost in despair. "Hard for a man to turn to God. It purely is."

"SID, WE NEED TO talk."

Sid had driven the wagon all day long, saying not one word to anybody. They had pulled up to their camp at night, and Edith had cooked a meal. "Come over and eat something."

"We can talk, but I don't want anything to eat. Not now."

"All right," Edith said. "Here's what we'll do. I don't know whether you know it or not, but your dad turned everything he had into cash. He sold out the land he owned, and he didn't trust banks so he brought it all along, hidden in the wagon."

"I didn't know that."

"It's quite a bit of money, Sid, and here's what I'd like to do. There are two wagons, and there are three of us, me and you two boys. Artie and I will take one wagon, and you take the other one. We'll divide up the goods in a way that's fair and divide the cash three ways, a third for you, a third for Artie, and a third for me."

"All right." Sid seemed lifeless, and suddenly Edith felt a faint stirring of compassion. She had never felt affection for Sid, but she saw his empty expression and pitied him. "You'll have to get over it, Sid."

"I don't know if I ever will. I had bad dreams last night about Pa and Clyde being killed by those redskins. It's going to be hard being alone."

"What do you think you'll do?"

"I don't know. I'm going on to Sacramento. I'll find something there."

"We haven't been very close, Sid, but I want you to know that I'll do anything I can to help you. The rest of the trip Artie and I will drive our wagon, and you drive yours, but we'll take our meals together."

A surprised look washed across his battered features. "All right," he said. "That'll be mighty nice of you, Edith." He hesitated. "What will you do?"

"I think Artie and I will pool our money and buy a farm. That's what he wants to do, and I'd like to help him all I can."

Sid glanced across the open space where Artie was talking to Jennie Pickett. "I'm sorry for what I done to Joelle and sorry I beat up on Artie. I hadn't any cause to do that."

"Well, that's over, and they hold no grudges, I'm sure. You need to find something good to do, Sid. Don't gamble your money away. Buy yourself a ranch or a farm. You might get a piece of land near us, and we could see each other."

"Maybe so. I can't think right now."

"All right. Here, I've divided the money. Here's your third of it." She handed him a wooden box and noticed that he didn't ask how much it was. He nodded, murmuring, "Thanks" and went back toward his wagon.

Edith watched him go and shook her head. *He's a miserable human being, and there's not much anybody can do to help him.*

Edith turned back to cooking the meal, and when Artie returned, his face was bright. "Jennie's folks are going to try to buy a place. Maybe we can move somewhere close to them. Might get a good buy on a good place and split it."

"You'd like that, wouldn't you?"

"I sure would."

Edith said, "Look, here's the money. I gave Sid his third and the wagon. You and I will have this wagon and the goods, and we'll have ten thousand dollars. That's what he had. About fifteen thousand."

"Gosh! That's a lot of money, Ma!"

"Enough to buy a good place, I'm sure, and get started." She saw Artie's eyes go involuntarily back toward Jennie Pickett where she was helping her mother at the campfire. Smiling, Edith said, "Why don't you ask Jennie to come over and eat with us tonight?"

"I'll do that, Ma. I'll do it right now."

Edith watched as the young man nearly ran across the camp, and she smiled slightly. "I don't need to be a gypsy to read your future, Artie Riker!"

THE NEXT WEEKS PASSED quickly, and the train was more than two-thirds of the way from Fort Ruby to Sacramento. Edith had expected Logan Temple to see her, but he seemed to be avoiding her. She didn't seek him out, and she was filled with long thoughts wondering how life would be for her and Artie. Considering Jennie Pickett, Edith had a clearer idea of Artie's future. She went about her work and drove the wagon while Artie helped herd cattle.

When they were only three days out of Sacramento, she stayed up late one night. Artie was on night watch, and she was alone. Sid had eaten with them and said little, but she had done all she could to encourage him. She wanted to be able to help him, but the three Riker men had been difficult. Artie was cut from a different cloth.

For a while she nursed the fire and made a pot of tea, which she had brought all the way with her. As she sipped it, she started to grow sleepy. Suddenly, she heard footsteps and turned to see Logan appear out of the darkness.

"It's late for you to be out, Logan."

"I can't sleep."

"I'm having trouble myself."

He pulled up one of the wooden boxes and sat down beside her. "Be glad to get somewhere we can sit in a chair and sleep in a real bed. I guess I'm no pioneer. I like my comforts."

"You're used to them. Tell me about your family, Logan."

"All right. My father was a doctor. My mother was the best woman I ever knew, and I had two brothers and one sister."

Logan's voice was soft, and Edith faced him. She gave him a cup of tea at one point, and he drank it, and as he continued to sketch his life, she studied him again. Finally he gave an embarrassed half laugh and said, "I don't know what's got me talking like an old woman here."

"You had a good family."

"Yes. My parents are gone now and one of my brothers too. I have a sister in Cincinnati, and my brother lives in St. Louis. We don't see each other very often. What about you?"

"Not much to tell," Edith said, and Logan saw that she was reluctant to speak about her life. "We weren't close in my family. My mother died when I was nine, and I had to help raise my brothers and sisters. My dad wasn't much help. He was a trifling man, a gambler. It was feast or famine. Sometimes he'd come in with money in every pocket, gifts for all of us, and sometimes we didn't have anything to eat."

"I'm sorry."

Edith shook her head. "That's all past." She placed a stick in the fire and watched until the tip caught flame. Then she held it up like a candle, and Logan noticed how fine her features were. He knew she had strength; he had seen that. He had the feeling that if necessary she could shoot a man down and not go to pieces afterward.

"You probably wonder why I married Lyman."

"It always seemed like an odd match to me."

"To everybody. To me most of all. He was different when he was younger, at least when he was courting me. I knew he had some hard spots in his life, but I was lonely. I lost my family pretty young, and he had a good home, a nice farm, a place for me to go. I told him at the beginning that I didn't love him as a woman should love a man she's married to. But he only laughed at that." She crossed her arms and looked up at the skies for a moment, then back at Logan. "He wasn't a loving man, Logan. Mostly he wanted somebody to take care of his house."

Logan didn't answer. Behind those few words he saw the skeleton of an unhappy marriage, but he had known this. He took her hand and saw her look of surprise. "I've been making up this speech for two or three days now. I guess you know what it's going to be."

"I'd like to hear it, Logan."

Logan Temple was an educated man, but somehow he found himself searching for words. "I can't say what I really feel. I went downhill and became a drunk. I'm glad to tell you I haven't even missed it on this train. I think that's because I made a bad mistake. When I was drinking, I hurt some people. Don't like to think about that."

Edith was conscious of his hands holding hers. She waited, and when he looked up, she saw honesty in his eyes. "I guess all I can do is tell you, Edith, that I love you. Maybe you already knew that."

"I saw something in your eyes for me, Logan."

"I know it's too soon, but would you think about marrying me? I wish you would. I'd like to spend the rest of my life with you."

Edith's eyes filled with tears. His honesty, simple and plain, was obvious. Logan Temple was a thing of beauty in her sight. She had seen some of the same sensitivity in Artie and none at all in Lyman or his two older sons. "Yes, I will marry you. There's no point in waiting."

"You'd marry me now?"

"Well, not tonight," Edith suddenly laughed. She stood up and he stood with her. "When we get to Sacramento. It'll be the shortest engagement on record. We'll find a preacher, and we'll get married. I promised Artie I'd help him buy a farm with the money that Lyman left."

"I can't farm, but I'll help you look. I like that young man."

Edith laughed again, a lighthearted sound.

"What are you laughing about?"

"You're about the worst man at courting a woman I ever saw."

"Well, what do you want me to do, Edith? Quote poetry and play a guitar and sing songs?"

"Yes, that's what I want. Come courting me."

"I can't do that, but I can do this."

He put his arms around her, and she came closer. Her eyes, he saw, were round, wide, and expressive, and there was an excitement in them he hadn't seen before. The hint of a smile was at the corners of her mouth and in the tilt of her head. He pulled her forward and kissed her lightly.

"I'll court you any way you want, Edith. I love you. Do you feel the same way?" She didn't answer him, and when he pulled her forward and kissed her again, she held him tightly. *This is what I want,* she thought. *This is what I've wanted all my life.*

℮∽

"WELL, RECKON WE OUGHT to be in Sacramento day after tomorrow." Chad had joined Owen who was still ahead of the train, his eyes still searching. He didn't think there'd be Indians this close to Sacramento, but one never knew. "Been a pretty easy trip. We didn't lose anybody to cholera."

"Too bad about Riker and Clyde," Owen commented dryly.

"I guess we were lucky. They shouldn't have gone off that way by themselves."

"Lyman was a strong-minded fellow. Nobody could tell him what to do."

The two rode silently for a time. Suddenly, Chad spoke. "How do you feel about Joelle, Owen?"

The question surprised Owen, and he turned to Chad, who was watching him cautiously. "What do you mean?"

"I mean I'm going to court her unless you've got ideas in that direction."

"Why are you telling me this?"

"You've been the best friend I've had, Owen, and I don't want to do anything to hurt that. You feel anything for the girl?"

"Well, I feel responsible for her."

"Sure, sure, I know about all that. But I'm talking about I want to marry her. So, I guess I'm asking if you'd be in the way."

335

Owen could not answer for a moment, but the question stirred him. "If you love her, tell her so."

"It won't bother you?"

"The only thing that would bother me is if she got mistreated, and I know you'd never do that."

Chad studied Owen Majors's profile. He knew the man wasn't saying all that was in his heart, but Owen had always been guarded. Chad said, "I'm taking that as a yes. Guess I'll go back and start my courting in earnest." He wheeled his horse.

Owen turned in the saddle to watch him go. For one moment he nearly spurred his horse forward to catch Chad and tell him—tell him what? He couldn't find the words, and his head seemed to hum with thoughts. Confused, he finally spurred the big horse into a gallop as if he could run away from something.

$e\sim$

JOELLE HAD RECEIVED CHAD'S visit the night before. He had, once again, announced his intention of courting her in a way she could barely resist. He had been joking, but he was also serious, she saw that. Laughing, she put him off. "You don't even know me, Chad."

He had argued that he knew her well enough, that she was just what he wanted. But when he tried to kiss her, she had moved away, saying, "Don't you start that."

The next day she watched Owen carefully, for Chad had told her he had mentioned his courting intentions to Owen. She was disappointed when Owen said nothing about it.

Later that evening, she went to a small stream to fill water buckets. She bent over and was filling them when she heard a sound. She whirled quickly, thinking of Indians, but Owen approached her. He had a guarded look on his face, and when he stood before her, she couldn't imagine what was on his mind.

"I've got to talk to you, Joelle."

"All right, Owen. What is it?" Her voice was calm, but she felt nervous. "Something's bothering you."

"Well, a couple of things." Owen took off his hat and moved his hand across his brow. "I can't get away from the Rikers' dying."

"You've seen men die before."

"Quite a few, but somehow it got to me. They got up in the morning just like always. Had no idea they'd be dead before the sun set." He dropped his head and was silent for a long moment, then looked up at her. "And when Harry talked about what comes after death, it hit me hard. I haven't been able to get away from what he read from the Bible."

Joelle said at once, "You need Jesus, Owen, just like we all do. He's my only hope."

"I—I know you're right. Maybe it's time for me to find God."

"I wish you'd talk to Harry, Owen. He's a good man and he wants to see you find the Lord. He's told me so more than once."

"I'll do that, right away." He hesitated. "There's something else I wanted to talk to you about." He fidgeted uncomfortably and then blurted out, "Chad told me he is going to ask you to marry him."

"He already has."

"What did you tell him?"

"Why are you asking these questions, Owen?"

Owen shrugged his shoulders and kept his eyes fixed on her face. He seemed to be searching for exactly the right words, and finally he said, "You don't need a man like Chad."

"What are you talking about? He's your friend."

"He's footloose."

"Why, so are you, Owen."

"Not anymore. I've had enough wandering around."

"That's what Chad says."

"I think he means it, but he's the wanderingest man I ever saw. He could never be still more than a day or two at a time. He's not the man for you."

"And you've decided this, have you?" She had hoped Owen might say a word about his feelings for her, and when he didn't, anger rose in her. "It's none of your business who I marry. I'll marry Chad if I want to."

Owen reached out and took her by the arm. "I don't want anything bad to happen to you."

"Nothing bad is going to happen to me. Chad is a good man. If I marry him, he'll be good to me."

Owen shook his head. "He's a good man, and he'd be good to you, but he'd be gone. He'd drag you all over creation. Why, he's already talked about moving on."

"Turn me loose, Owen." She waited until he removed his grip and then turned away.

Joelle Mitchell was dejected. She knew she was in love with Owen Majors, but apparently he felt like only a surrogate father to her. She was not in love with Chad and knew she would never marry him. Owen was right. Chad was romantic, but he had talked already about going to Panama, of all places, and other things. He thought she wanted to go travel and see the world, but she'd had enough travel. She wanted a house and a home, a place where she could set down roots, and Chad wasn't likely to give her that. Tears rose in her eyes and she sobbed once.

Owen turned her around. "What's to cry for, Joelle?"

"I'm afraid, Owen."

"Afraid of what? Nothing's going to happen."

"I know. That's the story of my life. Nothing's ever happened."

Suddenly, sorrow, disappointment, and the strain of the trip boiled over. She began to weep openly. Owen stared at her with astonishment. Then his face changed, and he pulled her forward. She put her head on his chest, and his arm was around her, and he was stroking her hair. He said nothing, but she wept as she had not wept since her mother died.

"I don't like to see you sad, Joelle," Owen said gently.

Joelle waited for him to say something. She longed to hear him speak of love, but he didn't. She pulled away from him and said, "I'm going to bed."

Owen Majors felt helpless and knew he had failed her. When she disappeared, he returned to the wagon and tried to sleep, but sleep would not come. Finally he whispered bitterly to the stars, "Well, I made a mess out of this as I usually do!"

Chapter Twenty-Four

"THIS IS THE UGLIEST place I've ever seen!" Joelle exclaimed. She was seated on Blackie, riding alongside Chad and Owen. The three of them were in the lead as they approached the mining area of Sacramento. Indeed, it was a sorry sight.

A multitude of men were passing, and the landscape looked like a hive of diggers scurrying everywhere.

"Looks like a huge anthill," Chad said. "They sure are uglifying things."

Owen raised himself in the saddle and took in the sight before him. With its great deep holes and high heaps of dirt, the town was literally turned inside out. "I've never seen anything like it," he said. "You suppose all those fellows are finding gold?"

"It'd take a lot of gold to satisfy all of them," Chad murmured. "There must be a thousand of them."

"Well, I guess we'll be separating here. For most of the train this is exactly what they've come for. There's a man who looks like he's in charge."

The man was wearing a black alpaca coat and carried a shotgun almost as long as he was tall. He was a short individual, broad and stocky, and his eyes peered at them from under his hat brim. He carried the shotgun at parade rest as he advanced toward them, and he seemed to be taking their measure. "Howdy," he said finally. "Just getting to the digging?"

"Came all the way from Independence," Owen said. He looked over the wild melee of workers who seemed to have little time for one another as they dug furiously. "Does this go on all the time?"

"Yep, it does," he said. "My name's Columbus Jergins."

"I'm Owen Majors. This is Chad Hardin and Miss Joelle Mitchell."

"Came to get rich, did you?"

"Wouldn't mind it a bit," Chad smiled. "Maybe you could tell me how to go about it."

The man with the strange name of Columbus pulled his coat back and exposed a badge. "I'm the deputy sheriff of Sacramento. Got to keep order."

"I guess that's quite a chore with this many men."

"Oh, there's shootin's pretty regular. Jail's not big enough to hold them all yet. The judge fines them and turns them loose pretty much."

"Some of our folks are going to be looking for farmland. Don't see anything that looks good around here," Owen said.

"No, you need to go down into the valley. Plenty of good farmland there. Pretty cheap too. Everybody's gone crazy over gold."

Joelle was watching with fascination as men made the dirt fly. "Do they just dig gold up in chunks?"

"Not likely, Miss." Jergins grinned, which made him look like a catfish, with his broad face and wide mouth. "There are several ways of finding gold, but none of them guaranteed. There's placer mining."

"What's that?" Joelle asked.

"Well, you got to separate the loose gold from the dirt it's settled into. You don't find it in chunks. It's tiny little flakes called 'colors.' Sometimes a piece will be as large as a grain of wheat, and sometimes you find a lump called a nugget."

"What are those things over there?" Chad asked.

"They're called sluices. The usual way is to just take a pan and dig it down in a stream to pick up some gravel and sand. You turn your pan around and pour it out, and sometimes there'll be gold settled at the bottom. You put the dirt in, and the water rushes down over them, and the gold gets caught as the dirt goes down the sluice. Sometimes you use a cradle. It's a box so that water and gravel can be rocked and shaken, and the coarse material separates from the gold." Jergins seemed to enjoy his lecture. "It won't last long though."

"People getting rich?"

"Well, a man named Steadland and his partners dug out two thousand dollars' worth in two days, but, of course, most men don't even make as much as a hired hand."

"It looks like they've all gone crazy."

Jergins removed his hat, exposing a thatch of salt-and-pepper hair. He pulled a plug of tobacco from his pocket and bit off a chew. "Men are plum fools about it. They'll do anything for gold. I guess you've seen lots of wagons coming west. Well, you'll see them going east some of these days. These rushes don't last too long. Then a big mining company will buy it, bring in rock-crushing equipment, and run the small prospectors out of business."

The three listened as Jergins spoke, and finally he nodded and said, "I've got to go on my rounds. Haven't heard a gunshot so I guess nobody got killed. There probably will be before supper time. Good to see you fellas. Ma'am, you be careful. It ain't safe for a woman to walk alone."

"Pretty blunt fellow," Chad grinned as the stocky deputy walked away. "Sounds like a wide-open town."

"Well, let's pull the train off somewhere. We can talk about gold later."

Owen returned to the wagons and spoke to Ralph, and the train moved on through the diggings. The wagons stopped a mile away from the activity, although the travelers could see men working at small streams.

"Don't guess we'll get ambushed by Indians," Owen said to Ralph.

"Nope. We made it fine. You done a good job."

"We were lucky—all except Lyman and Clyde."

The train drew up in a circle, and some of the miners had already left. Artie Riker approached and said, "What do we do now, Owen?"

"Well, pretty much anything we want to. I'm going into Sacramento to see the sights."

"I'm going to find somebody who knows about the farming country around here. Me and Ma are going to buy us a nice place."

"What about Sid?"

"He's already left. He's looking for a saloon, I think."

"I expect he'll find them," Chad nodded. "Where there's this many footloose men, there's bound to be lots of sin. You watch yourself, Artie. Don't let any of these dance hall girls get their hands on you. A fine young fellow like you, why you'd be a target."

Artie flushed and glared at Chad. "I'm not starting anything like that." He turned and walked away.

"You shouldn't tease him, Chad," Joelle said. "He's so easy to embarrass."

"Well, he'll toughen up, I expect. What do you say we go on into Sacramento and see what she looks like."

"That suits me. Will you come, Owen?"

"No, I'll hang around here. You two go on."

Joelle gave him a long look and saw that he would not meet her gaze. "All right. We'll see you later."

She and Chad rode off, and Owen watched them go. He was disturbed about Joelle, and somehow the idea of her riding off didn't please him. He had told her the absolute truth about his friend. He had nothing against Chad, who was simply a man who liked to see what was over the next hill. He had been that way himself for a time, but now he had changed, and he knew it. But he didn't think Chad was ready to settle down yet.

℮

"NOT MUCH OF A town. More saloons than anything else," Chad remarked. The two found Sacramento to be busy, which they had fully expected. They walked up and down the main street, and Chad took her into a café where they sat at a table with a red-and-white checked tablecloth and had a store-bought meal. "Not as good as your cooking," Chad grinned as he ate his steak. "There's probably a fancier place we'll find."

"It's not bad," Joelle said. Her mind was on Owen, and she only half-listened to Chad's teasing. Finally he said, "You wait right here. I'll be back in a few minutes."

"Where you going?"

"I'm a man of mystery. Don't try to figure me out. Sit still here. Some of these ugly miners get fresh with you, just pull out that little .38 and shoot them. I don't think anybody would care."

Joelle smiled for he teased her often about the .38 she carried. She sat alone and drank a few more cups of coffee. Indeed, many men eyed her boldly, and more than one spoke to her, but she returned their greetings coolly.

Chad came back, his eyes dancing. "Come on. It's Christmas—or will be pretty soon. I've got a little present for you."

He paid the bill, led her outside, and said, "It's working out just fine. Come on. Let me show you what I've found." He led her down the main street and off the busy thoroughfare to the edge of town and an area of houses. He pointed to a small house painted white with green shutters. "Here's where you'll be living," he said with a swing of his hand.

Joelle stared at the house and then turned to face Chad. "What are you talking about?"

"I asked a fellow if there were any houses to be had, and he told me about this one. I rented it for you."

"Why, Chad, I can't let you put me up." A thought came to her, and she grew still. "You—you didn't think I'd live there with you, did you?"

"Only after we get married."

"Chad, you're not ready to marry me or anybody."

"I don't know why you'd say that. You've hurt my feelings."

"It would take a stick of dynamite to hurt your feelings!"

"Well, I guess you're right. But houses are pretty hard to find, and I know you're sick of that wagon. So I rented it for a month. You can pay me back sometime, but I want to give you a place to be by yourself and think."

"What a sweet thing to do, Chad! I'll take you up on it."

"Come on. Let's look at the inside. Supposed to be furnished. The fellow that lived here was a dentist, but he got killed."

"Who killed him?"

"Oh, it wasn't intentional. Somebody took a shot at another fellow he was having an argument with. He missed and hit the dentist. His widow's gone back East, and she left the place with the newspaper office here. Come on, let's take a look."

They went inside, and Joelle took a deep breath and felt a great relief. She had wondered what she would do. There was bound to be some work she could do here. Maybe taking care of a stable as she had done before. They looked the house over.

"Don't I get some kind of reward for this?" Chad smiled at her, his eyes dancing.

"Yes. Here, you deserve a reward." She put her hand out, Chad took it, and she pumped it up and down. "Thank you very much, Chad. You can take your meals here. That's a nice stove, and it'll be a place of refuge. I really appreciate it. I haven't had anybody to look out for me in a long time."

"Well, you think I'm joshing you about getting married, but I'm not." His face suddenly grew sober. "I know Owen thinks I'm not through running around, but I'm mighty fond of you, Joelle. You're a fine-looking young lady and smart and tough. I admire that. We'll talk about that. I'll come courting every day. I'll wear your patience down." He smiled, and before she could move, he leaned forward and kissed her on the cheek. "You want to stay here and look at your house or go back to the camp? I guess folks will be saying good-byes."

"I'll go with you."

She shut the door; he locked it and gave her a key. They mounted their horses and rode back toward the camp. Joelle was relieved to have a place, even for a short time, and she was wondering what Owen would think of it.

❧

OWEN FIRST HEARD OF what Chad had done from Harry. He listened as Jump told him about the house, how Chad had found and rented it, and that Joelle was moving into it.

"That's not right," Owen said instantly.

"What's wrong with it? She needs a place to stay."

"Why, it doesn't look right."

"I swan, Owen, you'd complain if they hung you with new rope! There's nothing wrong with that. I kind of admire Chad for looking out for her. She needs a little bit of that."

"Where is she now?"

"She bought some stuff for the house and went back to put up curtains or something."

"I'm going to go talk to her, and I'll have a word for Chad too. He ought to know better. You know how gossip is. Everybody in the camp will think that they're living together."

Jump watched him leave and then went to tell Lily what had happened. "Owen's so mixed up he can't see straight."

"It's easy enough. He loves that girl, and he doesn't know what to do about it."

"He made a commitment to a woman once. I knew her. She was pretty as a woman can get, but she betrayed Owen. He's been offish with women ever since."

"Well, Joelle wouldn't betray anybody."

"Neither would you, Lily. Now, about time you and me talk serious."

"All right, start talking," Lily smiled at him. "I've never had a man come after me like you have, Harry. I like it. I think I'll play hard to get for a while."

"Oh, Lily, don't be that way. Rachel needs a dad and you need a husband and I sure need a wife. We're going to make a nice family. I don't think I told you. I want six kids, all of them boys."

Lily laughed. "Well, we'll have to talk about that when it's proper."

❧

JUMP HAD TOLD OWEN the location of the house, and he identified it at once when he saw Chad sitting on the front porch. He was seated in a chair and leaning back with his hat pulled over his eyes, but he straightened up when Owen dismounted in front of the house. "Hey, Owen, you come to help with the housewarming?"

Owen was upset with Chad. They had their ups and downs before, and now he said, "Chad, you're a fool."

Chad stared at him. "What are you talking about?"

"It's not right, you renting a house for Joelle."

"Well, Owen, she's got to have a place to stay. She can't live in that wagon forever."

"Where is she?"

"Why, she's in the house."

Owen walked past Chad and found Joelle standing on a chair and putting up curtains. She turned to him, and her face was pleased. "You come to see my new house, Owen? Isn't it nice?"

Owen stopped dead still, and seeing one glimpse of his face brought Joelle down off of the chair. "What's the matter? Is something wrong?"

"Yes, something's wrong! You shouldn't be moving into Chad's house."

Chad had followed him in. "It's not my house. It's her house."

"You paid the rent, didn't you?"

"She's going to pay me back."

"You step outside, Chad. I need to talk to Joelle."

Chad's smile disappeared. "Nope, I reckon I'll stay right here."

For a moment Joelle thought Owen would challenge that, but then he turned to her and said, "You shouldn't have moved in here. It's unseemly."

Two red spots appeared in Joelle's cheek, and she stared at him. "You think I'm doing something wrong?"

"It's wrong to live in a man's house when you're not married to him."

Chad said, "Owen, you're being a fool. You've been a fool before but not like this."

"You keep out of this, Chad, and I've told you before. Get out of here. I need to talk to Joelle."

"I'll leave when Joelle asks me to." Chad's temper was somewhat short at times. He hated being told what to do, and it irritated him that Majors would impugn Joelle. "You're loco, Owen. Joelle's straight as a string. I mean her no harm."

"What do you think the town will say?"

"The town will say whatever it wants to say. It's none of their business."

"I've told you twice to leave, and now I'm telling you one more time."

Chad's lips drew tight. "You can go to grass, Owen! It's not your house. Not mine either. I'll leave when Joelle tells me to."

Anger flared in Owen, and he suddenly stepped forward and shoved Chad toward the door. Taken off-guard, Chad staggered backward, and then his face flushed, and his eyes seemed to glitter. "Don't put your hands on me, Owen. We're friends, but—"

"Get out of here! I've got to talk to Joelle." Owen seemed past reasoning and gave another shove, but Chad Hardin was not a man to take shoving. He suddenly swung, and his fist caught Owen right in the chest and drove him backward.

"I told you not to put your hands on me!"

Owen's temper was short, and he threw himself at Chad with the intent of wrestling him out the door. The two men were evenly matched, both tall and strong, and they wrestled around the kitchen. They ran into a table and knocked it over, breaking the legs off. Then Chad threw a punch that caught Owen right in the mouth.

Chad yelled, "You're crazy, man!!"

The two got to their feet and began slugging at each other. Joelle tried to break them up, but she was thrown to one side by the violence of their quarrel. The two men were deadly serious now, all thought of friendship gone. Blows were given and taken, and both of them were marked. Finally Chad ran at Owen and wrestled him to the floor, but Owen rolled him over and hit him square in the mouth.

Joelle watched the two and stopped pleading. She saw a bucket of dirty water she used to mop the floor. The two men were struggling on the floor. Joelle poured the water over the back of Chad's head, but most of it went into Owen's face. Chad leaped to his feet.

"What'd you do that for?"

Owen was wiping his eyes. He started to speak, but Joelle was furious. "Get out of here! You're not going to fight over me like two dogs over a bone! I don't want to ever see either one of you again!"

She hit Owen with a broom, and he threw up his hands in defense. "Wait a minute, Joelle—"

"I don't want to hear you, Owen Majors! Get out of my house! And you, too, Chad! Both of you get out!"

The two men saw that the young woman was furious. Chad said, "I think we'd better go, Owen. I think we made a mistake." He turned and walked out the door, and Owen opened his mouth, but she hit at him with the broom.

"Get out, Owen!" she shouted. He followed Chad.

The two men stood on the porch for a moment, then Chad said, "Well, you sure made a mess out of that."

"What do you mean? It wasn't my fault."

"You're the one who started the fight. You ought to know better. What's the matter with you? You know that girl is true as steel. She'd never do a bad thing."

"I know she wouldn't, but—"

"Well, that's not what she thought, and that's not what you said. You as much as accused her and me of living in sin. That was the furthest thing from my mind, and she sure wouldn't put up with it even if I was trying to do a low-down thing like that. You've loosened one of my teeth, Owen. I don't want to talk to you for a while."

Owen watched Chad walk away and felt like a complete fool. He hesitated and wiped the water from his face and put his hat on his head. He wanted to go back inside, but he knew that now was not the time. Instead, he walked to his horse, mounted, and for a moment looked at the house, and then he shook his head. "Owen Majors, you are the biggest fool God ever made. What is wrong with you?" He jerked the horse's head around, dug his spurs in, and shot off down the street at a dead run.

OWEN DIDN'T SEE JOELLE for two days. He did see Chad, who managed to laugh at the whole thing. "Well, you and me just bound to be foolish at times."

"I was dead wrong, Chad."

"You sure were. Not the first time neither. Joelle speaking to you yet?"

"No, I haven't seen her. Have you?"

"Oh, I went by yesterday and told her how sorry I was about the way I acted. Couldn't apologize for you though."

"Did she say anything about me?"

"Not a word. She's looking for work. She's probably going to be a cook at that restaurant on Front Street."

"That's a rough place for her."

"She's tough enough. She'll take it." He studied Owen thoughtfully and said, "Look, I figured all this out. The reason you came roaring in like you did, making all those vile charges against Joelle and me, is because you care for her. Now, ain't that so, Owen?"

Owen stood for a minute, and finally he said, "I guess you're right, Chad, but she'll never have anything to do with me now."

"Don't be a fool. She was mad, and she should have been. We deserve worse than we got, but when I talk to her about you, I see a soft light in her eyes." Chad placed his hand on Owen's shoulder. "Go talk to her. It'll be all right. You're right about me. I've been thinking about heading down the coast. I'd like to see San Francisco. They say that's a wide-open place. I guess I'm just not ready to settle down, but I think you are."

"I couldn't face her, Chad."

"My stars, Owen! You've faced wild Comanche. She's just a little woman. She's not going to shoot you or anything— although she was mad enough to when we tore her house up. Go offer to help her fix it up. She's lonesome. Besides, you two formed a pretty good bond coming all the way across. She told me about how she took care of you when you were hurt, how you have been taking care of her even when you thought she was a man. Don't see how you could have thought that unless you're half-blind. Anyway, go see her."

"Thanks for the advice, Chad. You won't be leaving right away, will you?"

"No, no. I'm going to try dabbling around, prospecting a little bit. You want to go with me?"

"No, I've got another idea I'm working on, but I'll see you later."

Chad walked away, and Owen moved down the street. By the saloon he heard a voice call. Cherry Valance stepped outside. "Where you going, Owen? You might come in and have a drink."

"No, I've got some business, Cherry." He looked at the saloon and said, "Ash buy this place?"

"Yep."

"Seems like a nice enough place."

"It's a saloon."

Owen looked down at the woman. Her face had lines that hadn't been there when he first knew her, and it saddened him for he had once fancied himself in love with her. He still felt a fondness for her. "You ought to get out of this life, Cherry."

355

"And do what?"

"Marry a good man?"

"And wash dishes and change diapers? No thanks."

Owen tried to find a response, a way to persuade her. He saw that her lips were tight, and she suddenly laughed. "Don't try to convert me. Harry Jump tried it, and he couldn't make it."

"There's worse things than being converted. I've been thinking a lot about that lately."

"Oh, you're going to hit the glory trail, and you're going to marry that little girl that you couldn't even tell was a girl. You're not hard to figure out, Owen."

"I doubt if she would have me."

"She'd have you all right. She watched you all the time. Nobody could miss it—except somebody as dumb as you are."

"Well, I wish you the best, Cherry."

"Are you staying here?"

"I think so."

"Well, we probably won't be meeting much, but I'll always be glad to see you, Owen. I'll always have a good memory of our time together."

Owen watched her as she turned and walked back into the saloon. He felt a sense of a loss, not because he wanted her. But he hated to see her throwing her life away.

℮⁓

FOUR DAYS HAD PASSED since Joelle had driven Chad and Owen from her house. Chad had come back the next day and sheepishly confessed his wrongdoing. She had forgiven him at once. When he started to talk about going to San Francisco, she knew Owen had been right about him.

She had grown more miserable each day. On a Friday night she fixed a meal for herself and found she wasn't hungry. She sat at the table, drinking coffee, and tried to think about where she was going and what she would do. *I'll have to take that job cooking. I can do it.*

She walked around the room, pleased enough with the house, but it was only a house. She was unhappy and felt isolated and alone in a strange land. *I was this miserable back home with a stepfather trying to get at me. Now I'm two thousand miles away and still unhappy.* The friends she had made on the wagon train were separating, and she herself had nowhere to go and no plan. The thought of cooking for a bunch of men didn't thrill her, but she was strong enough to do it.

Finally she washed her face, brushed her hair, put on her nightgown, and went to bed. She had not been there thirty minutes and was almost asleep when she heard a sound. Some-body's on the front porch.

She picked up the .38 she kept beside her bed, and carrying a lamp, she moved into the large front room. She put the lamp down. At the door she listened. A faint knock startled her. "Go away," she said. "I have a gun."

"It's me, Joelle—Owen."

"Owen?"

"Can I come in? I need to see you."

"I'm not dressed. Wait a minute." She went back to the bedroom, put the gun down, and threw on the robe she had bought. She returned and slid the door open. "What are you doing here this time of the night, Owen? Something wrong?" She saw that his face was tense with emotion. "What is it?"

"I came to tell you something. Two things really."

"Why didn't you come earlier? It's the middle of the night."

"I felt like a fool. That's one thing," Owen said. "I was wrong to make all those crazy accusations about you and Chad. I think I lost my mind. You should have shot me."

"Oh, it wasn't that bad."

"Yes, it was. You could never do anything wrong, Joelle."

The words pleased her, and she smiled slightly. "You'll find out that's not true if we stay friends."

"Well, that's the other thing I've come about, but first, I've got to tell you I got a job here. Remember that deputy sheriff we met, the one named Columbus?"

"Yes. What about him?"

"I've got his job as deputy sheriff. The sheriff is an old man. Good fellow, but he's seen his best days. If I do a good job, I'll be sheriff of the county."

"Is that what you want, Owen?"

"I've done it before. I kind of like it."

"Then I'm glad, but it'll be dangerous. I don't like that."

"I'll be all right."

Joelle saw that he was nervously turning his hat around and said, "Give me your hat. You're going to tear the brim off of it." She took the hat away from him and turned to face him. "Now, you could have told me about the job tomorrow."

"Well, I've been four days working up nerve enough to apologize, but now I want to tell you something else. You know why I acted like a fool, don't you?"

"Because you are a fool?"

"Probably, but I was jealous. Joelle, I just couldn't stand the thought of you being with another man, not even Chad. He's the best friend I ever had, but I was blind jealous."

Suddenly Joelle felt a happy warmth. "Were you, Owen?"

"Yes. A woman misused me once, and I let it make me bitter. But since I've known you, that's all ancient history. You could never deceive anyone."

"I deceived you pretending to be a boy."

"Oh, that was something you had to do."

Owen stopped and put his arms around her. "I guess there's nothing to do but tell you that I love you, and I want you to marry me, and I want us to be together always."

At that instant Joelle Mitchell knew she had found her life. Owen was anxious, but his anxiety pleased her for it meant he was afraid he might lose her. She reached up, put her arms around him, and pulled his head down. And when he kissed her, she sensed the hunger in both of them. She knew she had a power over him, to offer him the feelings they could share. His arms tightened around her, and then when he lowered his lips to hers, she said, "I thought I had lost you, Owen."

"No, you're never going to lose me. Even when I act like a foolish fellow, I'll always be there. I feel like I got the whole world in my arms, Joelle. You're all that a man could want."

She walked to the stove and began to build the fire, and Owen watched her. When the fire was going, he said, "When can we get married?"

Joelle's eyes danced as she smiled. "I can't marry you before tomorrow, Owen."

He laughed and went to her. "That's about right, I think." He kissed her and said, "Now, I know it's late, but fix supper, woman. I'm starving to death!"